THE FOSSILARCHY

BY
TOM CLARK

First published in Australia by Aurora House
www.aurorahouse.com.au

This edition published 2022
Copyright © Tom Clark 2022

Cover design: Donika Mishineva | www.artofdonika.com
Typesetting and e-book design: Amit Dey

The right of Tom Clark to be identified as Author of the Work has been asserted in accordance with the Copyright, Designs and Patents Act 1988.

ISBN number: 978-1-922697-08-0 (Paperback)

All rights reserved. No part of this publication may be reproduced, stored in a retrieval system, or transmitted, in any form or by any means without the prior written permission of the publisher, nor be otherwise circulated in any form of binding or cover other than that in which it is published and without a similar condition being imposed on the subsequent purchaser.

A catalogue record for this book is available from the National Library of Australia

Distributed by: Ingram Content: www.ingramcontent.com
Australia: phone +613 9765 4800 |
email lsiaustralia@ingramcontent.com
Milton Keynes UK: phone +44 (0)845 121 4567 |
email enquiries@ingramcontent.com
La Vergne, TN USA: phone +1 800 509 4156 |
email inquiry@lightningsource.com

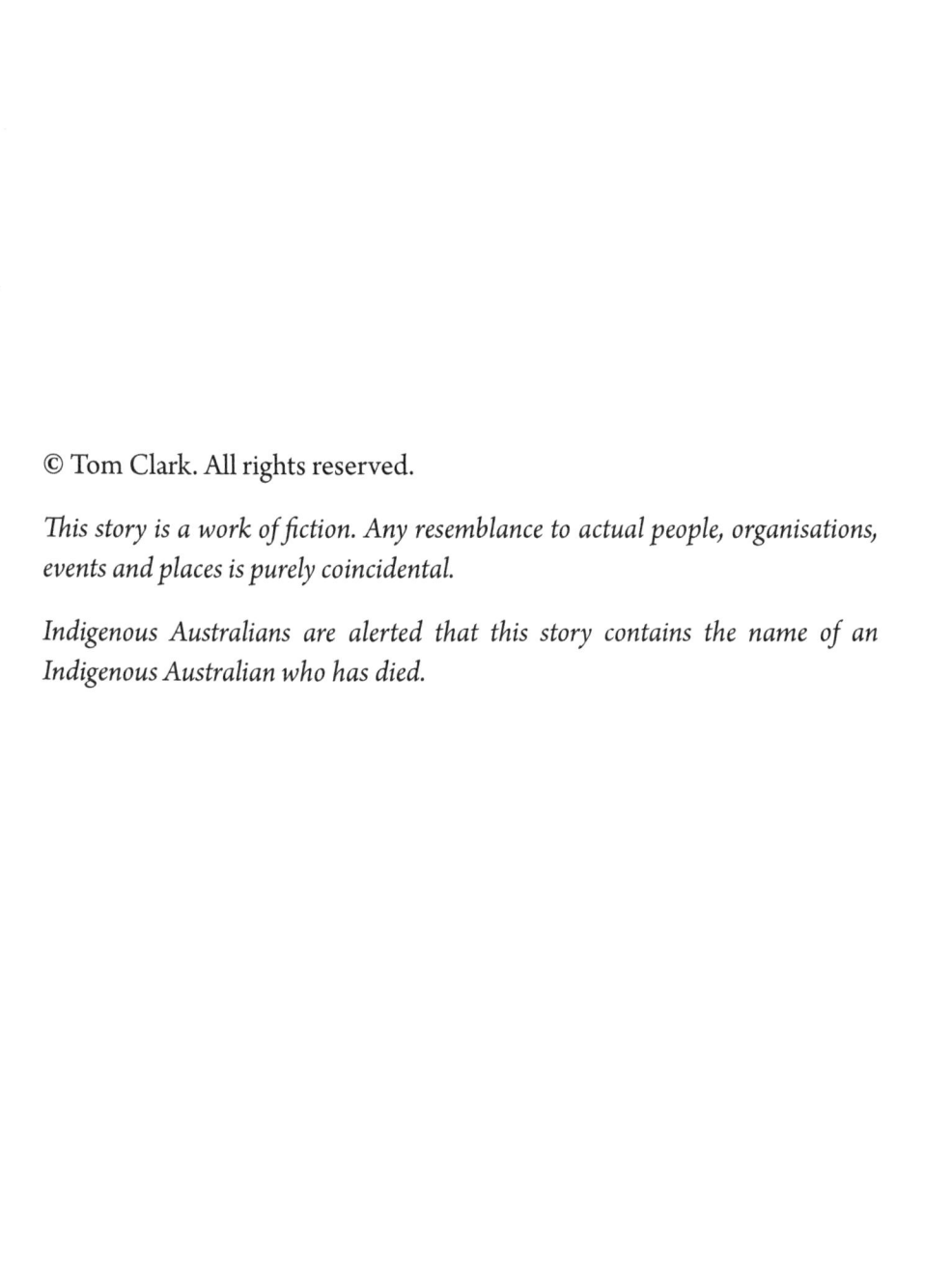

© Tom Clark. All rights reserved.

This story is a work of fiction. Any resemblance to actual people, organisations, events and places is purely coincidental.

Indigenous Australians are alerted that this story contains the name of an Indigenous Australian who has died.

To Pauline, Sarah and Alexandra

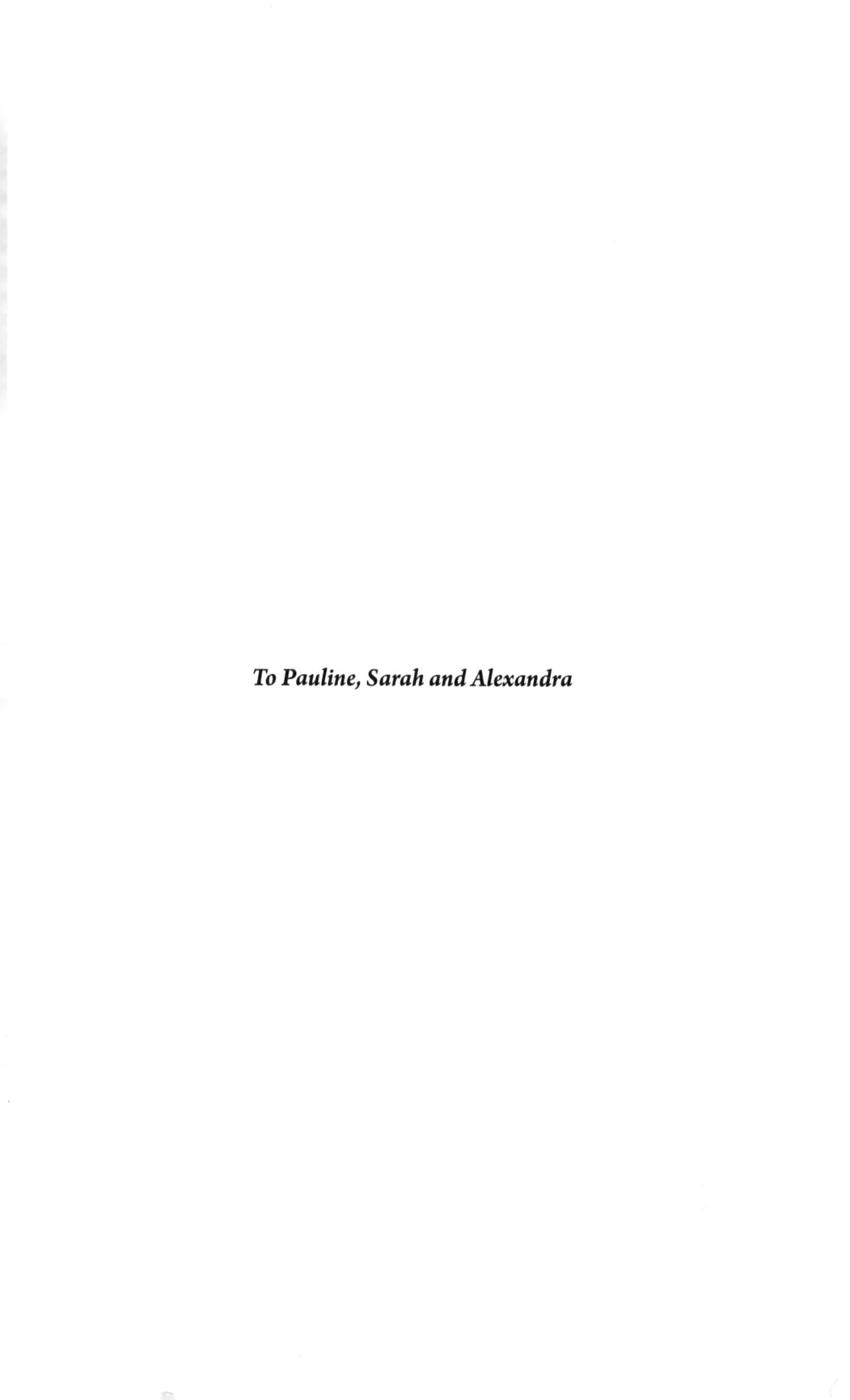

To Dili
TIMOR SEA
Darwin
From Port Moresby
GREAT BARRIER REEF
Kununurra
Port Douglas
Broome
Townsville
Callow Island
Mercury LNG
Monk's Point
Karratha
NORTHERN TERRITORY
Daghawi Mine
Mackay
Straw's Point
NINGALOO REEF
Onslow
Exmouth
Pilbara
QUEENSLAND
Rockhampton
Gladstone
WESTERN AUSTRALIA
Carnarvon
SOUTH AUSTRALIA
Brisbane
INDIAN OCEAN
Geraldton
NEW SOUTH WALES
PACIFIC OCEAN
Perth
Fremantle
Newcastle
Esperance
GREAT AUSTRALIAN BIGHT
Sydney
Albany
Adelaide
Canberra
VICTORIA
Melbourne
1000 kilometres
N
Route of the *New Endeavour II*
Notable incidents
TASMANIA
Hobart
SOUTHERN OCEAN

CHAPTER 1

May 30, Bernese Oberland, Switzerland

The six guests arrived discreetly and separately, by private planes to nearby airfields and waiting limousines for the last leg of their journeys. They had been requested to come alone, without PAs, bag carriers, cell phones, recording or other trackable communication devices. The meeting was never to have taken place.

Wolfgang Dreiser awaited each guest on the steps of his summer house, a mansion by anyone else's standards. Hidden security cameras down the road alerted him to approaching vehicles. He could see anyone coming up the glaciated hanging valley long before their arrival.

The house was surrounded by mountains, the views striking, although there was little snow on the peaks. Europe was engulfed in another heatwave—the new normal.

But they weren't coming to admire the scenery or to discuss the weather.

He greeted each guest as an old and trusted friend, to the extent that such men could have friends. Each carried a case containing a very large sum of money, although this counted as loose change for some of the richest men on Earth.

He had spoken to each guest privately during and since the last Davos World Economic Forum. It was now time for final commitment, time for the deposits to be paid.

After a light lunch, he opened the meeting.

"Gentlemen, thank you for coming. I don't need to remind you of the gravity of the situation or why we are here. Over thirty years of warnings have been ignored as the world has pursued the fairy tale of eternal economic growth. Instead of action, we have had fine words. Fine words and lip service from governments and corporate leaders, with all their excuses for doing little or nothing. Fine words from scientists, too timid to tell the truth or risk their careers. Fine words from self-important sustainability gurus, armies of parasitic consultants with all their fairy dust and incantations. Fine words from NGOs who think they're Jesus, sent to save us, all preaching to each other while most of the world has ignored them. Fine words and inaction have led the world to the brink of catastrophe.

"Now, as we stare into the abyss, there is no time to step back. Now, as never before, humanity needs to recognise its predicament, its peril, and be guided by science, knowledge, wisdom, compassion and cooperation. Instead, we have anti-science, lies, stupidity, ignorance, greed, hatred and conflict. Now, as never before, we need great leaders to steer the world to safety. Instead, we have psychopaths, megalomaniacs, narcissists, imbeciles, marketing hacks and religious zealots—nonentities put and kept in power by their own kind and by populations too stupid or ignorant to know what's going on. We are not on a road to human progress and enlightenment, but to a new dark age.

"The climate crisis is much, much worse than the COVID crisis, which lost vital time for action as the world was distracted. It stalled growth and emissions briefly, but now the world is ramping up again on the same trajectory of plundering the Earth—the cause of both crises. A desperate situation demands desperate measures. Without drastic action, there is no prospect of saving the world in the time we have left.

"Governments will not act decisively—therefore, we must. A million species face extinction. The young are fighting for their future; fighting for their lives."

Two hours later, Dreiser was summing up what had been discussed. He had presented a business case, feasibility study and outline plan. Standard practice when you present a multi-billion-dollar business opportunity to investors.

"Are there any final questions before we conclude our meeting?"

He paused. He knew what they were thinking. The guests looked at each other, scarcely able to believe what they had agreed to. They all knew it would give capitalism a bad name if they were ever found out, not to mention result in very long jail sentences. They knew from past hands-on experience that it was fair enough—perfectly legal and acceptable—for the investment community to finance the destruction of Planet Earth, all its life support systems and non-human inhabitants. Even worse, to bring the world economy to its knees with dodgy derivatives. But damaging property assets would be frowned upon.

Dreiser understood their concerns. "As I have stressed to you all, you will be protected. That is why we are adhering to the utmost confidentiality and why you will all have no further involvement beyond financing the venture and agreeing to the overall plan. I am grateful for your contributions today as an initial token of your commitment. Execution will be tasked to military strategists and operatives. Even as we speak, preparations are under way."

May 30, South Kensington, London

Alex Burns relaxed in his apartment off Prince's Gardens. The streets around were quiet. It was a Saturday afternoon, and the nearby Imperial College was semi-dormant for the summer. It was still sweltering outside.

He was once again in the job market. Since being pensioned off from Her Majesty's Special Air Service he'd tried a few 'executive' and 'management consultant' jobs, but pen-pushing and talking bullshit weren't for him. He'd killed better people, scraped from his boot less odious materials than some of the types he'd come across in the London business world.

He could kill a pint. He'd head to the Queen's Arms a bit later.

He had no ties now that his divorce had been finalised and his son James had flown the coop, now living in New York. He looked at the picture of Lottie on his desk. He loved and missed her, but after being away so much and doing what he had done—called 'serving his country'—there was no recapturing what they'd once had. There were now just pictures, memories, and associations—like everyone's past, good or bad.

He was enjoying being free, starting afresh, having a flat in town, visiting the nearby museums, going to concerts. He'd even started dating again—internet introductions were a new experience. He was keeping fit and could still pass the 'tall, dark and handsome' test, apart from a few grey hairs. He was enjoying meeting new women—enjoying the company, the conversation, being able to try 'minimum two people' set menus. But he was wary of dates who seemed to interview him as a prospective marriage partner, and so he gave them little to go on. He'd been trained to resist probing questions even when tortured.

There seemed to be a lot of Russian women in town. Tatyana was a gold-digger and had taken some time to shake off, but there was something about Galina. He'd see her again.

It was good to be participating in the normal world again, but the novelty was wearing off and he hankered for adventure once more. All the same, he was particular. He'd spent too much time doing things he didn't especially want to do, being in places he hadn't especially wanted to be in: Northern Ireland, Iraq, Africa, Afghanistan, Leatherhead. Just for a change, he felt like doing something good, something useful even—but no opportunities had arisen. Maybe he'd join a charity, something that had to do with land mines. He'd seen what they did to people. Maybe he'd work with disabled war veterans. He knew a few and knew about helping people with PTSD—too many of his mates had topped themselves. What had it all been for? What about animals? He'd adopted Gus the cat and Pongo the dog in Afghanistan—or rather, they'd adopted him—and brought them back to England, to do six months in quarantine. There was no lack of things he could do.

The call came in on his private number. Not many people knew it.

"Alex? Piers Hadley. How are you? I heard you were still looking. Might have something interesting for you. But can't talk over the phone. What about a spot of lunch? Friday suit you?"

They had met once before and Burns was on his books. Hadley liked to call himself a 'broker'. It was evidently easier to say this, when asked the 'so, what do you do, then?' question at parties, than saying 'arms dealer and mercenary recruitment agent for subversive and surreptitious operations worldwide. No task too tough.'

Which was also somewhat long for a business card.

Burns was intrigued. He wasn't one to turn down the offer of a free lunch.

"Glad to. Where and when?"

The late afternoon sun shone through the trees as the limousines lined up, their tyres crunching on the gravel.

"The destiny of the world depends on our success," said Dreiser. "I propose that the project is code-named Operation Phoenix, symbolising new life, new hope emerging from the ashes of a world on fire." The guests nodded in agreement as Dreiser poured seven glasses of schnapps. "Gentlemen, I give you a toast. To Phoenix!"

"Phoenix!" They all responded in unison, downing their glasses in one.

Dreiser embraced and bade farewell to each guest in turn before they were driven away. He watched them disappear down the valley.

He knew that if they were discovered and convicted, he would, as the ringleader, receive the harshest sentence. People would say he was crazy, a madman, a Bond villain out to destroy the world, not save it. His lawyers would no doubt get him to plead insanity and he would spend his last years cared for by nice young men in clean white coats.

Yes, he was mad—mad about the condition of the Earth, mad that people could let it get into this state and still carry on as before. That was the true insanity. Appeals to reason, to listen to the science had failed. You couldn't reason with stupid. He recalled a quote of Albert Einstein, a distant relative on his mother's side. 'There are only two things that are infinite: the universe and human capacity for stupidity, and I'm not sure about the universe.' Another great physicist, Max Planck, said that you could not change deeply held beliefs by reasoning. You had to wait for the holders to die in order for new truths to be accepted by a new generation. Old white males were the dominant climate deniers—the Robert Moorcocks of this world and their followers—but there was no time to sit around waiting for them to kick the bucket.

The older generation in rich countries had caused the climate crisis and done nothing to avert it. He did not care about them. He recalled reading the words in a German officer's letter sent home during the insanity of the First World War. 'This generation has no future and deserves none.' His concern was for the young and the nightmare that his generation would leave them in.

Throughout history, young men had been sent off to fight and die for the beliefs of the old, those in power. Today, not only the present generation of young were being sacrificed, but all future generations.

He knew that many shared his concerns, especially those who were taking to the streets—this Friday's protests around the world would be the biggest yet. The difference was that he and his colleagues had the Kohle, the money to do something about it.

The last of the limousines disappeared from sight. He would see his guests at the next Davos—or in court for war crimes.

CHAPTER 2

Friday, June 5

Dreiser watched the trees flash by. He and his driver, Johannes, had left before dawn and the sun was rising over the mountains. He usually liked to work from the back of his Rolls-Royce Phantom, but this time, he relaxed, deep in thought. Johannes would always wait for a cue to engage in conversation, and so he was left in peace.

Dreiser was returning to Zürich for a final board meeting. For the next six months, he would reduce his business commitments 'for health reasons', so that he could devote his attention to Phoenix.

He had not lightly decided on this course of action, but there was no going back now. It was a risky and dangerous enterprise and people were going to die. He felt bad about that. But many more would die if he did nothing. He would feel worse if he'd backed down, as he nearly had in the early days of planning.

He had not succeeded in business and amassed considerable wealth without making hard, sometimes ruthless decisions, but he'd always done what he believed was morally right. He'd been a thought leader in corporate social responsibility, helped establish the World Business Council for Sustainable Development, set up charitable foundations, supported environmental and social causes, loved animals and nature. What he had planned was out of character. He was no Blofeld—apart from having Heidi, his white

Persian cat. She didn't mind travelling and was sleeping in her basket next to him. He opened the door of the basket and tickled her under her chin. She liked that. Her purr was louder than that of his Phantom's engine.

But he saw no other way. Without saying why, he had spoken in confidence with some of the world's leading climate scientists. Publicly, they put on brave faces, telling the world that there was still time if they acted now. Privately, they were in despair. The world had not only run out of time but was on borrowed time. What were once worst-case scenarios were now increasingly likely. The new worst case was unimaginable.

There were no precise scientific terms for the two main options humanity now faced for the road ahead. The closest were 'Fucked'—even with emergency action—and 'Totally Fucked, Up the Arse', with business as usual. Some choice. In the circumstances, Phoenix was a sound and rational solution.

He'd told the sponsors his reasons for the venture but not the whole story. In his presentation, he'd shown pictures of his grandchildren and the ravaged world they would be bequeathed. Eighteen months earlier, he'd re-visited his beloved Australia. He'd been away too long, had fond memories of his carefree travels there as a young backpacker, picking grapes, swimming with Jan on the Great Barrier Reef. She was so lovely. Why had he left her to return to Switzerland all those years ago? Ah. Money, ambition, that sort of thing. He wondered what had happened to her. Maybe it was better not to know, to just keep her as a memory.

He'd been shocked by what he'd seen and experienced during that recent visit. It was the trigger for all of this. He'd seen huge tracts of bleached coral on the reef, that international treasure dying while the climate-denying Australian Government pretended it wasn't happening and continued to prop up and expand the coal industry, one of the chief culprits. Returning to Sydney, he'd seen vast clouds of smoke as he looked out of the plane window. It was like an erupting volcano and an atomic explosion combined. Vast areas were on fire from heat and drought. In Sydney, he'd choked on the smoke and had had to leave prematurely, flying on to New Zealand. In Christchurch, he could smell the smoke over two thousand kilometres away. He'd visited the Franz Josef and Fox Glaciers in the Southern Alps.

They had turned pink from the ash on them, causing them to absorb more heat, which accelerated their melting. He had a long and special interest in glaciers—over his lifetime, he had watched the retreat of those in Switzerland and Austria.

Australia's idiot politicians and the Moorcock media had dismissed the intense heat and fires as nature's cycle. They'd blamed arsonists, blamed greenies for stopping back-burning. How stupid could anyone be? Since then, fires had raged all over the world, even in the Arctic, where there had been record temperatures. Were the same arsonists at work up there?

These were the outward motivations, the triggers. But there was something else, something personal—atoning for the crime of his father, for the tainted money he had inherited. He would do some good with it this time—he'd not only save six million people, but millions more.

Over the past year, he'd spent much time alone with his thoughts, concerns, plans. This was not something he could share. The fewer people that knew, the better. He thought of the World War II poster he had once seen at the Imperial War Museum in London. 'Careless talk costs lives.' He'd only told the sponsors the bare minimum for their financial and moral support. He couldn't endanger Phoenix or the sponsors by telling them too much. It was going to be an even lonelier time as the momentum and danger mounted, but it was for a purpose.

Whatever the outcome, he would have to live with the consequences. Even if they were successful and he wasn't caught, he'd spend the rest of his days being hunted, always looking over his shoulder. Those in power would never forgive and forget what he was about to do.

He checked his Chopard LUC watch. They were making good time.

Friday June 5, Brisbane Central Station, Australia

Emma Johnson checked the time on the station clock. *He's late. Where is he? He'd better not have chickened out. He promised he'd come.*

"Move along! You're causing an obstruction!" shouted the policeman.

"That *is* the general idea today, you know, officer. Civil disobedience is all the people have against the mindless forces of corrupt governments and their corporate paymasters." Emma said it under her breath. Her cheek had got her into trouble in the past. She smiled at the officer, her hand to her ear, suggesting she was hard of hearing. Anyway, he wasn't speaking to just her, but to the crowd around her. *He called this an obstruction? Wait till they saw what was planned for later.*

She had arranged to meet David under the station clock, as lovers do in the movies. She was surrounded by people with placards, also waiting. Maybe they'd seen the same movies. She recognised some of the other Extinction Rebels from previous climate protests. She'd been arrested with them for blocking the traffic at the George and Margaret Street intersection. She smiled and waved. They waved back. The camaraderie was great. She'd never experienced anything like it before. Bonding with people who shared a common cause—a common fight—was exhilarating, even though fighting for climate action seemed hopeless at times.

She knew about facing extinction. The climate crisis was as big as it got, but she could handle it. For once, it wasn't a crisis within herself, something that had plagued her adolescent years. She'd ticked most of the boxes—anxiety, depression, anorexia, self-harm, and suicide ideation, but luckily hadn't ticked the 'doing it' box. The counselling and medication had helped a bit, but not much. After her dad had died when she was sixteen, she'd fallen in with a bad crowd, binged on drugs and alcohol and flunked out of school. She'd hated her mother for remarrying so soon after and couldn't stand her stepfather. She'd left home for a string of dead-end jobs and three months in juvey for repeated shoplifting. She shouldn't have cheeked the magistrate, but time out in detention had dried her out and arrested her downward spiral. She'd realised how lucky she was to have had a nice home and loving parents. Most of the poor kids there never stood a chance, had never known anything but violence, abuse and broken homes.

She'd since turned her life around, forgiving her mother and learning to tolerate her stepfather. Alright, he was still a bit of a dick, but he was kind and Mum was happy, and that was what mattered. She'd rediscovered music and had taken up the violin once more. Above all, she'd found a new purpose, a new passion—saving the planet—and had buried herself in study, going on to do a degree in environmental science. She was now doing a master's at the University of Brisbane. It was there that she met other XRs and had decided that protest and civil disobedience was necessary to draw public attention to the mounting climate crisis and government inaction. She had gone from being a rebel without a cause to a rebel with one.

She didn't feel good about the state of Planet Earth, but at least she'd finally come to feel good about herself. She couldn't remember feeling this happy since she was a young girl. She also felt good because she was in love. Where was he? Why hadn't he messaged? She'd kill him if he didn't come.

She'd met David after he'd given a seminar at the uni and shown a film on the Great Barrier Reef. He was doing post-doc research on it. She'd known the reef was in poor shape but was still shocked to see all the coral bleaching, which David had filmed himself. He was cute and afterwards she'd summoned the courage to go and speak to him. She'd had to wait her turn and was nearly trampled in the rush. The gasbag tarts in front just wouldn't shut up. She was about to go when he'd come over to her. "Hello," he'd said. "Would you like to meet for coffee?"

She hadn't expected that. "Er, yes. I'd love to," she'd replied, forgetting about what she was going to ask. It was only an excuse to speak anyway. He had told her sometime after that he'd spotted her in the audience and couldn't take his eyes off her.

They'd met for coffee and one thing had led to another. That was six months ago. Six months of bliss. He was so brilliantly intelligent and witty, kind and gentle, and *very* good in bed. He was very earnest, and boy could he rant, but he was passionate about his work. They did so many things together; they were like soul mates. Both missed much-loved parents—she, her dad, he, his mother who'd died three years before. He thought her fondness for Bartók was weird—maybe it was the Hungarian on her mother's side—and refused to come to chamber music concerts, but they both liked indie rock. Only two days before, they'd heard local band Ball Park Music, and she still had their song 'Cherub' stuck in her head. It reminded her of everything that was good and lovely.

She admired David's knowledge and passion for the reef, and he'd taken her snorkelling there, showing her the bad bits as well as the bits still alive.

He wasn't into protesting, but it was good that he'd agreed to come today. Where was he? He was never late.

Anxiety never went away if you were prone to it.

"I said move on!" repeated the policeman. "Now!" More police had arrived. They didn't look friendly.

She'd heard on the news that there would be a lot of police here today, and the government was promising to come down hard on protesters. *They're all talk and no action,* she thought. *They won't do anything.*

She received David's text and replied to tell him that she would meet him at the front of the station. So much for romantic meetings under clocks.

The train came to a halt just outside Brisbane Central Station, the signal at red. David Mallon texted Emma to say that his train was running late, but he'd soon be there.

The train was crowded with people going to the climate protest. People were talking and laughing, some dressed up. There were all ages of people. It was like a fun family outing, as if they were going to the Brisbane Pageant.

One group was dressed as marsupials. 'Protect the Quiet Australians', said their placards, which showed pictures of blackened koalas during the great fires, now happening every summer. He knew they'd borrowed a term the Prime Minister used a lot to describe his voters and supporters.

He hadn't wanted to come. He wasn't into protesting, and definitely not into sitting down in the traffic and getting arrested, as Emma had been that time. But she'd persisted. "It'll be amazing! Climate protests will be happening around the world. It will be the biggest yet in Brisbane. Thousands will be there to make their concerns known, all sorts of people, not just Extinction Rebels and schoolkids. You don't have to block the streets. Just be there! Be in King George Square!"

He'd relented and decided to come. She was very persuasive. How could a fellow resist eyes and lips like hers? He figured he had better come, if only to keep her out of trouble.

He knew he had every reason to be there. As a marine biologist, for the past two years, he'd been researching the condition of the Great Barrier Reef. It was like watching an old friend slowly turn into a skeleton.

He found himself getting worked up about it a lot these days, especially after a couple of beers. How could the climate deniers pretend it wasn't happening and claim that the reef was alive and well, as if that proved that climate change wasn't happening? They were like the pet shop owner in Monty Python's dead parrot sketch. 'It's not dead, just resting. It's a Norwegian Blue, pining for the fjords.' Were they blind or stupid or what? How could they be willing to sacrifice something so priceless for their stupid right-wing ideology and a few miserable jobs in the coal industry? Shouldn't conservatives want to conserve? The last straw was when the Federal Environment Minister, Sussan Cashmore, had recently gone snorkelling in one of the last intact areas and declared the Reef to be in 'good shape'. How could the government ignore all the research of even its own scientists?

I'll tell you why, he thought. *It's so that they can lie to tourists.* Of course, it would be bad for the economy if they stopped coming. What could you expect from that bunch of tossers? Sussan Cashmore was the one who'd dismissed the last IPCC Report as 'drawing a long bow' in warnings of dire consequences if urgent climate action wasn't taken, then admitted that she hadn't actually read it. How did people like that get to run the country? How could they get away with supporting Daghawi, the biggest coal mine in the world, and massive coal expansion elsewhere? And subsidising it with taxpayers' money?

Because the industry was the biggest donor to the Coalition, geddit, and Robert Moorcock made sure they kept getting elected. That was why. There'd be thousands more coal ships through the reef. Ships had already run aground and spilled fuel. It was madness.

"I love it when you have a good rant," Emma would tell him. "It makes me horny." Just thinking of her made him smile and gave him a hard-on. God, she was so beautiful. How could she want someone like him?

He had every reason to come today, but he felt uneasy. He'd heard in the news that the Federal Minister for Home Security, old Potato Head, had ordered zero tolerance towards climate protesters breaking the law after previous disruptions around Australia. The Queensland Premier had also ordered jail sentences of up to two years for protesters locking on or super-gluing themselves to the road and fines up to thirty thousand dollars. What, had they become some sort of Kafkaesque state whose highest purpose was freedom of traffic movement, where free speech was dangerously deviant? He felt another rant coming on.

He was mostly worried about Emma, concerned that they wouldn't be as lenient this time. He'd heard in the news that there would be a strong police presence, which meant drafting in many officers from the country. They could be redneck, Our Nation sympathisers. They might not take kindly to urban, woke greenies.

There could also be far-right extremists looking for trouble. There had already been isolated attacks at previous protests. Derisory comments by politicians and the media had helped stir up aggression. He'd read that one shock-jock TV presenter, Petanda de Ville, had suggested using the protesters as speed bumps. "Just a joke," she'd later insisted, when pulled up on it.

The whole thing could turn ugly.

He saw a group of men in the carriage staring at the protesters. If looks could kill.

The signal turned green, the air brakes hissed as they were released, and the train lurched forward as it drew into the station.

CHAPTER 3

They were now on the A3/A13 motorway, hitting the early morning traffic towards Zürich. There was a call on Dreiser's private phone.

"Thank you, that is very good." He turned off the phone.

Phoenix was so far progressing according to plan. Over the past year, he had done much investigation, analysis and planning. What he had in mind was not something for the back of an envelope. He had established a secure line of communication with Command and was being kept informed on progress.

Recruitment and procurement were well underway. Team leaders and operatives were needed. Phoenix presented ideal career progression for mercenaries, ex-military, ex-special forces, ex-etcetera. The jobs were not something that could readily be advertised on Indeed.com. *Do you want to make a difference? Exciting opportunities for energetic self-starters, previous experience with drones, rocket launchers and missiles welcome but not necessary, as training will be provided. Competitive basic pay and generous bonus. Equal opportunity employer. No time wasters.*

He had correctly anticipated that hiring would not prove too difficult using mercenary recruitment and other networks, such as trusted contacts. In a world where 'love thy neighbour' was not always observed, there were plenty of people with professional skills. There would be no shortage of motivated people with scores to settle, grudges, mortgages.

He had anticipated that Yemenis would be especially enthusiastic about the Saudi assignment. Besides sponsoring Zürich Grasshoppers, he was a fan of Tottenham Hotspur and a follower of English football. He'd often thought that if the Saudi Arabian government was a football team, it would have the chant of Millwall FC supporters, not known for their empathic tendencies. 'No one likes us. We don't care.' Because the world needed its oil, it could get away with murder. Besides being a leading opponent of action on climate change, it had been bombing the long-suffering Yemen since 2015—one more chapter in that country's sixty-year story of conflict and misery. One such recruit was Abdulaziz Saeed. His family were all dead, killed in a recent air raid.

For the Iran job, there would also be no shortage of candidates. It wasn't necessary to do much, to say much, to be persecuted by the authorities. It helped to be Kurdish, Sunni or to have protested for Kurdish independence. Arman Farhat had ticked all those boxes and had suffered for it, eventually escaping. He had done compulsory military service.

Nepalis would be especially attracted to the Qatar job. Only the terminally insane would hold a football World Cup in that country, and Dreiser had opposed it, but money had no mental or moral compass. Construction for the football World Cup stadium and other facilities had cost the lives of nearly four thousand migrant workers. Toiling for ten hours a day in temperatures up to forty-five degrees Celsius, most died from heatstroke. The son of Chitavake Bhattarai was one of over two thousand Nepalis who did not return home. Bhattarai was an ex-Gurkha, a proud tradition in his family. The British Army's Brigade of Gurkhas was one the most feared military units in the world.

Then there was the Indian assignment. The Sikh minority had long been persecuted, and Muslims were new victims of a Prime Minister stirring old divisions and old hatreds to enhance his political power. The father of Dilsher Singh had been killed by a Hindu mob when he was twelve. His family had emigrated to Toronto, but he carried the scar. He had served with the Canadian Armed Forces.

Other assignments were on the list, the targets stretching around the world. The Ogoni and Jiwa people would be especially enthusiastic about the Nigerian project, and Ukrainians about the Russian venture.

For security, project teams would be kept small and separate. No one, except those at the top, would know the bigger picture. Only the team leaders would know their targets in advance. A franchise business model would be employed. Besides training, military ordnance would be supplied as opposed to hamburgers, frozen fries and kitchen equipment.

They were approaching Zürich.

"It looks like another hot one, Johannes."

The sun was up and strong.

"Indeed, sir," said Johannes.

Emma spotted David squeezing through the crowd. She smiled and waved.

David spotted her blonde hair and waving hat. He waved back.

"Sorry I'm late," he said. They hugged and kissed.

"Never mind. You're here, that's what matters. Let's go."

They walked hand-in-hand along the crowded George Street sidewalk towards King George Square, where the rally was being held. She stopped to stare at the rings in a jeweller's window.

"I like that one." She laughed as he pulled her hat over her face.

Police lined the roadside, ensuring that people stayed on the path.

Thousands were already in the square as they arrived. There was a sea of faces and placards below the grand old buildings of the museum. A rock band played on a platform. People were making announcements.

David saw that Emma was right. There were not only XRs, but many others. They were mostly young, but there were representatives of all ages, parents with their children, grandparents with their grandchildren. There were schoolkid strikers in their uniforms, anti-Daghawi mine people dressed as lumps of coal, assorted anti-capitalists, animal rights representatives and others. There were professionals, business types in suits, doctors in white coats concerned about the impact of climate change on human health and mortality.

"Why are they red?" asked David. A group of XRs were dressed and painted in red from head to toe.

"They're the Red Rebels," said Emma." It's to signify the blood of all the animals that'll die from climate change. This way." She pulled him around the edge of the crowd, towards the Ann Street side. She knew that's where the action would be.

As they got closer, David didn't like what he saw. There were large numbers of police, many on horseback, many in riot gear. He could feel the simmering anger—hatred, even—of the police and many of the onlookers. He could see it in their faces.

Far-right groups were shouting insults and throwing things while the police looked the other way. He recognised the men from the train.

"Quiet Australians," he said. "Come on, Emma." He held her hand tightly as he tried to lead her away from potential trouble.

The organisers had assured the authorities that the protest would be peaceful and confined to the square, but the XRs had other plans. The text went out and a large group broke away through a gap in the police line and into Ann Street. Traffic had stopped at a pedestrian crossing and there was a gap in the road ahead. The crowd poured into it, Emma pulling David along with her.

"Stop! We're not doing this!"

"It'll be alright," said Emma. "There are loads of people. We have to stand up for what's right." A woman gave a signal, and everyone sat down in the road, except David, who stood out like a sore thumb.

"Sit!" said Emma.

"I'm not a cocker spaniel." David reluctantly joined her on the tarmac.

A traffic jam had built up and drivers were honking their horns. Some got out of their cars to shout at the protesters.

A police loudspeaker blared a warning to the crowd. "You are causing an … obstruction … breach of … disperse now … forcibly removed … arrested."

The mounted police had formed a line, the horses pacing impatiently. Behind them, lines of helmeted police stood in riot gear. The order was given, and the mounted police advanced at a canter, the sound of horses' hooves echoing above the cacophony. The riot police followed, banging their batons on their shields.

Protesters on the perimeter saw the horses coming first and leapt to their feet, as if sitting on nests of bull ants, trying to get out of the way as the police line drove forward.

Then foot police went into the crowd, many in riot gear. "Get off the road or you will all be arrested," said the police loudspeaker. Some protesters got up and tried to get away. Many stayed on the ground and were lifted or violently dragged to waiting vans, young and old being hit if they resisted. The protesters were shocked, many in tears of disbelief. How could this happen in Australia, land of the fair go, free speech, right to protest, where the disrespectful larrikin was a cherished mythical hero?

The police had been ordered to target smaller, lighter people, especially women, for lifting off the road before being arrested and taken away. There was less risk of back injuries and workers' compensation. For health and safety reasons, bigger people could be kicked. That would get them up.

Some protesters started fighting back, some using their placards as weapons. The riot police weighed into them. It was now a melee.

"We have to get out of this!" David was pulling Emma up when two officers grabbed her. They didn't expect her to put up a fight.

"Get your filthy hands off me, you pigs."

The officers were manhandling her, one pulling her hair. She bit his hand.

"You fucking bitch! You're coming with us. I'll have you for assault."

"Leave her alone!" shouted David, wrestling with and punching one of them.

The other let go of Emma, pulled out his baton and hit David on the side of his head. David crumpled, banging his head on the road as he fell. He lay motionless, blood oozing from his hair.

Emma struggled free and dropped to her knees, cradling him in her arms, gently slapping him on his cheek. "David! Wake up! Wake up!"

She looked up at the policemen, tears welling in her eyes "Don't just stand there!" she screamed. "Call an ambulance!" She crouched over David, sobbing.

Two St John's first aiders arrived, a man and a woman. One checked his pulse.

"He's concussed, but hopefully he'll be okay. At least the bleeding has stopped. We've already called ambulances for the other casualties."

Ten minutes later the road was being cleared of protesters, the arrested being loaded into police vans, the wounded into ambulances.

Emma was still clinging to David as the ambulance crew moved him onto a stretcher and loaded him in. "Can I come with him?"

"Sure, love. Jump in."

The ambulance drove off, light flashing, siren wailing.

A policeman looked around. Where was that fucking greenie bitch? She'd drawn blood and he'd needed a band-aid. Was his tetanus up to date? Toowoomba girls weren't like that. He should have arrested her.

All that remained on the road were broken placards being collected by police—*Stop Daghawi, Protect the Quiet Australians*—and blood stains.

A police traffic controller gave the order and the backed-up traffic started moving again. Civilisation was restored.

⁓

Emma sat in the back of the ambulance as it raced to Royal Brisbane Hospital. Oh please, God, let him be alright.

The ambulance crew wheeled David into Emergency. Emma followed.

"Wait over there, love. He's in good hands. The staff here are brilliant."

After an initial examination, David was taken in for an MRI and CAT scan.

A neurosurgeon arrived to assess the results. "There's been ICH, intracerebral haemorrhaging. We must operate. There's a serious clot."

⁓

June 5

"How good is coal!" declared Prime Minister Maurice Turbott. "We, the Australian Government, rejoice in coal, provided by God to make Australia prosperous, the lucky country, to deliver jobs and growth for many decades to come."

"Gobshite, ya fuckin' donkey!" Sean Mallon begged to differ.

Turbott was addressing the Australian Parliament in Canberra during Question Time. Mallon was over three-thousand-and-seven-hundred kilometres away in Fremantle, Western Australia. He was watching the national news and bouncing his grandson, Kieran, on his knee. The boy was eighteen months old.

"Language, Dad!" said Siobhan, Kieran's mother.

"Sorry. *Feckin'*. Look now, he doesn't mind." Mallon blew a raspberry on Kieran's tummy as the boy squealed with delight.

Earlier that day

PM Turbott brandished a lump of coal at the opposition benches as his colleagues smirked like mischievous schoolboys. The piece of fossilised plant matter, provided by coal industry lobbyists, had been carefully sprayed with a sealant so that he would not get his hands dirty. He checked his hands to make sure.

"Unlike the opposition, this government is not afraid of coal. That is why the Daghawi mine has had and will continue to have our full support. As will the Australian coal industry, the bread of life for our great nation." He was a devout believer. Coal was a gift from the Almighty and to not to dig it up and burn it would be a sin against God, not to mention his party's donors.

"There'll be no feckin' jobs and growth on a feckin' dead planet," Mallon remarked. "The Prime Minister of Tuvalu said that. Something like that, anyway."

"Where's Tuvalu?" asked Siobhan. "Sounds like someone saying goodbye."

"Somewhere in the Pacific Ocean. The Islanders will soon be kissing their arses goodbye if the sea goes on rising, and they keep getting blown away by cyclones. But never mind, says Barney McDuff. They can come here and pick fruit. That's very generous of him! I don't know, how can they make such an eejit Deputy Prime Minister just because he's leader of the Nationwide Party. They call him Cousin Jethro in Canberra. He comes out with something stupid every time he opens his mouth."

"You're such a greenie, Dad. I love it when you get on your high horse." Siobhan planted a kiss on his head and took Kieran.

"Greener than a feckin' leprechaun, that's me."

The news continued:

"Climate protests continued today in major cities around the world. Brisbane saw violent clashes between police and protesters with many arrests. A police spokesman denied accusations of excessive use of force."

The Minister of Home Security appeared on the screen.

"Today's events have been regrettable, but the police have been outstanding in the face of provocation," the minister said. "Breaking the law will not be tolerated. The Australian people have a right to go about their business without being disrupted by green-left terrorists."

"I hope David wasn't there," said Siobhan. "It looked nasty. I'll be happier when we know he's alright. It'll be late there but I'll call him." She had always been protective towards her younger brother.

"Ah, he's very sensible. I'm sure he's kept out of trouble." Mallon poured himself a Guinness. "Slainte." As a FIFO, fly-in-fly-out, shot firer at an iron ore mine in the Pilbara, he was enjoying being at home, relaxing with his family and favourite tipple.

The phone rang and Siobhan answered.

"It's the Royal Brisbane Hospital, Dad. You'd better take it."

"Yes … yes … oh, God! Tell him I'm coming! Tell him to hang on." Mallon hung up. "It's David. He's had a head injury and is unconscious. I have to be with him. I'll go on the red-eye tonight."

"Get yourself some hand luggage and I'll find a flight." Siobhan tried to keep calm. Kieran was crying for both of them. She was a nurse and had dealt with trauma injuries. It had to be bad for them to call. Fingers crossed he'd be okay.

There was one seat left on Virgin at 23:50. Siobhan booked it.

CHAPTER 4

Friday June 5, Trafalgar Sq, London

"Sorry, guv," said the taxi driver to Burns. "Looks like more bloody climate protesters blockin' the traffic an' that. I'd lock 'em all up an' frow away the key, I would. It's all a load of bollocks if you ask me. Wevver's always changin', innit? What's wrong wiv a bit of 'ot wevver for a change?" London was, once again, like the rest of Europe, sweltering in record temperatures.

Burns saw that the road ahead was blocked by a police line turning traffic around. Beyond was a large crowd of people standing, seated or lying on the ground.

"Drop me here, please," he said, deciding to walk the rest of the way. "Keep the change."

"All the best, guv. You're a gentleman."

He saw large, unmarked, dark blue buses with grilled windows disgorging lines of police in high-viz jackets, no doubt so that tourists could easily spot them to ask for cheery directions to London's many historic treasures. Large, unmarked vans were arriving, almost certainly to offer the protesters courtesy rides home. There was never a policeman around when you needed one.

He picked his way through the crowd. There were banners and placards galore demanding or commenting on this or that. Many of them were the usual best sellers: *There is no Planet B* and *I'll go back to school when the government learns some science*. Some were more original: *Climate change is worse than homework*. Was there an unstated competition for the wittiest slogan? A Booker Prize for *bons mots*? He reckoned that they were all suggesting more or less the same thing: that it would not, on balance, be a great idea for humanity to commit collective suicide and that the kids would like to have a future. If it wasn't too much to ask, that is.

Away from the protest, the streets were even more crowded than usual as swarms of people avoided descending into the poorly ventilated hell of the Underground, instead braving the surface heat.

"Mad dogs and Englishmen go out in the midday sun." Burns hummed the Flanders and Swan classic as he pounded the pavement. He noticed among the crowds an unpleasantly large number of pink, paunchy, topless men. He thought this had to be one of the worst things about global warming.

He stopped at a news stand. There was something for everyone in the headlines. 'It's Bikini Weather!' declared *The Moon*, Britain's best-selling newspaper. It had once been a favourite of his lads, especially when it showcased tits on page three. Whoever its owner, Robert Moorcock, told its readers to vote for was invariably elected to government. Funny that.

'Climate Bombshell: Earth Cooling Says Scientist,' claimed *The Daily Post*, Britain's flagship for climate denial. He'd read that its lead columnist on climate, James Uppole, also wrote for the RightWhat News, which was influential in US politics.

'Climate Catastrophe as Greenland Melts,' lamented *The Sentinel*. He bought a copy. He knew it was a fringe rag for thinkers and depressives—these days one and the same—but he liked its crossword.

Ten minutes later he was relieved to be in the reception of the Dominion Club on St James St. He was impressed by the craftmanship in its late Victorian stone and its marble and oak finishing. But above all, he was impressed by its air-conditioning.

Hadley was already waiting.

"Ah, Alex, so glad you could come. It's good to see you again."

"Likewise."

They shook hands.

"Come this way. I've booked a private dining room. I'm reliably informed that the Dover sole is excellent today."

"Sounds splendid. I was feeling a bit flat," said Burns. Hadley pretended not to have heard.

"We're in here," said Hadley. The waiter showed them to their seats.

"Pouilly fuissé?" suggested Hadley, scrutinising the wine list.

"Excellent choice," said Burns.

"I won't beat about the bush," Hadley began, when the waiter was out of the room. "I have a client who's rather concerned about the state of the world."

"I came across a few others on my way here."

"You did?" Hadley had a 'please don't interrupt until I've finished' look on his face. "He considers—and I understand he has sought the best and frankest scientific advice—that as things stand, we have almost no chance of avoiding climate meltdown within the next two or three decades. It will mean the end of most vestiges of civilisation, and most other creatures, bless 'em."

"This is all pretty grim, but isn't exactly news, at least for people who care to know. It's why the kids are back on the streets after COVID. What does your client propose to do, anyway? And how does it involve me?"

Hadley paused to top up their wine glasses. "He wants to take out the fossil fuel industry." He mentioned it casually, as if his client wanted to take out a home loan.

Burns raised an eyebrow. "The fossil fuel industry? That's a tall order. I understand there's rather a lot of it. What does he have in mind?"

"He considers the industry to be the basic problem, along with its political cronies. Apparently, we might have had a fighting chance of an orderly transition to low carbon if we'd started when the first IPCC report came out in 1990, but they've spent millions, billions on misinformation and blocking action. Since then, more carbon has been put into the atmosphere than in the whole of human history. Governments have been ladling out trillions in subsidies and recent COVID recovery bailouts to the industry. Then there are the financial boys and girls—several trillion in fossil fuel investment even since the Paris Agreement."

"Does he really expect to take it all out?"

"His intention is not to destroy it altogether—life has to go on—but to prune it, cull it, as it were. Disrupt and cut production and supply, curtail further expansion, run it down while renewables take off, send a supply and price shock around the world that will not just curb consumption and emissions from fossil fuels but also spike the guns of other harmful industries which run on it, like plastics. Above all, he wants to break the industry's power."

"I'm assuming he's thinking of sabotage."

"Funny you should say that. Yes. If you recall, just a few exploding drones on the Abqaiq and Khurais refineries in Saudi 2018 did a lot of damage and sent an immediate shock to world markets and oil prices. But they were soon repaired. Think of what a much bigger attack on many refineries would do."

"Aside from the military logistics—defence systems and what not, has he—have they—considered that it will have pretty dramatic consequences for the world economy and billions of ordinary people?"

"He knows that. Apparently, so will frying the planet and melting the polar ice caps. The Saudis might have spent a bit on defences since that attack, but petroleum installations are very hard to defend. Most in the world have little or no defence. They're soft targets."

"Governments are going to take it badly, as acts of terrorism and national security or worse. War, even."

"Alex, terrorism is relative to who has the upper hand, to who rules. There's already a war of terror going on, though most people don't know it or want to admit it. The fossil fuel industry has effectively declared a war of terror on civilisation, the future and all life on Earth in order to hold on to power and make a last buck. There's a war of terror on the world and those who want to save it by those who want to carry on profiting or consuming until there's nothing left. There's a war of terror by the older generation who want to carry on stuffing the planet, against the young who will pick up the tab." Hadley paused. "... I'm sounding quite the greenie anarchist in my old age, aren't I? But I have grandchildren. I wouldn't take this one on if I didn't think it was a goer. As far as I'm concerned, if an industry behaves like this then it shouldn't be too surprised if, sooner or later, someone comes along and kicks its arse. Especially if its arse—its assets—are highly exposed and vulnerable. And in most cases, highly flammable.

"The industry and its political goons have the upper hand now and are beating down protest, but as the kids realise protest isn't working and no one's listening, it will turn into a real war of resistance. A guerrilla war. Sooner or later, kids and others will realise that sabotage is all that's left. Unless, God help us, we have to resort to geoengineering, like filling the sky with particles as some maniacs want to do. We'll never see a blue sky again, I understand."

"They won't notice much in Britain," said Burns.

Hadley remained poker-faced. He didn't do humour.

"So why are you telling me all this?" asked Burns.

Hadley poured more wine. "We want you on board for a particular target."

"Don't tell me—it's in the Middle East."

"I rather thought you'd feel at home there … No, they're making other arrangements, you'll be pleased to know. I'm proposing Australia for you."

Burns thought Hadley sounded like the Hogwarts Sorting Hat choosing Gryffindor.

"Australia? I've been to worse places." Everywhere he'd been on active service.

"My client has made it a key target. It's soon to be the biggest coal exporter and it's overtaken Qatar as the biggest in LNG. That's liquefied natural gas. It's been one of the worst offenders in blocking climate action and is planning massive expansion of its coal and gas industries. It's also one of the worst affected by climate change. My client, like many others, has a soft spot for it and has been shocked by the devastation of its wildlife—images of cremated koalas and all that—and the stupidity of its climate denier politicians. Not to mention the stupidity of people who keep voting them back in. Thinks the Aussies need shaking up."

"A bit of a reverse swing usually does the trick," said Burns.

Hadley managed a smile—he had a season ticket at Lord's. But was Burns taking this seriously?

"The remuneration will be generous, of course, up-front and on results. Usual thing—through a Swiss bank. And of course, if we reach an agreement, it won't be in writing and we've never met. Interested?"

"I might be," said Burns. "Tell me more. Who's it for and what are the other targets and proposed attack methods?"

"I couldn't tell you who the ultimate client is, even if I knew, and I can't tell you all of the precise targets and attack strategies which, needless to say, have to be hush-hush."

"Okay, when will the attacks happen?"

"Attacks will be simultaneous or close together to maximise surprise, so that key countries and installations have little or no time to prepare their defences. They will be at night to provide cover for operators to act and exit. Going around the global time zones, Australia will be first followed by East Asia, Russia, the Middle East, Africa, Europe and North America. It's a bit like New Years' eve rotating around the world. First strike in Australia will also be symbolic—a Western country taking a first hit, to show it's not just a plot to destroy the power of the Middle East and Asia, that it's a shared thing. A chance for Australia to show a lead on climate action for a change."

"This all sounds pretty big if it's going to make a difference. Where will all the hardware and personnel come from?"

"It's big, alright. It's already being financed and arranged. Money seems to be no object. The personnel will be professionals like you and specially recruited individuals, who can blend in, speak the lingo, look the part. In the ME, especially, we can't do it all with people like you, with boot polish on their faces and tea towels on their heads. Around those parts there's no shortage of people with a grudge against the targets, who would probably do it for nothing, except of course they'll be paid."

"What attack methods are you thinking of?"

"Most will be direct, real-time, using drones, missiles or other methods. Australia will be an exception, given its size and geography, coal in the east, gas in the west, with timed explosives to allow multiple planting and escape. Here we're arranging a boat and a midget sub for the job. The bombs, like the attacks elsewhere, will be timed for what we're calling C-Day. Like D-day, it will be marked in history. C for climate action. C for Christmas when installations will have minimum people around."

"That's nice," said Burns "C for corporate responsibility?" The firm he had recently worked for was always banging on about it while behaving as if it thought ethics was a county in England. "And where will I and my team be when the shit hits the fan?"

After lunch, they agreed to meet again for a more detailed discussion.

Burns headed towards Trafalgar Square to see what was happening. Police cars—lights flashing—rushed past, followed by plain dark blue vans, no doubt containing protesters to be detained at Her Majesty's displeasure.

Nearby, the British Prime Minister was briefing the media from a lectern positioned outside Number 10 Downing Street.

"What do you think of the climate protesters?" asked a reporter.

"Uncooperative crusties, I call 'em," the PM replied, with the scathing wit only an expensive private-school education could confer.

Larry, the Number Ten cat, looked on disdainfully before deciding to wash his paws of it all.

On the way home, Burns stopped at the Queen's Arms in Queensgate Mews for a pint and a ponder.

He'd be doing what came naturally, what he was good at—leading a small group of highly trained professionals in intense covert action. It would be dangerous, but that's where the thrill was. If all went well, they could do the job undetected. He would assemble the best team of old mates he could find. He knew they'd jump at the chance of a last fling before becoming too old for it. The money was eye-watering. It would set them all up for life. What were the snags? Possible life imprisonment? Getting shot? Death? The decision was a no-brainer. 'Who dares wins'—the SAS motto.

CHAPTER 5

After a four-hour operation, David was taken from theatre to Intensive Care and was placed on life support.

"He's in a coma," said the nurse to Emma, who had been waiting, beside herself with worry. "It's too soon to say. He could be like this for some time. You might want to go home and get some sleep, then come back in the morning."

Emma held his hand. He looked so peaceful. She knew she had to be there for him.

"I'll stay."

The nurse arranged a chair and some pillows.

Exhausted, Emma dozed off.

Mallon was squeezed into his seat on the crowded aircraft for the five-hour flight to Brisbane. The red-eye was an unpleasant experience at the best of times—people jammed in for the cheaper overnight fares, faces long with dread, grizzly kids in pyjamas, awake way past their bedtime. There was no movie option on the screens, no food, and it was hard to sleep. Mallon was stout, like his favourite drink, but stocky—muscular rather than podgy. He knew they had to get as many people in as possible, but had they used leprechauns as seating designers and test pilots?

He wasn't usually a worrier, but he was anxious about David. No. He'd be alright. Medics were amazing these days. He was in good hands. He'd be okay.

Helped by the earlier Guinness, he dozed off, sleeping fitfully.

The nightmare often went away for a while, sometimes for months, but would always recur: the flash of the explosion, dust, screams, ambulances, bloodied faces staring at him through the dust, hands reaching out to him. The shrill laughter of the bearded man: "That's the way to do it! That's the way to do it!" Like in the scary Punch and Judy show he'd seen at the seaside as a small boy.

He awoke, sweating, then drifted off again. This time he saw bright light surrounded by blue. He was swimming with David. He wanted to hold his hand, but something was stopping him, making his son drift further away. He awoke and rubbed his eyes. It was now light outside, the bright rising sun in the east.

"This is your pilot, Peter Wells. We have now commenced our descent into Brisbane. We hope you have had a very pleasant flight and look forward to seeing you again soon …"

Mallon rushed out of the Domestic Terminal at Brisbane Airport and grabbed a cab.

"The Royal Hospital and step on it."

The cab hit the morning rush hour into the city and moved slowly.

"The traffic is getting really terrible," said the driver, apologetically. "Worse and worse. All the time, more cars and trucks on the roads." He took a shortcut, followed a flashing ambulance and raced into the hospital drop-off. "I hope all is well, sir."

"Thanks, mate. Keep the change."

Mallon ran into Emergency. Wrong entrance. *Go to Intensive Care.*

Emma felt the nurse waking her. Where was she? There must be good news! *Tell me David's awake!*

"I'm so very sorry. We lost him."

"What? No! No! No!"

She held David, kissing him, covering his face with her tears. "Forgive me, darling ... forgive me ..."

The nurse led her outside and sat her down. "Wait there, pet, and someone will be with you shortly."

She banged her head against the wall. Her face was red with tears. "What have I done? What have I done?"

"Mr Mallon?" said the young registrar. "We did all we could. Please accept our condolences."

In shock, Mallon could not at first take it in and had to sit down. As the realisation hit, tears welled up and streamed down his cheeks. He buried his face in his hands and cried.

A nurse patted him and gave him a box of tissues.

"Here, take these, love. Stay as long as you want."

"Thanks," he said, staring ahead.

He sat for a while, not knowing what to do. He took deep breaths, tried to compose himself. David would want him to be strong.

He heard the sound of crying and looked up. There was a girl sitting around the corner. David had mentioned that he'd had a girlfriend and would soon bring her to meet the family. He got up and sat next to her.

"Excuse me ... Are you Emma?"

She stopped sobbing. "Yes ... You must be David's dad. I ... It's all my fault ... I'm ... I'm ..."

"What happened? Please tell me."

She tried talking, convulsing as she spoke. "He didn't want to come ... did it for me ... it was peaceful ... people happy ... then it went bad, there was so much hate from the police, those watching ... the police just attacked, went for us ... hit David ... he was just trying to protect me, to protect the reef." She broke down and cried on his shoulder. As he patted her, his tears fell on her hair.

"Don't blame yourself. He was doing what he thought was right. Thank you for staying with him all night so he wasn't alone." He grabbed a box of tissues. "Here, take these."

"Thanks." She dabbed her eyes, blew her nose and straightened her dishevelled hair.

"Look, there's nothing more you can do here. Go home and get some sleep ... take this for a cab." He squeezed some notes into her hand.

"That's kind of you," said Emma. "... is there anything I can do?"

"Write your number here and I'll be in touch."

After Emma had gone, he asked to see David and was taken to an anteroom. The nurse lifted the cover, and he kissed his son's head.

"I'm so very sorry," said the nurse. He recognised her soft Irish accent.

"Thank you. I know you all did your best."

He was still taking it all in, his head spinning from the shock, the total body blow. He was fatigued after the overnight flight, needed coffee, hot and sweet. He went to the lift, down to the main lobby and on to the cafeteria. He ordered and sat down, finishing his coffee in a few mouthfuls. Thoughts flashed through his head, memories of David's life, the beautiful child, undergrad and doctorate graduations at the University of Western Australia, going diving with him at the Ningaloo Reef, their last conversation. Had he remembered to say, 'I love you'? *We should all do that to anyone we love, all the time, in case we never see them again,* he thought. He remembered his wife Laura, telling her goodbye as she died of cancer three years ago, even though she was unconscious from the morphine. At least she was spared this.

He hated hospitals. For many, they were places of reassurance and hope after accidents or unhealthy lives. He could see it in the faces of patients and visitors. But for him they were places of death. He needed to get out, get away, but felt he couldn't leave the hospital, couldn't leave David. He ordered another coffee and sat for a while, thinking about what Emma had told him. Why did they have to do that to his son?

He went out for some fresh air and paced for a while. There was a line of cabs. He decided to see what the police had to say, what they were going to do about it.

The cab dropped him outside Brisbane Central Police Station. He went into the reception.

He stood in the queue, which moved slowly towards two disinterested-looking duty officers. Mallon watched the citizens baring their little lives. Someone was going on loudly about their neighbour's anti-social behaviour. Do they need to describe in detail every incident, every insult? Why couldn't people get on? Life was so short and precious. Didn't they know the police couldn't waste their scarce resources on people calling each other names? Another was upset about losing her handbag, as if it was the worst loss of her life. "But the bag and contents are irreplaceable. Why aren't the police doing more about crime?"

He eventually spoke to one of the officers.

"My son David was one of those injured yesterday at the climate protest. He died earlier this morning. I want to know what you will be doing about it, about the officer responsible."

"Please take a seat over there. Someone will attend to you as soon as possible."

Mallon waited, brooding. They were taking their time sending someone out. They wouldn't have known that David was dead until now. They'd be considering their legal position.

Eventually a young female officer showed him into a meeting room.

"Rest assured, the incident will be fully investigated. There will need to be a post-mortem and coroner's report. If you wish to register a formal complaint, then I will take a statement from you now."

He kept his patience as he completed and signed the form. It wasn't her fault he was being fobbed off. He knew that they wouldn't do anything. That they'd pretend to investigate it, and that those responsible would be cleared of any wrongdoing. David would be blamed for protesting, as rape victims were blamed for being raped, as Indigenous Australians were blamed for their deaths in police custody.

"You'll be hearing from me!" he shouted as he stormed out of the main reception area. He had not yet considered the details, but it would be more than filing a complaint. He knew what he felt like doing to the police who had killed his son, the politicians who had set the police on him and the voters who'd put them in power.

The people in the queue looked at each other as if wondering whether the threat included them. "You get such unpleasant people in police stations," said one to another.

"Next," said a duty officer as Mallon left the building.

Dazed, he wandered around and sat down. It was now dawn in Perth. He'd better call Siobhan. She'd be worried sick, wouldn't have slept a wink. How was he going to break the news?

She called first. "How is he?"

"Siobhan, my love … he didn't come round. He passed in his sleep."

He could hear her sobbing.

"Look, darlin', I'm coming back today. It's a terrible thing and we need to help each other through this. I can't bring David home until after the inquest. I'll return here then to sort out his things and affairs."

"Okay, Dad. Let me know when you're arriving, and we'll pick you up. Love you."

Siobhan held Kieran and smothered him with kisses. She didn't want him to see her crying. She looked at the pictures of David on the mantelpiece, on the wall, and had to turn away. How could they do that to someone so beautiful, to her brother? Dad would take it badly. He still hadn't gotten over Mum going. He wouldn't take it lying down. He might seem calm and gentle on the surface, but people didn't want to get on the wrong side of him. He had amazing hands. He could do such fine delicate work, like electronics for his work, but he also had fists like sledgehammers. She hoped he wouldn't do anything he might regret.

June 6, evening, Perth Airport

Siobhan and Kieran were waiting at Terminal Three. The flight was on time and had just landed.

The arriving passengers streamed past. Siobhan spotted him, his head bowed disconsolately. He perked up when he saw her with Kieran.

They hugged and kissed, holding back the tears for Kieran's sake.

"Have you been a good boy, Kieran? Look, I got you this koala! They have them in Queensland."

Kieran smiled and held the toy in his arms.

"Come on, Dad. Let's get you home."

June 6, Zürich

Dreiser read that climate protests around the world had been mostly peaceful, but that Extinction Rebels had been arrested in London and in Australian cities. There had been a violent confrontation in Brisbane, with many protesters hurt and arrested. One had died. What must the young man's family be going through? It seemed he was a researcher studying the Great Barrier Reef. He was the first casualty of this war but wouldn't be the last.

He received a message that they had an outstanding candidate for the Australian Mission. Excellent.

When in Zürich, Dreiser stayed at his eighteenth-century villa in the exclusive Zürichberg district. He didn't see much of his ex-wives, Angelika and Claudine, these days, but his daughter Bernadine visited occasionally and left her children with him while she did her business in the city.

He loved to spend time with his grandchildren. Heidi didn't care for the children pulling her tail or carrying her like a sack of potatoes, but she was gentle with them and hid when they were around.

"Please can we play Red Riding Hood, Grandpa Wolfgang? Please?" asked Sofia, four.

"Oh, very well." She draped a cloth over his head.

"Just pretend I've come to visit you and the big bad wolf has locked you in the closet."

"My word! What a bad old wolf!"

"My, what big eyes you have!"

"All the better to see you with."

"My, what a big nose you have!"

"All the better to smell you with."

"My, what big teeth you have!"

"All the better to eat you with! Grrr!" She squealed with delight as he tickled her.

What he was doing was especially for them. There was such sweetness, such innocence in them. Yet, here they were, with their primeval fear of monsters, creatures of the night with beady eyes and sharp teeth, while most wild animals that might be the origin of such fears had practically been exterminated.

The real monsters they should be afraid of were those resembling human beings, cold-blooded, calculating psychopaths. People, mostly men, with no empathy, who would destroy the world for ideology, profit and power.

CHAPTER 6

June 8, National Press Club Melbourne

"In conclusion, we need to need to get the gas from under our feet."

PM Turbott was delivering a speech announcing a major expansion of natural gas production and exports, onshore and offshore. Offshore gas production in Western Australia, already the world's biggest exporter, would be greatly expanded. Bans would be lifted on onshore fracking and drilling for oil and gas around Australia's coast, including in World Heritage Shark Bay and the Ningaloo Reef in the west. Why would God have provided the bounty if He didn't want it to be exploited?

"This will build on our gas-led recovery, already highly successful in delivering jobs and growth. Are there any questions?"

"Louise Brailly, *The Sentinel Australia*."

She saw Turbott turn to take her question, with an 'oh her again' expression on his face. She'd given up pointing out that the gas-led recovery had provided almost no jobs and was a scam for Turbott's gas executive chums and party donors to line their pockets with taxpayers' money. She decided to stick to the new announcement.

"Prime Minister, how do you justify greatly expanding gas production when the world is heating up and Australia is on fire every summer? How will Australia ever reduce its greenhouse emissions?"

"I'm very glad you asked that, Louise."

From experience, Brailly knew that Turbott, an ex-marketing man, was always ready with a well-rehearsed answer, as if an answering machine had been switched on.

"Gas is the clean bridging fuel to the future. Thanks to our clean energy, Australia is all set to achieve our emissions reduction targets at a canter. What's more, by increasing the production and export of our fuels, we're reducing other countries' emissions. This is why there will be no reduction in our domestic emissions beyond our already world-beating targets."

OMG, thought Brailly. How can he be repeating that when Australia is at the bottom of the OECD league on climate action? Ranked at number fifty-seven, to be precise, like the old Heinz logo. It was an apt number. She'd wanted to write that this government had more farts in it than a tin of baked beans, but it wasn't house style at *The Sentinel*.

"There's time for one more question," said the Convener.

"Richard Evans, Australian Institute for Policy Research. Why isn't your government expanding renewables when Australia is the world capital for sun worship?"

It was a rhetorical question. Evans and others knew why. The answering machine switched on.

"Australia is a world leader in renewables and this government will ensure it remains so. But as an industry, it can stand on its own two feet."

Blah, blah. *That means being cut and thrown to the wolves*, thought Evans.

"Australia is also a world leader in technology innovation, which is the central plank of our emissions strategy."

That meant magic dust technologies like carbon farming and carbon capture and storage. Anything to avoid reducing fossil fuel emissions. Evans persisted. "I understand that your government plans to tax electric vehicles to replace lost income from fuel taxes. Why is this when other countries are supporting EVs?"

"Australians work hard and need reliable cars for employment and relaxation. My government won't be telling people what they can or can't buy and use if they want to go camping or fishing and tow boats and caravans. We won't be the government that ends the Great Australian Weekend."

Hamish Tallone, Turbott's scandal-ridden Energy Minister stood next to him, nodding sagely.

Evans caught Brailly rolling her eyes. They knew that renewables were not part of the government's plans. There were no political donations from that industry, none of the nice revolving door post-political career directorships that went with supporting their fossil friends.

June 8, Fremantle, Western Australia

Mallon took compassionate leave from work to wait for the inquest and David's funeral. His grief was overwhelming, and his mind wouldn't have been on the job. In his work at the mine there was no margin of error for lapses of concentration. There was comfort at least in being with Siobhan and Kieran.

"How's my best girl today?" He gave her and Kieran a hug.

"Better for having you around, Dad. I'll head off to work now. You know what to do for Kieran. His dinner's in the fridge and there's a beef and Guinness pie for you, your favourite."

Already a busy mother, she found that keeping active helped take her mind off things and so she was carrying on with her part-time nursing job at Fremantle Hospital. She wanted to get on with arranging the funeral, wanted to make it something fitting, something special, but couldn't do that until David was brought home and she could firm up the date.

Sitting at home all day, Mallon was moping, his grief turning to growing, festering anger. David's death was all over the papers, TV and radio, a talking point. Why couldn't they just allow quiet mourning? Oh no, they couldn't let a good story like this go, could they? They were opinion formers, after all, and everyone had to have an opinion on David and climate protest. Their fucking opinion. They couldn't resist an opportunity to put down the protesters, to blame them. It was David's own fault, they were saying. Of course, that Greta Thunberg was ultimately to blame for inciting people to riot. Why didn't they want to know why he was at the protest, what he had died for, why he cared so much about the reef, the future?

His tears of grief were turning to tears of rage. Most of all he hated the smarmy Coalition politicians with all their condescending disapproval. They were dining out on it. They'd all been sent on empathy training, of course, since all the abuse of women stuff. They knew that appearing to be human made good PR. "I regret that this has happened and extend my condolences to his family," they were saying. They liked to use the word 'regret' rather than 'sorry', didn't they? But they weren't sorry at all. In the same breath, they were saying: "But we are the government of law and order and will not tolerate anti-social behaviour." It was a great opportunity to pander to voters and show they were tough on protest. This was the way to go. To make an example of the protesters and to put the fear of God into them. He was disgusted by all the trolls calling for the police to kill more of these green-left terrorists, as the government and media liked to call them. He and Siobhan started receiving anonymous hate mail. Siobhan reported it to the police, but they did nothing.

A TV crew turned up at the Mallon home as they returned from the shops. Siobhan hurried indoors with Kieran.

"How do you feel about David's death? Do you blame the protesters for leading him on?"

"How would you feel about a punch in the face?" enquired Mallon, assisting the reporter and his cameraman into more relaxed positions on the ground. He was glad they didn't press charges and that the TV company didn't send the bill for a replacement camera. It must have been insured.

He was worried that Emma was beating herself up as well as grieving and called to check that she was alright. "Look, it wasn't your fault. You and David were doing what's right, standing up to this bleedin' government. I'm proud of you both. It's them that were in the wrong … Here, Siobhan would like to say hello."

"Hi, Emma. I'm Siobhan, David's sister. He said such lovely things about you … yes … I know how you feel … he was very special to us both …" They had a long chat. "Yes, I know … I know …"

Mallon turned on the ABC, one of the few Australian news sources he could stand, one of the few not owned by Moorcock News. The ever-frowning Resources Minister, Brad Callaghan, was being interviewed on the 7:30 Report. "Why do you say that young people shouldn't protest?" asked Leigh Sales.

Callaghan: "Protest will lead to the dole queue. I want them learning how to build mines and how to drill for oil and gas, which is one of the most remarkable science exploits in the world. Look at what happened to that protester. Ex-protester, I should say." A hint of a smirk. "This is what can happen if you don't learn science, if you blindly follow others instead of thinking for yourself."

Sales: "It seems that the young man who died was in fact a scientist."

Callaghan: "Protesters should make their point through proper, acceptable political processes. Through debate and the ballot box, which is the Australian way, not social disruption and blocking traffic, which amounts to terrorism. Look, the Coalition Government has an electoral mandate from the Australian people to support the Daghawi mine and exploit the nation's natural resources—coal, gas and oil—for the benefit of all. And that is that."

Sales: "Many people don't agree, and consider that in Australia, climate and energy policy is made on the basis of political donation. Some are protesting against the government's inaction on climate. Is that any reason to use violence against them?"

"If people don't want to get hurt, they should stop protesting. If people fail to respect the law, they must accept the consequences. I hope no one is foolish enough to make him into some kind of martyr."

"Thank you for joining us this evening, Minister."

"It's always a pleasure, Leigh."

"What a twat," said Siobhan. "He looks like he's just eaten an onion."

"His brain must be about the same size," said Mallon. "It seems to be a necessary qualification for this government. How can they make him Resources Minister when his family is in the coal mining business and he wants massive public investment in coal power since the private sector won't touch it with a flippin' barge pole? I thought the Coalition were all about free markets."

"More like free manna for their mates," said Siobhan. "They know they can get away with anything. Most Aussies don't seem to mind or care and just keep voting them back in."

Mallon saw that the PM's and Government's rating in the polls—already high—had gone up in response to taking a hard line on protest. Evidently the Australian public approved of them killing his son.

June 10, Brisbane

Emma cried for days, until she felt that her tear ducts had run dry. She'd been unable to do anything, go anywhere.

Her best friend and housemate, Kate, was a big help, making sure she ate, keeping her supplied with necessities—mainly tissues and alcohol. When moments were particularly hard, Kate sent her boyfriend Paul to the bottle-o.

"Chardy okay?" Paul would ask.

"Perfect," said Kate.

Emma thought it was kind of Sean, David's dad, to call to see how she was, and to say when the hearing would be held—that's if she wanted to come. She would. She had offered to testify but hadn't been called as a witness. She had had a lovely chat with Siobhan, David's big sister. She was nice, had made her feel better about herself—or at least, less bad.

Then she had snapped out of beating herself up and had started worrying about all her friends who'd been arrested. They were out on bail, due to appear in court, awaiting hefty fines, jail even. Some anonymous donor had paid for the bail. That was kind of them.

She'd read about that stupid pig Brad Callaghan saying they should all get jobs in coal mines, that they'd cop it if they tried protesting again, and that David shouldn't be made a martyr.

She met some of her XR friends at the Albion Hotel.

"We'll first see what the outcome of the inquest is. In the meantime, I'll start crowd funding to pay the fines. David won't be forgotten. He won't have died for nothing. The world is watching. I say we fight on. If the government and their coal cronies want to declare war on us, on the planet, they'll get one."

June 12

Dreiser was reviewing his shopping list for Christmas. His list wasn't small. It was enough to start a small war.

A major task and budget item for Phoenix was the procurement of ordnance. Some things had to be ordered well in advance, manufactured to order. He knew that even in the US you couldn't just wander into a store and buy the sort of hardware off the shelf that this operation needed—drones, lots of them, explosives of the high kind, with a few missiles and rocket launchers for luck. Oh, and while you were at it, don't forget the survey ship, midget submarine and mines for Australia.

He had not anticipated a supply problem. In a world where arms production and spending were among the top human enterprises, weapons were one of the main 'must haves' for nations. He knew that almost any item could be acquired at a price, maybe even a nuke if you showed ID. No, that would be overkill.

There was no shortage of ordnance around. The arms industry, euphemistically calling itself 'defence', depended on war and conflict to sustain itself and needed to export to recover the R&D and other investment, make a buck or two, exert political influence. It couldn't always be too fussy about its customers. After the US, Russia and China were the biggest manufacturers and these two were decidedly unfussy. Nasty customers were preferred—less scrutiny, fewer questions.

The world demand for weapons was always healthy. Many of the world's leaders and governments were like boys with toys, especially military and other dictators. They needed armies and arms to stay in power, show strength, impress the people, eliminate the opposition. Best of all, having a war took peoples' minds off domestic, economic and social failure, and boosted popularity, as long as you won. It was the oldest trick in the book.

You needed arms for all this, the right tools for the job. You couldn't do war with bows and arrows. You needed the latest kit even if you couldn't afford it. Finance? No collateral? No problem. Like any large, prestige hardware industry, there were networks of dealers and middlemen, long supply chains, and a healthy market for previously loved equipment, often with just one careful owner. But, unlike auto trading, there was little paperwork and no requirements for a licence or ownership records. Things could easily go missing or be sold on. Getting stuff into countries through customs? There was no one who couldn't be bought. They could pretend it was drugs. They could bribe the wharfies, customs, cops, whoever. Everyone has their price.

The hardware and logistics were being sorted by military procurement, intermediaries and fixers. Dreiser's job was to pick up the tab and deal with the bigger picture.

"Bang, bang, you're dead!" said Deiter, aged six, dressed in his cowboy suit, a present from last Christmas.

"You got me, Sheriff!" Still palpitating, Dreiser slumped over his desk. He hadn't expected to be creeped up on like that. Why couldn't Dieter play with dolls, like his brother Gunter?

CHAPTER 7

June 12, Oxford, England

Burns took a train to meet with Hadley to discuss financial arrangements and logistics and to begin detailed planning. Hadley lived in Headington and asked if they could meet at the Turf Tavern. In conversation, they'd discovered it was one of their mutually favourite drinking haunts as students, when Hadley was at Magdalen College, Burns at Pembroke. They both knew its illustrious student drinking alumni included former US President Bill Clinton and Bob Hawke, former Australian PM.

"Apparently, Hawke still holds a world time record for drinking a yard of ale here," said Burns. "That what you call a leader? I understand the present Aussie PM likes to make out he's a bloke's bloke but struggles with half a lager."

"The ship's crew will come with the boat," said Hadley. "But I'm sure you'll want to recruit your own operational team. You'll know one or two ex-colleagues, SAS and what-not?"

"I'll need to do some reconnaissance," said Burns.

"Naturally," said Hadley. "I'll see to things this end. You'll need to let me know what ordnance you think you'll need. Another pint?"

Burns worked on his homework late into the night, with the help of a glass or two of Scotch. Nobbling the Australian coal export industry would be most effectively achieved by taking out the coal ports - sinking ships in them or wrecking the jetties. A Google Maps search of satellite images showed the Queensland jetties to be very long, some of them up to several kilometres. They'd be easy targets. The New South Wales ports were traditional onshore wharves, more problematic.

What about the LNG plants in Western Australia? You wouldn't want to be too close to them when they go off. Boat and midget submarine access would be the ideal solution for all targets. They'd need limpet and other mines, rocket launchers, as well as light weapons—pistols, machine guns, grenades, knives—in case they got into a scrap. Hopefully, it wouldn't come to that, and they'd do the whole job incognito. He started preparing a Christmas list but would finalise it after reconnaissance.

June 19

Siobhan dropped her father off at the Perth airport. He was returning to Brisbane for the inquest. Nothing could bring David back, but some sort of recognition of wrong, ensuring it didn't happen again to someone else, would be something at least.

"Bye, love," he said. "See you Thursday. Look after yourself and Kieran."

"I will. You take care." He went through Departure.

She loved her dad to bits. Well, everything except his suggestion for her name, which Mum had agreed to. It was quite nice really, but if she had a dollar for every time she had had to spell or pronounce it, she'd be a rich girl. 'It's Shi-vawn. It's Gaelic. No, not garlic. Oh, for fuck's sake. Why didn't he call me Stacey or Tracey, Ayleen or Eileen? Anything but Siobhan.' She sympathised with Johnny Cash's 'boy named Sue'.

They had become especially close since Mum had died. He'd bought the house for all three of them. It was handy for her part-time agency nursing work at Fremantle Hospital and for her to be close to friends and the local hippy, arty community. It was a nice home for him when he was on leave from the mines, near to his favourite pubs. She was no longer bothered by Wayne, her ex and Kieran's father. After Wayne had started beating her, Dad had said, "You don't get a black eye like that from walking into a door," and had taken him outside. After treatment at Emergency, Wayne had packed his bags, and she hadn't seen him since.

June 20, Brisbane Coroner's Court

"The verdict is death by misadventure," declared the Coroner. "David Mallon's death was caused by fracture of the skull and contrecoup brain injury from hitting the road. Coup injury from the alleged baton blow to the head was minor and consistent with the statement of Constable Hall that he hardly touched Mallon, that Mallon stumbled and fell while attacking Hall's colleague Constable James Wright. Police witnesses testified that Hall was defending Wright."

"That's a lie!" yelled Emma. "I was there. David was bashed. He was murdered!" The court room was packed with David's friends, muttering or calling out.

"I demand justice for my son," shouted Mallon. "Is that too much to ask, even in Queensland?"

"Silence in court, or you will be removed."

On the steps outside, Mallon hugged Emma. "Thanks for coming and speaking up today. I hope you and your friends can come to the funeral. Let me know if any of youse need help with the fare or somewhere to stay. You don't have to, but would you be able to help me sort out his things?"

"Of course."

A man came up to him and shook his hand. Mallon had noticed him sitting at the back of the gallery.

"Hello, I'm John Grey, David's supervisor … We've all been devastated, and now this. We miss him desperately. Our deepest condolences."

"Thanks. David thought the world of you."

"I've packed his things into some crates. Do you want me to send them, or do you want to collect them? I'd like to come to his funeral if it's not private."

"I'll collect his things. Please do come."

Mallon finalised the arrangements for transporting David's body to Perth.

With Emma's help, he attended to David's affairs, cleared his flat and collected the crates from the uni. Most items went to the bin or the op shop, some he gave to Emma and her friends to keep or sell on Gumtree, and some things he shipped home.

"Thanks a million, Emma. Stay with us when you come over. We have a spare room."

He carried small items in his suitcase—mementos, memories, all that was left of a precious life.

He noticed a large sign outside a Baptist church: 'God so loved the world that he gave his only son.'

"Now the world has taken mine," muttered Mallon. "What's to love about it? The world can get fucked."

He returned to Perth that evening.

Over the following week, Siobhan busied herself with making the arrangements for David's funeral: sending the invitations, organising the food, the flowers, the wake.

Mallon helped, in between bouts of brooding and ever-mounting anger. He was further enraged to read that the Minister for Home Security and the media applauded the outcome of the inquest: 'Our police were magnificent under extreme provocation.' It was obviously a test case for the government's new approach to climate policy—bashing protesters. The trolls also cheered. 'On yer, cops. Spare the rod, spoil the child.'

He knew what had ultimately killed his son—climate denial. The police had done the deed, but it was a climate-denying government that had set the police on the protesters, a government continuing to do nothing about climate change except make it worse, a government put in power by a mostly climate-denying or uninterested public, a public told what to think by a climate-denying media, fed lies by the fossil fuel industry and its political cronies. All this contributed to the climate crisis and, out of desperation, the protests which had led to David's death.

Mallon loved Australia. It had been good to him, at least until now. But its climate denial, its sheer stupidity—except among the young—was annoying the shit out of him. Australia's dominant culture of climate denial was no secret—it wore this on its sleeve. It was a badge of what the country had become—stupid and proud of it, immune to reason, like its fellow travellers in the US. It wasn't just about climate denial; it was a tribal culture war against 'the other'—the intelligentsia, intellectuals, experts, progressives, lefties, arty farties, bleeding heart greenies, and 'inner-city woke lunatics', as Deputy PM Barney McDuff had called climate activists during the great fires. How much did Australia have to burn before the bulk of its people woke up?

David had taught Mallon a lot about the climate crisis—the causes, the threats to Australia, the reef and the planet. He had also instructed him on dealing with climate deniers. In Australia, almost everyone had an opinion, mostly denying the threat—or downplaying it, which amounted to the same. They easily bought the lies they were fed.

He had long avoided talking politics and climate change with mates at work or in the pub. He knew where their opinions had come from. Only the other day, in Clancy's, his favourite local pub, Derek had said, "I read that there was more carbon in the atmosphere twelve thousand years ago than there is now."

What had he said? Mallon had replied: "Where did you read that, then, Derek? *Right Wing Nutjob Weekly*?" You didn't keep friends by abusing them or slapping them in the mouth. Now, with all their opinions on the protests and his son, he had started going to pubs he didn't usually frequent, where he wasn't known and didn't have to speak to anyone. He'd even gone once to the Peninsula.

July 3, Zürich

Sofia was crying.

"What's wrong, Sofia?" asked Dreiser.

"Dieter ate all the chocowat."

"Did you, Dieter?"

"No, Grandpa Wolfgang."

"Look at me, Dieter. You know it's important to always tell the truth and not to tell lies. Did you?"

Dieter looked down. "Yes, Grandpa Wolfgang."

"Thank you for owning up, Dieter. I want you to promise to always be truthful and always to share."

"I promise."

"I will find more chocolate for you, Sofia. Here, dry your tears."

He wanted to tell Dieter that truth and trust were the foundation of civilisation and that when we lost them to lies, everything fell apart. But that would go over the head of a child.

Lies were why Phoenix was necessary, why efforts to reduce emissions from fossil fuels had failed. Too much time had been lost. After more than thirty years of lies from the fossil fuel industry and its cronies, climate denial was now too deeply entrenched, a tribal badge of the political right, of angry old men, of the incurably stupid, the incurably nasty. The world was full of them all. Populism, where the lunatics had taken over the asylum, had made things worse.

Since the fossil industry couldn't argue with the science, it had employed the classic football strategy of cloggers when playing better, classier teams.

He'd seen a lot of it against the Grasshoppers and Spurs. 'Go for the man, not the ball.' The industry had used lies to relentlessly attacked the integrity of climate scientists and by implication, all science and scientists. It had worked so well that it had helped propel the world back to a pre-scientific dark age, where the opinion of any fool counted as much as scientific knowledge and truth.

Lies were by no means new in human affairs, but the new anti-science playbook was a watershed, an infamous defining moment in human history, an end to the Age of Enlightenment for science. Lies created by the fossil fuel industry—to cling onto short-term power and profits—now threatened human survival. In a saner world, this might be considered a crime, an act of terrorism. Terrorists normally liked to claim responsibility for their handiwork, but the fossil fuel industry never did. No industry had done more to create the climate crisis. None was more deserving of payback.

He had received word that inspection of targets was about to begin, starting with Australia—the most complex mission. Besides the main oil states, Australia was a prime target—a leading fossil fuel producer and contributor to global emissions and a leading blocker of international action on climate change. Its perennial role as America's vassal, its poodle, had for a long while greatly strengthened the obstructive position of the US. No one liked to be isolated.

But underlying the fossil industry's power in Australia was the country's toxic level of climate denial. In this, the US was still number one. It had written the script, the playbook for the world to follow. But if the US was the father of climate denial—the Führer of falsehood—then Australia was its right hand, the Mussolini, the Il Duce of denial, a leader in lies. It was already the country most ravaged by climate change, with the prospect of much worse to come. In releasing the fuels beneath its feet, would it—like Mussolini—end up hanging by them?

July 3, London

"That's remarkable! I never knew that!"

Burns was finding himself enjoying Galina's company more and more. As a tour guide for Russian tourists, she knew more about London than most Londoners did. Also a former teacher, she was intelligent, witty and warm, and had a simple beauty about her. London was now her home after she'd been dispossessed of her property in Rostov. On her own now, she'd had her son Ivan when she was very young. Now eighteen, he'd chosen to stay in Russia with her ex-husband.

"You still haven't really told me what you do," she said.

"Consultancy, this and that. You don't want to know. It's really not very exciting."

"You have been a soldier, I can tell. My father was in the army. He was killed in Afghanistan."

"I'm so sorry," he said. "You're right. I spent time there also. There's no end to the trouble in that country. Do you miss him?"

"I was very young, but yes, very much." She paused. "But I want to know about you. I think you are very brave, very strong, that you looked after your men. That you were destined to be a soldier but are now not sure what to do with yourself. You are a leader; you need to do something special, not bullshit consulting."

Burns smiled. "You could be right there."

They talked about their sons, who they rarely saw, and showed photos on their phones.

"He has your good looks." They said it together and laughed.

He saw her back to her apartment in Bayswater.

"Would you like to come in for coffee … and perhaps a Black Russian?" She smiled mischievously.

"I'd like that very much but have to be away for a few weeks on business and have an early flight. Next time."

"I hope to see you when you return," she said. "Have a very good trip."

"Thanks," he said. "I very much want to see you again."

They kissed and embraced. Her warmth and the scent of her perfume made him want to go with her, but he had a big job ahead. Too much was at stake. He'd better go before he was tempted any more. A cab was passing, and he hailed it down.

She stood waving as the cab drove off.

July 4, Heathrow Airport, London

"Have a very pleasant journey, Mr Phelps," said the nice lady at check-in.

Burns departed on the non-stop Dreamliner to Perth, First Class. George Phelps was the name on his passport, driver's licence, credit card, the works. He felt a new man.

Emma travelled with Kate, Paul and a few others to attend David's funeral. They had already started making plans for the campaign, which would be stepped up after the funeral. There had to be better ways than by disrupting traffic.

Siobhan was waiting at Perth Airport.

"It's so good to meet you, Emma. Thank you for coming." They hugged. "You'll stay with us. Our friends around the corner will accommodate Kate and Paul. We've also made arrangements for as many of David's other travelling friends as we can manage."

"Come on, Dad. You'd best have an early night. It's a big day tomorrow." Siobhan hoped that her dad would start recovering after the funeral. All this moping was eating away at him.

"Alright, love. Goodnight."

Mallon found no peace in sleep. His nights were becoming as disturbed as his days. Once again, he slept restlessly. Ideas had come into his head over the past few days and wouldn't go away. The nightmare returned—the laughing, bearded man. "That's the way to do it!" But this time there was something different. No one could see him. He had on his head a large, bin-like helmet with a slit.

He had long known that he was related to Ned Kelly. Like him, Kelly's mother had come from Northern Ireland. Kelly was his hero. As a boy, he had made a helmet and body armour out of cardboard.

Mallon had tried to forget his past, but it never went away. It was always there, in his nightmares. The idea that was forming made it all flood back.

He had grown up in Northern Ireland during the Troubles, in Newry, a town near the border with the Republic. It was a centre for IRA, Irish Republican Army, activity and sympathisers, and the border area was known as 'bandit country'. His own troubles had started soon after leaving school—he hadn't been quick enough getting away. If you didn't leave for university or whatever else, you stayed and joined the unemployed or the IRA. In the Provisional Wing of the IRA, the Provos, you had a good chance of being shot or ending up in the Maze Prison. You could be shot by the British Army, the Royal Ulster Constabulary, loyalist paramilitaries like the Ulster Volunteer Force—or if you did anything wrong, by your own side. You were spoilt for choice. He'd chosen the IRA, or rather the IRA had chosen him. "I hear you're handy fixing things. Electronics and the like. We've something in mind for you," they'd said.

He hadn't wanted to kill anyone, although he had basic training with firearms, so he'd jumped at the chance to join the railway bombing campaign during the late nineteen-eighties and early nineteen-nineties. The campaign had involved repeated bombings of the main, double-track line between Belfast and Dublin, especially in the border area from Dundalk, in the Republic, to Newry. During question time in Westminster and the Dáil, the Irish Parliament, an open question had been asked of the IRA and its American paymasters enquiring how, if a united Ireland was their aim, it was helpful to blow up the Dublin to Belfast railway, the most unifying thing in Ireland. No one ever quite knew the answer. He was not party to the strategy. He'd just blown the track.

This experience and his twenty-five years as an expert shot firer in the quarries and iron ore mines of WA had given him an idea which was disturbing every waking and sleeping moment, like exhuming his past.

CHAPTER 8

July 5, Karrakata Cemetery, Perth

The funeral chapel was packed, or rammed as they say in Ireland, with most people watching on a big screen outside. Many were David's friends from the marine biology department at the nearby University of Western Australia, where he had been an undergraduate and PhD student. More still were friends and colleagues from the University of Brisbane, including John Grey, David's post-doc supervisor. Mallon's small family sat in the front row: Siobhan, Kieran, his sister-in-law Kate, her husband Kelvin and their daughters, Sharon and Karen. Emma had been invited to sit with them, too.

Mallon, two students and one funeral assistant entered with the coffin, and the young priest began the service. "We are gathered here today to celebrate the life of David James Mallon …"

Mallon looked straight ahead, barely able to take it all in. The last time his family were here, it had been for Laura's funeral nearly three years ago. How he missed her.

He hardly looked at the pictures of David displayed on the screen, showing his life from childhood to becoming a brilliant student and researcher. There were many images of him doing what he loved best—diving expeditions, exploring the wonders of nature. David had taught him to snorkel and scuba dive and had taken him on trips to the spectacular Ningaloo Reef off the North West Cape. While working in the Pilbara, Mallon had taken himself diving and had reported to David what he had seen.

The priest said the right things, knowing the circumstances of David's death "… tragic and premature … great promise … brilliant mind … much loved … friends and colleagues will continue his work … keep his memory and spirit alive … Jesus said … forgiveness."

Matt, David's best friend and long-time diving buddy, delivered the eulogy, knowing how hard it would have been for Mallon. "You will always be in our hearts," he said. "Your work will continue."

Mallon said a few words, reading from a few scribbled notes. "Thank you all so much for being here, I'm so deeply touched by the love and respect David inspired … My boy …" He had to sit down.

Emma read an extract from Shakespeare's love sonnet eighteen. "… So long as men can breathe or eyes can see. So long lives this, and this gives life to thee … I loved—will always love—David so much, although we only had a short time together. I'm so proud to have known him and I will carry on the struggle for climate action for him."

⁓

The wake was held in the Irish Club, Subiaco. There was a band playing jigs and reels, Paddy laments. People were drinking and mingling. No one could do a wake like the Irish.

John Grey was sharing a beer with some of his University colleagues. The conversation was reflective, respectful, with people attempting smiles. *He'd want a good send-off where everyone got trolleyed,* thought Grey. "Here's to David," he said.

"To David!" said the others.

He went to top up his glass. "Oh, hi, Emma," he said, when he noticed the young woman standing beside him at the bar. He'd met her briefly a few times, back when David had brought her to university functions and when she'd helped Sean to collect David's things.

"Hi," she said.

He saw that her glass was empty. "Can I get you something?"

"Yes ... A chardonnay, please."

"Your speech was very moving."

"Thanks," she said. "He was a beautiful person. He thought the world of you ... He ... Have you met Kate and Paul?"

⁓

As the evening went on, Mallon become well-oiled and was now drinking alone.

"Fuck forgiveness, thash what I say," he muttered, after quite a few Guinnesses and Bushmills. He preferred the more vengeful, less tolerant Old Testament God—the one who was justifiably hacked off with the world, who liked to smite the Philistines in the hindermost parts, who wouldn't have given the world a pot to piss in, never mind His only son.

He had already thought of a way to honour David's memory. He wasn't going to have died for nothing. "Fuck the fuckin' lot of 'em!" he shouted aloud.

Everyone turned and looked.

"Come on, Dad," said Siobhan, quietly. "It's time we went home. I'll call an Uber."

⁓

July 6

After the seventeen-hour direct flight, Burns was glad to arrive at Perth International Airport.

He took a taxi to the Esplanade Hotel, in Fremantle. After settling in, he went and had a beer at the nearby Little Creatures brewery. He learned that it was so named because it had once been a crocodile farm. While sitting at his bar table, he planned his trip north. It was a shame he would be unable to pay his respects at the SAS Campbell Barracks in Swanbourne, just up the road from Fremantle. The Aussies had been great messmates in Iraq and Afghanistan—'mess' meaning the wars, not the military catering facilities.

Afterwards, Burns fancied a pint in a proper pub. "I recommend Clancy's," said a barman.

As he arrived, he noticed a man sitting alone in a corner of the pub. Burns vaguely recognised him from somewhere but couldn't think where."

"Pint of Guinness, please."

After sleeping off his well-earned hangover, Mallon went for a hair of the dog at Clancy's.

"Fuckin' government, fuckin' Queenslanders killed David," he muttered to himself. "They've all got coal between their ears. Nothing will upset the lot of them more than their precious coal industry being stuffed. And I know how to stuff it and stuff it good."

"What can I get you, Sean. The usual?"

"Yes, please, Jim. Pint of Guinness."

As his head cleared, so did his thoughts. He would wreck the Queensland coal mining industry. The New South Wales industry was just as guilty but not as big, or influential. Queensland would do nicely. They would pay for David in financial losses, in reparations. He would make them dig deep.

Even a cursory web search told him that Queensland's huge coal export industry depended on a network of railways to various coal ports. His plan was simple—to bomb the crap out of the coal railways.

He was an expert in explosives from his years in the mining industry, but it was his IRA days that gave him the railway bombing idea. They were also bringing back bad memories.

It had gone well for a while. He'd considered it a sort of work experience and technical training, an apprenticeship, if not with a certificate you could frame. The IRA bomb schools and units were acknowledged by MI5 and army bomb disposal squads as the most sophisticated in the world. By comparison, the average jihadist was a kid with a toy chemistry set.

He was a natural—people said he could make a bomb with a potato—and found it fun, keeping the authorities guessing where and when they'd blow, then blowing again as soon as the line was repaired. He became the platoon leader. Sometimes they blew the track, sometimes freight trains too—they really made a mess to clear up—but always in the middle of the train, so the crew didn't get hurt.

But none of it had been enough for the liking of the commanders and paymasters. Mallon had been replaced by someone of a less empathic disposition, who went from attacking the track to bombing civilians in passenger trains and stations. Many people were killed or maimed.

He'd known who had replaced him, too. Sickened, he'd handed himself in to the army and had grassed in exchange for protection. He was given a new identity in England. Still not feeling safe, he'd applied for a new life in Australia.

His name had once been Patrick Mooney.

July 7

Burns checked out of the Esplanade and bought a campervan. He'd found it online before departing and it was in good nick, with up-to-date inspections and service reports. Some Swiss tourists were selling it before returning home. It still had a big sticker on the rear window: 'We're from Switzerland, how about you?'

As if anyone gives a rat's, he thought as he rubbed it off.

He paid in cash. "Oh, it's House, Michael M. House. H-O-U-S E." It was the first name that came into his head, for the license transfer papers. "I thought I'd see a bit of Oz."

With the help of hair dye, he'd donned the appearance of a grey nomad, which was an Aussie term for retired and semi-retired people who wandered the highways of Australia in campervans or towing caravans, the restless undead.

He headed north to his first port of call, Onslow, home of the Oatstone LNG plant. It was only a fifteen-hour drive. He took the Great Northern Highway. He'd read that it was a better road and more scenic than the coast road, where all you could see was scrub. He knew he had to watch out for the road trains and giant dump trucks, which took up two lanes while heading to and from the mines.

He stopped for a morning coffee at New Norcia, the only monastic town in Australia, which had been founded by Spanish Benedictine missionaries in 1847 to bring Jesus to the Aboriginals. There was an eerie silence in the place, but a peaceful beauty in the Abbey and other buildings, old by Australian standards. There was no one around—just a few pink galahs and warbling magpies.

Only a few monks remained, most old. Choosing the monastic life had long gone out of fashion. He wondered if the COVID-19 pandemic would bring it back, with all that practice in self-isolation. You'd escape all the nagging, demanding offspring, and if you chose the right Order, you'd also get to make booze. He'd once read that the traditional Belgian Trappist brews were under threat because of the growing shortage of monks who made the beer. No wonder they had a vow of silence—after drinking some of that stuff you could hardly speak.

The eeriness betrayed a place that was haunted by its past. The missionary work had long ceased, the orphanage long closed. New Norcia had been named in a Royal Commission investigation into sexual abuse in the Australian Catholic Church.

He recalled his own experience of the worst side of religion—his tour of duty in Northern Ireland. He'd seen what bigotry and hate did to people.

He was so young, then. He thought about his life and what Galina had said: being in the army had been his destiny. Sure, he'd been in the Oxford Uni Officers' Training Corps, but that was just for a bit of a laugh, to get fresh air on weekends. He hadn't planned to make a career of it; he didn't really know what he wanted to do. Studying history didn't really equip you for anything. It was getting dumped by Sylvia that had made him join up after graduating. He hadn't cared whether he lived or died, and had just wanted to get away, to forget. He also hadn't fancied the French Foreign Legion.

Northern Ireland had been an eye opener and he had had some close shaves, but at least it was an adventure—a desk job would have killed him. He knew that leading in moments of intense action was his calling, when he felt most alive.

He had gotten involved in intelligence and undercover work and it hadn't been long before he had come into contact with the SAS. He'd long known about them from growing up near Hereford, where they were based. You never saw them in town, but they were there. The police and pub landlords loved them. Hereford was peaceful, even on a Friday or Saturday night. Any troublemakers simply ended up down a dark alleyway.

Someone had suggested he apply. He didn't know if he should—he'd heard they lost more men in training than in combat—but he'd given it a go and the rest was history.

He wondered how Galina was going with her tours of London's history. *She's nice,* he thought. *She's something special.*

But he couldn't send a postcard since he wasn't technically here.

CHAPTER 9

July 8

Emma returned to Brisbane the day after the funeral, and the next day, she met with other XRs at The Albion. They were planning another traffic-blocking protest. She wanted to carry on the fight—to do it for David—but she didn't think this was the way anymore. She wasn't ready to sit in the road again and see people bashed. Her nerves were still raw.

"We need to do something cleverer—hit them where it hurts them most, in their pockets. We need to do things that actually stop emissions. Sitting in the road is just annoying the public, alienating them."

"That's the whole point," said Nigel, self-appointed leader of the strictly non-hierarchical, democratic group. "Blocking city streets maximises publicity and public attention to the climate crisis. It wakes them out of their sleepwalk to catastrophe. It's what XR does. It's our brand. If you want to block coal railways, or whatever, you're welcome to go and do it."

For the next few days, Mallon worked on his desk research, gathering a lot of information on the Queensland coal rail network. Blowing up the railways would be just the ticket.

"You okay, Dad?" asked Siobhan. "Shall I turn off the lights?"

"I'm alright. I might just have a nightcap."

He found out a lot just by Googling and looking at satellite images. Disabling the coal mines was one possible option. In Queensland, most were open cuts with giant excavators—he could bugger up the diggers big time. But he'd have to break in, and there was an even chance of being caught.

Bombing the tracks was a much better option—they were much more vulnerable. He examined the rail routes from maps and GIS. The routes were long. Some were hundreds of kilometres from mine to port. There was a mix of double and single tracks, and some were even double duplicates, allowing two trains to move in the same direction at once. That was unusual.

There was a mix of overhead electric and diesel hauled. Trains were typically hauled by two, sometimes three locomotives, and could be seven hundred metres long with a hundred and twenty rail cars. Each full car weighed up to a hundred and forty-three tonnes, and trains were about eighteen thousand tonnes when fully loaded. They'd make a mess when they left the track.

The average speed was eighty kilometres per hour—not too fast, so there would be a good chance of hitting them. Some coal went to local power stations, but most was exported, over two hundred million tonnes a year. *We'll see about that,* he thought.

His plan was simple. All of the mines were well inland. He would blow up the rail infrastructure at key points. He wouldn't hurt any train crew. Instead, he'd detonate the trains a few wagons away so that trains, and not locomotives, would be derailed. Derailing trains on bridges would make the biggest mess. It would be harder and take longer to clean up and repair. It would also be good for placing charges without having to dig away ballast. Then there were the electrified lines with poles and wires. They'd be fun. He hadn't bombed one of those—hadn't derailed an electric train since playing with his model railway as a boy.

Since all trains were timetabled and computer-controlled, he'd need to do a bit of trainspotting—not for collecting engine numbers, but to know where trains would be and when, and how late in the day they ran till. Setting the charges and detonating after dark would be safer for him and would maximise the chaos.

The new Daghawi mine was nearly ready to start shipping and would be the ultimate prize. Stuffing its railway would really piss them off. But the rest of the industry was much larger when combined together, so why wait for Daghawi?

His initial research was solid, but he'd needed to see the sites first-hand before getting to work. Another trip to Queensland was called for.

⁓

"Goal, Grandpa Wolfgang!"

Dreiser was playing football on the lawn with the boys and Dieter had just kicked the ball between his legs. In his day, he had been quite a good goalie. His reflexes weren't so good these days, but he needed to keep his eye on the ball for Phoenix.

Every large project needed a vision, a goal, feasibility study and a plan— strategy, options evaluation, risk assessment, models, scenarios, cost-benefit analysis, project plans, Gantt charts, that sort of thing. Over the past months, Dreiser had done his homework. He was a details man as well as a strategy man.

His goal for Phoenix was clear: he wanted to break the power of the fossil fuel industry, to break its ability to keep growing, developing, producing, generating emissions without constraint, buying off governments, funding climate lies and misinformation, and blocking climate action. Without this, there could be no rapid greenhouse emissions reduction. Without this, the world could not be saved.

He knew this would not be easy. The industry was at its zenith, in the heyday of its power and influence. The world was in its grip, serving its interests, fed by and dependant on the drug it supplied—the drug its customers and middlemen craved: carbon. Industry executives were drug barons in all but name, like mobsters, with franchises and syndicates throughout the world. The industry's middlemen—fossil friendly governments—were central to creating and sustaining the web at all levels. The industry drove and dominated the world economy, feeding directly or indirectly into most economic activities. Many countries had become 'fossilarchies', a form of oligarchy where nations and peoples were dictated to and ruled by the interests of private and national fossil fuel corporations.

The top dog fossilarchy was the US. Here fossil fuel executives and lobbyists filled the top slots in government as the revolving door spun round at ever-dizzying speeds. The industry had made, or—more often in the environmental case—watered or repealed laws to suit its interests. It had started wars, even. The US would hardly be concerned about democracy and regime change in Iraq if all that country produced was broccoli.

The death, destruction and continuing conflict from that illegal invasion so undermined the standing of the US that it has been regarded as the greatest blunder in American history.

In dealing with the drug industry, the most effective strategy was to choke supply, destroy the sources, poppy fields and labs. Dreiser had concluded that breaking the fossil industry's power meant doing the same: wrecking its assets.

July 9, Canberra

Resources Minister Brad Callaghan had simple but strong colour preferences. He loved anything dark and hated anything green. A frown momentarily crossed his face, to be quickly replaced by a sickly smirk, as he prepared to make a statement that he knew would upset a lot of people. This would be the icing on the Australian fossil fuel cake. Salt in the wound for the greenies. Sea salt.

He had decided to make the announcement to the media to maximise outrage in Australia and internationally and to maximise attention for himself.

"I'm delighted to announce that my department has approved exploratory drilling for oil in the Great Australian Bight. Australia needs to increase oil production capacity to ensure security of supply."

He knew that the announcement would really piss off the greenie tree huggers. Until now, the Bight had been out of bounds to drilling because of its unique environmental sensitivity and rough, deep waters. The risks of a catastrophic Deepwater Horizon type of spill had been considered too great. But vast oil reserves were believed to lie beneath the ocean bed, so fuck the lot of them.

"Contracts have been signed and the rig will arrive later this year. Are there any questions?"

"Lloyd George, *The Antipodean*. Can I be the first to congratulate the Government on this exciting venture, on its wise use of our national resources and on its world energy leadership?" George knew his master, Robert Moorcock, would approve.

"Thank you, Lloyd."

"Louise Brailly, *The Sentinel*." She was nearly speechless. "Can I ask why your government has approved this when previous governments have considered the risk of a disastrous spill too great? What has changed?"

"Technology, that's what, Louise. We're satisfied that with the remarkable new drilling technology, proposed by the Norwegian company, Energor, there will be zero risk."

PM Turbott stood smirking. It was his idea. It's what God would have wanted. Australia had to get the oil from beneath its feet.

Dreiser read about the announcement. "Mein Gott! What is wrong with that country? Are they insane? This must be stopped!"

He estimated that the rig would arrive off Australia around the same time as the Australian mission was under way.

Burns drove on through Mt Magnet, Meekatharra and other towns, topping up at every opportunity. There were sometimes hundreds of kilometres between filling stations.

Winter rains had brought green to the normally parched brown landscape of the Murchison. He reached the Hammersley Range and Pilbara, home to vast iron ore deposits, and rested overnight at Newman, a mining town. Neat and clean, it had a community feel, having been established before most mine workers became FIFO.

The next day he drove on to the Oatstone plant. He'd been briefed that this and other LNG plants in the north were fed by the one of the largest offshore gas fields in the world. Through a planned new offshore hub, production was due to be expanded still more. Apparently, Australia had to get the gas out from beneath its feet.

Wearing a twitcher's bird watching hat, he was able to approach the LNG plant quite closely and view it through binoculars.

He'd already done his homework on the WA gas industry and had read a brochure. *Natural gas and condensate, a light oil, are gathered from offshore gas fields and wells via hubs and separators. Some condensate is offloaded to ships at floating platforms. The gas, and the rest of the condensate, is piped to onshore liquefied natural gas (LNG) plants, where the gas and condensate are further treated before export. Some gas is processed for domestic use. The export gas, the main product, is liquefied to minus one hundred and sixty degrees Celsius using large compressors driven by gas turbines. The gas is stored in large, pressurised steel tanks and then loaded onto special carrier ships via jetties. The condensate is stored in concrete tanks and loaded onto tankers. Each process line is called a train and is in essence a giant refrigerator.*

Sitting duck, thought Burns

He drove to the gatehouse, parked and went to the reception desk.

"A very good morning to you," he said. "I've heard that tours of the plant are available."

"Sorry, sir," said the security guard. "I can't imagine where you got that idea."

Burns pointed at the sign stating that all cell phones had to be left with security. "Is that because photos aren't allowed?"

"No, sir. It's like at filling stations. The slightest electronic discharge could send the place up like Hiroshima."

"Goodness, we wouldn't want that!" said Burns. *Interesting,* he thought. "Mind you, it did end World War Two."

"Beg your pardon, sir?" said the guard.

July 10

The next day, Burns went on an all-day nature tour to Callow Island to check out the huge Medusa LNG plant. He had researched its history, how it had only fairly recently come to be built on a Class A nature reserve of international importance for its unique fauna and flora. It was a mini-Galapagos, and strict quarantine had long been applied to prevent the incursion of invasive animals and weeds.

He'd researched that Callow island was fifty kilometres off the north-west coast of Western Australia. The Medusa LNG plant had been built to process and export gas from the huge Medusa gas field. The plant's US owners, Dunoron Corporation, had bullied the fawning and compliant Australian federal and state governments into allowing the plant to be built on the island. The company had insisted it be there for the 'economical optimisation of the capturing, processing and exportation' of natural gas from its offshore gas fields.

It had to be there or nowhere. They'd threatened to pull out of the project if the EPA insisted on them piping the gas to a mainland processing facility. Government agencies had not only acquiesced but had thrown in generous tax breaks and royalty holidays for good measure. Dunoron had subsequently made no secret that the real reason was to demonstrate their impeccable green credentials in sensitive areas. They wanted to make sure that when the 2048 moratorium ended, the Antarctic could be opened up to oil, gas and mining. If Dunoron and other oil companies had their way, it would be.

Fossil companies were apparently salivating at the prospect of the ice-free poles they had been helping to create. The US, Canada and Russia were already in the Arctic—nearly clear of ice in summer—and had their eyes on the vast reserves to come when it was all open for business. The Antarctic would be next. People were apparently more important than penguins, and profits more important than both.

Burns viewed the LNG plant through binoculars while pretending to follow a Grey-Tailed Tattler, one of the many species of terrestrial and migratory birds regularly seen on the island. *It shouldn't be here at all*, he thought—meaning the gas plant, not the bird.

He pondered the best attack method.

"Spoilt for choice," he said. "A box of matches should be enough to send this lot to the Antarctic."

Mallon decided to drive his Land Cruiser to Queensland, then leave it and fly back to Perth, then return east with his campervan and 'munitions'.

He'd told Siobhan he needed time out from work, from everything. In a month's time, after giving notice, he would quit his job and go travelling. He wanted to spend time in Queensland, to explore the Great Barrier Reef while it was still there—something he had planned to do with David. He would require the Land Cruiser for the Daintree Rain Forest and other places like it, and the camper for just otherwise cruising around.

"Okay, Dad," she'd said. "It'll do you good to get away."

She was concerned about what was going on with her dad. He wasn't his usual joking self. But why would he be? They were both still upset, numb from David's death. But there was something more—it was like he was planning something. It must be his trip. That had to be it. It was a big step, taking time off work. His job was so much a part of him, but he had made a lot of money at the iron ore mines and didn't have to work. Getting away would be good for him. He'd so wanted to go to the Great Barrier Reef with David.

It was still winter in Perth. Going to the warmth of Queensland would pick him up—he'd been so down. But what if something happened to him in the middle of nowhere? Siobhan was a worrier. As long as he called or texted to say he was okay, everything should be alright.

Although close, she didn't know about her father's past. When younger, both she and David had asked him whether they had any aunties, uncles or cousins, and he'd said no. All his family had been killed in the Troubles and he never wanted to go back. She and David had left it at that.

July 12

"Bye, Dad. Take care. Love you."

"Love you, too." Mallon kissed Siobhan and Kieran.

Mallon set off in his Land Cruiser for the three-day drive from Perth to check out his quarry—the Queensland coal railways.

CHAPTER 10

Wrecking the fossil fuel industry sounded simple on paper, but the business was vast and complex. Dreiser needed a strategy to achieve his goal.

For better or worse, fossil fuels had driven modern civilisation and human development. But the industry had generated more than a carbon addiction. It had become a malignant, symbiotic, parasitic growth that had taken over the cardiovascular system and vital organs of the world economy. How and where could the industry be hit? Eased out without immediately killing the patient? It would be like blowing up a tall chimney without bringing it down on the factory. What should be the necessary scale of an operation like this? What would make a difference without causing total economic and social breakdown, alongside a humanitarian crisis fomenting an all-out war and the total collapse of civilisation? What could prevent the cure from being worse than the disease?

Although the problem was complex, he had thought through the high-level strategy. The focus had to be on oil: the life blood of the world economy. Oil also had the most concentrated and vulnerable targets—refineries. Due to international trading and commodity pricing, it was also a single entity, the circulatory system. Coal was huge, and while it was the biggest greenhouse gas source, production was often dispersed in domestic industries. It was the same for much of the gas industry. LNG was different. Processing plants were perfect targets—they would go up like bombs.

Strategic coal targets like major ports would be considered, but even without climate change coal was a deadly, dinosaur industry, its pollution alone killing nearly a million people prematurely each year, seriously harming many millions more. But hit oil and you hit everything—not only oil production, prices and demand, but every activity and industry depending on cheap oil for trashing the planet, including shipping coal. Some oil and gas was still needed for maintaining vital, beneficial industries and activities, for the transition to a more sustainable future, so it wouldn't do to destroy it all.

In his feasibility study, he'd wanted to know how many refineries needed to be disabled and for how long, the impact on emissions and the economy and the political risks. He'd wanted to know the costs, how to get the best bang for his bucks.

July 12

Burns inspected the single train Mercury LNG plant near Karratha before driving south to Perth via the coast road, on the way stopping briefly at Exmouth, Carnarvon, and Geraldton. It was not as scenic as the Great Northern, but it was useful reconnaissance for later in the year.

During the north and southbound legs of the WA trip, he liked to stop at roadhouses for refreshment. He would also pick up copies of *GoWest*, the local newspaper for WA.

He'd noticed *GoWest*'s climate denial and pro-fossil industry stance. 'Out of their Mines! EPA Economy Wreckers!' screamed the front page of one edition he saw. The head of WA's Environmental Protection Agency had apparently drafted a very tentative discussion paper on introducing a modest state carbon pricing scheme and carbon offsetting for the gas industry. For his trouble, he had been keel-hauled by the State Premier at the behest of the CEO of Stoneside.

That fellow has had a good spanking, thought Burns. *Let's see how Stoneside likes it when they get one.*

Burns was interested in political history. In researching Stoneside, he had read that it was not only Australia's leading gas producer, but also had more than a cosy relationship with the Australian government. The former Foreign Minister, Alexander Upham, had apparently authorised the Australian Secret Service to bug the East Timor delegation in Dili to gain commercial advantage for Australia and Stoneside in negotiations over Timor Sea oil and gas rights. The losers were Timor-Leste, one of the poorest nations in the world, and the Secret Service whistle-blower, facing trial behind closed doors and a possible life sentence for treason. The winners were Australia, Stoneside and Upham, with a lucrative revolving door position with Stoneside. *It's bad form to screw your neighbours*, thought Burns. *We'll stick one on them for you, East Timor. We'll be heading your way at the end of the mission. Get the beers in.*

On arrival in Perth, Burns left the campervan in a secure car park in Fremantle. The van would be needed later. He flew to Brisbane. It was time to check out the coal ports in the east.

Western Queensland

As Mallon drove, he couldn't help thinking about David and about Siobhan and Kieran, his only remaining family. He thought about his past and the family and friends he hadn't seen for over twenty-five years. They couldn't know who or where he was, for their safety and his.

It was a long time ago. Maybe it was safe to contact them now. Maybe what he had done had been forgiven, forgotten.

But in Northern Ireland, memories and grudges lingered.

Mallon tuned his car radio as he headed east. He was feeling tired and needed something to help him stay awake. It had been a long drive from Perth with little rest. There was no time to lose, but driving at dusk was dangerous when the roos and other creatures were out on the roads. Hours earlier he had crossed the border from the Northern Territory, but there was still some way to go before he reached the coalfields.

He was trying to find a station that didn't play country music. *Damn hillbillies,* he thought.

He found the ABC and listened to the garbled, crackly news. "Drought in Queensland continues ... New South Wales also badly affected ... emergency cattle feed from ... farmer Bill Wright can't go on like this ... scientist ... worst in memory ... climate change ..."

The signal improved for the PM's comment: "This is all part of nature's cycle. We have to remember that Australia is a land of drought and flood and always has been. My thoughts and prayers are with the farmers. We can only pray for rain."

Prayer—Turbott's only climate policy. *God help us!*

Through David, Mallon knew the standard checklist: 'Global warming isn't happening. Look, here's a snowball to prove it.' A US senator had used that stunt, copied by Turbott with his coal lump. A fave was 'there has been no warming for such-and-such number of years,' even as temperatures soared, records were broken year on year. 'Antarctic ice, glaciers and polar bears are increasing,' was said even as the ice was melting like buggery. 'The models are flawed. Conspiracy theories. It's a hoax by scientists, the Chinese, the UN, Jewish bankers. It's happening but humans are not to blame. The climate has always changed. Natural cycle. Sunspots. Volcanoes. It's happening, humans are to blame, but it's not significant, it's even beneficial. Crops will grow better. Fewer people will die of cold.'

The lies had all been debunked and easily refuted, but climate deniers still kept repeating them like brainwashed robots. David had coached him on what to say, calmly, without getting annoyed. "First take a deep breath. Imagine you're free diving. Only then, if all else fails, hit 'em." He knew David was joking; he wouldn't hurt a fly. He, on the other hand, up at the mine, had spent a lot of time killing flies.

The sun was starting to set as Mallon cruised into a small country town. He caught the name, Bilebola. *Sounds like a liver complaint,* he thought. *Or one of those African diseases where your dick drops off.*

He'd been sleeping in his swag for two nights. It wouldn't hurt him to have a good night's sleep. He checked into a motel, showered and walked to the only bar in town. The heat and humidity outside were oppressive. Inside, the A/C was turned up to full and the cool of the bar was welcome.

"Good evening, sir. What can I get you?" asked the young woman at the bar.

"Hello. A pint of that, thank you very much," said Mallon, pointing at the frostiest-looking tap

The beer barely touched the sides. He ordered another.

An okker type at the bar pretended to be an interested father-figure, rather than the drooling, late middle-aged man he was. "So, Ulla, have you gotten to travel around 'Stralia much?" he enquired.

"Oh, ja. I went to New South Wales and went skiing. It was wonderful. We have had no ski snow in Germany for five years due to climate change."

"Aw, you don't believe all that shit, do you?" said the okker.

"Ja, it's true. You can see it's true. Australia is on fire. The world is on fire. That's why people are protesting."

"It's a loada rubbish. Mass hysteria. Bunch of leftie anarchists. I'd shoot the lot of 'em. Boy, did I laugh when I heard they'd killed one. They should kill more of 'em."

Mallon stared ahead and finished his beer. He nodded a thank you to Ulla. Nice girl.

He waited in the dark outside.

He had always wondered how some older Aussies could sit for hours staring at their beer, sometimes with ponies—glasses so small they were not much more than a couple of swigs. "What's wrong with a pint?" he would often ask. Apparently, it was so they could sit in pubs all day and eke out their beer without it getting too warm, as would a larger glass.

The okker was in no hurry, as long as there was free eye candy.

But eventually he came out and headed for the carpark. There was no one around.

"Excuse me," said Mallon. "I'd like to debate climate science with you." He recalled David's guidance on dealing with climate deniers.

"What the …?"

Mallon's headbutt—a Glaswegian kiss—effectively and succinctly addressed the issue of the greenhouse effect and radiative forcing. His knee in the okker's groin addressed the overwhelming scientific evidence of human causality in global warming and climate change. His kick in the okker's ribs was for David. The other kick was for the reef. GBR had inflicted GBH.

Mallon returned to the motel and fell into a deep, dreamless sleep as soon as his head hit the pillow.

Heading east the next day, he turned on the radio. His ears perked up as the ABC reported their newest story:

"Earlier today, a middle-aged man, Clyde Palmer, was found semi-conscious in a waste skip in Bilebola. No theft was involved, and no motive has been established. The attacker was believed to be a climate scientist. Police are appealing for witnesses or information. Mr Palmer received multiple facial and bodily injuries. His condition is reported as 'comfortable.'"

Mallon was starting to feel remorse. *Maybe I shouldn't have hit him so hard. I hope he'll be alright ... It was a good debate, though.*

July 15, Queensland coast

Burns began his tour of the coal ports of Queensland, driving along the coast from Townsville to Brisbane. Using satellite images, he already had a good idea of the layouts and facilities. The four target ports were, from north to south, Monk's Point, Straw's Point, Sadstone and Brisbane.

He had agreed with Hadley that taking out the East Coast coal ports would be the most effective way to stuff the Australian coal industry. Having trained as a frogman with limpet mines, he'd initially favoured crippling the ports by sinking coal ships in them. It was a simple idea, but it would be hard to do. Ships moved. You had to mine and blow them quickly, with not much time to get way.

He agreed with Hadley's suggestion to take out the jetties and coal-loading gantries. They were much more accommodating. They stayed still. Planting mines under the jetties with timed and remote detonation would be better—much more flexible with much less chance of being caught.

Monk's Point, the newest target point and still expanding, was built to ship coal from the Daghawi mine and other large new mines in the Jordan Basin. The other ports were older. All were big, each similar in concept and design—a railhead and offloading to long conveyors, which fed into handling gantries and chutes. The jetties were nearly all long—on average two kilometres, the longest four kilometres.

Monk's Point had one jetty, the others two. From the maps, there were multiple loading crane handlers and berthing for four ships. There were eight at the other target points.

He disguised himself as a fisherman to hire boats and masqueraded as a birdwatcher with binoculars while he conducted his inspections.

Big buggers, he thought, seeing the three-hundred-metre-long coal ships.

He viewed the jetties. They stuck out like sore thumbs. There were steel piles, too—ideal for limpet mines.

While in Sadstone, he checked out the LNG plant on Durtis Island. This plant processed and exported coal seam gas from thousands of wells around Queensland. A full attack would have to be forgone. Being caught breaking in early could jeopardise the rest of the mission; blowing the loading jetty would have to do. But what if a loading pipeline caught fire and acted as a touch paper to the plant … ?

He flew from Brisbane to Newcastle to check out the coal ports in New South Wales.

CHAPTER 11

Dreiser had carefully considered where his hits would have the most impact. There were many oil producers, both private and national companies throughout many countries. But the industry was highly concentrated. The top ten countries accounted for more than half of the world's production—Saudi Arabia, Russia, the US and others, including China.

China? Really? It was a top producer on paper, but half of its fossil fuel production took place in Iran. Interesting.

The top ten state or corporate companies accounted for half of production and a large chunk of the world's carbon emissions. There were around six hundred and fifty refineries, mostly small or medium ones, but with a few mega refineries producing half to one million barrels a day. The biggest was Jamnagar, in India, producing one and a half million.

Singapore supplied much of Asia and nearly all of Australia, which had closed almost all of its refining capacity. Interesting again.

What about consumption? This was measured by the size of economies, of course, but who supplied whom? Most US imports come not from Saudi but from Canada.

Besides refineries, there were other promising targets, including some tank farms in the US as big as small towns.

There was lot of data and a lot of potential targets. Identifying target installations for cutting supply required modelling against impact. There were complex factors to consider: the economics and politics of supply and demand, the reaction of traders and markets. How will the attacks impact production, demand and pricing?

It was not logistically or financially possible to attack every installation, but too limited an attack would be ineffective and as good as failure. It was complex. How could the problem be solved?

Heidi ran in and jumped onto his lap. Sheriff Dieter must have ridden into town.

July 16, Queensland, inland

Mallon waited patiently. The sun was setting, the flies were clocking off and the mossies clocking on. Australia was renowned for its wildlife. "What do the nasty little beggars do when there's no one here? Bite each other?"

He had begun his tour of the coalfields using printed maps and GIS. He'd checked the dedicated coal-only railways, which were mainly networks of mine-specific lines fanning from final lines to the four main ports. By hanging around on the home straight, he now knew the total numbers of trains that came down laden from the mines. By dividing up the trains by feeder line, he assumed an average speed of fifty to sixty kilometres per hour. Operations would be computerised to synchronise all of the trains to and from the feeder lines and to tie in with loading at the ports.

Trainspotting is fun, he thought.

He had earlier chosen a few possible locations for charges and had checked them out. For the first, he parked his car off-road in a concealed location along a rail inspection track then walked to a viewing position and waited for the train to pass at the estimated time.

He heard the long blast of a horn and soon the headlight. His timing estimate was spot on. The train, headed by two large diesel-electric locomotives, thundered past. He hid in the scrub, resisting the temptation to wave at the driver.

"Damn, forgot to get the engine numbers."

July 16, Brisbane Crown Court

Emma sat anxiously in the public gallery for the verdict. The trial for those arrested in the Battle of Brisbane and other sit-down protests had been expedited by the Attorney General, Christopher Lee, so that the full weight of the law could be thrown at them. Hefty fines and jail sentences awaited.

Top human rights lawyer, Tim Gleeson, had been prepared to act pro bono for the defendants but didn't complain when a fund mysteriously appeared to appoint him and pay his costs and any fines. Australian banks had become accustomed to processing laundered money from unknown sources, more often than not via Switzerland.

Emma watched in awe as he made mincemeat of the prosecution. Gleeson was summing up: "I put to the court that the laws under which the defendants are to be prosecuted are in breach of the constitutional right to freedom of dissent and protest. They were hastily cobbled together without due consideration for what is reasonable, fair or even intelligent. The penalties provided are extraordinarily excessive compared to other offences. As for intelligence, I will give you an example. Several of the defendants have already been issued with orders barring them from the CBD, as well as orders to face trial in this court, which just happens to be in the CBD. Would any of the police officers present care to arrest the offenders for breach of the aforementioned order?" There was a ripple of laughter.

"Silence in court!" declared the Judge.

"I also put to the court that obstructing free traffic movement is not the heinous crime that the prosecution would have us believe. If that were the case, every commuter contributing to this city's traffic jams would be arrested and sent down for a very long time." More laughter as the judge banged his gavel.

"I put to the court that this is a political trial on behalf of the State and Commonwealth governments, who have failed to act on climate change and seek to punish young people who dare to protest against them, instead of applying duty of care in protecting them. People are rightly concerned and have the right to peaceful protest without being violently assaulted by police, as many of the defendants were. I rest my case."

The judge found them all not guilty of any criminal offence under the anti-protest laws. They were issued with small fines for wilful traffic obstruction under by-laws and cautioned against repeating the offence.

Dreiser read of the result. It was money well spent.

Emma later met Kate, Paul and others at The Albion. She was hugely relieved that the XRs had gotten off lightly but knew that most of them couldn't organise a piss-up in a brewery. They had no vision—no strategy. She would take a lead now, form her own protest and direct-action group, gather like-minded people, hatch plans, do things to make a difference. She thought of a name: 'the Climate Commandos'.

"I really like it," said Kate.

First up for the CCs was stopping Bjerk Jarlsberg's Centre of Consensus being set up at the University of Brisbane. Protests had stopped it in its tracks at UWA in Perth, and at Flinders University in Adelaide, and so she would do the same. She knew that Jarlsberg was a good friend of the Australian government, who still had a pot of money for any uni that would take it to house the centre. His shift from outright denying climate change to becoming lukewarm about it—'climate change is happening but it's not serious and technology will solve everything'—fitted with the government's narrative and that of the fossil fuel industry. The centre was to be modelled on Jarlsberg's facility in Copenhagen, where hand-picked conservatives would sit around agreeing to conservative solutions to the world's problems. Emma thought a good name for it would be 'the Facility for Universal Consensus and Knowledge Development'. Kate and Paul thought that was funny. Emma was good at coming up with names.

Apparently, the Vice Chancellor had accepted the four-million-dollar handout without seeking consensus. Well, times were hard, and they needed the cash, he'd said.

She organised a petition and a protest rally on campus to demand the VC hand the money back.

"It's an outrage," said Emma. "Jarlsberg is a wolf in sheep's clothing. He's a climate denier and always has been; that's why he gets a regular column in *The Antipodean*. He's not a climate scientist but a statistician who knows how to lie with stats. Universities should be centres for knowledge and truth, not the lies of people like him. I hear he's coming to speak on campus about how climate change is not a problem. We'll give him a warm welcome."

July 19

Associate Professor John Grey was disgusted to hear that the VC had accepted the cash for the Consensus Centre and was one of the many members of staff to have signed the petition opposing it. He'd go to the rally on campus today. He read that Bjerk Jarlsbeg was in Australia promoting his book, *The Sceptical Climate Scientist*, and had been invited to address the Federation of Conservative Students tonight. He wouldn't be going to that.

He was missing David—their shared love of marine biology, diving together, and their mutual passion for research. If he'd lived, David might have published even more than him. He was missing their beery rants about the state of the reef, climate politics, how the world was fucked, that sort of thing. If it weren't for climate denial and inaction, David would still be alive.

A climate denying scumbag had no business here. He hated pseudo-scientists like Jarlsberg, narcissistic attention-seekers with no scientific qualifications or peer-reviewed publications, who made a living peddling optimism and telling people what they wanted to hear. He'd read that Jarlsberg had been inspired by the late Princeton academic Julian

Simon. Simon's best-selling book, *The Ultimate Resource*—a response to the 1970s warnings about overpopulation and limits to growth. Simon had said that the world was a cornucopia of unlimited resources, that humans were the ultimate resource, that the Earth could comfortably accommodate forty billion people, that the economy could keep growing for ever. The more people, the more geniuses there would be to solve problems, including presumably those that would arise as a result of having forty billion people on Earth. *No one does crazy quite like the USA*, thought Grey.

He wandered over to where the rally was being held, nodding to fellow staff who were already there.

A petite, blonde-haired girl was making a speech on the steps, holding a megaphone. It was probably one of the students—staff had to be careful about being too political. "Say no to Jarlsberg!" the girl chanted. He recognised her as Emma and went over.

"Hello," he said. "How are you?"

"So-so," she replied. "You?"

"Oh, you know, still getting over David, bearing up. The same for you, I'm sure. Well done for organising this. I can't believe the VC would even consider it. I hear he's trying to back off without getting too much egg on his face." He hesitated for a moment. "Err, would you like to meet for coffee sometime?"

"I'd like that," she said.

Emma and the others weren't allowed into Jarlsberg's talk, which was by invitation only. They were anticipating green-left protesters. "We don't want your sort here," said one of the young men 'on security' at the door.

They waited until Jarlsberg came out, with his black T-shirt uniform, blond hair, and boyish, cheesy grin. He had come to sign autographs. The unexpected egg hit him squarely on his forehead and ran down his face. The grin disappeared as he glared at Emma.

"Eggsellent shot," said Kate.

"The yoke's on you, you … climate criminal!" shouted Emma. She'd got the idea from what John had said about the VC getting egg on his face, remembering that Egg Boy had become famous a couple of years before for egging a racist senator.

"Go home, you Danish dickhead," said Paul. He'd learnt about alliteration at school and thought that it was pretty good. He saw the conservative students coming. "Quick, let's get out of here."

Jarlsberg's egging and the cancelling of the Consensus Centre made the headlines of the Moorcock Media: *Crazed eggheads attack free speech*.

The shock jocks were apoplectic about the attack on their hero. "They need whipping," said Andrew Nutt on SkyHigh News.

"I'd stuff a sock up them and feed them to the sharks," said Alan Williams on Radio 2GBH. "What do our listeners think?"

The line became jammed with his septuagenarian listeners suggesting torture methods so cruel that even Williams had to change the subject.

July 20, Newcastle, New South Wales

From satellite images and research, Burns already knew that the NSW coal ports were different. They were older, and a lot of traditional, solid onshore wharves approached from a natural deep-water inlet. There was no long jetty. Newcastle was huge, with many wharves and ships at any time. It would be hard to mine every wharf and limpet every ship. It needed another solution.

At Newcastle, all vessels had to enter via a two-lane channel in the Hunter River. Burns observed the lines of coal ships entering and leaving port, and the minimum separation distances when leaving or arriving together. With a few magnetic sea-bed mines activated at just the right time, sunken coal ships could be used to block the port.

In less than a week in the east of Australia, he had retrieved all the information he needed, and he flew to London from Sydney. He would return in October with the boat and his team.

CHAPTER 12

Project preparation required site inspection for the many targets Dreiser had identified, and this phase was well underway.

Petroleum and other plants could be studied from satellite images, but you needed to know the terrain, the lie of the land—or the water—approaches, escape routes, security, hiding places. Apparently, drones, like large birds, hated electricity pylons and transmission lines.

Environmental and social impacts were a consideration. Greenhouse gas emissions from explosions and fires? Sure, this was important to keep in mind, but the emissions from the bombed refineries would be much less than from all the fuel they produced. Would the bombs harm sensitive ecosystems, habitats or species? Would they hurt many people in the plants? These were all serious considerations.

Dreiser read about the egg attack in Australia and the outrage it had caused. He smiled. Jarlsberg was a super spreader of lies, a mayonnaise of misinformation.

July 20, Eastern Province, Saudi Arabia

James Gryll—ex-SAS, fluent in Arabic—was disguised in tradesman clothing and inspecting the Saudi Arabian oil refineries and oilfields. He had started with the Ghawar, by far the largest conventional oil field in the world, which accounted for roughly a third of the cumulative national oil production.

There was no getting near to facilities on public roads. Barbed wire fences and military checkpoints were everywhere since the 2018 drone attack by Yemen, Iran or both. Saudi was the world's biggest arms buyer, an armed camp.

But GIS was all-seeing. Defensive barriers? If you couldn't go through, you could go over. *Like we're going on a bear hunt*, thought Gryll, remembering his favourite children's story. Drones would be perfect. *Who dares, wins.*

July 20, Baton Rouge, Louisiana,

Matt Coburg, ex-Navy Seal and leader of Louisiana ops, hired a boat. "I'd like to do some shrimp fishing."

To the west were oil refineries as far as the eye could see.

"Go east, boy," said the boat owner, spitting his chewing tobacco. "You don't wanna go west. Won't find nothin' there, leastaways nothin' you'd wanna eat. 'Specially since our beloved president cut them there environmental laws 'n all. Although them laws weren't much to speak of in the first place."

July 20, Qatar

Dan Moyer, ex-Australian SAS, leader of Qatar ops, parked by the roadside. With binoculars, he viewed the LNG plant, which shimmered like a mirage in the intense summer heat. There were no worries about impacts on the local wildlife—there was little wildlife to speak of, unless you included the feral camels. *They'll shit themselves when this goes off, as will the locals,* he thought. *At least it will be a bit cooler in December.*

July 20, Fort McMurray, Northern Alberta

Peter Daley had been in the Canadian Special Forces before it was disbanded due to some unfortunate incidents. He drove the five hours from Edmonton to view the tar sands project. There was no missing it. It was where the boreal forest abruptly disappeared and was replaced by moonscape. One of the dirtiest projects on the planet. There were a lot of targets, but they were all over the place.

The storage tanks were promising. Hitting them would be messy, but there was mess everywhere anyway. *Humans, the only creature that shits in its nest,* thought Daley.

July 22, University of Brisbane

Waiting in the cafe, Grey spotted her coming across the quadrangle. He couldn't help inspecting her. She was beautiful. She'd put on a pretty dress. Was it for him? *No, don't even think about it. She's too young, I'm too old.* No, thirty-one wasn't old. She was twenty-two or -three, not a teenager.

You couldn't mess around with students. But she wasn't in his department. Not that she'd be interested in him anyway. She'd have her own friends—there'd be a waiting list for her. No, it was too soon after David. What would she think of him showing the slightest interest?

This is just a social catch-up, to honour David, he told himself.

Emma didn't know why, but she was really looking forward to seeing him. And there he was, waiting. Her heart started to flutter. *Stop it, this is ridiculous,* she told herself. Why would he be interested in her? She was too young, too immature. He'd have a string of academic highflyers after him, women much more attractive than her. He might be spoken for, anyway—married even.

Why had she put on her nice dress? No, it was too soon after David. What would he think of her thinking these things?

"Hi," she said.

"Hi," he said, standing up and offering her a seat. *That's nice, he's a gentleman, making me feel like a lady.* You wouldn't catch the students doing that.

"Pretty dress … the one you wore at David's … funeral?"

"Thanks … yes," she said. He was observant, like David. Must be all that watching corals, fish and stuff.

"Coffee?"

"Cappuccino, please," she said.

He placed the order and sat down. They smiled at each other. There was an awkward pause. "I see you got in the news," he said. "That was a brilliant shot, potting Jarlsberg. Where did you learn to throw like that?"

She laughed. "Darts. In the student bar."

"Well, no one deserved it more, and good work getting his centre kicked into touch. Enough of that, anyway. Don't get me going on climate deniers. Tell me about yourself. How's your course going? What are your interests?"

"I'm really enjoying studying. That and campaigning seem to be taking all my time. I have a lot of interests: music …" *Where was this going?* "What about you?"

"Oh, well, I seem to have spent most of my life studying, researching and teaching, but I love diving—I guess my hobby is my work really. But I love all kinds of music: rock n' roll, jazz, but especially classical."

"Do you like chamber music?" she asked.

"I love it."

"There's a concert next week," she said. "Would you like to come? I should warn you it's Bartók and Kodály."

"I'd love to. I'm very fond of Hungarian music."

"How do you know about them? Do you have any Hungarian in you?"

Braving biting insects, over the next few days Mallon learned about coal train routes, timetables and the locations of main creeks and bridges. There was a mix of coal types and grades, depending on the mine and coal seam, including thermal and metallurgical coal.

He had decided to focus on dusk and night attacks. This made for a lesser chance of being spotted and more time before police and inspection crews would arrive post-detonation.

While in the area, he inspected the route of the Daghawi mine railway, which was nearly complete. He noted that it was fenced and fitted with security cameras due to continuing protests against the mine.

"Do the bastards think a few fences will keep me out?"

In less than a week, he'd gathered all of the information he needed.

He drove to Townsville and rented a lock-up garage for a modest sum. The owner had been more than happy to receive six months' cash in advance. Mallon had given a false name, address and phone number.

Being near to the reef made him think all the more about David. It also made him think about what David had told him about the coral bleaching deniers. David had told him how the Australian climate denial machine and songbook were nearly identical to those of the US, who owned the copyright, but reef denial was uniquely and proudly Australian.

"Like Vegemite and pavlova?" he'd joked to David.

"Actually, Dad, Vegemite is US-owned, and the Kiwis claim pav, but you know what I mean." David could be a bit of a know-all.

Getting one back for the reef would be good.

Given the complexity of the problem, Dreiser had done what any self-respecting corporate leader or government in the past forty years would do. He'd hired management consultants.

He'd carefully considered how to phrase the brief, the questions. He could hardly have issued an RFQ and commission for someone to conduct a feasibility and cost-benefit study into wrecking the oil industry and world economy. Although, if he had done, he wouldn't put it past many firms to bid and have all the answers. Most were already in the oil business, albeit snake oil, run by salesmen who would sell their grandmother for a fee.

And what use would they be? Dreiser knew that consultants and advisers were part of the world's problems, not the solution. They were behind many of the smart ideas and theories that had gone so horribly wrong. He knew all this but needed advice all the same and especially clever modelling. He knew that consultancies could do 'clever' in abundance, luring bright young things away from useful careers with the scent of money and self-importance.

He'd phrased the questions innocuously. He'd divided the tasks among different firms so that no one would see where it was leading. It was about modelling supply and demand.

What would be the impacts of a large cut in production on demand and the economy? What would be the risks to supply and economies if key refineries were lost due to catastrophic events, such as extreme weather, tsunamis, war or terrorist attacks, pestilence or plagues, Horsemen of the Apocalypse? These were the sorts of questions any insurer or investor might reasonably ask.

By piecing together the individual pieces of the jigsaw, Dreiser got the answers he wanted on the big picture: scenarios, sensitivity analyses, the works. Above all, he'd identified the key targets.

"Would you like a drink before the concert?" asked Grey.

"Yes, please," said Emma.

"Chardonnay?"

She smiled. He remembered. "Lovely."

The orchestra played a variety of pieces by Bartók, Kodály and other composers. Grey and Emma looked ahead. He glanced at her. She was deep in thought but in a calm way. She caught him looking and smiled. She was thinking about how to attack the coal industry and had just had an idea.

After the concert, they had dinner at a bistro, and he saw her home.

"That was a lovely evening," she said. "Thank you."

"It was wonderful," said Grey. "Thank you for inviting me. Err, can I see you again?"

"Yes, I'd like that very much."

They kissed.

"I'd better go now." Emma went inside.

There were some things that Dreiser hadn't asked the management consultants. What about the military aspects? How would *you* do it? What hardware would be needed? How many operators? What would it all cost? Drones seemed to be the obvious answer.

Some homework and lunch with a drone expert suggested that it was feasible and affordable. Again, his questions were innocuous: drones as a business opportunity. What could drones do? What could they carry and how far? What did it take to operate them?

The project would require military expertise for implementation. By then, he and his colleagues would have distanced themselves. But he knew enough about management, strategy and tactics to understand the options. Key to successful implementation would be local project teams and franchises. Central control and management would be too hard and risky. Some might fail. Most would win.

The oil industry was big. Even a major attack would only take out a part of it. Funds weren't a problem, but availability of operators and hardware was not unlimited. Key to the strategy would be attacking the hubs; the mega refineries; the most vulnerable. Key too would be to use leverage—just as in martial arts, the energy of opponents could be turned against themselves. They could use existing enmities and weaponry, especially in the Middle East. Most Saudi missiles were already aimed at Iran and vice versa.

The Middle East would be the biggest challenge. It was bristling with security, military checkpoints and surveillance systems, especially near to oil and gas installations.

Mallon left the Land Cruiser at the lockup and flew to Brisbane for a connecting flight to Perth.

He didn't contact Emma. It would have been nice to see her, but it was better she didn't know he was around or know what he was planning. What would she think of him?

After working his notice, he would return in early September with the necessary ordnance.

CHAPTER 13

August 5, Zürich Tonhalle

Dreiser attended a concert played by the Zürich Symphony Orchestra. He had a box seat reserved, and so he'd invited Anna Schwarz, his private secretary of nine years.

They were having an interval drink after the first half of Elgar's Cello Concerto.

"I hope you don't mind me dragging you along, Anna. You see too much of me as it is, but it's a shame to have a spare ticket go to waste."

"Your company is always a pleasure, Herr Dreiser, and I love music. That performance was so moving."

He had for long been a generous patron of the arts and music but had been more generously throwing his wealth into the industry since the performing arts had suffered so much during the lockdown. He was concerned that, around the world, classical music was dying off.

"It's a delight to share this with someone who appreciates it. So many people don't seem to care for classical music, except in film scores, yet it's among humanity's greatest achievements—a mark of our civilisation. You can understand why it's been transmitted into outer space to tell the universe we're here and civilised. Thank God it's not that awful, whiney, repetitive earworm music of today."

Anna laughed. "Aliens would surely come and destroy the source if we were to broadcast that."

"But they might spare us if they heard the great rock n' roll we grew up with. Please excuse me while I take this call.

"Hello. This is Wolfgang Dreiser … Walter! How are you? … I'm sorry to hear that. I assure you that all will be well. Your continued support will be greatly valued. I'll see what I can do."

One of the project investors was getting cold feet and considering withdrawing.

They returned to their seats for the second half of the concert, Beethoven's Fifth Symphony.

The conductor came to the podium, bowed and, when the applause had stopped, the orchestra began the famous opening musical pattern of *short-short-short-long, short-short-short-long*. Dreiser recalled that this had been a powerful symbol for the Allied forces in World War II, broadcast on Radio-Londres to the French Resistance. In 1944, it was the first coded message to France warning them to prepare for the D-Day attack.

Could it be used for C-Day?

Soon after returning to London, Burns took Galina to the Royal Festival Hall for a concert of Rachmaninov music—the Symphonic Dances and Second Piano Concerto. Afterwards, they had dinner at the Archduke under the Waterloo railway arches. He ordered his favourite, the 'Archduke Trio', a medley of sausages, and she had the fish.

"I love it here, it's very atmospheric," she said. Every few minutes, trains to and from Charing Cross Station rumbled overhead.

"I thought you'd like it."

"It was a wonderful performance," said Galina. "Music is the soul of Russia—our greatest contribution to civilisation, soaring above all the barbarism in our history. This samphire is delicious, I've never tried it before."

"They get it from the Norfolk coast, I believe."

"Can I try a bit of your sausage?"

"Of course. German, French or English?"

Later, he saw her to her apartment. "It was a fantastic evening," she said. "Thank you."

They kissed.

Galina smiled at him. "Would you like to have a nightcap?"

He grinned. "Do you have a Black Russian by any chance?"

Fremantle, early August

Mallon completed his preparations. From the start, he had considered what explosives to use. What he didn't know about explosives and devices wasn't worth knowing. During his professional career, he had used many of the common types. In the mines, most often he'd used ANFO, anhydrous ammonium nitrate and fuel oil, sometimes with a Semtex primer. He'd used dynamite, nitroglycerine-based, in his earlier work in quarries. In the IRA, he had mainly worked with Semtex, a plastic explosive containing PETN and RDX.

For what he was thinking of, ANFO would be the handiest, and he could get enough of this or other materials from work or wherever. A little bit of this, a little bit of that, the ingredients were not too hard to obtain. Explosives had been around a long time, were part of human history and—including in war and terrorism—had long been used for political purposes. He had personal knowledge of that through the IRA.

Canberra

Coalition MP Craig Tooley was excited—very excited. He was in a library basement archive buried in meteorological records. He was determined to prove that climate change was a scam and was onto something big.

Tooley was proud to be one of the leading climate deniers, not just in Parliament, but in Australia and now the whole world. He had more

Facebook followers than many other politicians put together and was proud to be the unofficial spokesmen for the government on climate change, the go-to for his mates at Moorcock News. Now he was in the international TV hall of fame. During the really big bushfires, he'd been interviewed by that Pommie poofter, Piers Long, and that weather girl. They'd said it was due to climate change. What the fuck did they know? He'd put them straight—put the world straight. There had always been fires in Ozzie. Thousands of his followers had agreed: 'On yer, Craigie, those Poms should mind their own effin' business.'

Most of all, he was proud to have co-founded the Friends of Coal Exporters with his best mates Brad Callaghan and George Magnussen. No one was going to stop them from digging up and selling their coal. Things were just brilliant, as good as they could get. Coal-friendly federal and state governments, new mines galore and millions of tonnes of new production had been approved by that hot bit of kit Minister Sussan Cashmore during COVID, without all that green and Aboriginal Heritage assessment shit. Too bad if there was one above Sydney's main water supply and one or two buggering koala habitats, farmland and Aboriginal sacred sites. People had to make small sacrifices for the greater economic good. Best of all, there was billions of bucks in support of the industry—investment in the future, not subsidies as those lefty lunatics called it. The icing on the cake would be the opening of the Daghawi mine. It was not long now until the grand opening. He couldn't wait. It would be a famous victory. It'd be so big that Australia could say to other coal producers: 'Call that a mine? This is a mine!' Just like Crocodile Dundee whipping out his skinning knife at those muggers. Daghawi finally opening would really stick one on the warmist wanker girlie boys and lesbian losers who tried to stop it. He'd heard that so many people had been invited to the opening that there was going to be a grandstand, like at the races. He and the other Friends were expecting A-Reserve seats.

Galina was still asleep when Burns got up, showered and made coffee. She awoke and rubbed her eyes. "Must you go?"

"I must, I must, but I'll see you later." As he kissed her, she pulled him down on top of her.

―

Hadley was waiting at the Dominion Club. Burns and Hadley had arranged to meet to carry out some final detailed planning for Australian ops.

"Sorry I'm late," said Burns." I was a bit restless last night and overslept— not like me."

Hadley looked at him suspiciously. He knew that smug 'I've had the best shag ever and everything is right with the universe' look.

"There's coffee if you need it. Let's get down to business."

Hadley began. "The overall strategy and plan have been worked out and approved by Military Command. The gas plants have to blow on C-Day and not before. Any earlier attack on these could alert other target countries. The oil and gas industries are more like a single organism, an anthill. An attack on one is an attack on all. The coal industry is different and separate. There's more localised production. The attacks could seem more local and unrelated to oil and gas as long as no international force is detected. The coal targets can wait until C-Day but there would be considerable benefits from an earlier strike."

Burns's ears pricked up. He stopped thinking of Galina. "What do you mean by that? The more explosions before C-Day, the more investigation. The more risk that someone would join the dots regarding the movements of the boat before we've completed the task. Our earlier discussions were about planting the explosives and getting well clear before detonating them."

"Look, I know that," said Hadley, "but a key sponsor is anxious for an early result as a demonstration project, showing the capability of the global project as a condition for further funding. Another is anxious for an early result in Australia. Command sees benefit as the first move in a western country, a morale boost for other ops, to show what can be achieved. They're the ones to beat—only, of course, if it can be done without jeopardising the overall Australian operation."

"This is a different dimension. I'll need to consider that and the safety of my team."

"Naturally," said Hadley. "Deception will be vital, as you know. As it was before D-Day, when the Allies convinced the Germans that they would land in the Pas de Calais, the shortest Channel crossing, rather than Normandy. The boat is key to the deception. As discussed, the boat will arrive in Port Douglas on October twentieth with its core complement of ship's crew, captain, engineers and so on—and Mike Ryan, chief scientist. It will be fully kitted with the ordnance you need. Inspection should be minimal given the VIP welcome we've set up. But the kit will all be concealed—you can't be too careful. You and the other specialists will join the boat in Port Moresby, PNG. After arriving in Australia, you'll need to sail about a bit, look like you're surveying, in practice, doing a bit of training with the sub and mine laying. Then you start the mission proper. How does that sound?"

"Alright so far," said Burns. *Was this really such a good idea?*

"Will you have enough time to do the coal in Queensland and New South Wales, then get to the other side of the country to do the gas plants? It's a big country, but we figured that a boat and sub attack is the only way, and we couldn't manage two boats and teams. Survey ships and military-grade midget subs don't grow on trees, and we're very fortunate to have gotten hold of one of each. Can you do it all?"

"There's a lot to do," said Burns. "But it's feasible—provided we keep to schedule and don't have any serious holdups, mechanical problems, cyclones."

"How are you going with finding your ops team?"

"I've picked them, and they've all said yes," said Burns. "I'm arranging a briefing meeting shortly. A couple of them have to travel to the UK and need flights."

"Good."

For the next three hours they discussed the details of logistics and tactics.

"There's just one other thing," said Hadley.
"There is?"
"My client—who, as I have mentioned—is rather fond of Australia, is concerned that the Australian government has approved drilling for oil in the Great Australian Bight. It could be a Deepwater Horizon catastrophe again, only worse, if there's a spill. Anyway, they've torn up environmental protections and given a Norwegian company a licence to drill for oil. The rig will be towed from China soon. It seems that you'll be passing at some point. Anyhow, if it's safe to do so without detection and you have a few limpets left over after duffing up the coal industry ..."

Craig Tooley was determined to 'prove' that climate change wasn't happening, that it had been just as hot in the past and that the Australian Bureau of Meteorology was fiddling the books by reporting soaring temperatures as being unprecedented in human history. He claimed that they had deliberately destroyed past records to assist in their scam.

The story had been started by Lloyd George, environment correspondent to *The Antipodean*, Moorcock's flagship newspaper. The Bureau had been 'homogenising'. No one knew quite what that meant. Was it something to do with milk?

The allegation was front-page news and was megaphoned by the Moorcock Media and shock jocks. No one was interested in the Bureau's explanation of innocence in statistical methodology. In the Australian public's mind, the Bureau boffins had been caught cheating. It was up there with Climategate, also once eagerly reported as a scam by the Moorcock Media, even after the lie was debunked.

Have we done well, Master? Robert Moorcock was ever watchful over his media empire, like Tolkien's Eye of Sauron.

Nationwide Senator George Magnussen was the largest and loudest of the Friends of Coal Exporters. As a good Christian, God had called him to spend much time praying with his girlfriend in Manila. He posted Tooley's intrepid detective work to expose the Bureau's measurement fraud. "The boffin bureaucrats must be nervous. Very nervous."

Many trolls posted likes and tweets. 'On yer, Craigie, you'll nail the lying bastards.'

The boffins had every reason to be scared. Tooley was a former furniture salesman and an expert in examining tables.

Dreiser had often wondered what had prompted Einstein's remark about human stupidity. Was it his exasperation with people in general? Compared to him, everyone was thick. Relatively. Was it the folly of the First World War? Or was it the public reaction to his General Theory of Relativity?

Refusing to accept the science—ignorant people apparently knowing better—had a parallel in the past. Relativity, energy, matter, the speed of light had all become more than theoretical physics. The political and religious establishment had seen the theory as raising heretical questions about the very nature of the universe and God. At a time of political upheaval, it was a dangerous threat to the status quo. Conservatives needed an opinion on relativity even if they hadn't a clue about the science. Their response had been simple: they dismissed and denied it. Einstein had complained that he couldn't even go for a haircut without every barber having an opinion on it. Dreiser wondered if it was why, in pictures, Einstein had looked like he self-trimmed.

So was it with climate change. It was not just a threat to the fossil fuel industry, but to the established political and social order, the status quo, the exploitative basis of the world economy; to endless growth, development, consumption; to capitalism. If the scientists were right, then collective, cooperative solutions would be needed, which smelled of socialism. Conservatives everywhere had a duty to oppose, deny and have an opinion.

Dreiser knew that the theory of relativity had also led to the atomic bomb, which had a decisive role in ending World War II. The relativity deniers had gone quiet after Hiroshima and Nagasaki. Japan had not expected to be hammered like that. Nor would the fossil fools.

CHAPTER 14

Brisbane, late August

Government inaction and David's death had led to increased climate protest around Australia and to escalating conflict. Emma continued to go along to street protests in central Brisbane for solidarity, to help make up the numbers, but refused to sit in the road. If she was going to get arrested again, it was going to be for something useful, on her terms. She had planned what that would be; she just needed to recruit enough people.

She stood on the pavement as the XRs blocked the traffic.

"What's the matter, Emma?" asked Nigel. "Have you lost your bottle?"

There was a sound of breaking glass, a police siren. Emma was afraid of anarchists and 'smash capitalism' types joining in and taking over. World revolution was like eating an elephant; you had to do it in small bites. But they seemed to believe that smashing shop windows was a start.

"That's what's the matter," said Emma. "This sort of thing is giving the protests a bad name and an excuse for police violence. I'm out of here. I'll see you at The Albion when you've been released. I've got a better idea if you and the others want to talk about it. Not stopping traffic but stopping coal trains."

Mallon spent his last home week in Fremantle before heading north for his last tour at the mine and his trip to Queensland. He couldn't wait to start blowing up coal trains.

Siobhan noticed a change in him. He seemed more cheerful, more positive.

"You're really looking forward to this trip, aren't you? We'll miss you something rotten."

"Yes, I am. But the time will soon go." He hugged her.

He was looking forward to upsetting a lot of people. Half of Australia. He was especially looking forward to the outrage he'd cause in the media. He couldn't wait. He even started buying *GoWest* and *The Antipodean*. It helped with motivation—sports coaches encouraged focusing on the opponent, thinking mean about them, thinking no mercy. If you were a boxer, you imagined yourself battering them to a pulp. He'd already done a warm-up round with the okker in Bilebola.

"I thought you hated those papers," said Siobhan.

"It's for the crosswords. I want to get in some practice for my travels."

Before he executed the plan, Mallon had to stop buying these newspapers. Reading the climate-denying op-eds and letters made his blood boil, and the swear box that Siobhan had provided was always full to overflowing.

"Old farts with nothing better to do than write arsehat shit. Think they know better than real scientists. Armchair fucking Galileos. Some of the letter writers appear so often, they're treated as columnists." David had told him that reputable newspapers such as the Los Angeles Times banned letters from climate flat-earthers. *GoWest* not only gave them a platform, it encouraged them.

"I'll flatten the fucking flat-earth flatheads."

The last straw for Mallon came when *GoWest* started providing a weekly column for Melbourne shock-jock Andrew Nutt, who appeared daily on SkyHigh News TV. With his suit and tie and opinionated manner, Nutt offered reassuring certainties to his many followers, who lapped up every bigoted opinion and climate denial lie in the book. Nutt had long insisted that Australia was not warming and that the Bureau of Meteorology was fiddling the books. Now that Australia was having an obvious hot flush, he insisted that warming would be good for the nation and the world.

"I'll shock the fucking shock-jocks," he grumbled.

At least *GoWest* didn't pretend to be anything more than a provincial rag—mostly sport and ads. Mallon detested *The Antipodean* for its pretence of being a quality newspaper. As if it was from an alternate universe, there was barely a mention of the global environmental and climate crisis, except in dismissive terms. Every other copy had a climate denial opinion piece from its own journalists or from Australian and international guests. Its own journalists, men and women, were all long in the tooth, all die-hard deniers. There was always a staring, unflattering photo, but it was always too small to show the foam around their mouths. Did they really think that, or was it to please their audience? To please Robert Moorcock?

"How are the new laws going, Peter?" enquired PM Turbott.

"Not as well as expected, Prime Minister," said Scroton, Minister for Home Security. "The police are having to exercise caution. That David Mallon has been made into something of a martyr by the green-left terrorists. Worse, a person or persons unknown has been funding top lawyers to defend climate protesters, and that's given our prosecutors a thumping."

"Can't we stop them? Make a law for it to be it illegal? Freeze the account?"

"It seems it's from Switzerland. It would mean stopping laundered money coming in. Our banking friends wouldn't like that."

Grey and Emma started seeing each other regularly, at first, just for musical events—chamber, jazz, rock. Then he took her snorkelling, showing her the reef, as David had done.

It brought back memories for her, painful, when thinking of losing David, but happy, remembering the good times they'd had together. She thought they were so alike in many ways, John and David, and she liked doing things with him.

"That was amazing, seeing that loggerhead," she said in the boat afterwards.

"Yes, it was," he said, thinking: *God, you're beautiful.*

But it was so soon after David's death and both were keeping their distance, taking things gently. They were both dealing with their own frustrations and internal tensions.

Emma was determined to protest, to make a difference and knew he wanted to do something too.

"Why don't you come to the protest in town?" she suggested. "Other professionals go to these things."

"Thanks, but I'll pass." He didn't say why, not wanting to discourage her, but he believed it was all a bit futile. Then again, he was beginning to think that about his life's work—to advance scientific knowledge on marine biology, especially around the deteriorating Great Barrier Reef. From a young age, growing up in country Victoria, he'd been determined to pursue an academic career and get to the top, but he felt a failure.

He was one of the small but growing number of scientists around the world frustrated by the scientific community's failure to confront and speak out on the growing climate and ecological crisis facing the world. He knew that science and scientists had to be strictly objective and that their work shouldn't be clouded by politics, emotions, values, right and wrong. To go against these protocols was professional suicide.

But he was starting to believe that saving the reef, the world, was more important than saving his academic career. Since David's death, he had started to speak out in blogs and articles. He had taken badly to losing his most gifted post-doc researcher, as well as his friend and diving buddy, and was getting fits of depression.

Emma had cooked dinner for them at her place.

"What's it all been for? The reef is dying, David's dead, the government gets away with murder … Literally, and no one cares."

"I care. Don't give up, John," said Emma. "You have such a brilliant mind. The world needs you … I need you." The words slipped out unexpectedly.

"You do … ? Oh, Emma. I love you so much."

"I love you too, John … I, I want you."

Dreiser knew that the propaganda war had been lost for years. Trying to counter brainwashing and thirty years of lies—with reason, with scientific truth—was hopeless, like treating COVID-19 with an aspirin. The fossil fuels industry had shelled out billions in engineering mass climate denial and funding misinformation, all helped by a well-established power network of governments, lobbyists, front groups, tame scientists, the media, right-wing think tanks and the Moorcock Media. Boch Industries alone had spent millions in the US. Lying was easy when many people were wilfully ignorant and stupid. A lie went halfway around the world before the truth had its pants on. Lies were easy. All you needed was for people to be gullible.

The lies had started in the US. There was no shortage of gullible people in a country where half of the population believed that the world had been created in four thousand BC. While studying for an MBA at Harvard Business School, Dreiser had dated a Seventh Day Adventist called Marti. He'd told her that someone had found a fossilised Supersaurus in Utah—it would have been sixty feet tall when alive.

"I don't believe in dinosaurs," she'd said. "Fossils are put there by the Devil to test our faith."

Dreiser thought about Marti. She was sweet and strikingly beautiful. It was a long time ago. He hadn't meant to test her faith. She hadn't minded; she had said it was God's will. He'd seen that she and her son—their son— were alright financially. He'd often wondered what had become of them. He had once thought to find out, but an initial trace drew a blank. She must have married and changed her surname. He hadn't pursued it—he had other family to consider, but he wondered all the same.

But gullibility was not confined to the US. Thanks to technology, the lies had soon spread around the world. The internet was supposed to be the information superhighway, spreading knowledge. Instead, it had become a septic sewer, the lies spreading faster than a malicious virus in the human Petri dish.

Spreading the lies especially depended on scientific Judases—super spreaders. In the US, especially, there was a seemingly inexhaustible supply of fifth-rate scientists and non-scientists eager to line their pockets with silver by giving superficial respectability to contrarian views—there wasn't a reputable, peer-reviewed publication between them.

Dreiser had done his research, spoken to scientists. Climate denial was a mental state, but there was no simple cause or cure, only theories. The lies were all too easily absorbed by the flawed human brain where the emotional part believes what it wants to believe and overrides the rational part.

There was no time to defeat the deniers, or counter the lies, with truth and education. Climate denial was a toxic plague, infecting the Earth with a terminal fever. There was no simple treatment, no vaccine, and no time to let it work its course. It had to be purged.

Nazi propaganda had not been countered by polite debate but by destroying the Nazi war machine.

Emma's breakaway group was growing, and she chose a few to be team leaders. She met with them at The Albion to discuss the plan. She showed them a map she had printed off.

"Here's where we'll lock and glue ourselves to the track, near Manstone. It's a double track line serving two feeder lines and coal mines. We'll block both tracks, stopping loaded trains to the Monk's Point port and empties from returning to the mines. It'll take hours to unlock us, and when they've done one team, another will lock on. It'll cause massive disruption." She had done her research and had driven out to pick the spot.

She wouldn't tell John what she was doing. This was her project, and it was better for him that he wasn't involved.

"Come, Dieter. Let us fetch Gunter and play trains."

"Yay!"

Dreiser took the boys into the room where he kept his model railway and turned on the lights.

"You sit here while I start it up." The boys sat, mouths and eyes wide open with excitement. They knew they weren't allowed to touch it or control it until they were older, apart from their own small area with Lego trains. Dreiser turned on the controls.

The layout was large and scenic, with Märklin, Fleischmann and other locomotives and rolling stock. Passenger and freight trains whizzed around a double-track mainline. A small train went on a branch line into the mountain. There was a cable-car, a tram, stations, signals, villages with people …

"I like the little people and moo cows," said Gunter.

Suddenly there was a crash—a freight train was derailed in a station, the locomotive and wagons on their side.

"Goodness, there must have been something blocking the track," said Dreiser. "I'll soon fix that. Look, it's one of the little people from the platform. How did it get there, Dieter?"

Mallon did a final review of his plans and the logistics. Yes, he could blow those feeder lines near Manstone all in one night.

CHAPTER 15

Inspired by Emma, Grey stepped up his blogs and articles attacking the government's climate policy, fossil fuel industry and Moorcock News, and especially taking apart the work of climate denying pseudo-scientists. As a scientist, he had put up with them for long enough and had put up with abuse and death threats from trolls. Now he would go on the attack.

Then he was called to the office of his Departmental Head, Professor Peter Wolfe.

"You can't do this, John. It will harm the reputation of the university and your professional standing and career."

The meeting turned into an argument. In his frustration, Grey found himself shouting.

"The public are fed lies and bullshit every day by the media, politicians, industry and trolls, while we try to present peer-reviewed papers with all sorts of uncertainties and caveats, which only make people think we don't fucking know what we're talking about! The media jump on them as if there's still some sort of debate. We play by Marquess of Queensberry rules while they kick the shit out of us. Scientists are human. We can't completely detach right from wrong, sit on the fence. Nils Bohr, one of the greatest physicists of his time, refused to participate in the Nazi nuclear weapons programme."

"I think you need to reconsider your position. This is a friendly warning."

"Is this something to do with my objecting to Jarlsberg's centre and to the new minerals building?"

Grey knew that the VC was still smarting over losing the four-million-dollar government handout for the Consensus Centre and that oil and gas company funding for the new minerals and petroleum engineering building was dependent on curbing on-campus protests against accepting it, which Grey had been involved in. Wolfe had been leaned on from above.

Grey considered his position later that day. He especially loved Emma on top, where he could see her in all her beauty.

"Are you sure you're allowed to do this?" asked Emma, smiling down at him.

"I think so. I could, of course, get permission from the Ethics Committee and my Department Head if it helps," he joked. He kissed her breasts.

"That won't be necessary. All seems in order … Mmm, the only head you need is from me."

Thanks to Emma, Grey was feeling better about himself, better about life. But he wanted to do something bigger than blogs and articles. It was good to let off steam, but he was preaching to the converted, and not making any difference.

Then he got a call from Mike Ryan, an academic acquaintance in America. Ryan and Grey had communicated a lot about the need for urgent action on climate change and had expressed their frustration with scientific and academic niceties in countering the lies of the climate deniers.

Though young, not much older than Grey, Ryan was an eminent marine biologist. Until recently, he'd worked at the Woods Hole Oceanographic Institution, in Massachusetts.

"I'm now working for the International Marine Conservation Foundation, IMCF, based in Switzerland," he said. "I'll be visiting Australia on a research vessel, doing survey work along the coast. I need your local knowledge and local content for government approval and PR. The boat will arrive in Port Douglas on October twenty. Can you get time off for a bit of field work? Most of it will tie in with your academic recess, in December. You know the things we've been discussing ... Well, there's a chance to do something really big, and I mean big."

"What's that?"

"I can't say over the phone. I'll tell you when I see you. You may be interested to know that the visit of the boat, the *New Endeavour II*, has just been approved and endorsed at the highest level, by your Prime Minister."

"The IMCF *and* The Endeavour! How good is that!" declared PM Turbott.

He had been informed that the *NE2* was monitoring the condition of the ocean, especially plastic and other pollution, and impacts on the marine ecosystem. They had proposed to survey the waters of Australia.

Through him, the Australian government would extend a warm welcome. It had made action on marine plastic pollution a priority as an uncontroversial diversion from inaction on climate. "On condition they pay a few visits."

An ex-marketing man, he was quick to spot a PR opportunity in the 'Endeavour' part of *NE2*'s name, and the idea of it sailing around the coast. Three years before, he'd proposed that a replica of Captain Cook's *Endeavour* could sail around Australia and visit 39 places. It would not just honour Cook but, more importantly, the civilising effect of white European culture and the government's part in maintaining it. Good for keeping core voters onside. But that idea had been ridiculed. Okay, Captain Cook never actually circumnavigated Australia, it was going to cost a lot of money and it would take many months. As for it being racist—far from it. Here was an opportunity for a cheap, quick win. Tourism Australia could arrange a few welcoming parties and local publicity, lay on a few meat pies, quiches and snaggers. Great photo ops. "Haven't heard of the IMCF but sounds important. Swiss, eh? Swiss cheese will go with the burgers."

The IMCF was based in the fittingly named town of Gland, near Geneva, along with WWF and other worthy organisations. The IMCF was in turn funded by an anonymous donor not unconnected to Wolfgang Dreiser ...

Dreiser was reviewing final Christmas wish lists, which were swarming in. He felt like Santa Claus. But you wouldn't put ordnance and weapons like these in kiddies' stockings.

He was not short of a Swiss Franc or two. He'd inherited a lot of money and had made a great deal more. Like his father, he had made a fortune in finance and pharmaceuticals. On the face of it, he'd had a good and privileged life. Growing up in Zürich, he'd gained a doctorate in chemical engineering at the ETH Institute of Technology before going to Harvard. He'd worked hard and lived well. An accomplished skier even now, he was often to be found on the fashionable ski slopes, including Klosters, St Moritz, others. He had a taste for fine dining and wine and for women. *I was quite dashing in my day,* he thought, with a smile. *Had to fight them off. Still do. I'm sure they don't just want me for my money.* He saw himself in the mirror. He was silver-haired now but still the same inside.

He'd always wanted to do better, be better. For all the money and privilege, there had been a darkness over his life, a coldness in his father. His father had said they had had no choice but to cooperate in order to stay neutral. The Germans would have invaded otherwise. Switzerland had been bankers to the Nazis, had financed their war machine and had taken the gold from death camp victims' possessions, even from their teeth. He suspected that his father had been a Nazi sympathiser and that some of the money he'd inherited from him was not entirely kosher.

Dreiser wanted to do good with his money, unlike some he knew.

August 31, London

Burns hired a room at the Freemasons Arms in Holborn, opposite Freemasons Hall. He was not a Mason himself—he had no time for it—but he knew the pub was often frequented by members and that secrecy was guaranteed.

He had already spoken to each of his team personally and had arranged for them to meet and plan their mission together. Most of them already knew each other, but there would be an opportunity for pre-match bonding.

His team was small—enough for the job, with two on the bench at any one time. There was Paul 'Simmo' Sims, a cockney from London; Chris 'Jonesy' Jones, a Brummie from Birmingham; Barry 'Bazza' Senior, a Scouser from Liverpool; Ron Moody from Yorkshire and Bob Beattie from Scotland. Beattie would be his 2IC.

He had also chosen Jacques Grobbelaar and Jan Boonzaaier, ex-Recces, from the South African Special Forces. Two were new to him but came highly commended, Mick Mann and Bryce Martin, ex-US Navy Seals. They went with the sub.

He could have chosen a crack team many times over from the men he knew, but these men were a bit special. He had served with Beattie, Jones, Moody, Senior and Sims in Iraq and Afghanistan on many dangerous SAS missions. They had all been incredibly brave, calm under fire, one hundred percent reliable and always good-humoured. They had another thing in common—they had all saved his life. He owed them one.

None was doing that well financially. If all went well, this mission would be a doddle, and they'd be made. They just had to sail around the Aussie coast and blow up a few things without being caught …

Burns had chosen Grobbelaar and Boonzaaier as the best-suited professionals for a special land job. He had trained them and served with them on special missions in Africa and had been especially impressed by their fighting and survival skills. They could eat anything as long as it was meat and ideally hadn't been dead for too long. He knew that the South African Recces were the most difficult to join among the world's special forces, due to rigorous physical, mental and intellectual requirements. Operating completely separately from other South African armed forces, only a few got past the basic selection stage and fewer still made the grade. Only devout Christians needed to apply, although this was not formally stated but implied in the Operator's Creed. Their prayer and motto was 'We fear naught but God'.

Burns had told them to come at noon. One by one they arrived in time for the traditional English pub lunch that Burns had arranged. It was raining outside. As they came in, they shook themselves, like dogs of war.

Moody came in first, went straight to the bar and ordered a pint before spotting Burns. "Burnsie! Good to see you. Can I get you one?"

"Good to see you too, Ron. I'm alright, thanks. There's a bar tab, by the way—on expenses."

"Thank God for that. You need to take out a bloody mortgage to buy a pint in London. It's half that price in Leeds."

Simmo, Jonesy, Bazza and Beattie arrived soon after. Everyone exchanged handshakes, greetings and hugs. "Great to see you, it's been a while …" They'd been through a lot together. It was all coming back to them now that they were together again. "Do you remember when …"

Martin and Mann arrived.

"Gentlemen, allow me to introduce Mick Mann and Bryce Martin," said Burns. "They will be in charge of our special toy, and if you're very good boys, they'll teach you how to drive it."

They were closely followed by the Recces. "Jannie, Jacques!" said Burns. "How was your plane journey from Jo'Burg?"

"We've had worse," said Grobbelaar.

"Gentlemen, meet our special guests—Jacques Grobbelaar and Jan Boonzaaier."

"Welcome to London, lads," said Simmo. "Have you ever tried … ?" They all started exchanging stories about the exotic creatures they had eaten in survival situations.

"Lunch is served," said Burns. "Beef and Guinness pie. You can bring your drinks into the meeting room.

"'Dis is 'orraait, Jannie," said Grobbelaar.

"Yaah, we've had worse jobs," said Boonzaaier.

There was a lot to discuss, to plan. They all knew they weren't as young as they once had been, but they weren't old crocks, either. They shouldn't need to do any armed combat unless absolutely necessary to fight their way out, but if they had to …

"Gentlemen, I trust you all still have good sea legs," began Burns. "As I've mentioned to you all, we're all going on a little voyage."

Seeing the team all together, Burns recalled one of the Duke of Wellington's remarks about his troops. "I don't know what effect these men will have on the enemy, but by God, they terrify me."

Burns had been on many missions with the ex-SAS members of his team, but one thing above all had influenced his choices. It had been a routine mission in A-stan to capture or take out a Taliban leader; it was the job they did, like plumbers coming to fix your drains. Intel had reported that the target and a small group were holed up at a village in Kandahar Province. You couldn't always trust Afghan informants; they could be working for both sides—they and their families would have to live with the Taliban when NATO forces eventually pulled out, and sometimes it was safer for them to do so. His team had had another job in the area, so they'd gone to check it out. They'd parked the APC in a concealed position, and Sims and Jones had stayed to guard it and would provide backup if needed. He'd gone in with Moody, Senior and Beattie, keeping under cover, spread out but in sight of each other.

The streets of the village were deserted in the heat of the day, but the village was occupied—it hadn't been bombed out like many. They'd sensed that they were being watched, like the Taliban were expecting them, and people were staying inside to keep out of trouble. There was going to be a fight.

A small boy had suddenly appeared from nowhere. He was out in the open and had sat down. He'd started to cry as if he was lost. Burns knew he could be a decoy, knew they should secure the area first, but he'd seen too many dead kids. He thought he could quickly get the kid to safety inside one of the houses.

He wasn't quick enough. A sniper had shot him in the leg, and he'd gone down in agony, bleeding buckets. The sniper could easily have finished him off but hadn't. He was obviously being used as bait for the others. Moody had run to get a better vantage point and bullets had poured in from all directions—there was more than a small group; it was more like a small army.

Senior and Beattie had watched with a source detection device, identifying the Taliban positions. Beattie had sent the locations to Moody and to Sims and Jones, who were coming into the village from the rear, dressed as locals. Beattie had roughly divvyed up the targets and the boys had taken them out one by one. Burns hadn't known what was happening, but he'd had an inkling. There had been the sounds of shooting. Grenades had gone off. He'd known the sniper and others had gone when he could move without being shot at.

Between them, the boys took out thirteen Taliban that day. Unlucky for some. No villagers were harmed, and only a few homes had needed rebuilding. The boys had used bullets and grenades sparingly. Knives were much quieter and didn't give away your position.

When it was safe, they'd called a helicopter to take Burns away.

"Try to be more careful in future, wack," Senior had said.

September 1, Area D, Pilbara Region, Western Australia

Mallon mopped the sweat from his brow and took a swig of water. At the bottom of the iron ore pit, the temperature was moving into the high forties. Although still spring, the heat was already building up.

The warning siren was still blaring as the blasting crew took their safety positions. Mallon squinted towards the face where his team had drilled holes for and placed multiple charges of ANFO.

The blasting zone had been cleared of people and equipment. One by one, the observers radioed that all was clear.

There was a pause as Mallon collected himself. This was to be his final blast before taking time out to go travelling.

"Okay, this is it lads. Counting. Five. Four. Three. Two. One. *Fire!*"

The electric spark initiated the chemical reaction in the explosives, generating intense energy, breaking up the ore body, throwing a large cloud of dust into the air and scattering debris. All the charges had gone together for greater effect.

"All charges fired. Well done, lads."

His colleagues lined up to shake his hand and give him big hugs. "Alright, that's enough of that. If you like me that much, you can buy me a beer in the wet mess."

His campervan was waiting for him at the mining camp.

He took the highway across the north of Australia, turning off towards the coalfields after Mt Isa.

Tempting as it was, he decided not to stop when passing through Bilebola. Nice girl, that Ulla.

CHAPTER 16

September 4, Townsville, Queensland,

After the long drive from the west, Mallon arrived at the lock-up garage. There was no one was around to ask questions, so he moved his 'preciouses' inside.

He acquired a workbench, chair and other sundries from Bunnings and other stores and made a start preparing the explosives and electronic equipment. He was doing what he did best. Every man needed a hobby.

September 6

Mallon left his campervan at dusk and, when nearing the railway, killed his lights and drove by moonlight along the rail maintenance track. Knowing when the less frequent night and early morning trains passed, he knew when he could work unimpeded—except by mosquitoes. The air was thick with them.

Thank Christ for repellent, he thought. He had sprayed himself with the strongest he could find. *The mossies won't bite your arm if they dissolve before your arm does.*

He planted two sets of charges in a single night—one on each of two of the lines to Monk's Point, not far from the junction with the main line.

His two chosen locations were just over an hour apart by road. He carefully concealed each bomb under a bridge. As well as the explosives and remotely controlled detonators, he placed sensors under rails so that he would remotely know if the train was passing and could fire them at a distance if need be. Computerised train control and long trains meant that the time of passing would be consistent, but he wasn't taking any chances on a delay.

After he had placed the second charge and sensor, he looked up at the night sky. It was completely clear and filled with stars. *Fucking amazing*, he thought.

In the distance, a locomotive horn blew, and its headlight cut through the darkness.

September 7, early morning

Emma had organised a group of fifty-two protesters to drive in separate vehicles to the agreed spot. She told them to come separately in plain cars, utes and the like, rather than rainbow or other whacky-looking hippie buses or kombis, which would invite police scrutiny and arrest. The police had orders to confiscate dangerous terrorist items, like tents and other camping equipment, which might be used by protesters. The police hunt was especially on for glue and other lock-on devices, but their focus was on cities and the prevention of traffic obstruction, so no one was picked up.

She had chosen the place to first assemble. She texted everyone to check they were all on the way: *OK, happy campers???*

They went in convoy for the last kilometre to some waste ground by a highway maintenance yard where they parked. It was a hundred metres from a level crossing on the main coal railway to the port, downtrack from the two lines that came in from the coalfields. The double track mainline was busier than the individual feeder lines.

Emma and thirty-four others put on suitable clothing and gathered the equipment they had brought. Others walked up the track to place flags and signs at a suitable location. The aim was for them to a stop a train without being run over.

Paul had attempted to estimate the stopping distance for trains applying brakes in an emergency. He'd researched that fully-loaded down trains weighed about eighteen thousand tonnes and travelled at sixty to seventy kilometres per hour. The necessary stopping distance would be less for empty trains returning from the port to the mines; they'd have less momentum. It was almost as important to disrupt them as it was to disrupt the full ones, as the loss would cause equal disruption to supply. While taking flags up the track, he tried to remember the applied mathematics he had done at school. He then remembered that his teacher, Mr Jackson, had never got the right answer when doing worked examples on the blackboard. The cases were always about billiard balls, cannons firing shells, never-stopping coal trains. "It'll all come out in the wash," Mr Jackson had always said.

Hang on, thought Paul. He remembered how Mr Jackson had always sucked a sweet while doing his sums. "He never once offered them around the class." Paul erred on the side of caution and gave it five hundred metres.

Emma and the others were meanwhile locking themselves to both tracks. She had already researched the timetable and knew that there would be a down train in thirty-five minutes and up train in forty-five minutes. The support crew took and hid the lock keys and concealed the vehicles.

As a keen rail buff, Paul had suggested getting hold of or making some track detonators, used by rail maintenance gangs to alert train crews, but no one knew how. Lookouts would wave flags and blow vuvuzelas to attract drivers' attention. They had also started fairly early in the day, so their presence would be known long before dark. Emma had thought of everything.

They waited. Emma smiled at Kate, who sat next to her and was very nervous.

"You okay, Kate? It'll be fine. This is our big chance to make a difference."

People said that a few people couldn't change things or make a difference in a big and complex world. She was determined to prove them wrong.

Mallon drove over the railway crossing. After doing some shopping for food, he was returning to his campervan to rest up before his busy night ahead.

He saw the lights begin to flash and heard the bells clanging. He accelerated to get across before the train—otherwise there'd be a wait. He glimpsed some people gathered near the crossing.

It was an old schoolboy trick to put your ear on a railway line in order to tell if there was a distant train coming. Emma and the others didn't need to do that. The down and up signals were both at green; crossing bells clanging loudly; the very ground vibrating as the down train thundered into view.

The driver, Wayne Simpson, was fortunately alert. Seeing the flags and waving people, he immediately released the dead man's handle while blowing the horn. The engines of the two giant locomotives were run down while power was generated for the air brakes. Sparks flew as steel ground on steel. The air was filled with the sound of wheel tyre screeching and banging wagon buffers.

The train came to a halt just before Emma and the others. They opened their eyes when they sensed the train had stopped. They hadn't been able to look.

Simpson first radioed to the control centre to alert the up train, which was on its way, and turn all the signals to red. He climbed out and strode down the side of the track.

"You stupid bloody idiots! Don't you know you could have been killed?"

"Don't you know you're helping kill the planet, kill all future generations?" Emma shouted back.

"Coal means death! Coal means death!" she chanted, and all the others joined in.

'That's my girl,' David would have said. 'Always has a smart answer to everything.'

There was the sound of cars honking at the level crossing.

"All right, everyone," said Nigel. "Sit down and glue on."

Emma had asked him and others to block the road crossing and get as many others as possible to drive out and clog the road. Traffic would build up and hamper the police and lock cutting crews.

September 7, 13:00

Greg Hutchings, CEO of King Coal, was on the phone to the PM as soon as he heard about the trains being blocked. "Maurice," he said. All of the PM's corporate chums and party donors were on first-name terms. "This is an outrage and a threat not only to my company and industry, but to our national economy." He thought of adding: *a threat to civilisation and the Australian way of life*, before the PM interjected.

"Greg, Greg, rest assured that we are onto it and will take all necessary steps."

"We face millions in penalties for late shipments, ship and port handling alone … not to mention loss of reputation and future orders."

"Greg, we …"

"I want the police, army, I don't care who, to get them cut out and arrested … or is it the other way round? Whatever … I don't want any kid gloves in dealing with them and I want long, maximum prison sentences to discourage others. And I don't want it in the news for other terrorists to copy the idea. You know the deal. We scratch your back, and you scratch ours."

"Greg, we'll do all we can. You can count on us."

"Prime Minister, there's another call on line six and one on seven," said the PM's Private Secretary. "More coal CEOs."

"Tell them I'm in a meeting."

There was no keeping events at Manstone out of the news. Long coal trains were hard to hide, even in the outback, and up track and down track, thirty-two trains were now motionless at red signals. The events were also immediately in the news because Emma had tipped off a friendly journalist to be there at a certain time. She wanted to maximise publicity and to have a witness if the police turned violent. Hopefully, the journo would arrive before the police.

"The fuzz are taking their time getting here," said Kate. "Sitting on railway tracks would be really uncomfortable without these cushions."

"I know, but the longer we're here, the more disruption, and the more it will cost the coal companies. The traffic blockers have done a good job. We have company."

They saw a woman and a man walking up the track.

"Hello, Emma," said Louise Brailly. "So, this is what you'd arranged. This will cause quite a stir. Oh, this my friend Eddie. He'll get a few shots if that's okay."

Eddie held a camera over his shoulder. "Hi," he said.

"Hi, thanks for coming," said Emma.

Emma had once met Brailly, a freelance journalist based in Brisbane, and had sent a tip off. She knew Brailly was a regular correspondent for *The Sentinel*.

"I guess we'll hang around and wait for the cops to arrive," said Brailly. "Eddie, do you want to get any shots of the people at the crossing?"

Hundreds of protesters were arriving, adding to the traffic chaos. Many drivers had tried to turn around, further blocking police and cutting crews.

"Ah, here they are." Police and cutters were walking up the track.

"What's all this, then?" said the officer in charge. "You're all under arrest for obstructing a railway. If I had my way, I'd …"

"You'd what, officer? Louise Brailly, *The Sentinel*."

The protesters on the crossing were easier to deal with than those locked to the track, so the police removed them first to get the traffic moving and to allow reinforcements. But it was slow; the police were being watched and filmed. The protesters had to be removed carefully; the police couldn't leave superglued body parts on the road.

More police and cutting crews were now arriving. As soon as the protesters were cut free, and taken away in buses, more appeared from the bushes and locked on to the track.

The last group to arrive was a flotilla of reporters from Moorcock News.

"What's it like to be a leftie bunny hugger? I mean, do you people ever take baths?"

Mallon dozed until well into the afternoon, then prepared his equipment, checking for functionality. *Don't forget the spare batteries*, he reminded himself.

He passed the level crossing once again in the late afternoon and realised there was a protest going on. He couldn't stop to look, but glimpsed police emergency crews and others on the track. There was a train stopped up the line.

Shit, this is going to throw everything. All the timetables will be fucked. He might have to postpone, but he didn't want to leave the charges another day. You couldn't leave explosives lying around. Not safe. "Fuckin' protesters!"

The protesters would be removed sooner or later, and the trains would get rolling, but at a reduced speed until the computerised control and signalling were fully operational.

He decided to wait in his usual place under cover, near the first target.

After the protesters were cleared, CEO Hutchings was anxious that all loading and train crews made up the lost time. He called the Operations Director.

"Yes … that's what I'm saying … Tell Control to override computerised train management and signals … fuck safety … time is money. They managed to run railways without computers for nearly two hundred years! Get those trains moving pronto, or I'll have your fucking arse."

September 7, 17:00

As the sun was setting, Mallon heard the horn of a train and saw its headlight. The train roared into view. *Okay, get ready.*

The slower running made it much easier to fire the charge at the right moment. Mallon activated the detonator as the locomotive passed over it, counted to ten instead of to five and turned the switch.

It all happened quickly. The charge was under the track on the bridge. There was a flash, a bang and a puff of smoke and dust as the ANFO blew the track apart. The wheels of the tenth wagon momentarily ran over the pre-stressed concrete sleepers, rattling loudly as the sleepers were sliced. The coupling to the ninth wagon was severed, along with the train's air braking system. Wagon ten was pushed from the track bed by the momentum of the fully laden ninety-one wagons behind it, assisted by the down grade. Wagon ten lurched and fell to its side, still being pushed along, spilling its carboniferous contents. The following wagons did the same and covered the ground with coal, in drifts like black snow.

"Holy shit!" said Mallon, grinning. "That'll take some cleaning up."

The locomotives with their surviving wagons were well down the line before the driver, Tony Hermoso, knew what had happened. With all the train and cab noise, bells and radio, he hadn't heard what was, deliberately, a relatively small explosion. The warning light indicated a failure in the air braking system. He stopped, climbed down and looked back down the line. Even in the fading light, he could see that most of his train had disappeared.

Hermoso radioed traffic control, who also knew something was wrong, although not exactly what. They turned the line signals to red as he walked back along the track. In Australian spring, the sun set quickly, and there was no long twilight. It was dark when he found the remains of his train. He shone his torch.

"Fuck me!"

―

Mallon didn't want to chance using the remote sensors to blow the second charge on the other line, so he decided to drive there.

It was now dark. The mossies weren't so bad. "Must be their night off." It was quite pleasant and balmy as he looked up at the clear sky.

He only had to wait thirty minutes for the train to come. The headlight cut through the night as the train roared past.

He did exactly the same as before. There was a huge din of crashing and banging wagons, but he couldn't see what was happening.

He thought he'd like to see the mess, but there would soon be a lot of police and emergency crews around, and he didn't want to be seen. He left immediately along the gravelled maintenance track and then onto the hard-top road and into the night.

Unknown to him, the train he had just blown was being followed closely by a second train.

He took backroads back to Townsville before locking away the Land Cruiser and resting in the camper. A good night's work.

He slept soundly and dreamed about the boy with the cardboard helmet.

CHAPTER 17

September 7, evening

Driver Fred Dibley wasn't happy running like this without central computer train and signalling control. The train was running slower than usual, but it was still faster than he liked and, in the dark, too close to the train he'd been following, watching for its taillight.

There was a big bend ahead, and the taillight disappeared from sight. Then the powerful beam of his headlight picked up something. *Fuck!* It was the train ahead, wagons piled up on the track,

Luckily, the cab door was open for fresh air. There was no choice. He leapt to the ground and felt a crack of pain in his right leg. He watched as his locomotive and the second driverless unit shunted into the wreckage of the first train.

After being cut free, Emma and the others were immediately arrested and driven to Brisbane Central Police Station, where most of them were already familiar with the police accommodation. In view of the new situation, they were held for questioning. None knew what had happened up the line.

Emma knew what to do if arrested and who to contact—human rights lawyer, Tim Gleeson.

She was called in for an interview first—the police suspected her of being the ringleader. Before the interview, Gleeson had a chance to brief Emma on what had happened and why she was under investigation.

"Three coal trains have been destroyed," said Gleeson. "Please tell me you had nothing to do with that."

"Wow! I don't believe it … I—we had no idea … What an amazing coincidence! Who can have done it?"

DCs Marina Towner and Brett Daley formally initiated the interview while DCI Shane Goss watched from behind the viewing window.

"Can I remind you of the seriousness of this investigation under the Prevention of Terrorism Act?" said Towner. "Being an accessory to an act of terrorism is an extremely serious offence. If you have any connection, any information about who committed this crime, it will help your case if you tell us now. What do you know about the railway bombings last night? I would ask you to take that smile off your face."

"I know nothing."

"How do you explain that the very day that you and others block the railway, two connecting lines and three trains are bombed?"

"I can't explain it."

"Whose idea was it to blow up the railway tracks? Was it yours?"

"Why would we bother to lock ourselves onto the track if we were going to blow it up?"

Gleeson gave a 'she's got you there' grin. She hardly needed him.

The police could find no evidence to connect her and the other protesters with the bombings and referred them to the usual processes and bail orders for obstruction. Bail was paid for by an anonymous fund.

The alleged protester connection to the bombings having drawn a blank, the police search widened. The investigation was now under Ministerial Control through the Australian Commonwealth Police. The Australian Secret Service were also alerted to look out for possible links to international terrorism.

"Green-left terrorists! What did we tell you!" screamed the popular media, accusing the protesters of being behind the bombings, demanding even longer jail sentences.

The bombings stirred considerable debate. Some senior members of the community suggested internment of the protesters. "That's what we did to the Japs, Germans and Italians during the war," suggested one caller on Radio 2GBH. "Course, we let 'em out after the war."

"Why let them out? I'd throw away the key," said Alan Williams, whose show was fuelled on outrage. Like a large part of the Australian media, its primary audience was angry, old, white males.

In *The Antipodean*, columnists foamed at the mouth. '… attack on civilisation … no punishment too harsh … need for the public to support the coal industry in its hour of need … threat to jobs and growth.'

"You're amazing," said Grey. "I mean, pulling off that stunt—even getting your picture on the front pages of the Moorcock tabloids. What did one say? 'Hot climate girl stops 'em in their tracks.' You'll be getting calls from modelling agencies next."

"I already have."

"I'm a bit worried that the police and government will throw the book at you. It will have cost the coal industry millions."

"Don't worry. Tim's preparing the defence. Thinks it's pretty solid, along the lines of preventing a greater harm."

Late September, London

Burns finalised his preparations and travel arrangements for himself and his team, ordnance and logistics. They would all join the NE2 in Port Moresby, Papua New Guinea, just across the Torres Strait from Australia.

He'd be on his way soon. He'd done all the planning he could, and hopefully all would go well. But the best laid plans could turn to shit. There was an outside chance he might not come back. He made his own personal arrangements.

Burns kept his distance from Galina. He liked her, and so he didn't want going away to be any harder, but she became concerned by his absence.

"Do you not care for me anymore? Is there someone else?"

"I think you're wonderful, Galina, and no, there's no one else ... It's just that I have to go away for a couple of months and will be offline. I'll miss you."

"It's a mission, isn't it?"

"You could say it's a sailing trip."

"You don't have to say any more. Promise me you'll come back. I'll wait for you."

"I promise ... I love you."

"Oh, Alex ... I love you too."

September 25, Weymouth, Massachusetts

The leaves were starting to turn gold when Mike Ryan visited his mother and stepfather.

"I thought I'd stop by as I'm off on a field trip for a couple of months, and calling will be difficult."

"That's nice, Mike," said his mother, Martha. "I'm sure you'll have a wonderful time. We're so proud of all you do, and we will pray for a safe journey and return."

Ryan was making his final preparations before flying to join the NE2 as Chief Scientist of the IMCF. He could hardly believe that he'd been selected for something so big. Was he crazy to accept? It was a chance to help save the world. He sure as hell wasn't doing that with his research work.

How did he get into this situation? It had all started with his love for humpback whales. He'd been brought up in Weymouth, on the Massachusetts coast, by his mother and stepfather, Jim. He never knew his real father. Martha, his mother, didn't talk about him. She just said that he was some guy at Harvard Business School who'd gone away. She said he was nice and had sent some money to pay for his education but had promised no one would come looking for him.

From a young age, his stepfather had taken him sailing and sea fishing. He was filled with awe when he saw the whales for the first time and was hooked on them from that moment. He'd gone on to study marine biology at UMass and MIT, had taught and researched before going on to work at Woods Hole Oceanographic Institute. His international reputation grew due to his work on rising ocean temperatures, climate change and their impacts on ocean currents and marine life.

Then he was approached by an English guy called Piers about something he'd written in his blog about the need for urgent, radical action. Piers's mission had needed a scientific front. He'd agreed to do it.

He now needed an Australian marine scientist for the mission, which would pretend to be a marine survey, and who better than John Grey? They'd met a couple of times at conferences and had really bonded, helped by beer. They cared about the same things, and agreed on the need for urgent action. But would he be ready to come on board when he learned how radical the mission would be? If not, he'd have to be just a shore-based adviser.

Mallon took off to Port Douglas to do some diving and snorkelling in the reef. He had heard and read about the chaos he had already caused and the outrage he had invoked. He picked up a copy of *The Antipodean*. His actions were front-page news. He wished he could see the foam around the journos' mouths.

"This is really annoying the bastards."

Over a Guinness at Paddy's Irish Pub, he changed his mind about it being a one-off attack.

He noticed someone on the front cover of a tabloid. "What the …? That's Emma! What do you know? That must have been her with those people at the crossing … what a coincidence. I hope she keeps out of trouble."

He had a mobile phone just for calls to Siobhan, but kept it switched off at other times so he couldn't be tracked.

"I'm having a lovely time, thanks. It's doing me a power of good … What bombings? Oh, those. I heard about them—inland somewhere. I'm on the coast. It's perfectly safe here. I think I'll hang around a bit longer."

The Queensland coal industry was damaged, but only temporarily. PM Turbott declared it a national emergency requiring public money be thrown at it, adding to the already generous public support for the industry.

Army engineers, as well as contractors and railway personnel, worked day and night to clear a way through the debris and reinstate the track. A full clean-up would have to wait. All lines would be operating again in less than two weeks, and surveillance would be stepped up.

CHAPTER 18

Early October

During the weeks after his first attack, Mallon settled into a routine, like a job, of making, planting and blowing up two coal trains every week, then relaxing at the reef to remind himself why he was doing it. There was danger, but it was also fun, keeping the fuckers guessing where and when and which train he'd strike. It took him back to his youth in Northern Ireland. They couldn't watch and inspect hundreds of kilometres of track all the time, especially at night.

Besides, there were all those nice, electrified lines with poles, wires and substations. Hours of fun—he hadn't played with an electric train set since he was a young lad.

However, he knew the dangers of what he was doing. The sulphur hexafluoride in high-voltage switch gear had a global warming potential that was twenty-eight thousand times that of carbon dioxide. Instantaneous switching was necessary in HV systems to prevent overloads, burnouts and power failure. He'd read that more and more renewables coming on stream meant more of a need for SF6 switching. No one had found a substitute as cheap and effective. Even small leaks could negate all the greenhouse benefits of renewables.

Who says there isn't a Devil? he thought.

His campaign was now into its fifth week and tenth bomb. He had hurt no one, apart from one broken leg, always bombing trains after the tenth wagon.

October 5, Police HQ, Brisbane

The Queensland Police were under pressure to apprehend the bomber or bombers before the Commonwealth Police, the ACP and Homeland Security completely took over. DCI Shane Goss was leading the investigating team, which had convened in the ops room. He was concerned. It had been over four weeks since the first bombs, and now there were two a week. The bomber or bombers were playing with them.

"Okay, what do we have on the bombings so far? Motive? Apparently intended to disrupt coal traffic, not kill. Not, it seems, directly connected to the climate protesters, but a connection can't be ruled out."

"Could be someone with a grudge against the coal industry," suggested DI Pettigrew.

"You could be right ..." Goss resisted a 'stupid boy' remark and continued. "Our bomb experts found little to go on, except that they started as simple ANFO devices and now are something else, possibly Semtex—we're assuming there was no more than one culprit. A pro, probably, but we can't rule out a gifted amateur."

Goss continued. "An appeal for witnesses or any signs of suspicious activity has drawn a blank. We've been ordered to do a check on every licenced blaster in the country and to check their whereabouts on the nights of the blasts. There's a watch on all ports and airports, which have stepped up checks with those poky explosives' detectors. The investigation is going to take time. There are hundreds of mines and quarries in Australia, so we'd better get cracking."

With each blown coal train, political, industry and media outrage intensified. Mouths foamed furiously. But Aussies liked a battler, a larrikin. Their favourite hero was Ned Kelly after all.

Louise Brailly spotted the parallel and wrote an article about it in *The Sentinel*.

Is the public warming to this mystery bomber? I believe they are. Is there a similarity to Ned Kelly? I believe there is. Kelly's exploits and images of his metal helmet, with that eye slit, and his body armour, have earned him a place in the hall of fame. Was he really an outlaw, the official view, or a fighter for the oppressed?

What of this mystery bomber? Like Kelly, he'd been giving the police the run around. They were assuming it was a 'he', since statistically there weren't as many female explosives professionals. He seemed to be fighting for a cause. Was he a climate activist or did he have a grudge against the coal industry?

There was even a cottage industry selling souvenirs, maps and pieces of coal. Brailly almost wrote that tourism was making a bomb as a result of renewed interest in the rural areas surrounding the railways, before thinking better of it.

Dare they call him Ned Coaly?

Sympathetic or not, the news media saw the sales opportunity. In days, Ned Coaly became world famous.

October 6, Belfast, Northern Ireland

In all the news surrounding the Australian bombings, George Moore recognised Patrick Mooney's trademark.

"Ned Coaly, are you, now? We all know how Ned Kelly finished up."

Moore had been released prematurely from the Maze Prison under the Good Friday Agreement but had done enough time to swear that one day he would pay his respects to the person who had put him there. In the IRA, grassing carried a mandatory death sentence.

While in prison, he was disappointed but not surprised to learn that Mooney had 'disappeared', no doubt to adopt a new identity somewhere or other. Australia, even. *It's where I'd go,* he thought. *As far as possible from me. Australia, Antarctica, the Moon.*

In the meantime, he'd had to content himself with killing other people.

Many people confused 'psychopathic'—zero empathy, liking power and control, compulsive lying—with 'psychotic'—mentally disturbed, in extreme cases nurturing a desire to kill. Moore erred towards the latter. He was proud of the diagnosis by the Maze Prison shrink, proud of his career progression to date.

After prison, he had tried a few jobs. For a while, he'd become a management consultant with one of the Big Four, specialising in 'change management'. This involved being paid to go into organisations and sack everyone in sight, because the management didn't have the balls to do it themselves. It had been alright—fun for a while. Scorched earth, he'd even sacked the potted plants.

But all those people blubbing got on his nerves. He'd then discovered that as a contract killer, you could kill people and get paid for it. It was more than job satisfaction; it was Maslow's self-actualisation.

In the IRA, he'd had no time for Mooney. He was of the view that setting off a bomb without killing at least half a dozen people was a waste of a perfectly good bomb. Bombing railway tracks and the rear half of freight trains was, to him, the equivalent of non-violent protest. *Gandhi shit,* he had called it. "Mooney, you're a fucking big girl's blouse," he had sneered in front of the platoon.

It was now time to go and find his nemesis. But he would get someone to pay for his trip.

Moore always found his work through middlemen so that his role and his clients were anonymous. The clients were usually looking for someone like him to do their dirty work, and contracts were arranged through a network of fixers. It was like being an Uber driver, except that you killed people for your customers instead of giving them a ride or a takeaway meal.

In this case, Moore decided to make a direct approach to a customer who might be glad of his services. He had Googled for information on the Australian Coal Council.

A YouTube video came up on what appeared to be a promotion of the Australian coal industry's corporate responsibility credentials. A slick-looking business type in a pinstripe shirt and tie declared, "We, the Australian coal industry, are responsible global citizens. We recognise climate change, and our need to reduce our contribution, for the future of our children. At the same time, we have to make a profit for our shareholders. How do we resolve this quandary?" The business type paused and stuck up his finger. "By saying *fuck you!*"

I suppose that's meant to be funny, thought Moore.

He was not surprised that ACC initially declined his offer. People who were squeamish about killing people always did at first, although mostly in response to the possibility of going to jail, rather than the ethics. Until they saw the benefits; until they did the cost-benefit analysis. It was human nature.

He guessed that the longer things went on without the police catching Mooney—or whatever his name was now—the more they'd be financially hurting. Then they'd see sense.

Greg Hutchings had asked the Australian Coal Council to call an emergency meeting of its members, coal industry owners and CEOs. He knew they were all nervous and angry that the police had failed to catch the bomber. The disruption in Queensland had already lost many millions in revenue, even after insurance and government support, and the costs were mounting daily. It had also created instability in coal share prices. Even before the attacks, coal was increasingly being seen as a dinosaur stock, only propped up by demand from economic expansion in China and India and nuclear replacement in Japan.

"This has seriously impacted on our profits and future contracts," said Tina Nulhart, multi-billionaire coal and iron magnate.

"More attacks will be bad news," said Hutchings. "We also have the Daghawi opening coming up. The biggest day ever for our industry. We don't want anyone spoiling the party."

The Coal Council knew that with the world heating up at an accelerating rate, their industry was on notice. They had to expand as much as possible to maximise short-term profits. New strategies would be needed. Opponents had to be attacked with more than just lies and propaganda.

"If the police can't find whoever's doing the bombings and put a stop to it, we need to pay someone."

As one of the richest women in the world, there was nothing Nulhart wanted that couldn't be bought.

Emma was inspired by the mystery railway bomber—*Ned Coaly, what a great name*—and his first attack on a power system. She suggested that the Climate Commandos do the same.

"Why didn't we think of it before? Obstructing coal lines is decidedly dangerous if the trains don't stop, and if we keep getting arrested, we might not get off so lightly next time. A lot of the coal railways are electrified. It won't take much to disrupt power systems without being caught."

"I have an idea," said Paul. "Kites. We just need to short-circuit the overhead power lines for electric locos and the power lines to signals for diesel locos. Without power and signals, the trains can't run." Paul knew about railways—he still had his electric train set—and knew how to fly kites.

Days later, Emma and Grey were eating takeaway pizza and had just watched the ABC news.

"All these power lines and coal trains being stuffed," started Grey. "I hope it isn't anything to do with you. I'd miss you desperately if you were in jail."

"Would you, darling? You could visit me, and we'd kiss through the screen. No, I wouldn't do anything like that."

He didn't notice as she looked away and released the deep breath she'd been holding.

Mallon followed his story on ABC Radio National:

"There was another coal railway disruption in Queensland yesterday evening. Power supplies were disrupted for a major section of the route. Police investigations are continuing, and they are appealing for witnesses, but it has been attributed to the attacker being dubbed 'Ned Coaly'."

"Ned Coaly, am I now? I like it—a nice family connection; Kelly would be proud."

Attacking power and signalling systems was fun, easy and added variety, but he still preferred to blow up coal trains. It was messier and harder for them to fix. They were his trademark.

The next day, Mallon's ears picked up when he heard something unexpected on the radio:

"There was another disruption to power supply of a coal railway in Queensland yesterday evening, bringing shipments to a standstill. Ned Coaly is suspected."

"That wasn't one of mine, not at all," said Mallon. "That's a copycat attack!"

October 15, Townsville, Queensland

Mallon was once again lying low. Until the police cry died down, he would blend in with the tourists visiting the reef. He was probably safe for now. He'd heard nothing more on the news.

There was little to connect him with the railway bombings. He'd covered his tracks. He'd had his phone turned off, used call boxes to phone home, and had paid with cash when outside of tourist areas. It would be a long shot for the police to check every blaster in the country and you didn't need to be licenced or even professional to make a bomb. If they did ask at the mine, they'd say he'd left and was sightseeing and diving in Queensland—whereabouts unknown.

He was enjoying a beer at sunset. Looking east, it wasn't quite like the spectacular sunsets over the Indian Ocean in Western Australia, but it was good all the same. He was missing his family and home. He was missing his son.

But you couldn't have everything. Nothing lasted for ever, and the more you loved it, the more heartache when it was gone. He wiped away a tear. He was going on another organised dive the following day and would imagine David was with him.

He couldn't go on bombing for ever. He had made his point. He would carry on travelling around Australia. But there was one last railway he had to see to—for David and the protesters, for Kieran, for the Reef. Then he'd call it quits.

Daghawi.

He had earlier read that the grand opening was confirmed for the fifth of November and would be broadcast on TV. "Guy Fawkes Night," he'd said out loud. "You're kidding me."

CHAPTER 19

October 15, Switzerland

Dreiser went for his customary afternoon walk. Autumn leaves were thickening on the ground, and the mountain peaks were whitening.

Military operations were in the hands of Command. For security, only one member of Command—'the General'—communicated directly with him and gave regular updates. All seemed well, to the extent that Phoenix was a good thing. But there were still things keeping him awake at night.

A big concern was the security risk. There was the risk of detection, the risk of him and his colleagues being caught and punished. If it succeeded, it would be worth it—they weren't so young. They could hire smart lawyers playing 'to prevent a greater crime', insanity or whatever.

Insanity. At worst, they'd do time in a five-star prison or a loony bin.

The important thing was protecting Phoenix, protecting the operators from detection before and after execution. They would be up against security and intelligence agencies, in some countries, no mere boy scouts. They could be subject to torture or even death. It was necessary to keep what they knew to the minimum and to make maximum use of deception and initiative while keeping to the overall plan.

Another worry was the population dynamics, collateral damage and the casualties. Oil and gas processing plants were large but not big employers. Still, there would be casualties in the targets. It would not be possible to phone ahead and politely suggest evacuation. There could be casualties among the plant operators and neighbours; it would be tantamount to murder, an act of war. Around the world, there might be deprivation, starvation if food supplies and production were badly affected ... Against that, if no drastic measures were taken, millions would die from the ravages of climate change, billions eventually, extinction in the worst-case scenario.

He read that the Daghawi mine was about to open and that there would be a big party to celebrate. There was a picture of that idiot Turbott grinning about how he had made Daghawi happen—how opening it would be his greatest moment, his finest hour.

"How bad is this?" PM Turbott had been deeply disturbed and shocked by the coal railway bombings and other attacks on the coal industry. It was surely the work of Satan.

He was making sure that the Australian government was sparing no expense in hunting down the perpetrators. An attack on their best friend donors in the coal industry was an attack on them. Although not written into the constitution, a fundamental principle of Australian democracy was that policy was made with the bribe, not the bomb.

"This Ned Coaly and his gang must and will be brought to justice," he declared to Parliament. "Look what happened to Ned Kelly."

But he was concerned that there were still no clues, no leads. He had to make sure that there was no threat to the Daghawi opening. For years, the warmists had tried to stop it. Thanks to him, they had failed. This was going to be his finest Churchillian moment.

With his government's financial support, the railway had been designed so that there were no level crossings—only overpass bridges—and it had been heavily fenced with barbed wire and detectors as well as CCTV for the entire route. For the opening, there would be an army of police and private security, helicopters, the works. That Ned Coaly wouldn't get anywhere near it.

He called his Finance Minister, Senator Herman Hormann.

"How are the Daghawi arrangements going, Herman?"

"Very well, indeed, Prime Minister. All of the invitees have accepted and there's a waiting list. We might need another grandstand."

"Good. We need to do all we can to support our friends. By the way, thank you again for finding the money for the DFAT delegation to London …"

October 15, Cumberland Hotel, Marble Arch, London

Australia was seizing every opportunity to promote its products. A major international conference was being held on the future sustainability of the fossil fuel industry. Australia was well-represented in speakers and attendees.

Damian Sproake had spoken on the benefits and necessity of gas. He proudly represented a major fossil fuel lobby, the Australian Petroleum Industry Group. "In conclusion, natural gas is the clean bridging fuel to a sustainable future." Applause.

"Are there any questions?" asked the chairperson. The mike was handed to someone who stood up.

"George Toynbee, journalist, *The Sentinel*. I have three questions on three of your lies. First, do you seriously expect anyone to believe that clean fuel rubbish anymore, which your industry has been spruiking longer than anyone can remember? Numerous studies have shown that when gas is liquefied, vented and burnt in open cycle gas turbines, it's almost as dirty as coal. Second, if gas is a bridging fuel, why are you planning for a hundred more years of it and expanding the industry when climate science says it has to stay in the ground? Third, is it not true that your expansion is designed to push out renewables, not displace coal? Gas might have been a bridging fuel once, but it's at the end of the bridge. Claiming that gas is good compared to coal is like saying that heroin is much healthier than meth. But if you're a major pusher of both, as Australia is, then hey, that's good business!" At least some of the audience laughed.

"Can questioners please stick to one question in future?" requested the chairperson.

Greg Hutchings waxed lyrical on clean coal and carbon capture and storage. "In conclusion, coal is good for humanity, lifting millions out of energy poverty. It will have an important role in benefiting the global economy and people for many decades to come. I'm happy to take questions."

The mike went out.

"George Toynbee, journalist, *The Sentinel*. Why has your industry suddenly become interested in the poor when for centuries it has been using them as slaves and poisoning their lungs, when the poor will be the worst hit by the climate change it has caused?"

Was that one question? thought the chairperson? *I'll let it go.*

"Can you please repeat the question?" asked Hutchings. He was stalling while he thought of an answer. Personally, he thought the poor were disgusting. He hated those commie arseholes at *The Sentinel*. That Louise Brailly was always pissing him off, siding with the climate protesters, making a hero out of the bomber of his trains. He'd have them all lined up and shot if he had his way.

The closing panel discussion focused on scenarios. A question came from the floor. "In view of recent events in Australia, does the panel believe there could be more attacks on the fossil fuel industry? Or is this a one-off issue?"

"Would you like to take this one, Jonathon?" asked the chairperson.

Panellist and sustainability guru Jonathon Polkington had been in overdrive with sage head-nodding and handwringing. Polkington was good at being Polkington—a living legend to some, an insufferably smug, name-dropping know-it-all to others.

"It's not known what's behind the Queensland bombings—whether it's a grudge attack or eco-terrorism. It's possible that protesters might try to disrupt more infrastructure, like Earth First in the nineteen-eighties.

We've seen people try to turn off a valve station on the Keystone Pipeline in the USA. The CIA once predicted that eco-terrorism could become a bigger threat than jihadism. As I was saying to Jacques Delors, CEO of Nand Corporation only the other day ..."

As part of PM Turbott's trade delegation, Hutchings was also in London to visit the head office of King Coal's owners, TRX Resources. He had been summoned to explain his company's poor quarterly returns as a result of the bombings.

After the conference, he was approached outside by a man with a beard.

Back at his hotel, Hutchings called his CFO in Melbourne. "He says he knows who the bomber is—that he's a pro. The police will take time to catch him, if at all, and if they do, he'll be martyred, and we'll be the bad guys. He's already a folk hero, this Ned Coaly. He hasn't killed anyone, so he won't get a big sentence. He could come out and start again. I say we do it."

"Alright ... but we haven't had this conversation. We'll take it out of the slush fund. It was disappearing offshore anyway."

October 16, Port Moresby, Papua New Guinea

Burns had arranged for each member of his team to make their own way to the ship by noon. He arrived at the harbour by taxi, and there it was, the *New Endeavour II*.

He had done his research and felt like he already knew it. The oceanographic research and survey vessel was seventy-five metres long. It was weather-beaten but sleek, with powerful diesel engines, designed for severe ocean conditions. Built in Lübeck, Germany in 1986 as an Arctic fisheries protection vessel for the Icelandic Navy, it was later sold and refitted as a marine survey ship and available for contract commissions, operating crew included.

For this mission, some extra fixtures and fittings had been arranged. He could see something under wraps at the stern, ostensibly an ocean research submersible. It was the submarine. He knew that there was a subtle difference—submersibles were physically linked to the mother ship by an air, power and communication umbilical, whereas submarines were independent and free-moving. Handy if you wanted to drive around and do a bit of mine-laying.

Simmo, Jonesy, Bazza, Moody and Beattie were already there, as were Grobbelaar and Boonzaaier. Martin and Mann were just arriving.

"Hello, guys, glad you could all make it."

They boarded and were welcomed by the captain.

"Lars Hoemberg, at your service. Welcome aboard. I trust you will have a very pleasant journey. We are just waiting for one more. As soon as he's here, we will prepare to set sail."

He introduced them to the mostly German crew of seventeen—ships officers, mechanics, technicians and other support—and they were shown to their quarters.

A taxi arrived, and a young man came aboard with several bags.

"Doctor Ryan, I presume," said Burns.

"Sorry I'm late. You must be George Phelps. Pleased to meet you."

They shook hands.

"I've heard all about you, Mike. Come and meet the captain and crew. I think we're all ready to get going. Next stop, Port Douglas."

October 16, Canberra

At the request of PM Turbott, Senator Hormann was reviewing the final list of attendees for the grand opening of the Daghawi mine and railway. As Finance Minister, he was responsible for the budget.

Thanks to his government, its industry supporters and Robert Moorcock, Daghawi had become the flagship for anyone in Australia who was pro-coal, climate-sceptical and anti-green. This wasn't just the PM and his government, but more than half of Australia by voting preferences. Stopping and acting on climate change had been a top election issue at the last two federal elections, but the Coalition and its media supporters had been vociferously for the mine and against economy-wrecking climate-warmists. Even the Labor opposition had been ambivalent, not wanting to lose votes in Queensland and NSW coal seats or the financial support of mining unions.

Hormann thought it was all bloody marvellous. So many had wanted to come to the opening, to show their solidarity, to celebrate, that it had to be VIP only, and a special grandstand had been erected. Televised live, it would be a historical marketing moment for the prime minister, who would officially open the mine and railway.

There was a waiting list. WAGs had to be invited. They'd want to wear large hats, as if it was a day at the frigging races. The pitch of the seating had to be steep so that everyone got a view. No-one would be forgetting to bring the bubbly.

He saw that all the leading climate sceptics had been invited: the staunchest ministers and senators—Brad Callaghan, Craig Tooley, George Magnussen—the Coal Council, generous donors of the parliamentary coal lump, and other lobbyists. All the right media would be there to trumpet this triumph for the government and the Coalition.

Hormann was delighted that Australia's most eminent and outspoken climate sceptic could come—Cardinal Colin 'ding dong' Bell. Bell had only recently been acquitted and released from prison. Like the Australian cricket team, he'd been charged with ball tampering.

Among the other VIPs were the coal magnates—main donors to the Coalition. They would need Gold Class seats and service. The top invitee was the extraordinarily wealthy Tina Nulhart—who, by inheritance and acquisition, owned vast iron ore and coal interests.

Billionaire Clive Huntley was another Gold Class invitee. The government owed him one. As well as coal, he had money to burn on buying political influence. Although his own registered party, the Huntley United Nationalists, had failed miserably, his millions spent on ads attacking Labor had ensured the Conservative Coalition gained office. Which was good for what he had planned, the Wangha Coal Mine, four times bigger than Daghawi.

I hope the bloody grandstand is strong enough, thought Hormann, seeing the huge list of invitees.

Townsville

Mallon was relaxing at Paddy's. He read that there was going to be a grandstand at the opening, with a lot of guests and leading climate deniers. He would put on a special show for them …

He ordered another Guinness.

CHAPTER 20

The journey from Port Moresby to Port Douglas was smooth and uneventful.

"It's a fine ship, Mister Hoemberg."

"Indeed, it is, Mister Phelps."

Burns had time to check out the ordnance, all stowed and concealed or disguised in case of inspection. With all the expected VIP treatment, he hoped there wouldn't be too much scrutiny.

He was pleased that the boys were relaxing and bonding well before the action ahead. He'd known they would. They were happy with beer, banter and poker.

"Care to join us for a game, boss?" asked Bazza. They all knew his real name but calling him boss avoided letting it slip out if they were in company. His team also had false IDs and passports.

"Delighted."

Burns had been daydreaming, thinking of Galina, of making love to her. It was hard, leaving. He'd have to stop and concentrate on the job. He couldn't keep taking cold showers.

He'd read in online news about the railway bombings in Queensland. The pattern reminded him of events in Northern Ireland. No, it couldn't be. It had to be a coincidence.

October 20, Port Douglas, Queensland

A small crowd was waiting on the quayside as the *New Endeavour II* tied up. When the team came ashore, onlookers noticed that some of the crew didn't exactly look like research scientists, but then, what was a research scientist supposed to look like?

Two did look the part. The chief scientist for the expedition was Dr Mike Ryan of the IMCF. Dr John Grey, a local from the University of Brisbane, had also been invited to join and advise on marine ecosystems and marine topography along the coast.

"John, it's good to see you again," said Ryan. "It's really great that you could come."

"It's good to see you, too." Grey also noticed there was something different about the crew. Aside, he said to his friend, "What did you mean about … you know?" Grey knew that Ryan wouldn't be here, given his concerns and views, just to do some seawater sampling.

"I'll tell you later," muttered Ryan. "Before the boat leaves, so you're okay with it." Then louder, he said, "I'd like you to meet Lars Hoemberg, ship's captain, and George Phelps, survey mission leader."

They all exchanged greetings.

"Looks like the VIPs are here now," said Ryan.

Dignitaries arrived for the welcome ceremony. PM Turbott was going to milk this for all it was worth. He was unable to attend himself so had delegated it to his Minister of Tourism, Bronwyn Porter. After a welcome to country from the Mayor of Port Douglas and Indigenous Australian dancers, Porter took the mike. "The government and people of Australia are proud to welcome the *New Endeavour II*. Its voyage around Australia is the brainchild of our wonderful Prime Minister …" She went on to state the government's commitment to keeping Australia's waters clean and plastic-free, to preserving its rich coastal heritage and the country's proud connection to Captain Cook. "This is a historic moment. Ladies and gentlemen, I give you the *New Endeavour II*."

Ryan spoke. "Minister, ladies and gentlemen, boys and girls. I and all the crew thank you for your generous welcome. We are proud to be here and to help make Australia and the world a better and cleaner place."

Members of the public were allowed on for limited inspection. In the gushing welcome, two Border Force officers overlooked the submarine under wraps. They did not discern that it was a top-of-the-range military type and did not find other equipment that was unusual for oceanographic survey: limpet mines, rocket launchers, military-grade drones …

Ryan took Grey aside and told him what the basic plan was as far as he knew.

"So that's it. The crew here are going to sabotage the coal ports. Not us, of course—we're just the respectable front." He decided not to mention the LNG plants. That might be a bit too much to take in.

"What! Do you know what you're doing?"

"Yes. Perfectly. You know as well as I do—we've discussed it—that only drastic action will save the world now. This is it."

"I know—I mean I don't know," said Grey. "What if someone's hurt? What if you're caught? What if *we're* caught?"

"It will be done very discreetly with the midget sub and limpet mines. We'll be well out of the way and they'll be timed to avoid hurting anyone. The chances of being caught are small. And you needn't be around or implicated for the action. Just be around for the quiet legs of the voyage and shore visits. John, this project will make real difference. I don't know much, but I think it's part of a much bigger thing."

Grey knew what was happening to the reef, the world—that both were as good as dead without something very much like this.

"Okay … I guess. Hell, I'll do it." What did he have to lose? His career, freedom, life. "Something big, you say?"

Emma and Grey met the following day.

"You know that invitation to go on the *New Endeavour*?" asked Grey. "Well, it's all confirmed. I'll be away quite a bit over the next few weeks. Will you miss me?"

"Course I will, silly. Why the sudden interest in marine sampling?"

"It's good to be involved with international collaborative ocean projects. Something might come of it."

Dreiser received a message that the NE2 had arrived in Australia. He had become still more concerned about all the bombings in Queensland. Would they lead to extra intelligence, security and police activity? Would they be a threat to the Australian mission?

Everywhere, the utmost precautions were being taken. Security was paramount, but Phoenix had to proceed with the next stage in order to keep to schedule.

In the plan and budget, he had allowed for training in preparing for the attacks and operating the equipment. Practice made perfect.

"Come, Dieter and Gunter, today we will play with our toy drone."

"Yippee!" said Dieter.

"It's scary," said Gunter. "It's like a great big bee."

October 22, somewhere north of Lincoln, Nebraska

"Goddamn!" shouted the instructor, Louis Curran, as two drones collided mid-air.

Curran was an alumnus of Worcester Polytechnic Institute, Massachusetts, where he'd hated his nickname, Screwy Louie. He'd been determined to prove people wrong.

He'd achieved his ambition of setting up a training school for drone pilots. He'd found the ideal location in the middle of nowhere—cheap property, accommodation in an old barn, flat farm country, no hills and mountains in the way, no flight paths, none of those tall HV electricity pylons and transmission lines, which drones hated. There was one small snag—no customers. The business had been failing big time.

Then, out of the blue, he'd received an order for two hundred trainees, each for a week, spread over two months "Sure, but we'll need to hire extra staff for the duration. What's that? You'll provide some? Great! You'll supply drones too? Better still. What, you don't need certificates? If you say so ..."

He didn't enquire as to the sudden rush. There was a lot of interest in drones for all sorts of purposes—agricultural and forestry monitoring, surveying. He'd often used one to send out for a hamburger. It wasn't his business what it was for. The trainees weren't talking much anyway.

All the same, some of these guys looked a bit more muscular than your average farmer or hobby type. Some looked and sounded a bit foreign, with unusual names. And their drones—well, drones came in all shapes and sizes, but these were top of the range, fixed-wing, military-grade.

October 22, somewhere in Afghanistan

The first batch of trainees for ME ops had been given their initial theoretical instruction on drones in the classroom. Now it was time for some practice, starting with lightweight models.

Drones were not easy for beginners in hilly country. "No! Not like that!" shouted the instructor as a drone crashed into the mountainside.

He glared at the students for any signs of grinning—even the slightest smile.

Burns planned that, over the next few days, the NE2 would sail up and down the reef in order to look like it was doing what it was here to do—survey the ocean. In practice, it was for training the crew in how to use the midget submarine, for laying mines and for generally preparing for the tasks ahead. Burns suggested to Ryan and Grey that they could create some pretend research papers to keep themselves amused.

He briefed the team with PowerPoints and a whiteboard, taking each of the coal jetties in turn. He drew targets and arrows, like a football coach planning tactics. "This is the first call, Monk's Point. Our target is the jetty here, with berthing for four large coal ships and two coal handling gantries. We'll moor here, out of sight, two kilometres away. The sub will go in, we'll plant the mines." He showed a final elevation. "On the piers here, here, here and here … below the tidal water line. Then we'll beat it. With any luck, they'll also blow a hole in a ship's hull, if there's one around."

"Anything to add on local waters, Mike?" Grey was not involved in detailed attack briefings. It was better that he didn't know too much. Ryan would get separate briefings from Grey.

"There can be strong currents and tides to watch out for, but the sub will be away from these when submerged. Extreme storms can blow up—pardon the expression—but the forecast is good."

"Any questions?" asked Burns.

"What if a ship's on the move or they're loading?" asked Simmo.

"Ship loading is only done by day for safety and environmental regulation reasons," said Burns. "There may be a ship or two tied up. Hopefully, there won't be anyone on the jetties when the mines go off at night. We'll be well away by then."

Crew members removed the wraps from the sub and prepared it for its first test. They checked systems and practiced loading and unloading from the boat using the crane and winch on the stern.

Mann and Martin had driven similar midget subs and Ryan had driven oceanographic submersibles in the past. Others would receive necessary driver training as backup. All of the SAS crew had experience in working with midget subs and planting limpet mines. It was standard practice.

Burns had inspected the sub in detail and had been impressed. Midget subs were not new technology—they were widely used in World War II—but they had gone out of fashion before making a comeback in recent years. Hadley had informed him that it had a range of forty kilometres, and that if it were a car, it would be a shop-soiled demo model. He didn't know the exact arrangement, but some sort of loan, hire, sale or return deal had been done. Whatever. He was to return it if possible. Procurement had told the owner that it was for ocean research. They were not cheap, and you didn't find them on eBay or your average boating magazine. This one was state of the art.

"Okay, lower it now," said Burns. "Slow and steady."

When it was floating, Burns, Moody, Mann and Martin, wearing wet suits, climbed down and entered via the hatch and airlock. Mann and Martin switched on the power unit and controls while Burns established communication.

"Okay, testing. All systems on. We have power. We have control."

"Release the winch," said Burns.

"Charging ballasts one and two," said Mann.

The vessel sunk beneath the surface.

Burns was pleased to see that no one was observing their 'research' or had wanted to come aboard. No one had cause for suspicion. The coal railway bomber seemed to have gone quiet for now at least. They'd be looking for him inland and wouldn't be watching the coast. He hoped.

Surprise was critical. They couldn't be expecting an attack this big.

CHAPTER 21

Whenever the NE2 was moored near the reef for sub training, Grey showed Ryan around the coral. Ryan had not visited for a while, so Grey showed him the special places remaining as well as the devastation. He told his friend about David.

"I read about him," said Ryan. "You must miss him."

"Very much."

Ryan spoke of his work monitoring the death of the oceans as warming boiled them and dissolving carbon dioxide turned them to acid.

They already knew that they had a lot in common. They discussed at length the frustration and desperation that had brought them to this point, to becoming involved in this venture. They had both argued with their superiors on the need for scientists to make a stand, to take a moral position on the desperate situation the world faced.

They talked a lot about the state of the reef over beer.

"Hell, it's all enough to turn you to drink," said Ryan, cracking another brew.

Emma was missing John. She was happy for him, if he was doing something he liked and that cheered him up, but there was something odd about it. Wasn't he bored by marine sampling? And just how much more research needed to be done on the reef? What could this ship achieve by sailing around the coast? Why did communications have to be limited after the first two weeks except when they were in port? Her phone rang.

"John! Of course, I miss you, desperately. I only want you … Of course, I'll wait for you … John, you've only been gone three days."

She missed John, but her mind was on other things. She and the Climate Commandos had nearly been caught twice. There were security guards and CCTV everywhere within easy striking distance of the city.

She considered her next mission, the next big thing to attack: Brad Callaghan's oil rig en route to the Bight. It had to be stopped. But first, there was the big protest at the opening of the Daghawi mine. It was too late to stop the mine, and the track was so heavily fenced, patrolled and under CCTV surveillance, there was no getting near to block it. Hundreds were going. The best they could do was bear witness to this crime—maybe cause a road obstruction to hold up the opening, maybe stop the invitees getting through. At least, tell the world that not all Australians were proud of fucking up the planet.

October 28

After pouring a Guinness, Mallon sat down to watch TV in his campervan. Q&A was on. The host introduced the panellists.

"From your left to right, please welcome Louise Brailly, Environment and Climate Correspondent for *The Sentinel*." Applause "… Astrophysics professor, Brian Knox, visiting Australia for Science Week …"

"It's sickening," said Mallon. "How can anyone be that clever and good-looking?"

"Environment Minister Sussan Cashmore … Our Nation Senator, Mervin Herberts …"

Mallon had seen Herberts on previous shows. "This should be interesting. Him and Knox. Talk about opposite ends of the human gene pool."

Someone in the audience asked a question. "Is the government doing enough to address climate change?"

"Would you like to take that one, Minister?" asked the host.

"Indeed, we are … Look, we are meeting and beating our targets, developing technology solutions …"

"Blah, fucking blah," said Mallon. "Useless fucking cow."

It was Brailly's turn to speak. "It seems that the rest of the world doesn't agree, which is why we're ranked bottom of the league on climate action. The rest of the world regards us as climate pariahs, as free riders." She turned to Cashmore. "Why do you keep approving new coal mines?"

Mallon liked Brailly and had read her Ned Coaly article about him. "She's a feisty girl," he said.

Herberts was invited by the host to respond.

"Here we go," said Mallon, taking a swig of Guinness.

"There is no empirical evidence for human-induced climate change." Herberts liked to use the word 'empirical' as if it made him sound more scientific.

"What do you say to that, Brian?" asked the host, knowing that Knox had been briefed beforehand.

"It's funny you should say that. Here's the evidence." Knox heaved an armful of scientific reports on to the table.

"The data is corrupted," said Herberts.

"What?" said Knox. "You're saying that IPCC, NASA and all the world's national academies of science have falsified the data?"

"Yes. Jewish bankers have paid them to do it," said Herberts with serene, bug-eyed confidence. "They have a lot to answer for. It's a well-known fact that the Rothschilds started both world wars."

Knox had no answer to that conspiratorial nonsense. His mouth was wide open as the audience roared with laughter.

"Oh, for fuck's sake," said Mallon. "Eejits like that are making Australia a laughingstock."

"I believe that you have to keep an open mind on science," said Herberts, coldly.

"But not so open that your brain leaks out," said Brailly, smiling. Yes! An open goal.

"Nice one, Lou Lou," said Mallon.

The video clip of Herberts versus Knox went viral around the world.

Dreiser saw it and shook his head. "Mein Gott! How can someone so stupid be elected to office?"

October 30

Moore entered Australia via Brisbane on a holiday visa. He ticked 'visiting friends or relatives' on the immigration card. Well, Mooney *was* something like an old friend.

After hiring a car and checking into his hotel, he phoned a contact he had been given in the hardware trade. He couldn't take a gun in his luggage and knew that, in Australia, you couldn't just go into a shop and buy one. He'd read that after the Port Arthur massacre in 1996, there had been a bipartisan political agreement on introducing strict gun controls. These had held firm for over thirty years in spite of the efforts of gun lobbyists. But Australia had a healthy illicit trade and, especially in Melbourne, a well-established gangster industry. As a result, weapons were always available if you knew where to find them.

Moore collected his weapon in Brisbane, a Glock 17 with silencer.

"It's a pleasure doing business with you," said the local agent who sold him the gun.

"It's going to be pleasure doing business with you, Mooney, ya big fucking girl's blouse," muttered Moore. "I know exactly where you'll be. I can read you like a book."

He headed off towards the Daghawi Mine.

Hadley learned indirectly that George Moore was touting for business and had a target in Australia, who the coal industry would be happy to see dead. Hadley didn't do assassinations and had declined, but he guessed that the target had to be the coal train bomber. It could be a risk to their venture if Moore was retained for further work when sparks began to fly. Communications with Burns were strictly limited for security, but Hadley sent an urgent encrypted message: *Coal industry have hired a contract killer, George Moore. Probably to eliminate Ned Coaly, but watch your back.*

October 31, Townsville

With the training and submarine trials completed, the NE2 tied up in Townsville.

There was a welcome reception.

"Ladies and gentlemen, boys and girls …" Ryan gave a speech.

"We'll top up the fuel tanks here," Burns told his team afterwards. "That will see us through for the rest of the mission." He knew that fully fuelled and with steady running, the NE2 had a range of six thousand kilometres.

"You boys can relax for a couple of days before we get going. I have something to attend to."

His job was to execute and protect the mission, not to take unnecessary risks or get side-tracked. But he already had a hunch about who the bomber was, confirmed by the identity of the killer, who he had come across a long time ago. Moore could be a threat to the mission if the coal industry hired him for repeat work. And he couldn't let him just kill—what was he called? Mooney? He had to get to him before the killer and warn him, but how? Mooney, or whatever his name was now, had laid low lately. Would he be able to resist attacking the Daghawi opening? The killer wouldn't know his new identity but would probably hope to find him there.

He hired a car. It seemed that a lot of people were going to the opening. It was a fair drive, and he didn't want to be caught up in traffic. He would go the day before and stake it out. He collected a Smith and Wesson M&P 2.5, with silencer, from the small arms store. He briefed Beattie, his 2IC.

"No, it's better I go alone. This is for the mission and also personal. I'll be careful this time."

Moore followed the highway alongside the railway route. There was heavy fencing and security. It would be difficult, if not impossible, for Mooney to bomb the track. He'd try something at the mine, knowing they wouldn't be expecting that.

Burns followed the railway route, not far behind Moore. It would be tricky for Mooney to bomb the track, but he would definitely try something. Burns had to be prepared.

Emma and the others had headed to the mine in a convoy the day before, taking backroads to get there.

"There will be police roadblocks trying to stop us if we go on the day," she'd told them. She hoped they'd made the right decision.

Going via back roads and gravel tracks during the day, Mallon concealed his Landcruiser and laid low. It was now dark, and so he got to work.

He knew they'd be expecting him to attack the track somewhere along the line. Track bombings were his signature dish. They wouldn't necessarily be expecting him to walk across country and come through the back of the mine under cover of darkness. He knew from experience how slapdash fencing contractors could be. He was prepared to cut a small hole but didn't need to. Here was a gap he could squeeze under with his bag.

He walked on through the scrub. He could see ahead the locomotive shed, lit up like a Christmas tree. He crouched low and kept in the shadows. He knew there would be some night activity, but full production and loading would not ramp up until two days' time.

All was still in the yard, except for a maintenance worker entering the crib cabin. There was the engine pair, all spruced up and decorated, over an inspection pit. He had to work quickly. He went down the steps of the pit and fixed the Semtex under the chassis of the trailing locomotive, concealing the charge with grease.

He went back under the fence and walked to his car, which was concealed under bushes and trees. He would get some sleep before the big day. Nearby was a small hill from which he could see the grandstand and fire his charge.

"Come on, Eddie, wake up," said Brailly. "It's time to get going." Their relationship had become more than professional in recent weeks, although sharing a bed also helped with expenses.

They had stopped at a motel on the way to the Daghawi mine, nearly eight hundred kilometres from Brisbane.

"Uh, I need coffee. It's still dark."

"We'll get some on the way. It's still a few hours, and we don't want to miss the fun. We may not have been invited into the inner sanctum, but they can't stop us from covering the story. There'll be the protest outside and, who knows, Ned Coaly might strike."

Moore could see the grandstand through his binoculars. No, he wouldn't bomb that, he'd do the train. He wouldn't want to risk hurting anyone with a timed explosion; he'd want to fire in real time with visuals. Where better than that hill?

CHAPTER 22

November 5, East-Central Queensland

PM Turbott was excited. "How good is this?" The day of the grand opening of the Daghawi coal mine and railway had come at last.

Guests were arriving by car and via the specially constructed mine airfield. The guest list was a who's who of Australian politicians and other climate deniers and coal club VIPs. There were WAGs with large hats.

For Turbott and his government, this was a showpiece to the world that Australia, the land of the digger, was open for business—coal business—and that it was not going to be told what to do by warmist wankers. This mine was the big one—democracy in action, the people's will. They had voted for it. They would see it on TV with 'How Good is Coal' ads by the Coal Council. Grinning young employees in high viz and hard hats. 'Working for the Future.' Gold standard marketing.

After going through intense security checks, the guests mingled in the marquee where morning tea had been laid out. There was a big day ahead—the opening, a lavish lunch, a party. There was laughter, excited chatter, anticipation, a sense of victory. There was music. *"We are the champions … of the world."* There was much smiling. Even Brad Callaghan managed a small smirk.

Federal Member Craig Tooley brought copies of his report. It had lots of tables proving that it had sometimes been hot in the past. George

Magnussen also liked tables. Besides liking eating from them, he had brought his God-fearing girlfriend, Maria from Manila; they had met when she was dancing on one.

"It really put the wind up those bastards at the Bureau of Metrolology—Meteorlo …Weather," said Tooley. Tough to say even when sober. "Course the shitbags tried to take the piss out of it. I take that as a compliment. They laughed at Galileo."

There was much bowing and scraping towards special VIP Cardinal Colin Bell, although people were unsure of how to address him. "On yer, yer Grace. Always knew you were innocent. It was a bum rap."

Then it was time for what they had all been waiting for. "Ladies and gentlemen. Please take your seats. The show will begin in fifteen minutes."

When everyone was seated, PM Turbott and his special friend, multi-billionaire magnate, Mohan Daghawi, went to their places at the dais.

Australian and Indian flags adorned the grandstand. A fully loaded train with two shiny, black, brand spanking new locomotives stood by the dais, engines idling. The flags of both nations were on the nose of the leading engine, adorned with garlands.

Outside the security gate were thousands of uninvited guests, protesting about the existence of the mine. Hundreds of police pushed them away from the fence of the rail track and access road. Police had also been posted down the line at key viewing points, and railcars patrolled to watch for any intruders. Helicopters buzzed overhead. Bridges and culverts had earlier been inspected while CCTV watched throughout. With high-security fences all along the track and no level crossings, no one was taking chances after the recent attacks.

"Emma! Fancy seeing you here," said Brailly.

"Hi, Louise. Hi, Ed," said Emma. "It's really good to see you. It's a pity we didn't manage to stop this."

"Fellow Australians and distinguished guests," began Turbott. "How good is coal! This is a proud moment for our nation, the opening of the first of many mines to come in the Jordan Basin. It is a massive boost for the national economy and will create jobs and growth for decades to come, which is what this government and the Coalition is all about, unlike other political parties I could mention. The slogan for the green-left terrorists for all these years has been 'Stop Daghawi'. Well, we haven't been stopped. It's 'Go Daghawi'!"

He waited for the cheers and applause to subside. You could always milk a good slogan.

"Thank you. This is also a proud symbol of cooperation with our good friends from India, where millions will be lifted out of energy poverty. Coal is, and always has been—and always will be—good for humanity. Coal, my friends, is *Fair Dinkum Fuel!*" Rapturous applause. "Without further ado, I declare this mine and railway open."

A bottle of Aussie sparkling chardonnay pinot noir brut was smashed against the leading locomotive and the tape across the track was cut. A cluster of black balloons was released as the locomotives revved, two plumes of diesel smoke rising above them. The leading engine sounded its horn, and the train slowly moved off, a rattle and vibration moved down the train as the wagon couplings took up the slack.

The PM and guests stood shaking hands and congratulating each other as refreshments were poured.

It was a proud day for Tony Hermoso and Jamie Reilly, as they had been selected to drive the first train. Both had transferred from other routes where their trains had been blown up and were glad to transfer to a bomber-free line. The signal turned to green.

"Chocks away, here we go." Hermoso sounded the horn, and they returned the waves of all the people in the stand. Getting to wave at total strangers was one of the best things about being a train driver.

When the train was two hundred and fifty metres down the track, they heard the sound and felt the force of a massive explosion in the unmanned trailing locomotive.

"Fuck me," said Hermoso and Reilly in unison. There was a pall of dust, smoke and flames billowing from behind them. Hermoso instinctively released the dead man's handle. That should have cut the motors and applied the air brakes to the whole train, but all systems had failed. The explosion under the locomotive's chassis also blew the track and derailed the trailing bogie, as well as the following wagons. At the same time, the train was being pulled by the locomotives and pushed by the downgrade momentum of the heavily laden wagons. Their locomotive was tipping over.

"Jump for it!" shouted Hermoso.

The merriment on the grandstand was disturbed by the massive explosion and fire under the trailing locomotive and, in less than a minute, both locomotives on their sides, along with the first fifteen wagons. Coal was heaped like black sand dunes.

After the initial stunned, open-mouthed silence from the onlookers, the air filled with panicked shouts and screams and the tinkling of breaking champagne glasses as people instinctively hit the deck.

"Are you alright, Prime Minister?" called an aide, crawling over. "Yes, I think so. How good is that!" He kneeled, praying in thanks. God clearly wanted him for other business.

"Holy crap!" Thus spoke the Cardinal, fearing he may have stained more than his reputation.

"Gundmare!" said Daghawi.

People started to look up.

"Keep down, in case there's another!" shouted a security officer, not thinking that if the bombers had wanted to really spoil the party, they could have detonated in front of the grandstand, not down the track. But you couldn't be too careful.

"Another nice mess, Stanley," said Mallon.

He was watching the proceedings, through binoculars, from a hill a kilometre away. He was carefully concealed, so that he couldn't easily be seen by the helicopters, other surveillance or even sharpshooters. When the train was still stationary, he heard the horn and saw the balloons go up. *I could …* he thought. He was sorely tempted. *Nah. I'll wait a few minutes.*

He saw that the mine's emergency crew had arrived. Fireys were hosing down the engine, medics were attending to the drivers and anyone suffering from shock, cuts or bruises from falling about. The mine site was swarming with police and helicopters.

He was prepared to lie low until dusk or dark. Although not far from a blacktop road, his vehicle would be spotted by day if he drove away now. As it was, it was concealed.

He was about to find somewhere to rest when he sensed that he was not alone. He heard a voice that sent a chill down his spine.

"If it isn't Patrick Mooney. I don't believe it. What a small world."

Mallon turned to face George Moore, who was pointing a silenced gun at his face.

He instantly recognised the bearded man of his nightmares, even though the beard was now grey.

"It's been a long time. Too long," said Moore.

"Not long enough," said Mallon.

Thoughts rushed through Mallon's head. How could this be happening? He knew what Moore was like and that his time was up. The best he could hope for was a straight bullet, but Moore would want some fun first. At least a kneecapping, the traditional slapstick practical joke punishment of the Northern Ireland Troubles, employed by both sides. You never saw anything funnier than a victim trying to walk after one of those.

Ah well, he had struck a blow for David. And after all, he didn't have much to look forward to—the rest of his life on the run or in jail. If the government wanted two years for protesting on the streets, he would be sent down for several lifetimes.

A helicopter passed low over the trees, but there was no chance to wave.

"Don't even think about it," said Moore. But the aircraft was heading away, looking for anyone driving off, not expecting anyone to stay around.

Mallon decided he would at least die with pride. "I suppose you want me to say I'm sorry, to beg forgiveness for getting you locked up. Well, I'm not sorry. I probably saved a few lives. Evil, murdering scum like you don't deserve freedom. I'm only sorry they let you out."

"You will be. Aren't you interested to know how I found you?"

"Not especially."

"I spotted your trademark in the news. Bleeding heart nancy, not using bombs as they should be used. Even today you missed a huge open goal, with hundreds watching, but you didn't have the balls." Moore threw a shovel in his direction. "Just knew you'd be around here and within sight of the grandstand, so you didn't hurt anyone. Get digging."

Mallon knew he would be digging his own grave. No body, no crime. Moore was capable of anything, even burying him alive.

Earlier, Burns had concealed himself, watching for activity with binoculars before police and inevitable helicopters were out. One vehicle had come down the road and disappeared into the bush. An hour later came another. He would have to hike across the valley, staying under cover.

Mallon dug, biding his time, awaiting his moment. Maybe he'd catch Moore off his guard, swing at him with the shovel. But it was hot, and he was tiring.

"It's thirsty weather, don't you think?" enquired Moore. "How I longed for drink when I was in the Maze. In between thinking about you, of course."

Moore sat at the other end of the hole. *It's now or never*, thought Mallon. He pretended to be exhausted, sitting on the edge of the hole, head down. But he was used to working in extreme heat in the iron ore mines and had a powerful frame. He planned his swing without a tell-tale reverse swing. He flexed his torso and arm with all his might and swung the shovel.

Moore moved to the left to avoid it, but the tip of the shovel smashed his left hand. Moore yelled and leaped up, swearing.

"You'll be sorry for that. I don't need the hole anyway. It was just for amusement. The wildlife around here will soon remove any trace of you. This is where the fun really starts, when you'll wish you were never born, beg me to kill you."

Mallon stared defiantly at Moore, waiting for the first bullet.

Burns found the two concealed vehicles and walked through the bush. He heard voices and got closer, always concealed. He couldn't get a very close look, but one looked like he was about the meet his maker and the other, holding the gun, looked and sounded like a greying Gerry Adams. This was not just a contract killing. It was also an IRA vendetta.

Either way, it wouldn't be a pretty sight. There wouldn't be a second chance if he missed. He had to get him with one shot.

Moore pointed his pistol at various targets on Mallon, as if undecided where to shoot him, before aiming. "Let's see … No … I know!"

There was the crack of a silenced pistol, and Moore fell to the ground, half his head blown away.

"Sweet mother of Jesus!" Mallon crossed himself as a reflex, rather than as an act of religious devotion.

Mallon looked up, in a state of shock and disbelief.

He saw a tall man approach, two-handedly holding a silenced pistol. He lowered it when he saw that Moore had no head for fighting back.

"It's not … You're not …?"

"I believe I am," said Burns.

Mallon vaguely recognised Burns as the young army officer on duty when he had handed himself in nearly thirty years before. The one who had made sure that he'd had immediate protection before being interrogated and spirited away to a new identity in England.

"What … How?"

"Take it easy. Have some of this." Burns handed him a water bottle. "I've had the misfortune to come across this character before. I lost a few mates to him and his sort. We're well rid of him. I can't tell you how I knew about what he was doing here or why I'm here. We'll lie low and wait till after dark to get out of here, then part company."

"What'll we do with him?" asked Mallon.

"We might as well make good use of the hole," said Burns.

CHAPTER 23

Emma was standing with the crowd of protesters near the mine site. Hundreds of police, many mounted, had forced them off the road so they couldn't obstruct VIP and other traffic or get anywhere near the railway.

It was noon, time for the opening. They were all feeling down. Years of protest had failed, coming to nothing. No one could bear to watch the televised opening on their smart phones. They were dismayed to see the balloons go up and to hear the sound of distant loudspeakers, cheering, music and the horn of the train departing.

Then a plume of dust rose into the air, followed by a noise like thunder.

Those with a signal tuned in.

"It's chaos, unbelievable … people lying on the decks, crowding through the exits … we can't tell yet if there are any casualties … the Prime Minister seems to be praying … the locomotives have been destroyed, but the drivers are being attended to."

"It's Ned Coaly!" shouted Emma. "He's done it!"

Brailly was nearby. She had been watching on her phone. Ned had done it without hurting anyone.

"Yes!" She punched the air and hugged Eddie, then gave a thumbs-up to Emma.

There were a few more hours to kill, some time to catch up. Burns didn't offer any more on how he had come to be there that day or what he was doing in Australia, so Mallon didn't ask.

"Sorry, I don't remember your name," said Mallon. "It's kind of etiquette to introduce yourself, especially when you've been burying a stiff."

"George. George Phelps."

"George? Like him?" He nodded to the freshly turned pile of dirt.

"What are you called these days?" asked Burns.

"Call me Sean. I've been that longer than I was Patrick."

They talked about their days in Northern Ireland when they were younger.

"It's a beautiful country," said Burns, "but they were unhappy times."

"Don't I know it. I left it—home, family—forever. I couldn't even let them know where I was, how I was. The Provos would have tortured any knowledge out of them, killed them to stop them trying to warn me, so they had to know nothing."

"I know."

"My folks never even found out I have a family. *Had.* There's only my daughter and grandson now."

"Did something happen?"

"I lost my wife to cancer and my son to … Well, I call it murder, but the law has a different point of view. You?"

"Divorced, one son, grown up, living in New York. He's doing well. So, what have you done with yourself in Oz?"

Mallon told him about his career in the mining industry

"So, you kept your hand in. With explosives, I mean."

Burns looked through the binoculars at the mine site. Cranes and diggers were clearing the debris. A large crane had arrived, to lift the locomotives, along with a track repair train and crew.

He gazed towards the main gate. It looked like more TV reporters had arrived at the gate, and some had been allowed entry to the mine site. Most were arriving in poncy city cars.

"Looks like media reinforcements are here," said Mallon. A convoy of cars raced along the nearby road.

The Daghawi Mine bombing produced a flurry of police activity. DCI Goss and some of his team raced to the scene, along with forensics, but it was dark by the time they arrived.

"There probably won't be much to find in this mess. I want a full inspection of the perimeter fence, to see how and where they got in, and any DNA or other clues. They can make a start now and carry on tomorrow."

"D'you think they're still around? Still in the area?" asked DC Pettigrew.

"Maybe. Maybe not. They'd lie low until dark if they were. But the choppers didn't see any signs of coming and going, and patrol cars sent around the back roads didn't see anything. They may not have been around. It was pretty risky after all. They could have detonated remotely. The opening and timing weren't exactly secrets; they could have done it watching the TV live, eating popcorn. They could have picked a better day than the fifth of November. But hell, it could have been worse. At least they didn't put the bomb under the grandstand."

Also not a secret was the location of the police roadblocks Goss had ordered. They had been well-publicised on social media by campaigners returning home. Emma, Kate, Paul and Danny were among them, and had earlier been stopped at a checkpoint.

"You again," said the officer. She was well-known to the police.

"We were waiting for the train, but it didn't show up," said Emma. "Do you know when the next one will be along?"

"On your way."

Brailly and Eddie headed back to Brisbane, Eddie driving.

Brailly was composing her story in her head.

"He's amazing," she said.
"Who?" said Eddie.
"Ned Coaly."
"Yeah, amazing."
"I mean, taking on an army of police and security, then doing a precision bombing in front of Turbott and his cronies, humiliating them in front of the world, and not hurting anyone except whatever bones the engine drivers broke … Look, it's been a long day. What say we stop for a drink, dinner and motel somewhere soon?"

"That was a pretty impressive stunt," said Burns. "Your whole campaign has been impressive. I assume it's just you? Tell me, what made you start bombing railways again after all these years? I know a man needs a hobby, but …"

Mallon told him about David, his love of marine biology and how they would go scuba-diving at Ningaloo on the west coast. He told him how they'd planned to do the Great Barrier Reef together. He told Burns of David's death and why he'd decided to get one back at the guilty.

"You know, I would have done the same," said Burns. "Probably worse."

It was now dusk and getting dark. A police car had driven along the road some time earlier, but no more had followed. It was time to leave the scene. They pushed Moore's car into a gulley and covered it with brush wood.

They went in Mallon's Land Cruiser along the blacktop, to where there was a turnoff and a short trail to Burns's vehicle, also a Land Cruiser. In mining areas, ordinary saloons looked conspicuous.

"It's better we part company now, Sean. Safer if we travel alone—take separate routes. Where are you heading?"

"Townsville."

"That's where I'm going too, as it happens. But we can't have any contact there. We've never met. Okay?"

"Okay. You didn't say why you were in Oz. Can I help in any way? I feel I owe you one. I wouldn't still be here without you."

"You don't owe me anything, Sean. What I did was mutually beneficial. Look, you've done your bit—a truly heroic feat, a fantastic start, but the disruption will be temporary. After each bomb, the railways are soon back in action. Bigger forces are now at work to do more lasting damage. I can't say any more, but you don't need to do anything else. Lie low till the dust settles, then get on your way. Be around for your daughter and grandson."

"It's been good to see you again," said Mallon.

"You too. Take care."

They shook hands.

Mallon gave Burns a hug, got into his vehicle and drove off into the setting sun, headlights off. Burns went in the opposite direction.

Burns felt uneasy. What if someone paid Moore? What if they sent someone else? What if Sean was found out? The police would hunt him down like a dog if the next killer didn't get to him first. What about his family; were they in danger? Maybe he should have given Mallon a gun? No, it wouldn't look good if the police caught him. Maybe he should have sheltered Sean on the boat? No. He was in enough trouble as it was, without involving him. *You've done enough,* he thought. *You have a job to do, a crew to look after. You can't go around rescuing every stray dog and cat you come across. Gus and Pongo were one-offs.*

The media went wild with excited outrage. A small army of reporters descended on the mine gates. They drove around nearby roads, hampering police efforts to observe suspicious activity.

The police were only stopping people from leaving the area and had been expressly ordered to allow in the media so that the government could milk the event for political mileage.

'Assassination Attempt on PM', declared one headline. 'Bombing Outrage: Bring Back Capital Punishment,' suggested another. 'Rejoice, It's a Miracle: Spared PM a Hero.' 'Gunpowder Plot Foiled.'

There was speculation on anything the media could make up. No stone went unturned. Was it an assassination attempt on Cardinal Bell? He had friends in high places, but many enemies amongst those who had been molested in low places.

Always relying on the anti-Muslim vote, a government spokesman at an emergency press conference had replied to the question, "Could it have been a jihadist?" by stating that the possibility couldn't be ruled out.

The police were ordered to widen their search to the Islamic community, diverting their already stretched resources.

"What did I tell you about jihadists, Chief?" said DI Pettigrew at a team debriefing. "They want us to investigate that as well."

"What exactly did you tell me, Pettigrew?" snarled Goss. He had just been informed that Home Security and the ACP had fully taken over the investigation, and he and his team would be just foot soldiers from now on.

Mallon decided to lie low at Port Douglas for a week or so until the heat died down. It was a job done, but there were bound to be heightened random stops and searches until the police got tired of it and returned to their proper job of issuing speeding tickets.

It was time to call it quits. He had also pushed his luck with the police, covering his tracks, but it couldn't last forever. More worrying was George Moore finding him.

Moore thought he was still Pat Mooney. What if someone had paid him and would send someone else? What if they got to him through Siobhan and Kieran? They were probably all safe as long as no one knew who he was … He busied himself with packing and meticulously cleaning up the lockup in Townsville before vacating it. He cleaned the lockup and vehicles of all traces of explosives, just in case he was stopped at a check point with a Bruker Roadrunner or a DE-tector. From past training and experience, he knew how to get past sniffer dogs. He found a community recycling centre, which accepted recyclable waste, including e-waste from his electronics and household chemicals.

As far as he was concerned, his bombing days were done. He went for a Guinness.

He was relieved it was all over. He had read about World War II bomber crews celebrating after completing their last raid. He felt like that, except without the PTSD.

He would head west in the Land Cruiser and fly back for the camper. Maybe he'd sell it. It was a bit of a wreck now and not all that savoury after he'd been living in it for two months. He was glad to see the back of it.

Before he left, he would go for a dive on the reef. It might be his last chance for some time, if ever. He could see it was dying and wouldn't be around for much longer. He would remember David in other ways.

He was still having bad dreams sometimes. But the bearded man was gone.

While waiting in Townsville, Ryan and Grey caught up with professional colleagues at the Institute for Ocean Science. They all had a good whinge about the state of the reef, the state of the oceans, and the government's cuts in funding for marine research—so that it could give more tax cuts and other handouts to its corporate chums.

"You're lucky, being able to do any research at all," said one boffin. "Our boat's in mothballs. All dressed up and nowhere to go."

"So I hear," said Ryan.

"What sort of gear do you have on board?" enquired another boffin.
"Oh, you know," said Ryan. "Usual stuff."

Grey called Emma.

"How have you been?" asked Grey.

"I'm good but missing you."

"Miss you too. What have you been up to?"

"Nothing much. Getting on with my studies, you know."

"We're heading south to start fieldwork around the coast. I'll see you when we get to Brisbane?"

"I can't wait," said Emma.

November 6

Burns's team had been enjoying relaxing in Townsville and had discovered Paddy's bar. They all knew that it was their last R&R before the mission, and the boss would be back about now. They knew where he was and what he was up to. If, in the worst case, he didn't come back, they would continue the mission with Beattie in charge, and get Moore when the time was right. They couldn't delay any longer.

Moody was at the bar. It was his round.

"A pint of Guinness, please, Ron." He turned to see Burns.

"Sod it, just my luck … another Guinness," he said to the barwoman. "It's good to see you back, boss. You're a real worry. Did it go okay?"

"It was all good. Threat eliminated. I need this, though." He sank the pint in one. He was out of practice at killing people. "I'll have one more and then we'll go. Does anyone need topping up?"

They returned to the NE2 and completed preparations for sailing.

"Let's be under way, if you will, Mr Hoemberg."

"Very good, Mr Burns."

"Cast off!"

The NE2 slipped out of Townsville and headed south, like a bird migrating to lay its eggs.

Dreiser waited for news. It was the start of winter in Switzerland, but the start of summer in Australia. The word 'summer' had once had pleasant connotations: relaxing, enjoying the outdoors, holidays on the beach with the children … Now, everywhere, it meant new temperature records, fires, heatstroke. In many parts of Australia, it meant the onset of hell. The bushfires had already started.

He read about the Daghawi mine bombing. It was front page news around the world. "That Ned Coaly is something else. We could have done with him on board."

There would be more like him. The war was starting. Phoenix was not just a one-off attack on the fossil fuel industry, but was part of a greater war of beliefs, of ideology. The Second World War had been a war against fascism. Now it was time for a war for those who wanted to save the world, against those who would plunder it until there was nothing left. A war for the world.

The propaganda war was already lost. Thirty years of climate inaction and the dire condition of Planet Earth were testimony to the victory so far—ultimately Pyrrhic—of fossil fuels, the climate deniers and plunderers.

'Phoney War' was a term that had described the first few months of World War II when nothing much happened, the time before the Blitzkrieg of May 1940 when all hell had broken loose.

The phoney war for the world was over. The real war for the world was about to begin.

Dreiser received a message that the boat had just sailed. "Gott sei Dank," he whispered. *God Speed.*

CHAPTER 24

Early November, Queensland coast

Ryan and Grey went through the itinerary of east coast shore visits arranged with the Department of Tourism. Ryan didn't mention the other stopping points, the coal jetties. Grey didn't need to know too much about that.

Grey pointed to the chart on the wall. "As you'll know, we'll be following the East Australian Current, the three thousand kilometre oceanic river flowing down the east coast and on to the Antarctic. It hugely influences the climate, ecology and well-being of Australia and is rich in marine life. It helps marine turtles, which nest along the coast then follow it south before hangering left and swimming to South America. Migrating whales follow it from their breeding grounds in the tropics to their feeding grounds in the Antarctic Southern Ocean. At this time of the year, we should see quite a few humpbacks migrating south."

"We also see them along the Eastern Seaboard of the US," said Ryan. He told Grey about watching them as a boy, how they were the reason he was here.

They went out on deck. The sun was setting; there was a light breeze and swell.

"There!" said Grey. A pod of humpbacks was following the NE2, including some mothers with calves.

One came close and put on a spectacular show, as if it knew what they were up to. It breached and turned like a fighter plane doing a victory roll in an air display.

"Wow!" said Ryan. "No other whales can do it like that!"

November 15

Soon after one am, the NE2 anchored two kilometres south of the Monk's Point coal terminal. Lights on the boat had been killed an hour earlier. The sea was calm with a light breeze. A full moon lit up the night.

"Okay, boys," said Burns. "Let's get to work."

Crew members removed the wraps from the sub and prepared it, checking systems and loading it with its cargo of limpet mines and diving gear.

Following the now well-drilled procedure, the sub was lowered to floating.

"Alright, all aboard," said Burns. He, Simmo and Moody entered wearing wet suits. Mann and Martin took their places at the controls. When the final checks were done, the vessel submerged.

"All set," said Burns. "Take it away, Mr Mann."

"Aye aye, Cap'n"

Thirty minutes later, they were beneath one of the giant ships in berth and awaiting loading. There were lights above from the loader and three-hundred-metre-long ship. Maintaining radio silence, Burns and Simmo placed four limpet mines in the airlock and went through one at a time. They each carried one mine and a torch and swam to the first of the targeted jetty piles. There they placed the mines against the piles, below the tidal water line of any berthed vessel. They returned for the other two. The timers for the detonators had been pre-set. For a single jetty with two gantry loaders, four mines were sufficient to cause a lot of damage.

Burns code signalled to the NE2. "Eggs laid. Flying home now."

The sub returned and surfaced alongside the survey ship. "One down. Good work everyone."

The next day, the NE2 pulled into Mackay, where Ryan and Grey went ashore to keep up appearances. There was a small reception in honour of Captain Cook, attended by a few curious onlookers.

"Ladies and gentleman, boys and girls …" Ryan gave his speech. Two of the onlookers clapped—both mothers with prams. Grey said a few words.

"That went well," said Ryan, afterwards.

"You have to remember, Mackay is a coal town and port and doesn't take kindly to greenie types. 'Fuck the reef. Fuck climate change. The more coal ships, the better,' I'm afraid."

Later that evening, the NE2 moored two kilometres from Straw's Point and three hundred kilometres south of Monk's Point. It was a much larger terminal, with one two-kilometre jetty and one three-kilometre jetty, each with four berths and two loaders. This time, Burns took Moody, Jonesy and Bazza. "There are bigger jetties and more loaders. More hands make light work." Between them, they laid ten mines, all set to blow at the same time as at Monk's Point.

The NE2 sailed on to Rockhampton, four hundred kilometres south, for a short reception. Ryan and Grey made their speeches.

"They were as lukewarm as the meat pies," said Grey. "We're still in coal country. Maybe it's the way we tell 'em." Their jokes were going down like a lead balloon.

The NE2 sailed on to nearby Sadstone to repeat the mine-laying exercise under the single jetty at the coal port. Since they were passing, they left some calling cards under the LNG loading jetty at Durtis Island, a much shorter jetty. A tanker was being loaded.

"I wouldn't want to be around if one of these goes up with the jetty," said Jonesy.

"I would," said Moody. "To watch, that is."

"You know, I feel a bit of a fraud," said Grey. "Like a spare prick at an orgy. These guys are doing all the real work here. Everyone knows the oceans are full of plastic and well on the way to being totally fucked. Any research we do will only confirm what we already know—humans can't dump eight million tonnes a year in the oceans and then be surprised by the consequences."

"I know," said Ryan. "But they're all highly trained, battle-hardened military professionals. It's their job. We're the scientists. We have an important job: to look pretty and, being the scientific front, to make the deception possible."

"I guess."

"And hey, we get to have a free trip around Australia. See some of the marine life. Maybe even do some sampling; write some papers."

Grey smiled. "Yeah, I promised old Wolfey."

Along the way, Ryan and Grey, helped by members of the German crew, sampled plastic content in the waters and marine life. "What have we got so far?" said Grey. "Dead seabirds choked with pieces of bags, toothbrushes, lighters, pen lids and other human necessities. Ground-up plastics and microplastic in fish, everything. Plastics have become the web of death for all life on Earth. If climate change and pesticides didn't see us off, plastics will."

"Big Oil sold the lie that single-use plastics would be recycled," said Ryan. "Look here. The 'recyclable' arrows to prove it."

"Like climate change," said Grey. "Liars, liars, pants on fire."

November 18, Area D Mine, Pilbara, Western Australia

Mallon's former mine site had been going through its biennial inspection by the Department of Petroleum and Mines. Vibushitha 'VB' Bandaranayake, a member of the audit team, lived for poring through explosives purchase, reconciliation and stock records. His family had been Tamil refugees from Sri Lanka when Australia was more welcoming. As a boy, witnessing the conflict in his native country, he had marvelled at the power of bombs.

He, like many in Australia, had taken a keen interest in the Queensland bomber—it was in all the news—and wondered what explosives he was using and how he knew so much. He knew that the Queensland police had already alerted the Western Australian police to look out for any suspicious activity by shot blasters and had started the screening process for WA mines, enlisting the help of his department to do the legwork. *Lazy buggers, no doubt to allow them to concentrate on speeding fines and other real police work,* he thought. He had recently copped one. *Well, the joke's on them; I'm doing the detective work here. I'm going to be in the news. I'll be famous!*

"I'm telling you, there is an irregularity. Explosives and detonators are unaccounted for. There is a possible forged entry. Can I speak to the shot blaster who signed here? A Mister Se-a-n Mallon?"

"He's left," said Ron Mullins, the mine site manager. "Best I ever had. Trust him with my life."

"That is all very well, but unless you can explain it, I will have to report it to my superiors, who will be obliged to report it to the police."

Within days, Mallon's picture was all over the media, albeit one of him ten years younger, taken from his work photo ID.

Have you seen this man? Sean Mallon is wanted for questioning in connection with the recent Queensland bombing. If so, contact the police on the numbers below. Do not approach him. He may be dangerous.

"Like fuck am I dangerous!" Just as he had finished packing and was about to head west, Mallon turned on his car radio and heard the news. "Shit, that's it, then."

He had always known it was a matter of time. They would know he was somewhere in Queensland, and now they knew who to look for. They had probably traced his vehicle regos. They were probably visiting Siobhan, if they hadn't already, and tapping her phone. He couldn't even call without giving away his location. But he wouldn't be giving himself up for a lifetime in jail. All the same, he didn't fancy being shot away like Ned Kelly, Butch Cassidy and the Sundance Kid or Bonnie and Clyde.

He was cornered. How was he going to get out of this?

DCI Goss was relieved that finally they'd found a positive lead.

From questioning at the mine by the WA Police, it was quickly established that Mallon had gone to Queensland at the time of the bombings and was probably carrying explosives at that time—although they would have been used up by now.

In investigating Mallon's family history, the police also established the link to David Mallon.

"A clear motive," observed Goss.

Mallon's records showed that he had emigrated from England to Australia in 1995. He had no previous criminal record.

Fremantle

Siobhan was at first shocked to see her Dad all over the front pages and on the TV news.

"Bloody hell, Dad! So that's what you've been up to! You're Ned Coaly!" She remembered how he had been at the funeral and after, and then she felt proud. *You did all that for David,* she thought. Then the anxiety hit her. *They'll lock him away and throw away the key to make an example of him.* She needed to get in touch, to do what she could to help.

She saw a policeman and policewoman coming up the path. They knocked on the door and she opened it, holding Kieran in her arms.

"Are you Siobhan Mallon?"

"Yes."

"Your father Sean Mallon is wanted for questioning in connection with the Queensland bombings. Can you tell me his whereabouts?"

"I don't know anything about this. He said he was going travelling to Queensland. He always wanted to see the Great Barrier Reef. I don't know where he is."

"When did you last hear from him?"

"Last week, the week before. I can't remember."

"How often does he call?"

"It varies."

"I must warn you that it's a criminal offence to harbour him or withhold information on his whereabouts."

"I wouldn't tell you if I knew. And while we're on the subject, it was a criminal offence when you pigs murdered my brother. I'm proud of my dad. Now fuck off and leave us alone."

Kieran smiled.

Emma saw the news. "Bloody hell, Sean! You're amazing!"

She was immediately anxious for him. How could she help? How could she make contact?

PM Turbott was excited that the police had a firm lead and were closing in. Daghawi had been the greatest humiliation, and revenge would be sweet. But he had to gain marketing advantage by pursuing the 'strong against terrorism' angle, and not let the media be side-tracked. Terrorism was terrorism. He called the Attorney General, Christopher Lee. "Christopher, can you instruct the police and our friends in the media not to pursue the link between Mallon and his son's death? We don't want to make an even bigger hero out of him than he already is. We don't need Ned Coaly the Outlaw and Avenging Father. We don't want the media speculating, so can you serve an injunction? Potential jury members can't be prejudiced by what they hear in the media."

He knew that they could rely on the Moorcock media to pursue the line that Mallon was a dangerous green, anti-coal terrorist. He was as good as convicted. It was a pity the police weren't able to charge anyone without an arrest or sentence someone without a trial. Not yet at least, although he was pleased that Peter Scroton was working on it with the AG under prevention of terrorism laws.

AG Lee served the injunction too late.

Louise Brailly had spotted the Mallon surname link and had already published an article.

'Is Ned Coaly avenging his son?'

The father-son link hit the progressive and social media and flashed around the world. The mainstream media was always hungry for a story and couldn't help but join in, although to them, he was still a green anti-coal leftie terrorist, just one who happened to be a guilty, bad father with a grudge. Could they find a story about him on parental cruelty and sexual abuse?

PM Turbott and his followers were relieved and jubilant to hear that Ned Coaly was named, on the run and must be close to capture. The attacks must surely be at an end. It was time for a PR boost now, a Churchillian address to the nation on TV and radio.

"Terrorists must know they will never win against the will, courage, resilience and mateship of the Australian people—our ANZAC spirit. In spite of the setbacks, all of the railways are fully operational and Daghawi mine and exports are at full production, creating jobs and growth for the Australian people. We now have identified the key suspect. Ned Coaly, there is no hiding. We will bring you to justice. Give yourself up."

"Have we heard anything yet from our contractor, you know who?" enquired Hutchings.

"Not at all," said his CFO. "He seems to have gone to ground."

"I suppose we'll have to rely on the police to catch this Mallon character now that everyone knows who is. That's if our man didn't find him first. He should have stopped him before the Daghawi opening—what a humiliating day that was. It showed how useless the police are and why we're right to sort it ourselves. Have we paid him anything yet?"

"Just the upfront instalment. The rest is on proven results. If Mallon's still alive, I doubt he'll try anything else now. He'll be too busy hiding."

"Hmm. Either way, keep on it. I want Mallon to pay for what he's done, not end up in some care home jail and be out on parole in a couple of years."

Hutchings was known for his vengeful streak, especially if anyone did anything to affect his pride, power and pocket.

"If our man doesn't deliver the goods, get someone else on the case. At least we know who he is. Does he have any family?"

"Why do you ask?"

CHAPTER 25

Mallon heard Turbott's announcement. "The smirking git has won. The railways are operational again. It's all been for nothing!"

He stopped to pick up a newspaper and some food while getting fuel at a service station. He kept his head down. It was an old photo—his work ID—and he now had a beard and shades, but there was still a possibility he could be recognised. He averted his gaze while paying.

Desperate thoughts flashed through his head as he sat in his car. There was nowhere to go. He couldn't go home, but he couldn't hide forever. *My Aboriginal mates are kind and would look after me,* he thought. But the prospect of exile in a remote community in the Great Sandy Desert didn't appeal. He pictured himself hunting with a spear and doing a ritual dance. *No, I'd be hopeless at that sort of thing.*

Now it wasn't just the police who were after him … Maybe someone had paid Moore to kill him. *They might try again … Might try to get me through Siobhan and Kieran.* The police would be watching them with CCTV or whatever, but that wouldn't protect them. He needed to warn them, but how was he going to explain his IRA past? He needed to get to them, but how? There would be a trace on his cell phone and a box call to her number would be recorded. He couldn't fly—they'd be watching the airports. He couldn't drive the car or van—they'd have the regos by now. There'd be roadblocks. The camper was parked up and concealed, but they'd be looking for it and the Land Cruiser. They'd no direct proof, but they'd be looking for traces of explosives in it. What a fucking mess.

Who did he know in Queensland? Emma? He didn't have her phone or address. George, or whatever his name was? He didn't know where he was or where to contact him. John Grey? He thought the world of David. He worked at the university in Brisbane. It was late afternoon, but he might still be there.

He saw a call box across the road. He moved his car there and parked it off-road, concealed in the shade of trees and shrubs. A police car raced past, lights flashing. Another drew into the service station. An officer got out and went inside. They weren't there for fuel. Had he been spotted and reported?

He was on the road to Brisbane. Would they be expecting him to head there?

Mallon called the uni from the call box. The operator put him through. An answering machine told him that Grey was out of the office with a mobile number, emergencies only. It was an emergency. Mallon called him.

"Hello, this is John Grey." John was on the boat and hadn't heard the news. "Sean, really nice to hear from you …"

Mallon told him the story and about the situation in a nutshell. "Anyway, the police are after me and closing in."

"Bloody hell … So, you're Ned Coaly … How amazing!"

Mallon couldn't help noticing that Grey was surprisingly non-judgemental, but wasn't to know that his misdemeanors were small beer compared to what Grey was involved in.

"Of course I'll help. Look, we'll be pulling into Brisbane tomorrow. You know Emma. We're friends … sort of. She'll take care of you until then. We'll work something out. Here's her number."

Grey called Emma.

"Yes, I heard," she said. "What an amazing old bugger. All that for David! But yes, I'm worried about what'll happen to him. He needs to be sheltered."

"He can stay at my flat," said Grey. "I've told him to call you from a call box."

After the call, Grey told Burns about what was happening and was surprised by his response. What didn't this guy know?

"Yes, I know Sean. I won't explain now, but we go a long way back. All the same, it's a strange coincidence that you know him and here you are on the boat. It's a small world."

"Can we—*you*—help?" asked Grey.

"I've already helped him out. I was hoping he wouldn't need any more but was ready to offer him sanctuary on board if he needed it. I knew he wanted to get to his family, who could be in danger. Of course, I'll do all I can."

Mallon called Emma on the number that Grey had given him.

"Hello, Emma. It's Sean. I'm in a spot of bother, like, and I was wondering if …"

"Sean, I heard from John. Okay, get to the Eastlands Shopping Mall in Brisbane. There's a big carpark. Call me when you're there and I'll come and get you. Put your car somewhere out of sight."

Mallon rested and waited until it was getting dark before heading south towards Brisbane, looking out for police roadblocks. They were easier to spot ahead at night. There were none. He saw police cars, lights flashing, heading north.

Monk's Point, Queensland, an hour earlier

All was quiet at the end of the jetty. Except for the lapping of waves against the hulls of two coal ships tied up, the only sound was the hum of the vessels' power generators as fumes whisped into the cloudless sky. The coal handling gantries were still. A few lights punctured the darkness. Apart from two men keeping watch on the bridges of each ship, all of the crews were asleep.

At midnight, Burns remotely detonated the limpet mines, creating a caldera of water. The jetty collapsed into the foam. One of the coal loading gantries broke up and joined the jetty in the sea. The other collapsed forward onto one of the ships. The power of the explosions on the piles close to the hull opened a crack in the hull of one ship and it began to sink slowly. The ships' sirens blared as the crews took to the life rafts.

The Port Safety Officer, Greg Nuttall, and an emergency team drove up the two-kilometre jetty and arrived at the scene. With emergency generators, they shone arc lights and were able to see the extent of the wreckage. Nuttall recorded that, thanks to the night timing and good fortune, there were no direct casualties from the explosions, although the event had necessitated extensive requests from the ships' crews for a change of pants.

However, there was one indirect casualty away from the explosions: a maintenance sparky, Tyrone Smith, who was on night shift, repairing an electrical circuit on a coal conveyor belt motor. He was being helped by his offsider Brett Swanson.

"Yeah, nah," said Swanson. "His doc told him he was on borrowed time due to smoking and too many meat pies. The shock of the explosion must have short-circuited and fused his ticker. Anyway, he dropped and sank like a stone. I reckon he karked it before he hit the water. There was nothing anyone could do. I told him he should eat veggie like me."

Nuttall's investigation revealed that Smith wasn't wearing an over-water PPE life vest, and with steel toecap safety boots, he'd failed to float, and divers would be needed to recover his body. His case would later be used to develop an excellent PPE safety training study.

Tyrone Smith's body lay at rest in its watery grave. Next to it was one of the mines, which had failed to explode—also due to a timer circuit fault.

Before the Monk's Point incident, DCI Goss had ordered all forces to focus on Brisbane. There had been several sightings of Mallon or his vehicle, all up to a day old and all over the place. People liked to report shit; it made them feel important.

But most reports did suggest he was headed for Brisbane. A cordon was placed around the city centre. "I want all the hotels and motels checked," Goss said. "I want officers on the streets—yes, I mean actually walking ... yeah, you know, with feet ... alright, bikes are okay."

He was woken immediately after the bombing.

"What is he, this Ned Coaly? Fucking Superman? Sounds like it's much bigger than anything before, but we have to assume it's him. We know he can dive and is good with bombs. Get as many people as you can up to Monk's Point."

Still driving south to Brisbane, Mallon turned on the radio for the two-am news report.

"It has just been reported that there has been a large explosion at the Monk's Point Coal Terminal, which serves the Daghawi and other mines. Initial reports indicate extensive damage to the loading jetty and one ship sunk. One man is missing, presumed dead. Ned Coaly, believed to be Sean Mallon, has claimed responsibility. Police will issue a full statement when they have assessed the situation."

"Well, I'm buggered," said Mallon. "That'll take the smirk off his face."

The NE2

"That's opened the batting," said Burns, putting down the transmitter. "At least we'll know if this thing and the mines are working."

He took a calculated risk to protect Mallon, to throw the police off the scent, to give him time to get to Brisbane. The fellow deserved a break. Even if the police concluded that Mallon wasn't up to limpet mines and it was someone else, there should be no risk to the project and team. He'd informed the team beforehand. They'd hear it on the news anyway.

They were okay with it. It was what they were there for—commission for every ball potted. He waited until afterwards to inform Hadley by code. The client wanted an early result. Was it enough?

Before dawn, Mallon arrived in Brisbane and parked where Emma had told him to. Then he called her. Ten minutes later she was there.

"Hello, Sean. Follow me and we'll put your car somewhere out of sight." They drove to an overgrown derelict site and left it there. It would be of no more use to him, and a friend would deal with it. He retrieved his bag and got into her car.

She hugged him. "You silly old thing. What have you done?"

"Less of the 'old', young lady."

November 22

The NE2 put into Brisbane and was well received. The reception might not have been as welcoming if they knew that Burns and his team had not only been responsible for the mayhem at Monk's Point but had left some calling cards at the Brisbane coal port the night before.

"The condition of our oceans is a matter of grave concern," declared the Lord Mayor, greeting Ryan and Grey on the quayside. "You are doing good work indeed."

"Thank you. We like to think so," said Ryan.

Grey spotted Emma waving in the small crowd. When the brief formalities were over, she ran up. They kissed. Burns and the crew watched, smiling, from the deck.

"Fetch a bucket of water, someone," said Beattie.

"Lucky guy," said Ryan.

After reuniting with Emma, Grey went to his flat.

"Sean!"

"John! Sorry, thanks … What a mess. Look, I shouldn't be here, getting you into trouble for harbouring a criminal."

"Nonsense. Think nothing of it. Look, George Phelps will be along later to look after you."

"George? How? Oh yes, that's grand."

"Help yourself to anything you need. I have to go now …"

"Are you and Emma … ?"

"Yes … kind of."

"Good luck. She's a lovely girl."

Grey left the boat temporarily but would make token appearances at Newcastle, Sydney and Melbourne before rejoining at Adelaide for the south and west coast legs of the voyage. He'd found out that there was much more to come but was okay with it. He needed to attend to some matters at the university before the end of term.

"Glad to see that you're getting in some field research, instead of that all that activism nonsense." Professor Wolfe caught Grey as he rushed out of the departmental building. "I trust there will be some good papers forthcoming." *'Publish or perish', the first commandment of academia,* thought Grey. The other commandments were also-rans. 'Thou shalt not covet thy students' had to be in there somewhere.

He also needed to attend to Emma. They went to her flat.

"I missed you so much," he said, fumbling with her bra hook.

"Mmm, you too," she said, tugging at his belt, as they fell onto the bed.

They lay in each other's arms.

"That George Phelps and his crew ... they're up to something ... you're up to something ... aren't you? How come Monk's Point just blew up? Sean couldn't have done that. You don't have to tell me what, but are you in any danger?"

"No ... really. It's all quite safe. But I can't tell you."

"And will you still go on the rest of the voyage?"

"Yes, I will. On and off." They changed positions, him on, her off. "Why do you ask?"

"I've decided to go on a sea trip myself, in more or less the same direction as you ... You know how the government gave approval for oil drilling in the Bight? Well, the drilling rig is on its way. I'm going on the *Sea Horse* to try and stop it."

Grey sat up and looked at her. "What? How? Getting in the way, or what? Protesting is all very well, but this sounds really dangerous. I don't want you to go."

"Try stopping me." She pulled him down.

Burns arrived at Grey's flat after dark.

"George! I'm sorry to be troubling you again," said Mallon, "but John said you might be able to help."

"It's no trouble ... Look, I know you're anxious to get to your family, but you'll be no help to them if you're caught. I can't stop you taking your own car, and John has kindly offered to lend you his. But you know that, to the government, you're public enemy number one. You'll be lucky to get out of Brisbane, never mind Queensland. Then there could be others besides the police after you—maybe, maybe not. Either way, you have to stay out of sight. In the meantime, do you have a mate who can tell Siobhan you're alright, who can check in on her?"

"Well, there's my mate Stuie."

"That's good, so we'll do that. We'll communicate discreetly through him. But tell him to be careful what he says or texts, as they'll be listening to her phones. Best if he drops by personally."

"What else did you have in mind?"

"Your safest bet will be to come with us on the NE2. It'll take a little while to get to Fremantle, but you can see Siobhan and Kieran then. We'll find a way to sort you out, though I admit I haven't thought of it yet. One step at a time. We sail later tonight. Would you care to join us?"

"I don't know what to say," said Mallon. "It's very kind of you."

"It will be our pleasure to have you on board. The accommodation is pretty basic, but much nicer and more airy than the alternative. One of those stuffy old prisons."

"One thing …"

"Yes?"

"When you said there were bigger forces at work … Was it you who blew up Monk's Point?"

CHAPTER 26

Burns drove them to the NE2 and showed Mallon aboard.

"Gentlemen. Allow me to introduce Sean, our newest crew member. Sean, may I introduce you to Lars Hoemberg, captain of the good ship *New Endeavour the Second*—and Professor Mike Ryan, chief scientist of the expedition." They all exchanged greetings.

"Welcome aboard, Sean," said Hoemberg. "Your reputation precedes you."

"Let me introduce you to the crew," said Burns.

They don't look much like scientists, thought Mallon, as he shook Boonzaaier's hand, *but what would I know?*

"It's a pleasure, Sean," said Boonzaaier. "Did you ever think of joining the Special Forces?"

"Well now, you could say I was in the army once …"

The media was full of stories about the Monk's Point bombing and the hunt for Ned Coaly, aka Sean Mallon.

'Murder! Many killed in terrorist attack!' was the *SunHerald*'s headline.

The Antipodean's editorials and opinion pieces questioned people's fondness for Ned Coaly. Being an anarchistic larrikin was not being quintessentially Australian if that anarchistic larrikin was not only a green-left, anti-coal terrorist, but also a murderer. Justice required that an example be made of him. This bombing on Monk's Point, port for the Daghawi mine, was an attack on everyone, on the Australian way of life. The Daghawi project was a torch of freedom, a symbol of what Australia was, the Australia they all loved. He must not get away with it. No one should be allowed to bring down civilisation.

PM Turbott's phone didn't stop ringing. "It's Greg Hutchings again, Prime Minister, I think you should speak to him."

"Greg, Greg … I'm as upset about it as you are … Look, I know all about bankruptcy … I didn't know you had to pay for the sunken ship too … We're in the same boat there, no pun intended … What? Isn't insured? … Act of war? … I hardly think … Public funds are short, but I'll see what we can do when we've passed the cuts in youth dole bludger allowances … The police are closing in, and we're expecting an arrest any time soon."

Emma's friend Danny did as she asked. After dark, he found somewhere out of the way to douse the inside of the car with petrol and torch it. Gavin had followed and was waiting.

"We'd better get going before anyone sees us. Pity we can't stay and watch. This is fun."

Emma had also given them a key to the camper and its location near Townsville. They would do the same to it.

"He can't have just disappeared into thin air! Keep looking!" shouted DCI Goss down the phone, while getting an update. "And find his car! I want explosives traces and fingerprints as evidence.

"Actually, we found a car that could be it on a derelict site in Brisbane. Plates missing and burnt out."

The NE2 continued south along the East Coast, calling into Coffs Harbour for a warm reception, as arranged by the Department of Tourism.

Ryan gave his usual speech. "Ladies and gentlemen, boys and girls …"

Along the coast of New South Wales, the sky was filled with clouds of smoke billowing up into a giant mushroom, as if an atomic bomb had exploded. Australia was on fire once again—the new normal.

Mallon was talking to Burns and Ryan. "They're calling them the 'forever fires.'" Year-on-year record temperatures and drought were making Australia a tinderbox every summer. Summers and bushfire seasons grew ever longer. Flurries of rain and violent storms generated understory, which dried and became kindling for the next fires. "All the government and Moorcock News can think of is blaming the greenies for stopping back-burning, even though as much is done as possible, and firestorms have gone through even recently back-burned forest. They're even logging protected forest as an economic stimulus to help out their logging chums—even though three billion animals have died from fires in the past two summers. Of course, there's no fire risk from clear-felled moonscapes. Turbott's climate and bushfire policy are all marketing spin."

PM Turbott was concerned about the fires. It was bad PR when fireys told him to fuck off and homeless victims refused to shake his hand.

"We need more hazard reduction, not emissions reduction," he declared in a press announcement. "We need more adaptation and resilience."

"Louise Brailly, *The Sentinel Australia*. Are you saying, Prime Minister, that slogans will do the job, that we just have to get used to it?"

Burns didn't tell Mallon a lot about the mission—about what had been done or what was still planned. He didn't want to get him too involved. Mallon was in enough trouble already. But Mallon gathered that it had something to do with mining and blowing up the coal ports. They'd already laid mines in Queensland and had set off Monk's Point.

"Look, I really appreciate that you blew that and threw them off the scent, even though it might have broken your cover. Look, I know you're all professionals and all, but anything I can do to help … I might as well be hung for a sheep as a goat. Seems I'm wanted for murder now."

"You're very welcome, Sean. I might just take you up on that. You're clearly a dab hand with explosives and electronics. In the meantime, just enjoy the sea air."

Mallon was enjoying relaxing and enjoying the voyage, helping where he could and playing poker and laughing with the boys. It was soon clear that they were passengers with an unstated job to do. Military types, they all had their own tales to tell, diluting their harrowing experiences with the comical. They'd been through a lot in Iraq and Afghanistan. If you didn't laugh, you'd cry. What had it all been for? Ultimately, to protect US oil interests in the Middle East and obsequious British and Australian Prime Ministers so far up America's arse that all you could see was their feet.

It was clear that the team all had the highest respect for Burns, who always looked after them, while at the same time keeping his distance, often reading or listening to music—he had some weird tastes—or doing crosswords in his cabin.

The regular crew were pleasant enough, but efficiently got on with their jobs and didn't talk much to the passengers. They kept to themselves and conversed in German.

He was content that Stuie would check in on Siobhan and Kieran and tell them that he was safe and in hiding. He'd see them soon.

Fremantle

Stuie came over the back fence after dark and tapped on the window.

"What's going on, Stuie?" asked Siobhan. "Why all the cloak and dagger stuff?"

"There's a CCTV outside and I don't want to be seen. I'm to tell you that Sean's okay and in hiding. I can't tell you where, as I don't know. I'm to check you're okay. Are you okay?

"Yes, we're okay."

"He told me to tell you to call the police immediately if you see any suspicious strangers."

The NE2 was nearing Newcastle and Burns briefed the team.

"This will be the biggest and boldest attack so far. I've just received a message that the client needs an even bigger, more strategic first strike, especially now that Australia is on fire again, and the attention of the world is on it. A bigger attack will help divert attention from the build-up in other countries. The original intention was to delay detonation until C-Day. Early activation entails a risk so soon after Monk's Point and just down the coast. The authorities might smell a rat and link the two, so we'll need to be careful and cover our tracks."

In his July survey, Burns found that the big, much older coal port in Newcastle, north of Sydney, had a lot of onshore coal loading wharves, but no long jetties. They would be hard to disable without a shitload of mines or other explosives, and there were no strategic targets within the port itself. But Newcastle had a narrow, dredged deep-water channel in the Hunter River through which every ship had to pass. If they sank a ship or two in the channel, they could block the port until the ships were salvaged. Salvaging would be hard to do if they were laden with coal.

Sinking could be done with sea or limpet mines. Sea mines were invented to hit ships in sea lanes, but the old floating kind were large and visible. Modern magnetic mines could be anchored on the seabed and float up when activated. He had planned for this and had ordered some in his shopping list to Hadley.

There could be crew casualties, but single holing below the hull would give time for escape to life rafts. Crews were small. You couldn't make an omelette …

"Now, that's what I call a bomb." Mallon had taken a keen interest in the mines and explosives in the magazine. Burns explained the plan for the Hunter River and proposed a sequence for remote detonation later and possibly sooner. The mines had been adjusted so that they would sense large draught, low-lying, fully laden vessels, which would severely block the channel and be hard to salvage. They would ignore other, innocent vessels.

"Now, it's not for me to say," suggested Mallon, "but if you were to fire an outgoing boat, then wait for the next to overtake on the incoming lane … I know how these buggers think. Profits. They'll override caution and checking for more mines. Just like they overrode the railway signals. They'll turn the inbound into a two-way, like the roadworks, except for someone standing here with a stop-and-go pole. You then nab another loaded outgoer next to the wreck. You can also get a couple held at the traffic lights. Here's how to do it with the right sequencing …" Mallon was handy with electronics. "By the way, I was checking the timers and one or two are faulty. Simple connection error. They're fixed now."

November 25

The NE2 sailed through the Hunter River channel towards Newcastle port. There were lines of coal ships inbound and outbound. The ships in each line were stationary.

Ahead was a cordon of hundreds of kayaks and a dozen Pacific Island long war canoes. The River Police were also there and attempting to clear the boats. The sound of loudspeakers could be heard.

Angah Tupou, from the low-lying Tongan island of Ha'apai, had taken umbrage at the Deputy PM McDuff's 'let them pick fruit' remark about what would happen if the Pacific Islands drowned, especially as he had come to Australia to pick fruit since his home was disappearing beneath the waves. He'd had a hard time during COVID-19, as he couldn't go home, and the Australian government gave nothing to unemployed casual workers from overseas, even though the agricultural economy depended on the cheap labour they provided to ensure low prices for consumers and high profits for supermarkets. He had come to expect nothing from Australian politicians who could say things like that, who were so stupid as to say that the Pacific Islands were always coming and going. Weren't there minimum educational standards for the Australian Parliament?

Nothing surprised him anymore. A few years before, Maurice Turbott and Minister Scroton had been caught with the mike on, joking about sea-level rise being the reason Pacific Islander leaders were late for a meeting on climate change, when yet again, their pleas for assistance on adaptation would result in strings-attached minimum aid only. Environment Minister, Sussan Cashmore, had publicly berated the Islanders for always having their hands out and had dismissed their pleas for Australia to reduce its coal exports, which were making the situation worse. The Islands could all die and go to hell as far as Australia was concerned. Coal profits and a few jobs were more important.

Now Australia was going to hell. A fiery hell of its own making.

Tupou was a warrior, a fighter, with a proud heritage—not a fruit picker. Like many of his kin from Tonga and the other islands, he was proud to be built like a brick shithouse—an attribute put to good use by the rugby codes in Australia and elsewhere. But not only were his beloved Islands dying, so were his people. The western diet of junk food dumped on the Islanders was turning his people into Michelin men and women with the highest diabetes rates in the world.

Four years before, along with friends from Fiji, Tonga, Vanuatu, the Solomon Islands and Tuvalu, and sixty white Australians, Tupou had paddled out to attempt to block the Hunter River to coal ships. At the same time, some protesters had attempted to block the coal railway. But it wasn't a great success—not much publicity, nothing about the reason, just the usual images showing hippie weirdos being arrested. Most Australians didn't know about the protest, and many that did treated it as joke—a bunch of greenies and darkies out in boats. Didn't the lentil-eaters know that the Islanders might be cannibals and eat them as their vegetable course?

Now it was different. Climate change was biting Australia hard, just as hard as it had affected his own home. The drought was tearing the life out of the country's interior. There were dying rivers and communities, floods and cyclones in the north. Now the fires. Even smug Sydneysiders, with choking lungs, could not pretend that nothing was happening—or if it was, pretend it was happening somewhere else.

It was now time to fight and fight hard. There was nothing to lose and everything to fight for. Bravery won against cowardice, against bullies, and Australia was a regional bully. *Look at how they treated East Timor,* he thought.

That Ned Coaly was an inspiration. The eyes of the world were on Australia, on the fires. The message of the plight of the Islanders could be told to the world. Let Turbott and his cronies try smirking now. They could use the visit of the *New Endeavour* to Newcastle and Sydney as an opportunity for extra publicity, especially through the Captain Cook connection. Didn't Cook 'discover' them as well? It was why some Pacific Nations still had the Union Jack on their flags. Okay, they'd done him in and planned to eat him. It was a small misunderstanding. Shit happens.

The River Police were not having much success at breaking up the cordon. DC Shane Swann called for backup.

"Half our officers are in the water."

It was one thing to pull young people from kayaks, another thing to try and lift a feisty Fijian or testy Tongan from their war canoe.

The cordon parted to allow through the NE2, which followed the channel into the port and tied up.

There was a short reception, joined by Grey, who was waiting at the quayside with a small crowd of attendees. People were there for the reception, their numbers swelled by protesters about the coal industry.

Mallon had to stay out of sight on the boat.

"I'll fill my pockets and bring you a muffin," Burns told him.

Mallon put in a special request. "Can you manage a quiche if they have one?"

In his July visit, Burns had discovered that Newcastle was much deindustrialised and yuppified from the steel industrial powerhouse it once was, but it was still the biggest coal export port in the world.

"Once Australia made everything," said Grey. "But now it likes to just dig things up, priding itself on being a Quarry Economy. It likes to present a smiling, bronzed image to the world, but as it fries each summer, it's looking more and more as if it has itself been just dug up."

That evening the NE2 sailed and moored offshore. The submarine was used to lay eight mines on the seabed—four in each of the two main channels. The mines were set for daytime activation, when traffic was busiest, and evacuation safer. They were set for two days' time.

CHAPTER 27

November 26

The NE2 sailed into the Sydney Harbour.
"You can see why it's one of the greatest natural harbours of the world," said Burns, as they admired the view of its iconic bridge and the great sails of the Opera House.

"Have you ever been there?" asked Mallon. He'd caught Burns listening to opera in his cabin.

"Yes, once. It's nice that since this voyage is commemorating Captain Cook. Sydney was one of the places in Australia that he actually visited. He wouldn't recognise it today. Not just the buildings—all the smoke from the fires.

The NE2 tied up near to HMAS Kuttabul Naval Base in Pott's Point. There was to be a very special reception with a very special guest—the Prime Minister himself.

PM Turbott had loved summers as a kid—cricket, the beach, snaggers and prawns on the barbie. But summers weren't the same with the fires and all—not being allowed to sneak off for holidays in Hawaii, having to visit bushfire victims and force them to shake his hand, being told to fuck off by fireys, having to put up with 'where the bloody hell are ya?' jibes. Now his beloved Daghawi Project was up the spout—out for months. But the *Endeavour* visit would be a good news story at least—a chance for a good photo and TV op. He could pop out while staying at his Kirribilli House residence just across the harbour.

"How good is this!" he declared, while Burns and the crew posed for a picture behind him. Mallon stayed out of sight.

Turbott was shown on board.

"What's that under the wraps?" asked Turbott.

"This? Oh, it's our submersible. For surveying the ocean floor," said Burns.

Turbott moved on to pose serving snaggers on the quayside, wearing his baseball cap and holding a tinnie.

Burns took a hot dog to Mallon. "Guess who cooked this? He'd have sprinkled on some rat poison if he knew it was for you."

Burns remembered something he'd read and did a Google search. "D'you know it says the last time a midget submarine visited Sydney Harbour incognito was in May 1942? The Japanese Imperial Navy sent in three two-man midget subs from larger submarines that lurked outside the Heads. The first got caught up in anti-submarine nets and the crew deliberately blew themselves up. The second managed to sneak past the nets and fire two torpedoes, hitting a ferry and killing nineteen people, but never made it back to its mother sub. The third sub entered Sydney Harbour at around eleven pm. By this time, the Australian Navy was ready and dropped six depth charges, sinking the sub. Most Sydneysiders were spooked, fearing an imminent invasion, but many came to watch the submarines being hauled out of the harbour. Some people even waded into Taylors Bay to collect fish that had been killed by the shock of the depth charges. How about that?"

November 27, morning

Burns decided it was time to strike, while the iron was hot. The mines were in place and ready. Mallon and Grey had told him about the plight of the Pacific Islanders and why they were protesting. They'd be in jail by now and blocking the river would give them a lift. They wouldn't mind if someone claimed that they were responsible. *It'll confuse the authorities and it'll be a distraction from our presence in the area,* Burns thought. *They'll soon be let out, and it will buy us time.*

The fully laden coal bulk carrier, *Samantha*, entered the Hunter River narrows. Three hundred metres long and carrying one hundred and eighty-five thousand tonnes, it was en route to China. Two mines on the seabed detached from their anchors, rapidly found the hull and exploded. The vessel began to sink, sirens blared and the crew evacuated to the life rafts in a disorderly fashion, the all-Bangladeshi crew regretting foregoing the delicious lunch that was being prepared.

It was not obvious that the incident was caused by mines. It could have been an engine room explosion, a structural failure.

The following ship, *Belinda*, radioed. "Is assistance needed?" It didn't want to have to stop and turn around or wait for a rescue boat. It was on its way and had a schedule to keep. Time was money.

"No, we're all very fine," said the *Samantha*'s captain. The sea was calm. "We can wait for rescue." He could see a rescue craft speeding towards them.

The control tower had already been informed and halted incoming boats. The *Belinda* was permitted to overtake at reduced speed to reduce backwash.

Before it passed, a mine exploded underneath, and it came to rest alongside the *Samantha*, totally blocking the channel to large ships. Additional mines sank another full ship in the outbound channel and, for luck, an empty coming in.

"Here is the news: Today, four coal ships were sunk in the Hunter River, New South Wales, blocking the entrance to the Newcastle coal port, the largest in the world. There were no casualties. A group calling themselves the Fighting Fruitpickers Front has claimed responsibility. A number of men have been detained for questioning."

"It's the power of the Pacific Sea Gods, my ancestors," Tupou told the police. "Vengeance for what your people are doing to my people. It's justice, man. Do what the fuck you like."

The Australian government, coal industry and Moorcock media were apoplectic.

Deputy Prime Minister Barney McDuff was special guest on Alan Williams's Radio 2GBH. "You can't go around sinking other people's ships, just because your islands are sinking. They have to realise that the Australian economy and coal industry, and Australian jobs, matter more than they do. They should be grateful that we let them come here to pick our fruit."

The Friends of Coal Exporters were in mourning. Craig Tooley was on the Sunup breakfast TV show wearing a black armband. He was struggling to hold back a tear. "What kind of people could do this?"

Joel Cole, Federal MP for the Hunter Valley, was railing on radio about the Hunter River blockage. Although a Labor Member, he was a climate denier and member of the Friends. He had only had a narrow victory in his coal mining constituency and, with the backing of mining unions and corporate sponsors for Labor, led the Labor right-wing faction opposing action on climate change, as it had been a vote loser. He was a regular guest on 2GBH. "I regard the coal ship sinkings as an act of war by climate warmists, be they green-left terrorists from Australia or the Islands. Halting our coal exports is a dark day for the Hunter Valley and for Australia. It's costing the industry millions, but they won't win. We'll soon be back in the black."

The news also went further afield.

"It's the US President, Prime Minister," said Turbott's aide. Turbott was the President's best buddy, his soulmate. He still wasn't sure about the Brit.

"Maurice, what the hell is going on down there in Austria?" He had heard that Australia was ablaze once more and that someone called Ned Coaly and now Fijians had blown the coal ports. "Fiji. That's the swank fraternity Phi Gamma Delta. They wouldn't accept me when I was a student. Look at them sucking up to me now."

"Everything is fine. Everything is under control," said Turbott.

"Why don't you rake the leaves? It was my brilliant idea and it sure stopped the fires here." There was little left to burn in California after the recent wildfires. "That's not the reason I'm calling. Who cares anyway? Reason I'm calling is America has coal. Lots of beautiful, sweet, clean coal. I mean really clean coal. I thought you might need some. I can do a deal …"

The NE2 left Sydney and headed for Hobart, Tasmania, still on the Eastern Current. The wind became stronger, colder, the sea heavier as a storm blew in.

"We're on the route of the famous Sydney-Hobart yacht race," said Mallon. "Many a yacht has come to grief, sometimes lives lost."

The NE2 cut through the swell.

Mallon liked to check the news.

"I see there have been more bombings and other attacks on fossil fuels all over the world—in the US, Japan. There are even unconfirmed reports of attacks in Hong Kong and Tibet. And, get this, a mob has just wrecked the Daghawi power station in India that was burning coal from their mine here. We've certainly started something."

"You've started something, Sean. Ned Coaly is a hero. A revolutionary."

Louise Brailly was trying to understand what was going on and was preparing an article. The railway bombings had stopped, and Ned Coaly—Mallon—had gone to ground, as you'd expect if there was a massive manhunt for you.

But there had since been huge attacks on coal ports.

"What do you think, Eddie?"

"Uhh." He had gone back to sleep.

Sweet. I must be wearing him out, she thought. The bombings in Australia were definitely causing a stir around the world. It was interesting that George Toynbee had called from London only last night to discuss what they meant. *What a hunk of spunk. Pity he's so far away ...* "But I love you, don't I, Eddie?"

"Uhh."

She continued writing notes on her laptop. *Australia is normally ignored by international news except when it's on fire, but since other places are burning, even the Arctic, it's a ho-hum occurrence. Now, once again, Australia is the centre of attention. Yet international coverage is still mostly from the terrorism and anarchism angle. The Ned Coaly bombings received a lot of attention, but more for the vengeful father story. In mainstream news, the climate action possibility has been ignored. Climate change is still barely newsworthy, outside of* The Sentinel *and other progressive rags, even as the world burns and icecaps melt. The Hunter River protest and bombings have reminded the world of the plight of the Islanders, but no one cares much. Leaders of low-lying islands have been pleading with the world for years that their nations will die if the global temperature rise exceeds 1.5 degrees Celsius, but they've been ignored. They're expendable. The collapsing world environment is never more than a few lines on page six—even the direst of reports. The mainstream, majority view is still 'You can't stand in the way of progress. Jobs and the economy, people, have to come first. Doomsayers have always been prophesying the end of the world, crying wolf and always been wrong.'*

Eddie was stirring. "Are you coming back for more, darling?" He turned over. "Maybe not."

But to climate protesters around the world, it's clear what the bombings have been about. To them, Ned Coaly is a hero, a celebrity, a Che Guevara of the climate revolution, except with a mining hard hat instead of a beret and star. Australia has been showing the way with coal industry sabotage, and now attacks are happening all over the place. It's a copycat world. Look what the Aussies are doing. They're not just good at cricket. Governments, the fossil fuel industry and the media can dismiss it as copycat terrorism. They would say that. Their reign of terror towards the Earth is coming to an end. But has the revolution started? Revolutions are always preceded by tensions, like pressure building up under a volcano before it erupts.

Tensions are building as the climate crisis grows. Around the world, people are suffering and dying from the ravages of climate change. Increased frequency and intensity of wildfires, droughts, storms, cyclones, hurricanes, tidal surges and receding coastlines are rampant. Crops and harvests are failing, water resources dwindling, conflicts are flaring, people are starving and dying from heatstroke. The poor are the worst affected; storms and floods are washing away their homes, drowning their children, their animals. In the economic chaos, there is conflict and war, hundreds of thousands of climate refugees. Soon there will be millions on the move.

"Oh Eddie, you move me, but when will it move again."

Sympathetic governments continue to do nothing beyond talk. Unsympathetic governments—the US, Russia, Brazil, Saudi Arabia and Australia—continue to deny any problem and to do nothing but accelerate the plundering of resources and oppose international action. China and India are the last nails in the coffin, putting solutions beyond reach. China is planning to build forty coal power stations as part of its Belt and Road plan for colonising the world.

Delete; better not say that.

You cannot keep lying to all of the people all the time, when physical reality is washing the lies away, sending them up in smoke. When those who are not blind see the truth through the fog. When those who lie to keep their power, and oppress the people, lose the base of that power. All revolutions start with a few people. Individuals having thoughts, exchanging ideas. In the past, it took decades, centuries to throw off the ideas of the divine right of kings, the idea of colonial empires. The empires of old have been replaced by commercial empires—at the pinnacle, the fossil fuel empire. Will it be the last empire? The world is a tinderbox waiting for a spark. Are people beginning to think what was before unthinkable? Say what has been unsayable? Plan and do what has previously been undoable? Things are happening all around the world. Are the people awakening, beginning to rise up?

"Oh, Eddie! Are you ready?"

November 28

All down the coast of Victoria, smoke billowed up from the land, and after crossing the Bass Strait, distant smoke from the west of Tasmania.

"It's a catastrophe," Mallon told Burns and Ryan. He knew and loved Tasmania. "Those wet temperate forests in the west and alpine vegetation on the mountains—World Heritage—have no history of natural fire cycles. There's no role for fire in germination. And the King Billy Pines are hundreds of years old. Once they burn, they're gone forever. Yet the loggers still want to go on logging native forests until there's nothing left."

The NE2 tied up in Salamanca Harbour and, after the reception, Burns ordered takeaway fish and chips.

"Shame I can't go and look around," said Mallon. "There are some great pubs and restaurants, whisky tasting too. The Blue Eye Restaurant over there is really good. Don't let me stop you."

"Sounds nice, but I won't," said Burns. "We need to get on."

"Mind you, there's a dark side," said Mallon. "Unlike other places in Australia, there are hardly any Aboriginal people, not even place names. The British massacred the lot. Did you know the killing inspired H.G. Wells to write *The War of the Worlds*? He said to a friend in his club in London, 'What if Martians came and did to us what we've done to the Tasmanians?' It's like humans are now behaving like Martians, frying the planet with their fossil fuel death rays. It's not the war of the worlds, it's war *on* the world."

Later that day, the NE2 sailed on to Melbourne, following the west coast of Tasmania, smoke billowing from the wet temperate forests.

Dreiser intended that the project would be a one-off, the last chance for a surprise attack. After that, everyone's guards would be up. There would be a new and vindictive 'war on terror' as governments and the fossil industry closed ranks. It would be hard to repeat the attack at scale as a single event. But he'd always thought it could be a trigger for something much bigger. When many big targets had been hit, it could open the way for oppressed people to see the opportunity for breaking the power of the oppressors by knowing their weakness, their Achilles heel—their fossil fuel infrastructure and supplies. But he didn't expect it all to start so soon. It was premature.

He was well pleased that Australian operations were underway but had not anticipated the timing of the informal revolt happening all around the world. There would surely be a severe backlash from the authorities. He was concerned for the project—that it would be detected. He was concerned for the safety of the operatives. They would have to tread carefully, keep their heads down.

CHAPTER 28

Late November, Oregon, USA

Arnold Zimmerman was angry. An ageing hippy, he reckoned he'd been protesting more or less since modern environmentalism was born in the sixties. He was a veteran of the long defunct Earth First! campaign of the eighties in Oregon. In that campaign, he had driven steel spikes into redwoods to make them useless for logging and had put sugar into logging machinery fuel tanks. But it had come to nothing. The US and the world were fucked. The government and most Americans were climate deniers or lukewarmists, which amounted to the same. Protests had failed; direct action had failed. He'd joined sit-in protests against fracking and oil development in First Nation territory and had helped turn off a valve on the Keystone XL Pipeline, a major pipeline from Canada. He'd even protested outside the White House and had been gassed and bashed by police. He took solace in his home-grown weed.

Then he read about the bombings and other sabotage in Australia.

"Hey, we thought of this idea first. Isn't there some sort of copyright or patent?" But in spite of everything, he was still proud to be American. America should have been the leader, the number one in this. Americans had more energy than anyone else, a 'can do' mentality—even if, more often than not, it was channeled into 'can fuck things up'.

His first efforts achieved instant national fame. He watched NBC TV News:

"We've just heard that there was an explosion at a pumping station on the Pacific Connector Oil Pipeline. The police have not reported whether it was an accident or terrorism. Jim, do you have anything for us on today's sport?"

He was proud that many good Americans were soon following his lead with attacks on oil pumping stations, compressor stations on high-pressure gas pipelines, fracking infrastructure and those poor, defenceless, nodding donkeys. Derailing or bombing coal trains was soon popular, using the 'à la Ned Coaly' method. It was driving the police crazy. There were too many soft targets to defend. He felt good about himself. He puffed contentedly on his joint.

Honshu, Japan

Until now, Junichi Kamata had felt bad. Around the world, people had been made to feel guilty, told they were to blame for greenhouse emissions. But for years, they were told they could atone for their guilt by making a small difference—by turning things off, doing more of this, less of that, making sacrifices. With climate change getting worse, he had felt even guiltier, feeling he hadn't tried hard enough. Now there was a new way for people to make big cuts in emissions, the emissions of the truly guilty, the fossil fuel industry. That Ned Coary had started it, but Japan was good at doing things better. Why hadn't anyone thought of it before?

He had once been radical but had calmed down. He met with old friends for a Japanese Red Army Faction reunion. They all shared similar ideas and discussed plans. With bands around their heads, they toasted with sake. "Kampei!" They were all knowledgeable in electronics and explosives.

They had heard about isolated, small attacks in other countries, but the Japanese thought strategically. Within two weeks, they had sabotaged two large oil storage facilities, bringing half of Honshu to its knees and damaging power lines, causing two coal power stations to shut down. *Yes, everyone can make difference,* thought Kamata. He was pleased that young people were damaging coal plants under construction, curbing future emissions from Japan's major coal expansion. There was already a holdup in supplies from Australia.

Kyiv, Ukraine

Andriy Kolisnyk was not that concerned about climate change. All the same, he hated what Russia had done to his country. The attacks in other countries made him think about how he could do the most to annoy them. No one was more dependent on fossil fuel exports than Russia. He knew that one of the main gas pipelines to Western Europe went through Ukraine …

Hong Kong, China

Oppressed people were starting to see energy sabotage as a good way to annoy and undermine their oppressors. Hong Kongers, Tibetans and Uyghur struck back with attacks on power plants, power lines, pipelines and fuel storage tanks—all vulnerable and hard to defend.

Kwan Tung Chiang alone blacked out the government buildings of Hong Kong.

Sunderabans, Bangladesh

Debesh Rahman was angry that his country had signed up to the Belt and Road Project, effectively agreeing to be an indebted colony of the new Chinese Empire, after they spent all that time trying to get rid of the British. He was especially concerned that one of the many BRP coal power plants was being built on the edge of the home of and food source for many thousands of people. He couldn't believe that they would risk potentially polluting the Sunderabans and its World Heritage mangrove forest. The whole of the low-lying country was already threatened by sea-level rise.

He addressed a crowd of villagers and fishermen.

"Will we let this happen?"

"No, we will not!"

Overrunning security, a mob marched onto the construction site, carrying torches and scythes. Within an hour, they turned it to rubble.

Shiracha, Gujurat, India

Chetu Chowdhury and his family lived near to the Daghawi coal power station, built to burn coal from the Daghawi mine in Australia. To build it, his family and hundreds of people had been forcibly evicted from their homes and land without compensation. Since it had become operational, thousands had been choking on the smoke, drinking poisoned water. The sudden stoppage of supplies from Australia had led to the plant being temporarily shut down, reminding everyone of what clean air was like. He organised a meeting.

"In India, coal power expansion is for industrialisation and the enrichment of the Prime Minister and his wealthy backers, not the poor who will live with the polluted skies and waters." He knew that, normally, Indians were peaceful, easy-going people. But when they were displeased about something, they didn't write letters of complaint to the newspapers. They rioted.

He led a mob to the plant. Police could not hold them back. Army reinforcements had to be called in, but extensive damage had been done by the time they arrived.

Mohan Daghawi visited by helicopter to calm things down but was obliged to make himself scarce.

December 1

The NE2 visited Melbourne for a short stop, tying up in Docklands. Not wanting to be outdone by Sydney, its fierce rival, the city laid on a lavish reception with quiches to die for.

Grey joined them for the reception. To protect him, it had been arranged that if the attacks were ever discovered, he would have an alibi, always being somewhere else when they occurred.

"Ladies and gentleman, boys and girls …"

Agron Hoxha was proud to be an Albanian Australian, proud that his people had contributed to Melbourne being the most culturally diverse city in Australia, if not the world, through their rich traditions. In Albania, being a gangster was as normal and respected a career choice as being a CPA in other countries. What was wrong with that? He knew the history of emigrants from his country. They'd sought their fortune in Australia and had naturally gravitated to Melbourne, where there was a well-established syndicate industry and career opportunities, all thanks to the Italians. Over time the Albanians had taken over the business. Younger Italians had become lazy, living off the hard work and investments of their parents, nonnos and nonnas. The Albanians had more enthusiasm and natural flair, more hunger.

He had arrived as a boy and had ascended to the top, a rags to riches Aussie success story. Good-looking and a charmer, he was someone in this city. A box seat at Collingwood footy games or seats at the Melbourne Cup were always on standby for him.

There had been no lack of opportunity in a vibrant, enterprising country like Australia. Such friendly, nice people; accommodating politicians and police. The usual DPP. Drugs, prostitution, protection. Core business. Then there were sidelines like assassination. Profitable, but one-offs. Not so much repeat business.

Most assassination contracts were to rub out fellow gangsters for encroachment on territory, personal vendettas and family matters. Then, through a middle-man, Hoxha was contacted to see off an unusual target.

"The police are after him too," said the middleman.

"It will cost extra," said Hoxha. Standard tariff. Conditions applied. There was more risk. The cops investigated and snooped around more if a killing was outside of gangland. They welcomed it inside the circle. *One less crim.*

"He's famous. Someone called Mallon. You know, Ned Coaly."

"Never heard of him." Hoxha was too busy to read the papers and watch TV. "Famous is extra." The police would definitely investigate.

He assigned the job to Urt 'Coca' Kola and Zef Dervishi. Coca was his nephew—very reliable, resourceful and a ruthless, cold-blooded thug. Hoxha had high hopes for him.

"Where is this Coaly?" asked Kola.

"We don't know," said Hoxha. "It's up to you to find him."

"Can we get a tip-off from the police?" Hoxha had a network of police informants. The cops weren't paid much, and the extra cash in hand was always welcome in these hard times.

"It's like this. If the cops knew where he was, they'd arrest him, and we're out of a job—unless we can get a prison hit contract. We need to get to him first. See if he has any family."

It was business. Nothing personal. Cash, no GST.

"Don't tell me any more. They'll have to do," said Greg Hutchings, who had been concerned that their man had not been in contact and that Mallon was still on the loose and a threat. Now Newcastle was out of action, losing him even more.

"I don't want to know their names—probably couldn't pronounce them anyway … No, I'm not cultural stereotyping, biasing the selection process—it's what the Albanians do best. In economics, it's called the comparative advantage of nations." He remembered that from *Economics for Dummies* in his MBA course. "Anyhow, at least they're Australian. We wouldn't want to break any visa and employment laws. Did we pay the last one a retainer? Nothing more upfront, this is on results. I want Mallon eliminated. Call it revenge. I don't care what they do as long as I'm not implicated."

The paparazzi and TV crews found and mobbed Siobhan at her home in Fremantle.

"How does it feel being the daughter of Ned Coaly? Where is he now?"

She recognised him and the cameraman as the ones her dad had duffed up. The TV camera was held together with tape.

The NE2 sailed on along the coast of Victoria and South Australia where, once again, fire came down to the sea and people were being rescued, Dunkirk-like, from the beaches by the Navy. So much for the famed beach lifestyle, which would be gone anyway in a few years with sea-level rise.

"We'll see if we can help," said Burns.

Some of the crew put dinghies in the water and ferried people to the naval boat.

"I'd like to help," said Mallon. "I don't think anyone will recognise me. This is the closest thing to hell I've seen—like *Dante's Inferno*. I'm sure it's where I'm heading, so it'll be practice. Acclimatisation."

Hutchings's middleman saw Siobhan on the news and passed the intel onto Hoxha's middleman who passed it onto Hoxha.

Hoxha briefed Kola and Dervishi. "They saw it on TV. Daughter—nice-looking kid too. Easy to smoke him out now. But you'll have to drive. No good flying, as you need to take artillery. Can't subcontract to our associates in Perth—as useful as an ashtray on a motorbike. The police keep taking away their guns … Hey, that's good—they *are* bikies."

Kola and Dervishi prepared for the long drive to Fremantle.

CHAPTER 29

Early December, Queensland

DCI Goss had to admit that the nationwide manhunt for Ned Coaly, presumed to be Mallon, was not going so well after all. He had disappeared into thin air and was lying low. There was circumstantial—but still no firm—evidence to link him to the railway bombings. At the bomb sites, forensics had found small fragments of devices that possibly matched what had been taken from the Area D mine, but they couldn't be sure. They had found the burnt-out remains of what appeared to be his two vehicles but no clues. They'd found the lockup in Townsville but no trace of explosives. Failure to hand himself in for questioning was incriminating, but that was not enough in itself.

Then there was the Monk's Point bombing. There was nothing to link him, except that he was capable, had the motive and the equipment and was in Queensland when it had all happened. There was no obvious link to the Hunter River sinkings and the Fighting Fruitpickers Front.

Above all, they had no idea where he was. They would find something to pin on him if only he could be found.

"He's got to be still in Queensland," insisted Goss, when reporting progress to the Australian Commonwealth Police, the ACP. "Unless he left the state off-road or stowed away on a ship. His own vehicles were still around, but he could have stolen a car or hitched a ride. Queensland is a big state, but there aren't that many roads out, and all have been watched, vehicles searched. He has to show himself. Has to eat. There have been a lot of fake sightings and reports around the country, but all have come to nothing. Someone must be sheltering him. Anyhow, if you're so clever, why don't you find him? That's if you're not too busy beating up journos."

He couldn't stand the ACP. In coordinating national efforts, they were leaning on state forces to get results, stretching local resources, as if the state forces had nothing better to do—no other crimes to solve, speeding fines to issue. The ACP liked to do exciting stuff like mass surveillance and midnight raids on the ABC and journalists' offices and homes. They wanted to leave the boring stuff, the legwork, to the poor state plods.

He knew that, besides the hunt for Mallon, the investigation into the Monk's Point and Hunter River bombings were continuing, but also not going well. After questioning many Islanders in Sydney and Newcastle, the NSW Police had concluded that the FFF was a fictitious organisation and that there was no clue as to who was responsible or how the perpetrators had obtained the mines. Mallon could be involved, but it couldn't be all his work. He knew how to dive, but it wasn't his hallmark. It was one thing to blow up railways with regular explosives, but Hunter River was something else and on a much bigger scale.

But it isn't all bad, he thought. He was secretly pleased that NSW was copping it for a change, instead of just his state. *Cocky bastards.* NSW had won the last three State of Origin series. There had long been a fierce rivalry between NSW and Queensland. Rugby league was established in Australia as an alternative to outright war between the two states. It was marginally less violent.

The ACP were being leaned on by their Chief Commissioner, Andrew Robb, who was in turn being leaned on by the PM and Minister for Home Security.

"How is the investigation going?" enquired Turbott. "I'm beginning to lose patience. I want Mallon and any other culprits found. This has gone on long enough."

"We're onto it, Prime Minister," said Robb. "It's just a matter of time."

"I know I can rely on you." It was good to be Prime Minister, having his own private police force. The ACP were marvellous—always ready to raid the home of any journalist who dared criticise him or his government. He only had to ask. His Energy Minister, Hamish Tallone, had been accused of doctoring a City of Sydney report on its air travel spending so that he could rightly accuse them of hypocrisy in declaring a climate emergency. The ACP had found no wrongdoing and had dropped the investigation after a call from him to Andrew. What were a few zeros? That's what friends were for.

Robb and the ACP had their own theory. One, the supplier of the mines was most likely China. Two, the Islands had a grudge against Australia, a sure-fire motive—no sense of humour when Australia took the piss about sea-level rise. They were totally unreasonable in demanding that Australia stop increasing its coal exports. What did they expect?

Robb informed the PM of his secret concern. Turbott, in turn, informed the Australian Secret Service. If the police didn't find Mallon, they would have to. That was if they could spare the time from important work like bugging foreign trade delegations to gain favourable deals for Australia.

Emma and Grey were flying to Adelaide, she to join the *Sea Horse*, he to join the NE2.

"You okay, Emma?" He nodded. He could tell she was a bit nervous. He squeezed her hand.

"I'm going to see this through," she said. "We have to try to stop the rig—at least let the world know what's happening."

They snuggled up. He looked at her. She had dozed off. He couldn't bear it if anything happened to her. She'd told him she had been a supporter of the Sea Defender Marine Conservation Society for some time and had been on one campaign as a volunteer, helping in the galley and other work. She knew that one of its boats, the *Sea Horse*, would be aiming to stop the rig. Sea Defender had been involved in earlier publicity, but not confrontational campaigns against approving drilling in the Bight. She had been accepted for this campaign. He had given up trying to persuade her not to go, not that he was one to talk.

Mike Ryan had encouraged him to come on the second leg of the NE2's trip along the south and up the west coast. Well, it was now summer recess—he had time to spare and wasn't doing anything else, especially with Emma away for a couple of weeks. He didn't know what and where, but the NE2 would be blowing stuff up. For security and their later protection, Burns had only briefed Ryan and Grey on a need-to-know basis. He wondered if the NE2 might also out to stop the drilling rig.

Brad Callaghan had been frowning even more than usual lately with his beloved coal industry taking a severe beating. He felt at war, a war hero even. He had sustained minor bruising at the Daghawi opening and liked to show people his war wounds, even after they had healed. Oil was his new hope and dream. *Let's see the green left terrorists trying to get at his shiny new oil industry,* he thought. He had dreams of a Bight full of oil rigs, just like the Gulf of Mexico—Australia a new Saudi Arabia, himself a desert prince. Protesters would get their bits chopped off if they got anywhere near the rigs.

The rig flotilla was finally on its way from China. He and the Prime Minister had arranged for an armed naval ship to escort it from Perth to the Bight in case protesters tried anything.

December 4, Port of Adelaide

Grey and Emma were waiting in the large crowd by the quayside. Some of the people were there for the NE2 visit and reception, but most were there to see off the protest ship protecting *their* Bight.

"Emma! What are you doing here?" Emma saw it was Louise Brailly.

"Hi, Louise. Hi, Eddie. I could say the same about you. I'm going on the *Sea Horse*. This is my friend John Grey, from Brisbane Uni."

"Hi, John. I've heard of you and your involvement with the NE2. You write well. Weren't you David Mallon's supervisor …? Eddie and I are covering the drilling in the Bight story. I still can't believe the government is allowing it, but what can you expect from that lot? Anyhow, the best of luck, Emma. Take care."

The NE2 was coming in and tied up behind the *Sea Horse*, which was preparing to leave.

"This is my bus," said Grey. "You'd better go. Be careful, darling. Maybe I'll see you in Perth."

"You be careful, too. Oh, John, I love you so much."

They embraced and kissed until the *Sea Horse* blew its horn and Emma scuttled aboard. The gangplank was drawn up and the ship cast off. Emma waved at Grey, blowing kisses until he was a speck in the crowd. A flotilla of small boats followed until the water became too choppy for them.

It was exciting. She forgot her anxiety. There were familiar faces. The *Sea Horse* had a crew of thirty-six, a mix of old hands and younger volunteers. Everyone had a roster of tasks. Emma started in the galley.

After handing over to the first mate, Pete Adams, Captain Andrew Daniels came to greet the crew and welcome new members and old.

"It's good to have you on board again, Emma."

"It's good to be here," she said. She felt safe with him. He was a hero.

Daniels went back to the bridge and took the helm as the *Sea Horse* ploughed through the Bight. He knew that this could be its toughest mission yet. A converted trawler, it was built for rough seas and had confronted Japanese whalers in the mountainous seas of the Antarctic Southern Ocean. But it had never confronted ocean-going tugs manned by Norwegians.

He was a seasoned veteran from the Antarctic whaling wars, a long campaign every year for twelve years until the Japanese were finally forced to stop. He was glad that this was all over. .

He received a report from off the north-west coast of Australia. He had spotters tracking and reporting the drilling rig's progress. It was hard for them to miss. A fifty thousand tonne, heavy-lift semi-submersible, it was over a hundred metres tall when partially de-ballasted for transportation. Like all deep-water drilling rigs, it was fitted with dynamic thrusters so that, when in position, it could maintain its position without anchoring to the seabed. Built in China, it was being towed by two ocean-going tugs. An extra tug was acting as a free moving escort.

He knew a naval coastguard escort ship was waiting at HMAS Stirling, a major RAN base near Perth. His plan was to harass the oil rig convoy further north, down the calmer WA coast, before it was escorted, and not to wait until the rougher south west and Bight, when it would have the escort. They would slow the rig down, maybe get aboard and sabotage it. Maybe release the cables. Lock onto it. They'd do whatever gained maximum publicity and interfered the most.

Brailly spoke to Grey after the reception. "Did you know David Mallon's father—Ned Coaly?"

"I met him, very briefly, at David's inquest and at the funeral."

She had interviewed enough politicians to smell when someone wasn't telling the whole truth. It was odd, too, that only John Grey and Mike Ryan looked like scientists. The others were all hunks, though.

"Come on, Eddie. Let's have a drink while I work on my piece."

Over a G&T she began. *Beneath the seabed of the Bight are believed to be vast oil reserves. For a long time, its special nature, deep and rough waters, have made the Bight out of bounds to the oil industry, especially since Deepwater Horizon. The Bight is much rougher and oil drilling much riskier than in the Gulf of Mexico, making the chances of a devastating spill much higher. This hasn't stopped repeated applications by major oil companies, hoping that their persistence, influence, money and claims of safe technology will wear out ENEMA, the responsible federal agency, and wear out objectors to oil drilling. There aren't many—only all Aboriginal groups, more than thirty local councils, many community groups, fishing companies, conservationists, many thousands of members of the Australian public and global NGOs. Each time proposals have been rejected and various companies have pulled out. Until now. The government has torn up environmental controls and approved it. Apparently, Australia has to get the oil from beneath its feet ...*

She looked towards the quayside.

"It looks like the NE2 is about to head off." She finished her G&T.

"Come on, Eddie. Let's go back to the hotel."

―――

"Let's be under way and get this bit over with," said Burns. A storm was brewing. It was going to be rough, but they had to get a move on and keep to the visiting schedule. If they were going to intercept the rig, they had to get to it before it got to the Bight, before it had a naval escort and before Emma and the others on the *Sea Horse* got themselves killed.

He'd do the job if at all possible, but he couldn't risk the mission.

CHAPTER 30

The Norwegian Parliament

Greens representative Olaf Olafsen was outraged that Energor was proceeding with drilling in the Bight, but he was not surprised. Norway liked to make out that it was green but had one of the highest levels of climate denial in the world, seemingly a common syndrome in fossil fuel states. Fossilarchies would be a good name for them. He stood to speak.

"This is causing international embarrassment. A spill in this pristine environment will be a catastrophe. The Norwegian government, as a major shareholder, must intervene to stop it. Order the rig to turn back."

The Energy Minister, Jakob Johansen, rose.

"Contracts have been signed and exploratory drilling has the full approval of the Australian government. Energor has assured us that they have state-of-the-art technology, which is why they've been chosen, and the risks will be minimal.

"That's what they said about the Titanic!" shouted Olafsen, to uproar and sardonic laughter.

"Order!" called the Speaker.

Emma had never been in seas so rough or felt so ill. By comparison, the Bight had been like a duck pond during her previous voyage. She tried to eat and drink but couldn't hold anything down. She tried to sleep, but it was impossible with the violent tossing of the ship, the banging, the sound of waves crashing into it. How was the boat still afloat? *Oh, God!*

"Hang in there," said Jill, who was doing a bit better. "We'll be out of this in a few hours."

Pete Evans was at the helm, waves and spray lashing against the windows of the bridge.

"I'll take over now," said Daniels. "Get some rest. I've never seen it so choppy. The old tub is holding well."

Burns had just gone out to check that the submarine and other gear were secure and, after seeing that they were, came onto the bridge.

"How are we doing, Mister Hoemberg?"

"We are doing well. I've seen worse."

Mallon was suffering. He'd spent much of the Bight crossing so far with his head in the toilet.

In the mess, there was little conversation, and the galley crew had less demand for food than usual. The Recce Boys were nowhere to be seen, but the SAS and Navy Seals were toughing it out and keeping the poker going.

"I'll see you … ugh … excuse me …" said Beattie.

Ryan and Grey were born to the sea, but it was a tough crossing, a conversation killer even for them.

"Did you ever consider terrestrial ecology?" said Ryan.

The German crew members remained resolutely at their posts, taking their turns on watch.

National Highway A1, somewhere on the Nullarbor Plain

"Shit, Coca, this road is boring," said Zef Dervishi. "It's a shame we couldn't fly."

"Yeah," said Urt Kola. "But you know what the boss said. We have to deliver the hardware and we need irons ourselves to deal with this Ned Coaly."

"Hey, he sounds a bitta like you—Kola, Coaly—geddit?"

"I guess." Kola didn't think it was very funny.

"It was good to get some shuteye at the roadhouse last night," said Dervishi. "That guy said they were all booked up. The look on his face when you told him he had a room or else. Looked like he was gonna shit himself. *I'm sure something can be arranged. Oh, look someone has just cancelled.* Like fuck they had."

⌒

The *Sea Horse* put into Albany on the south coast of Western Australia.

"It's good to see some colour back in your cheeks, Emma," said Daniels. "It happens to the best of us. The waters will be calmer from now on."

"I'm much better now, thanks. I've got my sea legs back."

The *Sea Horse* had stopped to pick up two experienced crew before getting quickly on its way. The plan was to pick up more crew in Fremantle and to intercept the oil rig somewhere north of there. They were making good time. At least they wouldn't have to face the rig in the Bight, which would have been tough.

⌒

December 6, Esperance, Western Australia

To the relief of Mallon and the other landlubbers, NE2 reached calmer waters sheltered by Woody Island. The NE2 stopped briefly at Esperance port for a reception.

"Ladies and gentlemen, boys and girls ..." began Ryan.

Mallon watched from the boat. He had fond memories of camping here one summer with Laura and the children. He remembered that it was named after the French exploration vessel, *Espérance*, which had visited this part of the coast in 1792. An iconic tourist venue, as well as mineral export port, he recalled the long stretches of pure white sand, shimmering in the sun, the Cape Le Grand National Park coming down to the sea, with kangaroos on the beach. It was as Aussie a scene as you could get if the roos had stubbies, board shorts and hats with hanging corks. He sighed at the happy memory, those carefree days before all this. There was only him and Siobhan left now from that time—and little Kieran, of course.

While the reception was going on, with Burns's permission, he sneaked off the boat and called Stuie from a call box.

"She was okay yesterday," said Stuie. "I'll check again tomorrow."

December 7

The *Sea Horse* put into Fremantle, where a crowd had gathered to greet it. Sea Defender had a lot of supporters here. Daniels was proud that during the whaling wars, the vessel was accorded Freedom of the City of Fremantle as a gesture of solidarity. This was also an example to those gutless other Australian cities who, in the interests of trade, had banned it from refuelling under pressure from the Japanese. Four experienced crew joined, veterans of the anti-whaling campaign in the Antarctic Southern Ocean. Although shorter, this new campaign would be tough, the watches long, and reserves would need to be ready.

He ran through the plan with everyone.

"Is everyone okay with this? We'll follow all reasonable safety precautions, but I'm not going to pretend there's no danger. You all knew the score before joining the mission, but there's no shame if anyone wants to leave now. See me personally if anyone wants to discuss it."

Emma could see that some of the younger ones were feeling anxious, like her, but no one came forward.

They were preparing to sail. She called Grey, but there was no answer.

"Cast off," ordered Davis.

The rig had been sighted off Shark Bay. They would intercept off Geraldton.

December 7, Albany

The NE2 sailed between Michaelmas and Breaksea Islands, where they saw a pod of Southern Right Whales. Mallon pointed out the Cheynes Beach whaling station.

"It was the last in Australia, only closed in 1978. It was set up when Albany was founded, around 1830. Yankee whalers had been coming here since the 1790s."

"Damn Yankees," said Grey. Ryan smiled.

The NE2 put into Albany, a historic ships' bunkering port, for the scheduled reception.

"Ladies and gentlemen, boys and girls …"

Mallon was coming into his home territory.

"It's a pity we can't stop. You'd like the Earl Spencer, a National Trust building and one of the nicest pubs in Australia. It's way up that hill, with a great view of the town and the Sound. Did you ever go in the Crown in Belfast, George? That's National Trust—a different one of course."

"I did. Off duty, of course," said Burns. "A beautiful pub. Classic timber, marble and glass."

"Aye. It was fitted out by the same firm that fitted out the Titanic. As you'll know, it was never bombed. The IRA and Loyalists would all drink there without troubling each other. They maintained social distancing, of course. It was a place of truce and respect, as if the architecture soothed the soul."

"Not to mention the Guinness," added Burns. Mallon smiled wistfully.

"Now the Europa Hotel, the concrete monstrosity over the road, was bombed about six times."

"Deservedly so, in my opinion," said Burns. "I understand the provisional wing of the RIBA claimed responsibility."

"What?"

"The Royal Institute of British Architects."

"Right."

Mallon called Stuie from a call box. There was no answer.

"We'll check on Siobhan and Kieran when we get to Fremantle in two days," said Burns. "We can't do anything till then. I'm sure everything's alright."

The NE2 continued west along the coast, past West Cape Howe and Walpole. Mallon pointed in the direction of the great karri, jarrah and tingle forests of the south-west. Distant whisps of smoke were rising. "That'll be bush fires. It's the wrong time of the year for controlled burning. The forests are beautiful and unique—a remnant of Gondwanaland. The karri tree can grow to ninety metres—one of the tallest in the world. But the forests are slowly dying and drying out. They depend on very high rainfall, but it's been in long-term decline from climate change. Another thing we'll have fucked. Can you believe that publicly subsidised old growth logging is still going on? Turning the karris into a few dollars' worth of woodchips to make cardboard in Japan."

It was dark when the flashing of the lighthouse on Cape Leeuwin was sighted—the south-west tip of Australia, where the Southern Ocean meets the Indian Ocean. The NE2 turned to head north.

December 8, Geraldton

The small oil rig armada stopped at Geraldton for refuelling. After anchoring the rig, the tugs took turns to go in, so that there was always one on guard.

A few protesters had gathered outside the port gate but were not able to breach security. Some small boats tried to protest but got out of the way of the returning tugs, which evidently weren't taking prisoners. The armada was soon underway once more.

Later that day, South of Geraldton

"Jaevla greener," said Dag Wennevold to his first mate, Noah Gundersen. Wennevold, skipper of the free-range escort tug *Odin*, was a veteran seaman and one-time whaler. He had no time for fucking greenies. The *Sea Horse* had just come into view. They had been warned to expect protesters.

The tall superstructure of the rig had made it visible to the *Sea Horse* much sooner.

Emma and the others gathered at the gunwale as soon as it was sighted.

"Big, isn't it?" she said, feeling nervous.

"Yeah. Those are big tugs, too, and there's more of them than us," said Simon.

"We can live with that," said Dave, a veteran. "We took on the whole frigging Japanese whaling fleet. Anyway, two of those boats are tied to the rig and can't manoeuvre. And we have the RIBs." Three rigid, inflatable boats were being prepared. Fast and highly manoeuvrable, each with inflatable gunwales, they had been ideal for chasing and obstructing whalers. They would do the same to the tugs.

The RIBs were lowered into the water, engines started. Crews of three wearing wet suits, life jackets and crash helmets sat inside. They would try to board the rig.

When the armada was within two hundred metres, Daniels announced, "Hear this! Man your stations! We're going in!"

CHAPTER 31

Daniels steered the *Sea Horse* into the path of the towing tugs. They slowed but weren't going to stop.

"Full ahead. All you've got."

He accelerated out of the way, turned and repeated the manoeuvre.

Wennevold could see what they were doing and steered to intercept before they could get ahead of the towing tugs. The flotilla was being slowed enough for the RIBs to get close to the rig, but the hull was high, and ladders had been pulled up.

The RIB crews tried to board the tugs but were hit with water jets.

"You are endangering the safety of our crew," declared Wennevold by radio. "And you are contravening the International Marine Shipping Safety Convention. We request you cease your action immediately."

"You are endangering the safety of the planet," replied Daniels, "and all the creatures in the Great Australian Bight and Southern Ocean. We request that you fuck off back to Norway."

The confrontation went on for two hours. There were repeated near misses. Wennevold thought it was a strange term. To nearly miss was to hit, wasn't it?

He was not known for his patience. Something snapped.

"Full ahead. Brace yourselves, everyone," he called over the loudspeaker.

There was a grinding of steel on steel as the *Odin* hit the *Sea Horse* broadside, so hard that the protest ship tipped to forty-five degrees.

The tough hull of the *Odin* was built to withstand collisions. The *Sea Horse* was not and was listing badly.

Aw, shit, thought Wennevold, the red mist clearing. *Maybe it wasn't such a good idea.*

Daniels had not expected that they would hit them and was unable to steer out of the way. Only at the last minute, he shouted, "Brace yourselves!" over the loudspeaker.

Emma was helping in the galley. She tried to grab something but hit her head as she fell. She lay unconscious, her head bleeding. Others, too, were badly hurt. Jill was conscious but in pain. "Emma's hurt! Help!"

Daniels rushed to investigate. Fortunately, there was no one overboard. "Down here! There are people injured!"

First-aiders and one trained nurse attended to the casualties, while Daniels and the chief engineer inspected the damage. Water was pouring through a breach in the hull.

"Abandon ship!" ordered Daniels. The klaxon blared.

The crew took to the life rafts, stretchering the badly hurt into them. The RIBs arrived to help.

Daniels was the last to leave. Seeing that everyone was off safely, he got into one of the boats.

The *Odin* came alongside.

"Can we help?" called Wennevold over the loudspeaker. "Do you need medical assistance?" It was considered maritime etiquette to pick up survivors of sunken vessels, even if you'd just sunk them.

Daniels politely declined. "Go fuck yourselves, you fucking crazy Norgie knob-heads. You're up shit creek now."

"Where is this shit creek I keep hearing about, Noah?" Wennevold asked his first mate, Gundersen. "Is it in Australia, like *Wolf Creek*?"

Daniels was not one to put pride before the safety of his crew, but Rottnest Island was clearly visible, and the RIBs could get there before a tug. There would be a helicopter ambulance to nearby Perth, he thought. Aussies were good at that sort of thing. While Evans radioed an SOS, he drove the

RIB with Emma and the other worst hit to Rottnest. They were bouncing over the waves, but there was no time to lose. "Keep her head cushioned!" *Please, God, I've never lost anyone before. Don't let this be the first time.*

The RIBs reached the jetty. Daniels saw that Emma was still unconscious. He looked towards Perth, which was in the distance. There was a small speck in the sky. *Come on!* It got closer, louder. The air ambulance landed, its rotors slowing and stopping.

A medic and paramedic lifted Emma into a special stretcher and loaded her on before helping the others aboard.

The rotors spun furiously. The helicopter rose and roared off towards Perth.

Siobhan had settled Kieran down for the night and was having a glass of wine. She dozed off, then suddenly awoke. Had she heard something? She got up and went to check that Kieran was okay. There was a man sitting and holding the sleeping Kieran in his arms. Her mind raced with fear and panic.

"Oh my God! Please don't hurt him! What do you want …? I have money, jewels. Take that, but please don't …"

A hand and pad were around her face. As a nurse, she knew the smell of chloroform.

Kola and Dervishi bound and gagged Siobhan, put pantyhose over their heads and carried her and Kieran to a car outside, its licence plates covered. In scouting earlier, they had spotted the CCTV.

"That camera will be there to catch Coaly," said Kola, as they drove off. "Now we have our own bait to catch him. We can wait. Sooner or later, he's gonna turn up."

Stuie walked down the street as a car was passing. Sometimes he checked after dark. He could see if anyone was in.

The lights were off. He'd check again tomorrow.

The sinking quickly hit the news.

"This is the ABC News. Yesterday, off Rottnest Island near Perth, there was a collision between the environmental protest vessel, *Sea Horse*, and one of the three tugs escorting an oil drilling rig. The *Sea Horse* is reported to have sunk and several of its crew were injured, one critically. There were no casualties on the tug. The captains and crews of the oil rig flotilla have been ordered to remain in Fremantle, pending an investigation into the incident. The captain and crew members of the *Sea Horse* have been detained under the *Prevention of Terrorism Act*."

Louise Brailly heard the news and saw the papers. 'Gotcha!' was the headline of *SunMail*, one of Moorcock's tabloids. She knew from studying journalism that it was one of the most infamous headlines of its UK sister newspaper, *The Moon*, when the Royal Navy sank the Argentinian cruiser, *General Belgrano*, during the Falklands war in 1982. There was similar gloating commentary from other Moorcock media. "That's the way to deal with terrorists," said Andrew Nutt.

She was worried about Emma and the crew. What was going to happen to them? It was part of her story on efforts to protect the Bight.

"Eddie, darling. How do you fancy a trip to Perth?"

Canberra

Brad Callaghan was elated and punched the air. "Yes!" His face broke into a smile.

He phoned Brian 'Horatio' Nelson, Defence Minister.

"Brian! Have you heard the news? You can call off the naval escort. It won't be needed. I don't think anyone will try mixing it with these Norgies. They're like bloody Vikings. Just let anyone try stopping the rig now."

December 9, morning

The NE2 was south of Bunbury when they heard the news.

"I'm really worried about Emma," said Grey. He phoned Royal Perth Hospital. Emma had a serious head injury and was still in Critical Care.

"I've got to see her."

Mallon couldn't believe this was happening. First David, now Emma. He tried to be reassuring.

"Royal Perth has some of the best medical teams anywhere. Unlike the government, it doesn't need to keep bragging about everything it does being world-class."

"I'll put you off at Fremantle," said Burns. "We need to stop there. Sean is as anxious as you are to go ashore, and I have to go with him. After dark, of course."

"Aren't we due a visit and reception in Bunbury?" asked Captain Hoemberg.

"Bugger Bunbury." As he said it, Burns remembered the purported last words of King George V when told he would soon be well enough to visit the town of Bognor Regis for the sea air. "Bugger Bognor!"

The rig must be parked somewhere off Perth, thought Burns. *Perfect.*

December 9, afternoon

The NE2 entered Fremantle port via the Gage Roads sea lane. Mallon felt he'd come home.

After docking at C Wharf, Grey caught a taxi to the Royal Perth Hospital, and Burns went to collect the campervan parked nearby.

Emma opened her eyes. Where was she? Everything was blurred. She couldn't remember anything at first, then it all started coming back—the fight with the tugs, being in the galley when it all went black … She was worried. How were the others? Had anyone been killed?

The nurse saw that she was conscious and smiled.

A young neurologist came and examined her. "The MRI and CAT scans look good, but you've been badly concussed, so we'll keep you in for observation." He held a pencil in front of her face. "What do you see?"

"Two pencils."

"The double vision should go in a couple of days."

Grey arrived. The nurse smiled and drew the screens.

"You!"

"You!" They kissed.

"I told you I was worried," said Grey. "Was I right to be?"

"Of course not. What happened to the *Sea Horse*? How's everyone else? Was anyone hurt?"

"It sunk, unfortunately—rammed by one of the tugs. Apparently, there are a few in orthopaedics with fractures, and some people have been treated and let go. It seems that Andrew Daniels and some crew are being held in custody and others are on bail with orders not to leave Perth, presumably until there's some sort of hearing or trial."

"Does that mean I'll be arrested and have to stay in Perth for a while?"

"Possibly."

"I think you should let her rest now," said the nurse. "But you can stay beside her for visiting hours."

He watched over her while she slept.

After a while, two visitors arrived, a woman holding flowers and a man. He recognised Brailly and Eddie.

"Louise! Eddie! This is a nice surprise ... how?"

"We're covering the Bight story, as you know, and were worried when we heard the news, especially when we found out it was someone we know. How is she?"

"She's much better, but they're still not sure."

"We'll leave these and come back tomorrow. So happy the news is good, touch wood. Give her our love. How's your trip going? You'll be on your last leg now. It must be peaceful compared to Emma's trip, not having to fight with Viking marauders."

Burns and Mallon were outside Siobhan's house. Burns checked that the coast was clear. There was a CCTV in the street. "That'll be to look out for you," said Burns. Mallon went over the back fence. A dog barked.

"You should have been in the SAS," said Burns. "Okay, you have twenty minutes."

Mallon found the house empty. He came out to the fence. "You'd better come in."

There was a message and cell phone on the kitchen table. "You better ring your daughter on this number."

Mallon rang the number.

"Dad! Sorry, they've got me and Kieran! Don't come!"

Mallon heard the sound of a slap. "You bastards! Don't hurt them!" He guessed that the phone was on speaker.

"It's very nice to hear from you," said a voice. "We were expecting you to show up sooner or later. If you want to see your daughter and the brat again, you'd better pay us a visit. We do a swap. You for them. Understand?"

"Okay. Where to?"

"You better come alone. Somehow I don't think you'll be calling your friends the police." The voice gave an address.

"Where's Hamilton Hill?" asked Burns.

"It's not far. Look, I can't risk them. I'd better do as they say and go alone."

"If they've been hired by the same people as Moore, they'll want you dead. They'll kill you and Siobhan. They won't want any witnesses, even if they're wearing masks. They don't know I'm around. Let me deal with them."

"I didn't expect him to turn up so soon," said Kola. "I was hoping we'd have a nice long vacation here until Coaly turned up sometime later."

Kola knew they could stay as long as they liked in the house. The usual occupants, associates of Hoxha, were doing time in Casuarina Prison, WA's main maximum-security guesthouse.

"Now that he's on his way, go and put tape over their mouths to stop them squealing. Hey, and be careful. That woman bites."

He checked the band-aid on his hand.

CHAPTER 32

Burns and Mallon parked the van down the road from the house. "Wait here while I do a recce," said Burns.

He went through a hole in the back fence and could see a man smoking in the kitchen. Another appeared. There was no sign of anyone else. It looked like two of them. He couldn't see where Siobhan and Kieran might be. They must be locked in a back room or cellar.

He returned to the van. "Okay. Here's what we'll do."

Mallon knocked on the front door. A drawn curtain parted.

Dervishi opened the main door, pointing a gun through the fly screen. Kola was behind, in the hallway, also pointing a gun. Both guns were fitted with silencers.

"Get your hands up and get inside," snarled Dervishi. "And don't try anything."

"Frisk him," ordered Kola. Dervishi did a full body.

"He's clean, boss."

"So good of you to come," said Kola, smiling.

Mallon thought that if they had been cartoon characters, there would be dollar signs in their eyes. They were bounty hunters and their pay check—him—had just shown up.

Kola thought for a moment. What was it that the client had requested? Dead or alive? No, just dead. You had to get these things right.

"Let Siobhan and Kieran go. That's the deal," said Mallon.

"So sorry, but there's been a change of plan," said Kola. "We can't have witnesses, can we? Nothing personal. It's business."

"I really think you should reconsider. Especially as there's a unicorn behind you who gets mad when people are dishonest."

He was relieved to see that Burns had come through the kitchen and hoped he'd kept them talking just long enough.

"You crazy or what?"

Kola raised his Beretta to shoot. Before he could do so, Burns shot him in the back. As Dervishi turned, Burns shot him through the head.

There was blood everywhere.

"I wish you'd do this sort of thing with less noise and mess—like in the fillums," said Mallon. "You know I'm a bit squeamish."

He fingered his ears, which were ringing. Even with gas recoil sliders and suppressors, silenced guns were noisy, especially in a confined space.

They checked that there were no other mobsters around before looking for Siobhan and Kieran. They found them tied up and gagged in the basement.

"Oh, Dad. I was so scared. I was so worried," she sobbed. "I thought they were shooting you." They hugged.

"There. You're safe now."

He picked up Kieran and kissed him. "Such a brave boy."

He noticed her black eye and cut lip. "Did they … do anything else?"

She shook her head. "One tried. He didn't get very far."

"That's my girl. Siobhan, meet my friend and guardian angel, George."

"Thanks a million, George." She hugged him and planted a kiss on his cheek.

"The pleasure's all mine. I've heard so much about you."

"We'd better take you both home now," said Mallon. "We'll go out the back. You and Kieran had better not see what's in the hall."

Mallon led them through the kitchen and out through the backyard while Burns searched the bodies.

Burns had made an instinctive decision to kill both. He could have wounded one for questioning. From his training, he was well versed in getting people to talk. But these were foot soldiers. They wouldn't know who the client was or who was behind this. Even if they found out, he and Mallon were hardly going to go the police and appear in court.

Would they send more? As long as they were after Mallon, his daughter and grandson wouldn't be safe. Now there would be revenge in the mix. Those Albanians were vindictive buggers.

They all got into the campervan and drove on to Siobhan's house. They went in the back way.

It was good, but strange, for Mallon to be home. He was sad to see the pictures of David and Laura on the wall, sad that he could never return. He grabbed a few things.

"I'd like to stay, Siobhan, but you need to rest," said Mallon. "And we need to be on our way."

"Oh, Dad! What's happening? When will all this end? Will we ever see you again except in Casuarina?"

"Don't worry, I have a plan. You'll be safe tonight, but these two are bound to have friends. From tomorrow, you'll have to hide out where they can't find you and the police don't come snooping. Don't let neighbours or anyone know where you are. I'll be in touch and we'll all be together before too long."

In the dark, Burns hadn't spotted the concealed CCTV watching the road as they left the house in Hamilton Hill.

It was late, but Mallon took Burns for a Guinness at Clancy's where they could sit outside in the semi-darkness and he wouldn't be seen.

"Slainte," said Burns. They clinked glasses. "You know, we're not a bad team."

"I've enjoyed working with you, George. Mind, I've only got seven lives left. Ah, that's good. What if I need a leak? I'd better not show myself inside."

"Bushes over there," suggested Burns, always looking out for his team.

After their initial success in identifying Mallon as the chief Ned Coaly suspect, DCI John Papas, WA Police Lead Investigator, was disappointed that they were still having no luck on leads—no calls intercepted, no appearances or attempts to contact his daughter.

Assistants watching Siobhan Mallon's house on CCTV had seen what looked like her and her son being bundled into a car by two men at night. The licence plate was hidden. It was hard to make them out, but neither was Mallon.

Mallon could have arranged it. There was no reason to suspect anyone of wanting to harm them. A follow-up visit was made the next day, but Siobhan was out, and the neighbours knew nothing. If she didn't show up, they would investigate her whereabouts further. She was still the best lead to Mallon.

Then a new lead appeared. There was a hidden CCTV watch on the house in Hamilton Hill, which had been a centre for criminal activity involving bikies. Bikie gangs had given Papas's and other Australian police forces a lot of grief, often being associated with drug pushing, extortion and other shady activities. A vigilant police assistant spotted Siobhan, Kieran and Mallon. "There's also another man. They're all getting into a campervan leaving from across the road. It's dark, but you can just make out its rego."

On arrival in Hamilton Hill during the early hours, the police discovered the bodies.

Papas had a briefing session with his team.

"From their DLs, the deceased have been identified as from Melbourne and implicated in gangland killings. They're hit men. Why would they be in Freo? Why would the woman and boy be in that house if they hadn't been taken and kidnapped as hostages? Who was it to trap and kill, if not Mallon? Who would want Mallon dead?

Who would kill the mobsters if it wasn't Mallon? I want all traffic units alerted to look out for the campervan. I want the public alerted to look out for him too, but don't issue his rego. They might be tempted to confront him or even ask for a Ned Coaly autograph. More importantly, we need to use the advantage. Mallon won't know that we know about the van. Ask filling stations to look out for it. Focus on Perth. Why would he leave? He's close to his daughter and grandson and will want to protect them against a possible revenge attack. It's what mobsters do. They're bad losers."

December 10

The NE2 remained in Fremantle harbour, moored at C Wharf.

Nearby, the Rottnest Island Ferry prepared to depart, a catamaran with powerful, pulsating turbo engines. Happy Rotto campers were parked, offloading their luggage and bikes for loading onto the ferry. The air was charged with excitement.

Among the throng were Grobbelaar and Boonzaaier, helped by Moody, Jonesy and Beattie. They were loading drones, explosives, a rocket launcher and machine guns from the boat into the campervan. They'd have to sleep in swags. There would be no sleeping room in the van.

"Okay, boys. Off you go," said Burns. "We'll see you later."

"That's our holiday cruise over," said Boonzaaier as they drove off. "It's time to start earning our pay."

"Ja," said Grobbelaar.

They both knew the plan. They would shadow the NE2 up the coast. There was a growing risk that the NE2's involvement in bombings past and future would be discovered. Each port visit could be a police and security forces trap.

They would do reconnaissance, discretely checking before each visit, appearing as typical tourists browsing the unique Western Australian country. If the NE2 was intercepted at sea, they would take out one or two of the LNG plants from land. At least they'd have fulfilled quite a lot of the contract for the team.

They would drive at night and wait for the boat to catch up. It would be less visible if there was any tailing or later investigation. You couldn't be too careful.

"Pity we can't catch up with our old school rugby mates," said Boonzaaier. "There are more here in Perth than back home."

Brailly and Eddie were having a morning stroll along the quayside after breakfast at E-Shed Markets. They saw the camper being loaded and then driving off.

"That's odd," said Brailly.

There was a radio news bulletin.

"Earlier today two bodies were found at a house in Hamilton Hill, near Fremantle. Police are investigating, but it is believed that it was a gangland incident. The house has links to the Undertakers motorcycle gang. The incident also involved the kidnapping of the daughter and grandson of Sean Mallon, wanted in connection with the Ned Coaly bombings. Mallon was seen in Fremantle and the public are asked to contact the police if they see him. They are urged not to approach him, as he is believed to be armed and dangerous."

"That's a worry," said Burns. "We must have been picked up on CCTV somewhere. It didn't mention me or the van, so hopefully they didn't get an ID. It was dark, but we had to do it. We'll have to be more careful in future."

Later that morning, there was a welcome reception attended by the Mayor of Fremantle and other local dignitaries.

Grey came to say goodbye. "I have to be with Emma while she's still in hospital, and she's been ordered to stay in Perth while the investigation is going on."

"I understand," said Burns. "It's been really good having you with us. We couldn't have done it without you and Mike. He'll miss you for the last leg—we all will. Give my love to Emma and wish her a speedy recovery."

"I will," said Grey. "Good luck."

He didn't exactly know what the last leg was, except that it had something to do with the gas industry.

"Thanks," said Burns. They shook hands, and Burns patted him on the arm.

"I'd like to be at the final reception in Darwin if I can," said Grey.

"Please do, but don't worry if you have Christmas commitments." Burns hoped that things weren't getting too hairy by then. "You're a very lucky man to have Emma. She's a gutsy and lovely girl. Take good care of her."

"I know. I will."

Brailly and Eddie were at the hospital as Grey arrived.

"Hi, John. We're just leaving," said Brailly. "Thanks again for telling us your story, Emma. You and the other crew were incredibly brave. It's wonderful to see you getting better. We thought we'd stay around for the judicial hearing, so we'll see you soon. Did you hear that Sean Mallon was seen in Fremantle last night?"

"Was he? Really?" said Grey

The police did a check with the Department of Transport on the registered owner of the campervan—Michael M. House.

"Wasn't it pretty obvious to you that it was a false name?" enquired the police officer, DC Mal Power.

"How are we supposed to know every flippin' Aussie name?" replied the Department Licensing Officer, Tran Lim.

Brailly and Ed watched the NE2 leave.

"That's Rottnest Island," said Brailly, pointing. They could just see the island's silhouette twenty-three kilometres away. The flashing lights of its two lighthouses cut through the twilight.

"Dutch explorers called it *rottenest* or rat's nest, because of the quokkas. They're really cute marsupials, almost as cute as you." She kissed him. "There's something funny going on, Eddie. You know, when I mentioned that Sean Mallon had been seen in Freo, they didn't seem that surprised, like they knew something. Then there's the NE2. What were those men loading into that campervan? What's it really up to? Why is it that wherever it goes, things seem to blow up? Sunsets are so romantic, aren't they, Eddie? Shall we go back to the hotel?"

They were staying at the nearby Esplanade as a special treat.

CHAPTER 33

Dreiser had followed with dismay the story of the sinking of the *Sea Horse*—the people hurt; the girl nearly killed. It seems she was the same pretty young girl who'd been in the news for blocking the coal railway. She was very brave. Now they were out to punish the captain and crew, jail them for terrorism, while the *Sea Horse* captain said they were rammed. They needed a good lawyer.

He could only give suggestions and advice on military operations. Execution was not his competence or responsibility. They could only take out the rig if it was safe to do so.

"Alright, lower it now," said Burns.

They were preparing the sub.

"You're alright with doing this? You don't have to. The boys here are being paid for it."

"I wouldn't miss it for the world," said Mallon, ready in his wet suit.

Burns, Bazza and Mallon loaded the mines and climbed inside. Martin and Mann were already on board, checking the controls.

"Full steam ahead, Mister Mann."

"Aye, aye, Cap'n."

"You okay, Sean?" asked Burns.

"It's exciting. I've got Yellow Submarine playing in my head."

"Same here," said Bazza. "Me gran knew Ringo Starr."

Mann steered the sub towards the west side of Rottnest Island, where the rig and three tugs where anchored. Burns observed them through the periscope, silhouetted against the western glow of the setting sun.

He decided that two mines would do the job and lifted them into the airlock. In turn, he, Bazza and Mallon went through. He and Bazza carried the mines. He checked that Mallon was okay and Mallon gave a thumbs up. By torchlight, he led them under the hull of the rig, and they positioned the mines on either side. For each, Bazza positioned the mine while Mallon activated the magnetic clamping control.

Burns led them back to the sub, and they returned to the NE2.

"Let's be under way, Mister Hoemberg."

"Very good, Mister Phelps."

The NE2 headed north.

When the NE2 was two hours away, Burns asked Mallon to do the honours of activating the remote firing device.

Off Rottnest Island, Western Australia

Dag Wennevold was in a deep sleep on the *Odin*. He'd had too much aquavit the night before. He was feeling bad about sinking that boat, even if it was full of green leftists. Now they were going to jail them all for terrorism. Thank God that kid hadn't been killed, but with her head injury, she could end up a vegetable. In his guilt, he had been dreaming about cabbages, broccoli and lettuce. He'd hated greens since he was a kid.

He awoke with a start, his ears ringing. He hoped it wasn't his tug. There was the sound of an emergency klaxon. He opened the outside door. There were searchlights on the rig. It was sinking fast. There were only three on watch on the rig, and he could see them on the emergency escape craft.

The submersible quickly submersed beneath the waves.

"Fuck me," said Wennevold.

"You enjoyed doing that, didn't you?" said Burns.

"I did as a matter of fact," said Mallon. "That one was for Emma. Do you think there was anyone on it?"

"Probably a couple on watch in case the protesters tried anything, but I don't imagine they stayed around to go down with the rig like the band on the Titanic."

"My great grandfather helped build it."

"What, the rig?"

"The Titanic," said Mallon. "It was built in Belfast. Before the partition in 1922, Catholics were allowed to work at Harland and Wolff."

There was a news announcement on the radio

"Last night, the oil drilling rig being towed to the Great Australian Bight sank off Rottnest Island, near Perth. Police suspect it may be a revenge attack for the earlier sinking of the protest ship, *Sea Horse*. Members of the Sea Defender protest organisation have been arrested for questioning.

Yesterday, the captains of the tugs escorting the drilling rig were exonerated from blame in the collision incident. Captain Andrew Daniels of the *Sea Horse* has been charged with dangerous conduct, under the *Marine Safety Act*, and with being an accessory to terrorism."

December 11, Zürich

"It has been a wonderful evening," said Anna. "I so enjoyed the opera. Madame Butterfly always makes me cry. And the dinner has been exquisite. Your company is always very agreeable, Herr Dreiser."

Dreiser suddenly felt shy. "Anna, I think you can call me Wolfgang after all these years."

"Wolfgang. There, I've said it." She smiled.

A message came through on his phone. He wanted to run around the restaurant, lifting his shirt as footballers do when they've scored a goal.

"You look very happy about something," said Anna.

"I have secured a very good business deal."

"They don't usually make you smile that much."

"The rig has been sunk!" said Grey.

Emma punched the air, dislodging her drip and monitoring lines from their clamps.

"That's amazing. I'm so happy ... Was anyone hurt?"

"Apparently not."

"Who can have done it. Did you have a hand in it?" She put on a deep policeman's voice. "Where were you between the hours of twelve and two," she laughed.

"I had nothing to do with it," said Grey. "Honest."

She looked at him suspiciously.

"Look, I can't say, as I don't know exactly what," said Grey. "But big things are at play; professionals are at work. You don't need to go protesting any more. I just want to look after you, keep you safe. You're more precious than anything to me. I love you."

"I love you, too."

"What the hell is going on down there?" enquired Jarl Bjornsen, CEO of Energor, calling PM Turbott from Oslo. "I thought you'd locked up all your greenies."

"Rest assured we will punish whoever is responsible, Jarl," replied Turbott.

He had developed a personal relationship with Bjornsen, as with all his corporate chums. He had personally intervened to ensure that drilling in the Bight was approved. It was all part of cutting 'green tape', all that unnecessary 'protecting the environment' nonsense. *God gave us dominion over nature, which means it's there for us to use to boost the economy, jobs and party coffers*, he reminded himself.

"I guarantee there will be full naval protection for future rigs. There will be no recurrence."

"You're damn right there won't be," said Bjornsen. "This has been terrible publicity for Energor and our Board has decided to pull out. I'll be sending you the bill for the rig."

"But ..."

Bjornsen hung up.

Turbott looked to the heavens for guidance.

The news came in:

"Today, Norwegian oil company Energor announced that it has discontinued its plans for oil drilling in the Great Australian Bight. Energor Australia Director, Sven Torstein, issued a statement at a press conference today. 'Following a holistic review of its exploration portfolio, Energor has concluded that the project's potential is not commercially competitive compared to other exploration opportunities in the company.'

"Damian Sproake of the Australian Petroleum Industry Group commented: 'The company's decision to dump the project was disappointing for South Australians, who would have benefited economically, and for the wider Australian community, which needs new energy supplies. The project exploration activity has been subject to an extreme campaign of false and exaggerated claims that deliberately overstated the risks and ignored the potential benefits. It is to be hoped that the government will continue to pursue development of this resource, which is vital for Australian energy security.'

"Resources Minister Brad Callaghan declined to comment on speculation that he had invited China to drill for oil if they would write off the cost of the lost rig. Yesterday, the Green Party put forward a proposal for legislation on World Heritage Protection for the Bight."

⁓

Siobhan had taken Kieran to stay with a friend near Kalamunda, in the Darling Hills. She came with Kieran to see Emma. Grey was at Emma's hospital bedside.

"Look, I heard what happened, and I'm sorry I didn't come to see you before, but I was otherwise detained. I was kidnapped and held hostage. You may have heard in the news."

"It must have been terrifying," said Emma.

"It was. Someone must have paid the murdering thugs to kill Dad, me and Kieran, and they'd have done it if not for Dad's friend … He dealt with them good and proper. It's better I don't say any more. The police haven't caught up with me yet, and I'm not telling them anything if they do. Dad said we had to go into hiding until he finishes a job and can meet up. I don't know what he's involved in or how he's going to get out of this if he's done even half of what they say he's done. Unless he can escape the country."

⁓

"I want someone nailed for this!" shouted ACP Commissioner Andrew Robb. "Do whatever it takes!"

WA Police Commissioner Jim Bertoloni held the phone away from his ear. "We're on it."

"It has to be these green-left terrorists," said Robb. "They're more than capable and they have a record. In 1980, a limpet mine was used to sink *Sierra*, an illegal whaling vessel, which docked in Lisbon after a confrontation with the *Sea Shepherd*. Later that year, about half the legal Spanish whaling fleet was sunk in a similar fashion. Evidence enough. If they could do it in 1980, then they can do it now. And what about this Ned Coaly? I understand there's been a sighting in Fremantle."

"There's a full watch for him and a vehicle," said Bertoloni. "We have the registration. Once again, he's gone underground, but rest assured we'll find him. After all, it was us, the WA force, who uncovered his identity."

"It's a bit of a coincidence that the rig sinking happened at the same time that Mallon was in town. See if there's any connection. Coal seems to be his thing. But maybe he supplied the greenies with mines. Maybe he got hold of some for Monk's Point and had a couple left over."

There was a major hunt for the perpetrators of the rig bombing. Extended security tests began at Perth Airport. The hunt for Mallon was stepped up.

Damian Sproake spotted the sequence. He was still furious over the sinking of the rig but also alarmed for oil and gas industry member companies and their projects. As part of the fossil fuel and climate denial club, he had felt for the coal industry, but coal was not his territory. Oil, on the other hand, was, and gas definitely was.

Mallon showing up in Fremantle just when the rig was sunk was too much of a coincidence. He had to be involved. He knew about bombs and could dive. The whale huggers were possible but unlikely suspects. If Mallon was now attacking oil, then gas could be next. He had to be stopped before he did any more harm, before others got the same idea. There had already been attacks on oil and gas pipelines in the US and elsewhere.

The kidnapping and shooting were clearly an attempt to flush Mallon out using paid assassins. Who would want Mallon eliminated?

He called Greg Hutchings. They had both gone to Geelong Grammar, one of Australia's most exclusive schools, Prince Charles and Robert

Moorcock among its illustrious old boys. You had to use your networks. Mateship—the spirit of Australia.

The police eventually traced Siobhan and Kieran to the Darling Hills.

"We know you and Kieran were forcibly abducted and have identified the felons. Who killed them?"

"I've nothing to say to you."

"Was it your father? Between you and me, he did a good job, ridding the world of scum like that. It won't count as murder if you say."

"I'm saying nothing."

"Who was the other man?"

"I've no idea who you're talking about. Now fuck off, and leave us alone."

In Melbourne, Hoxha was somewhat disappointed to hear of the result of the expedition to Fremantle. He sincerely hoped that no one had grassed. The police were snooping around in Melbourne, asking too many questions. They didn't seem to like people kidnapping women and kids. Fair enough. But they didn't mind professionals—his boys—being murdered. They dared to call them scum.

But if the boys snitched, well … Betraying client confidentiality was unethical, unforgivable. If they had, it would be just as well that Mallon had done the job.

The boys still had to be avenged, for honour. But the contract from the client remained unfulfilled—no results, no payment. So it might have to be pro bono. He would claim expenses as tax deductible. Wait, that was unnecessary. He didn't pay tax.

Then he received a call—not just a renewed contract for Mallon, but a new contract. It was unusual, but he wasn't complaining. Protection rackets were part and parcel of his core business portfolio. But protecting property? Normally, clients didn't ask for protection. You told them they were getting it or else. This was a new business—diversification. There was a lot of property to protect, most of it in the west. It would need extra resources, extra personnel. He had to set up this new business and attend to this Mallon once and for all. If you wanted something done properly, you had to do it yourself.

CHAPTER 34

December 13

As the NE2 sailed into view off Geraldton, the Recce Boys did a pass along The Esplanade and port area.

"I wish we knew where to find a good coffee," said Boonzaaier. He knew a liquid sandwich was out—they were on the job. There was no sign of police or spooks.

"All clear." He radioed to Burns and they waited in a side street, weapons ready. They drove on when the boat landed. They knew it was better not to be seen in the same place. You couldn't be too careful.

The NE2 tied up for a short visit and reception.

Ryan was missing his buddy, but the show had to go on.

"Ladies and gentlemen, boys and girls. First of all, Doctor John Grey sends his apologies that he can't be with you today. He had to leave the ship on account of a sick friend."

As usual, Mallon stayed hidden on the boat. He was having coffee with Burns. "Geraldton's most famous for its big crayfish export industry—that's lobster—especially to Asian markets. But it's also rich in maritime history. You could say it suffers from chronic wind; even the people and trees lean at forty-five degrees due to the relentless westerlies. It was discovered long before Captain Cook by ships crashing into it."

"Not to mention discovered by the Indigenous Australians who've only lived here for sixty thousand years," said Burns.

"Correct," said Mallon. "Anyways, this part of the coast and nearby islands and reefs are littered with shipwrecks. The most famous is the Dutch ship *Batavia*, wrecked on the Abrolhos Islands in the early 1600s on a voyage to Java. The tale of madness, mutiny and murder was infamous. I think it was a hundred and fifteen people murdered, making *Lord of the Flies* look like a school picnic."

Canberra

Brad Callaghan smirked as he signed federal approvals for oil and gas drilling in the Abrolhos Islands, Shark Bay and Ningaloo Reef.

His advisor, Colin Steadman, had noticed that Callaghan had developed a nervous twitch but didn't like to say anything. "Minister, you are aware that these are all World Heritage?"

"So is our oil and gas."

"I mean, people may protest. These sites have special protection."

"Let them. So does our oil and gas industry."

Hoxha decided to pay a visit to Perth. His police informant tipped him off that Mallon was believed to still be in town. He would get his drug networks looking for Mallon. They were much better at watching out than the police—always on the streets, looking over their shoulders, looking into cars for interesting things to finance their habit.

He felt like a trip to the warmth of the west, to do some business and see to his networks. He would see what he could find out about what happened to Coca and Dervishi. At least, they had done something useful. The airlines were funny about letting you take artillery on their planes, and the boys had taken extra irons and ammo and had stashed them somewhere safe. You never knew when things were going to come in handy.

Burns conducted his daily toolbox talk with the boys. "As you know, communications have had to be strictly limited throughout the mission. But we'll especially need to keep silent up the coast. As part of Australia's special relationship with the US, one of the spying stations in the US global Echelon network is near here and they have another up the coast at Exmouth. They're linked to the main Australian station at Pine Gap and then to Langham in the US. They listen for everything."

"Do they know who just farted?" asked Moody.

The NE2 sailed on, within sight of the Abrolhos Islands.

Ryan checked his notes. "I read that these are high conservation value; they have unique ecosystems, rare fauna and flora, as well as fisheries and tourism. But I heard on the news that the government has just torn up protections for here, Shark Bay and Ningaloo Reef, and the EPA has issued licences for oil and gas drilling."

"Why does that not surprise me?" said Mallon. "Useless twats. Just let anyone try drilling here or in Shark Bay and Ningaloo. Over my dead body." He thought of David and their times diving there. "There's another bit of history near here. In November 1941, the cruiser *HMAS Sydney* encountered the German raider *HSK Kormoran*, which was disguised as a Dutch merchant vessel. Although superior in armament, the *Sydney* allowed the *Kormoran* too close. With the advantage of surprise, the *Kormoran* uncovered its guns and used all of them, sinking the *Sydney* with all hands. In its last moments, the *Sydney* sank the *Kormoran*, killing half of its crew. They only found the wrecks in 2008. There's a memorial to the *Sydney* in Geraldton. Over a thousand young men died for the beliefs of one madman in Berlin."

"Not to mention eighty-five million others in the whole of World War Two," said Burns. "The madness of war. I know it well. It's a sad tale, but it shows the power of deception. We need to keep it up ourselves or we'll be sunk."

Hoxha and his cousin, Shefqet Shehu, arrived in Perth Airport, hired a car and checked in at the Esplanade Hotel, Fremantle.

"This is nice. Classy," said Shehu.

They collected hardware from a business associate. Coca and Dervishi had delivered a collection for safekeeping and wholesaling.

That evening, they paid a visit to Mallon's daughter's house in Fremantle. This time there would be no hostage-taking, this time an eye for an eye. *Kill a man, you kill him once. Kill someone he loves, he dies every day for the rest of his life.*

They were out. The neighbour said they had gone away, although he didn't know where. Too bad, but the business priority, the contract, was to find and kill Mallon. Hoxha had already organised for his network to be looking out for Mallon and the van. They could look for the bitch and brat as well.

Then there was also the new business. He couldn't immediately spare any of his compatriots from Melbourne. Locals would have to do. The bikies. They liked to cruise the highways. They were nasty, too—his kind of guys. The ideal solution.

Siobhan hadn't needed her dad's warning to lie low and stay out of sight. She knew that others could come after her and Kieran. She took time off from her agency nursing work so that no one would find her at Fremantle Hospital and didn't give them or anyone else her temporary address. It was safer away from Fremantle, but she needed something from the house.

She parked along the road and was just about to get out when she saw them outside her house. Her heart started pounding. They must have known what she looked like from all the publicity. She kept her head down until they'd gone, then drove to pick up Kieran. She'd left him with a friend.

She drove to the house in the hills, took Kieran inside, locked all the doors and windows and drew the curtains. She gave Kieran his dinner, put him to bed, turned down the lights and read for a while. When would this nightmare end?

It was after dark when Siobhan felt most vulnerable. With the lights on, she could be seen but not see out, so she had taken to going to bed early, but with a gap in the curtains so that she could see lights coming up the hill.

She was just dozing off when she heard the noise of motor bikes approaching. Beams from headlights flashed through the curtain.

She slept ready to go, with the beds looking like they were occupied and the globe in the bedroom removed so no one could take a close look. She picked up Kieran, went through the back door, hurried to the cubby in the bush and waited, her hand over Kieran's mouth in case he woke up.

There was also a van. She heard someone trying the front door. One came round the back. Then another. Voices. They shone a torch inside and then kicked in the door. She heard shooting with silencers—recognising the sound from the last time—and the sound of a metal can. She kept her head down. How did they know she was here? Only the police knew …

A flicker of light, then the inside burst into flame as the curtains caught alight. Soon the house was an inferno.

The bikes rode off, followed by the van, the headlights disappearing down the hill.

She called the police on Emergency and a patrol car eventually came with a fire truck.

"I want protection," she demanded. "It's pretty bleeding obvious that one of your lot is a mob informant. Or would you like me to tell the newspapers?"

She knew that although they had cleaned up their act, the WA police had a history of bent coppers, and the press was always game for a juicy story.

She and Kieran went to stay the night with another friend nearby. The mob were after her dad and were now out to get her and Kieran. The police wouldn't investigate in a hurry. They were always quick to protect their own; they'd say she let her address slip to someone. But she knew she hadn't. Here was a clear link to the bastards. She'd get them. She didn't want the publicity—the mob might think they'd killed them—but it would be in the news anyway. The police would be forced to investigate if exposed by the press.

Who did she know? Emma must have contacts—she'd been in the news enough. She was still in town to appear in court.

There was a news report: "In the Perth Hills last night, a house burned down in suspicious circumstances. Two occupants escaped unhurt. They are reported to be Siobhan and Kieran Mallon, relatives of Sean Mallon, the alleged Ned Coaly. The police are treating it as a possible arson attack. The attackers have not been identified, but motorcycles were heard in the area."

Brailly and Eddie were still in Perth for the Sea Defender judicial hearing. Brailly could still work remotely on her other projects and they were having a nice time, even though they'd downsized from the Esplanade to the Local Hotel in South Fremantle. Brailly had been concerned and puzzled when she'd heard about the kidnapping of Siobhan and Kieran

Mallon and the bikie gang link. It was another element of the Mallon mystery, and she had a sense that something else was going on, not just in Australia but elsewhere in the world. Now there was another incident involving them, another possible bikie gang involvement. Why would anyone go after a mother unless they were really after her father? Who would hold such a grudge against him, except the PM and half of Australia? If only she could speak to Siobhan …

Her phone rang.

"Louise Brailly? This is Siobhan Mallon."

CHAPTER 35

Siobhan left her car in Midland and took a train to Maylands. She waited in the Sherbert Café.

Brailly and Eddie arrived soon after. They had taken the train from Fremantle.

"Siobhan? I'm Louise, and this is Eddie … What a lovely cafe strip. This place is just delightful."

"Thanks for coming," said Siobhan. She shook their hands, and Brailly gave her a hug.

"What you've been through …" said Brailly.

"It's been hard and frightening. I've been out of my mind worrying about Dad. I'd have come see you in Freo, but I don't feel safe near my home. I know they're watching."

"They?"

"Look, I want what I say to be anonymous, off the record. Sorry, I know the ACP won't respect your journalistic rights and may come and do a raid on your knicker drawer." Eddie gave Brailly a knowing look. "I haven't told the police anything, and I'm not going to. I have no idea where he is, and I wouldn't tell you or anyone else if I did. He hasn't hurt anyone—alright, there's been a bit of property damage—but he did it because of what happened to David. Now someone's out to kill him, and they've tried to kill me and Kieran. I want to know who put them up to it. The police aren't trying hard in their investigation; they're out to get Dad. They won't admit it, but there's also an informant in the police. There has to be. That's how they found us."

"What can you say about the attackers?"

"The kidnappers were Balkan or something, maybe Albanians—hit men. I didn't get a good look at the attackers in the hills, but I reckon they were bikies."

"Two bodies were found at the bikie house. One with his head blown off, apparently. That doesn't sound like your Dad's style."

Siobhan knew something, thought Brailly, but she wasn't saying. She changed the subject.

"What, you mean you thought you'd killed them?" snarled Hoxha. "I said shoot them, then burn the house down to destroy the evidence."

"I can't explain it," said Dean Nalder. "We could see them in their beds, I swear. We did the job. Nothing could have got out of that fire."

Nalder was a proud leader of the Undertakers and a veteran of the WA bikie gang wars. In his younger years, he had been involved in the revenge attacks on a bent copper suspected of shooting a gang leader. These included firebombing the historic Ora Banda Inn near Kalgoorlie, bought by the copper upon retirement. He'd helped to blow up the copper's car with him in it.

Nalder and all of his gang had been regular guests of the Prison Service. A history of violent crime was the minimum qualification for membership of the Undertakers—documented failure of a Police Check an essential credential.

"Now it's all over the news!" shouted Hoxha. "Now she and the brat will have some kind of police protection. Protection! That's our job! Our informant was relying on you doing a clean job, and now he's having to watch his arse. We'll save the bitch and brat for later. We don't forget. For now, we concentrate on the main contracts, getting Coaly and the protection business. Don't fail me again if you know what's good for you."

"We won't. You can rely on us."

The NE2 followed the Ningaloo Coast on the way to Exmouth.

Being over the Ningaloo Reef was poignant for Mallon.

"It's where David taught me to dive. It's over two hundred and fifty kilometres long, and it's Australia's largest fringing coral reef, the only large reef positioned very close to a landmass. It's more accessible, and many say prettier, than the Great Barrier Reef."

He looked towards the coast. "The land is hot and harsh up here, semi-desert, but the Yinikutira people have inhabited this area for over thirty thousand years. I used to know an elder, Ann Preest—lovely lady. She told me a story about something that happened here involving a shipwreck. Around 1875, a sailing barque, the *Stefano*, left Dubrovnik and picked up a shipment of coal in Cardiff, Wales, for transport to Hong Kong. The crew of seventeen were all very young. In a terrible storm, the ship was wrecked on the reef, and seven of the crew drowned. The survivors headed south, helped by Aboriginal people who provided food and water. All but two perished in the desolate conditions and a cyclone. With no hope remaining, they headed inland and, close to death, found the Aboriginal people who had earlier helped them. They were nursed back to health, on occasion even carried by the women, until their strength returned. They were welcomed into the group, learning about the land, the customs and the language. Nearly six months after the wreck, they were picked up by a pearling boat and taken to Fremantle, where they were feted, before heading back north with gifts for their saviours. Later, they were repatriated to Croatia. Until then, the people up here were thought to be savages, cannibals even. It's a shame Europeans haven't been as generous to the First Nations. It's such a beautiful, special place, the reef. Besides the corals, the marine life is amazing—the turtles, dugongs, whales and whale sharks. The whale sharks come from March to August, so we won't see them."

"We're making good time," said Burns. "I think you deserve a dive, in memory of David."

The NE2 moored and Burns called time out for R&R. Mallon, Ryan and Burns swam together as Mallon had done with David, pointing out and acknowledging things as they went.

"It's simply wonderful," said Burns, as they relaxed on the deck afterwards.

"It certainly is," said Mallon.

"It must be hard for you, coming back."

"Yes, but special all the same. David was part of this." He paused. "It's hard to stomach that this will probably be gone in twenty or thirty years thanks to the fossil fools."

"Who knows where we'll all be," said Burns. "It's all going to turn ugly. I think we both know that."

They knew it was to be the last calm moment before the coming storm.

The NE2 put into the Exmouth Marina for a short reception.

"Ladies and gentlemen, boys and girls …"

On his reconnaissance in July, Burns had learned that Exmouth, on the North West Cape, was a fairly new township that had arisen from a World War II air and submarine base. It remained the home of a US Navy Communications Station. They would have to keep their heads down and keep communications to a minimum.

The Recce Boys did their routine pass-through in Exmouth and signalled the all clear before driving off.

"We're a bit low on fuel," said Boonzaaier. "We'd better top up."

The filling station CCTV in Carnarvon picked up the camper. It showed one man, tall, who didn't look like Mallon. Was the other man the one who'd been spotted in Hamilton Hill? The van was heading north.

"Get patrol cars on the lookout and tail them," said DCI John Papas. "See where they go. Tail them until we get reinforcements up there. We know they're armed."

Hoxha's police informant reported that the van had been spotted refuelling, not in Perth, but at Carnarvon, eight hundred and ninety kilometres north.

"Carnarvon? Where the fuck's that?" Hoxha was annoyed that he couldn't attend to Mallon in Perth.

"I haven't seen it, boss." Shehu thought Hoxha was talking about his fur hat.

Led by Nalder, six Undertakers headed north up the Brand Highway on their Harleys. There was no time for the scenic route.

Tim Gleeson had been asked anonymously to defend Captain Andrew Daniels and the crew of the *Sea Horse*. They had been charged with intent to commit a terrorist act for their attack on the oil rig flotilla and as accessories to the subsequent sinking of the rig. He'd heard about it in the news. *God, they've got balls,* he thought. He reviewed the case notes. Good Lord, there was Emma Johnson. She was a feisty thing—she'd now done coal and oil. Whatever was next? Gas?

He read on. The inquiry into the collision between the *Odin* and *Sea Horse* had found Captain Andrew Daniels and his crew guilty of dangerous misconduct under marine safety law. On the testimony of Dagmar Wennevold and the crew of the *Odin*, as well as the other crew of the other tugs, the investigation had found that the SH had deliberately blocked the path of the *Odin*, and Daniels was to blame for the collision. Daniels denied this and claimed that the *Odin* had turned to deliberately ram his ship, saying it was no accident. He said that the *Odin* had accelerated to hit his ship full on at speed, not slowing to a glancing collision, as would be the case if he'd crossed their path.

The extent of damage to his ship would prove this. Daniels stated that he was an experienced seaman with twenty-five years without an accident.

Why would he risk his ship and crew by attempting suicide? Only a general statement on damage to the *Sea Horse* had been provided to the inquiry, but underwater pictures and a detailed technical report had not been released. Energor's Australian director and a team of lawyers had made the case for the company. A local pro bono solicitor had acted for Sea Defender.

Besides Daniels, no other witnesses from the *Sea Horse* had been called, as they were accessories and unreliable witnesses. There was no video evidence from them. Phones had been lost in the survival situation. One claimed he had filmed the incident and that the police had confiscated his phone. They denied they had it. Now the government and Attorney General wanted to throw the anti-terrorism book at them.

It was clear to Gleeson that the prosecution was rigged.

Monk's Point

A frogman was inspecting the structural integrity of the remaining piles. It was difficult with all the steelwork and other debris from the coal gantries. He found an unexploded mine at the foot of a pile that was still standing.

Bomb Disposal later inspected the mine and decided not to remove it—limpets were always booby trapped to prevent removal. They decided on a controlled explosion with the approval of Commander Linda Crosby, head of the Australian Secret Service.

"The type and markings on the mine indicated it was Chinese-made and military-grade," said Crosby, briefing her team. "It doesn't look like the sort of thing Mallon could easily have gotten his hands on, and there were others at Monk's Point. Mallon's bombs were home-made. No, someone else is at work. Do we have any info on what might have been used on the oil rig?"

Grey climbed the stairs to the court viewing gallery. He spotted Brailly and Eddie and tried to avoid eye contact. She made him feel uncomfortable. She was smart, her brain always whirring round, thinking of questions and always probing. He sensed she suspected something about him.

"Oh, hello, John," said Brailly.

"Hi, Louise. Hi, Eddie."

"Come and join us," said Brailly. "Let's hope Gleeson can pull a rabbit out of the hat. He's pretty amazing."

Brailly, Eddie and Grey sat in the gallery, with supporters of Sea Defender and friends and family of the defendants.

They watched in awe as Gleeson demolished the prosecution and its witnesses.

He first questioned Daniels and key *Sea Horse* crew defendants, who had been on deck and seen the ramming. All corroborated Daniels's version of events.

He then proceeded to cross-examine the technical expert witness, Geoff Cooper. Gleeson had ordered all information to be released and had been briefed on the technical content.

"I ask the Court to view Exhibit A."

Ghostly images of the *Sea Horse* were shown on a screen. Emma and others were in tears.

"Mister Cooper, why were these photographs and this detailed report not released to the initial inquiry?"

"I ... it's complicated, very technical ..."

"I see. What's the technical term for that?" Gleeson pointed.

"It's a hole."

"Indeed, a very large one. Like the one Energor have dug for themselves, may I suggest?"

"Objection!" called the Crown Prosecutor.

"Objection overruled. Continue," said the Judge.

"Does the hole suggest that that the *Odin,* as the Prosecution and Energor witnesses have claimed, attempted to slow and take avoiding action?

Or, as has been alleged, does it suggest that it accelerated at the time of the collision?"

"It's hard to say ... it depends on ..."

"Could the *Odin* have accelerated? Yes or no?"

"Yes."

Dag Wennevold had been watching the proceedings, feeling uncomfortable and guilty. He and the other tug crews had been told to say nothing, to say it was an accident, that the *Sea Horse* was to blame for getting in the way. It was their word against Energor's. Who was going the believe a bunch of green terrorists? They shouldn't have been protesting, but they didn't deserve to go to jail for terrorism. They were so young, some of them. He'd been a hothead himself when he was young. They were warriors too, brave. He respected that. He'd felt guilty about nearly killing one of them. There she was with the other defendants. She looked like a nice girl.

If he admitted to it, he would lose his licence, but he could always get work for a flag of convenience in Panama or wherever. This Gleeson was going to make a meatball out of him in any case.

Wennevold was called and didn't wait for questioning.

"I did it! I rammed the *Sea Horse*. Everyone but those people have been lying. I can prove it." He held up his phone. "I videoed it." He looked towards the defendants. "Sorry guys ..."

People in the gallery, including Brailly, Eddie and Grey, stood and clapped. Wennevold wondered if he should take a bow.

"Silence in Court!" ordered the judge. "The proceedings are not finished. Does the Prosecution wish to pursue their case?"

The Crown Prosecutors conferred. With no act, intended act of violence or harm by the *Sea Horse*, their case under anti-terrorism law was weak. Cross examination or other evidence had not revealed any link to the rig sinking, as the ACP and the AG had alleged.

"No, your honour."

The defendants shook hand and people in the gallery cheered. "Silence in Court!"

⁓

"Today in Perth, all charges of intent to commit terrorism were dropped against Captain Andrew Daniels and the crew of the *Sea Horse* protest ship. All of the defendants have been bound over with an order to keep the peace. The captain of the *Odin* was charged with dangerous driving. The oil company Energor was ordered to compensate the ship's owners, Sea Defender, and to pay for court costs.

"Resources Minister Brad Callaghan commented on the outcome.

"'It's very disappointing to lose the case on a technicality. It's tantamount to inviting terrorists in. Clearly, we need to strengthen our laws against this sort of thing. We will bring to justice who was responsible for sinking the rig.'"

⁓

Burns and Mallon were listening to the news.

"I wish I could see his face," said Mallon. "He looks like he's just eaten an onion at the best of times."

"I'm very pleased for Emma and the others," said Burns. "I hope John has persuaded her to give protesting a rest. But with Sea Defender clearly exonerated, they'll be coming after the real culprits. We'll need to get a move on."

CHAPTER 36

Oregon, USA

Arnold Zimmermann was hiding in the woods near his home, living in his RV. They were after him, and he'd had to skedaddle. The fossil fuel sabotage movement had turned to shit.

It had started with events in Australia. But hell, he'd had the idea back in the eighties. The new movement had had some initial successes through surprise attacks around the world but most success in the US. *America is always number one.* There were more people trained, more ex-military, more access to hardware. More crazies. But here, too, they were in retreat after a big show of force by police and the FBI. Even the National Guard had turned out. There were many raids on suspects' homes. He had narrowly escaped.

But the movement was still small. It lacked weight of numbers, planning, organisation, financial and material resources—aka military hardware. It lacked skills. Unlike him, most were amateurs. There wasn't much going for it except destiny. But destiny took its time. It had now been a hundred and eighty years since Marx had predicted the imminent overthrow of capitalism.

He read that in China, Russia and other places, the authorities were rounding up and imprisoning people without charge or trial. *Thank God we have democracy in the USA, land of the free.*

PM Turbott was pleased to see the global war against green terrorists being won.

"Other countries have the right idea, Christopher!" he told the Attorney General. "They go after them. Round them up."

Dreiser was well pleased with the outcome in Perth. Once again it was money well spent. The Australian mission would have to be careful during the final leg of its voyage.

But his attention was on global operations. He had been informed that procurement, training and other preparation was complete. In other circumstances, drone operators might have been issued with an approved certificate of competence, satisfying aviation safety protocols. You didn't want just anybody flying drones around, especially when they were carrying high explosives.

Operations teams had been told to travel to within distance of their targets and to look out for the deliveries. They'd been told to wait, be patient, act normal and blend in. When they had the equipment, they were told to check it and practice with the drone and missile simulators. It could be any time in the next two weeks. No one but Command knew the exact time.

He was concerned about the backlash against the informal sabotage movement. He predicted it, and now the heightened security was a risk to the project.

He had known that security was already intense. Around the world, security forces, defence forces and intelligence networks maintained their eternal vigilance. They watched and waited for any threat to national interests while remaining indifferent to the attack on the world's failing life support systems, which was happening all around them.

In Saudi Arabia, security forces watched over the oil and gas installations like mothers watching over their babies, aided by US-supplied security systems. The US needed Saudi oil. Saudi weapons systems pointed towards Iran, the main threat.

In Iran, security forces and systems watched in turn, especially in the direction of Saudi Arabia. In Russia and China, security forces watched their own people as well as the rest of the world.

Now, with the attacks, agents for the Project had reported that security had been stepped up. The Middle East was always tense, but now the tension was palpable.

The informal campaign and subsequent backlash by the authorities was not welcome for the Project. At least not yet—it would be important later. It was making some operators nervous, having to go further underground and wait for the 'all go' to attack, with less chance for last minute training and prep. They could have done without all the scrutiny, the checks. Although dispersed, there was a lot of equipment to conceal.

US Intelligence, Langham, Maryland

"We're intercepting encrypted messages, but haven't deciphered them, except that it could involve Saudi. We'd better warn them that something might be happening. It's not news, I guess. They're always waiting for an attack from Iran or Yemen."

Somewhere in Saudi Arabia

Saudi Arabia was on red alert with tanks and truckloads of army personnel driving about, extra roadblocks and checks.

Yemeni Abdulaziz Saeed was stopped, searched and taken to a police station to await collection by the Secret Police for interrogation. Before he had his phone confiscated, he texted project leader James Gryll.

Suitably disguised, Gryll created a small diversion by blowing away the front wall of the police station. After overpowering the dazed guards, he took the key. He and Saeed escaped into the night.

"I only meant to blow the bloody door off," said Gryll. *Who dares wins.*

Their escape and the arrival of security forces was hampered by a dust storm.

December 15

Dreiser waited for news on the dust storm. It had reared up like a kraken from the deep, a reminder that Nature overruled the Lilliputian affairs of Man.

The storm had blotted out most of Saudi Arabia and its neighbours. It was reported by Al Jazeera as the worst for years, climate change making it more severe than usual. Desert storms could blow for weeks.

Now Dreiser and Command were becoming still more concerned. The heightened security was troubling enough, but conditions were not favourable for drones.

The Saudi attack might have to be postponed. Which meant global ops. Saudi was pivotal. The signal went out to stand by.

Conditions had to be right. The D-Day invasion had been postponed in early June of 1944 when the English Channel was rough and stormy. In spite of meticulous planning surrounding all other aspects of the invasion, the Allied commanders could not control the weather. Everything rested on the forecast of a break in the weather by the UK Met Office. Delaying for days or weeks could have been disastrous.

Burns received a short, encrypted message from Command. Any message was RUA—Requires Urgent Attention. Communications had been deliberately limited for security reasons, as well as trust that Burns would deliver. He had delivered so far.

The message read: *Consumer confidence down. ME market down. Client needs to close Aus sale. Request expedite if convenient.*

'Consumer confidence down' meant that there was a problem with the global project. Burns had read on online news about the random attacks around the world. He knew that they would lead to heightened security and could be a problem for operators.

'ME market down' meant that there was a problem in the Middle East. A quick check showed a major dust storm. Saudi was pivotal to the global project. C-day might have to be postponed until the storm subsided. But you couldn't keep teams on standby for long. They might have to be all stood down, the entire Project aborted. Either that, or teams elsewhere would have to fire at will and hope for the best.

'Closing Aus sale' meant completing the Australian job. 'Needs' meant 'urgent'. 'Expedite' meant 'do it now', and 'convenient' meant 'if it is safe and does not jeopardise the Australian and global projects'.

Burns considered the options. The original plan for Australia was to set the coal port and gas plant mines on timers, blow on C-Day and exit Australia before the authorities investigated and pursued. But contingency planning for Australia had included the possibility of changing the timing for one or all of the targets. There were four gas plants to go and the remaining Queensland coal ports and gas jetty waiting to blow. Blowing all carried risks now. For each of the bombings so far, the NE2's involvement was veiled. A much bigger series of blasts in Queensland would point to a bigger force at work. Joining the dots would link all attacks. Someone might spot the coincidental presence of the boat. There was the clockwise sequence: coal in Queensland, coal in NSW, oil in the south and west. *Gas next?*

But the rest of the coal ports had to go some time, and the sooner the better. It would be a lift for the kids in jail. Maybe they'd be let out if there was no coal export industry for them to wreck. He would blow them as soon as possible.

The gas plants were something else. Blowing any earlier would be a higher risk to the team. The explosions would be massive, and someone would surely connect the NE2. If they were in the area, the navy would come after them.

Blowing the gas plants could also be a risk to the global project. An attack on any gas plant could be seen as an attack on a much more connected industry. It could alert other LNG plants, especially Qatar. It could alert oil refineries. It could add risk to the teams involved. If they were ex-SAS, he might know one or two of them. But his priority was delivering his project while avoiding unnecessary risks to his own team. He would consider, but couldn't be responsible for, other teams and projects. Part of the strategy was that all project teams were semi-autonomous and led by resourceful people. They would have to look out for themselves. Having all projects sing together was a nice idea, an ideal. Some projects might fail, but if most succeeded, better half a loaf than no bread.

Delay was not on. He couldn't wait for the desert storm to subside before blowing the gas plants. The longer the NE2 was in Australian waters now, the greater the risk. They were now on a knife-edge; the risks of detection and capture increasing by the hour. They would need to make themselves scarce pretty soon.

But aborting was also not on. He was going to finish the job. They had come this far. He and the team weren't here for a nice cruise or the higher cause, but for money. They were to be paid on commission, paid to deliver the goods—for how many coal ports and gas plants they wrecked. There was no consolation prize for non-delivery.

He decided to set the timers in the Medusa and Oatstone gas plants, to blow on C-Day as planned, and to blow the remaining coal ports without delay. He also decided they could get away with blowing just one gas plant early. It would be another early win for the client and one in the bank, one less to break into. They could make it look like an accident or the work of Ned Coaly. Whatever. They might search the other gas plants for explosives, but they'd have to be well hidden anyway.

He briefed the team on the new development and options. He wasn't going to have them take on extra risks without consultation.

"Hopefully we'll be on our way home before they twig and come after us. Are you all okay with this? We wouldn't be asked if it wasn't important."

"It's what we're here to do. Fine with me," said Simmo.

"Me too," said Bazza. "Anyway, they might still think our mate Sean here did it."

Mallon smiled.

"Do we get an early completion bonus?" enquired Beattie.

Burns smiled. Scotsmen weren't mean, just canny with money. "I'll put in a request."

He contacted the Recce Boys for a brief progress update and to issue new instructions.

PM Turbott was envious of leaders in certain other countries being able to round up and imprison people at will. Australia was the land of the fair go—at least if you were one of them: his voters, his corporate chums. But he wished he could just lock up all green terrorists without all that 'no holding without charge' or 'trial by jury' nonsense.

Most of the Queensland coal industry, mines, railways and ports were still operating. But they were being frequently disrupted by sit-in protesters and the sabotage of power and signalling.

More worryingly, two thirds of NSW coal exports were out with the blocking of the Hunter River, and it could be weeks or months before it was reopened. The same went for the coal mines shipping through Monk's Point, all totally disabled. And there was no connection or capacity for shipping by alternative routes.

Above all, his beloved Daghawi project had been a double humiliation, with the opening *and* the port. It had made him a laughingstock around the world. It was bad marketing for him and Australian coal, and it was costing the industry shitloads now and losing future orders. He needed to assert his authority—for his coal friends and their customers and above all for the voters.

Then there was the oil rig. Jarl Bjornsen of Energor had given him the idea: "I thought you'd locked up all your greenies." Yes! Why hadn't he thought of it before?

What he had in mind would be applauded by his political supporters and voters—everyone loved a strong man—and the media. But would it be legal?

He consulted with Attorney General Christopher Lee, who was not unsympathetic. He was salivating, to be exact. There was just the thing under prevention of terrorism, the small print under 'Emergency Powers' …

He had one other question. Would it possible to use the special guest accommodation on Christmas Island?

CHAPTER 37

Brisbane, December 15

Emma and Grey had returned to Brisbane and were enjoying relaxing. It had been a stressful time for her, and she was still not quite herself, still getting headaches. She was catching up with her studies, and he with his work. She was giving protesting a rest—at least for now. But she was feeling anxious.

They went to a concert, their first for some time—a programme of Russian music, Prokoviev's Lieutenant Kijé and Symphony Number One.

"I feel like I'm being watched," said Emma at the interval.

"Well, you are rather nice to look at. Seriously, you were acquitted, they've nothing to pin on you, and you're going to keep your nose clean. Aren't you?"

"Yes."

"This isn't Russia, where the KGB come for you in the night. Poor old Prokoviev. He wrote such wonderful music, but it didn't take much to piss off Stalin, and he had it in for composers who produced work he didn't like. Prokoviev expected them to come any time. He even slept fully dressed with his overcoat on, a small suitcase packed for the one-way journey to Siberia."

"All the same, I wish you weren't going away. Kate's staying at Paul's tonight, and I don't like being alone in the house."

"You'll be alright. Lock the doors, and don't let anyone in. I have to go—boring family stuff—and I'll be back the day after tomorrow."

They came in the early hours, when people were least resistant, when there were no neighbours around to see them taken away. The KGB had perfected the art, but it was now international standard procedure.

"What's this?" said Emma, eventually waking and answering the door.

"Emma Johnson?"

"Yes."

"You're under arrest under Section fifty-three B: *The Prevention of Terrorism Act*. Get dressed and no funny business."

"Can I call my friend John Grey?"

The officer looked at his list. "Oh, him. So you can tip him off? No."

"I have the right to call a lawyer."

"You're a terrorist. You don't have the right to shit."

She was handcuffed and taken to Brisbane Central police station. To a large room, packed with other climate activists. She knew most of them.

"Hi, Kate. Hi, Paul. Do you know what's happening?"

"I don't know. They've already processed and taken away a bunch of guys."

Grey heard it on ABC Radio when he woke.

"Last night there were nationwide arrests in connection with recent coal and oil industry sabotage. The suspects have been detained under anti-terrorism emergency powers."

Grey called Emma. No answer. He called the police station. The switchboard was jammed. "Please hold. Your call is important to us. The average waiting time is …" He was eventually put through.

"Emma Johnson has been detained for questioning," said the voice. "I'm not at liberty to tell you more."

Grey called Ryan. Maybe something had gone wrong there. The arrests were all over the country.

He used his regular phone. His involvement with the NE2's 'research' activities were no secret, but he had to be careful about what he said. Communication had to be limited in case he was bugged.

"Hi, Mike. How's it all going? Just checking."

"We're all fine."

"That's good," said Grey

"How are you? I miss you."

"I'm good. Miss you all too."

"How's Emma?"

"She's made a good recovery, but I'm worried. Did you hear the news?"

"We sure did. What the fuck's going on in this country? I know they've sold half of it to China, but do they really need to start behaving like them?"

Grey called Tim Gleeson and then Louise Brailly.

"Job well done," said Turbott to ACP Commissioner Robb. "Have we got all of the terrorists and subversives?"

"Pretty well, except for a few stragglers."

"I think you'd better leave this one off," said PM Turbott. "It's one thing interning crazy inner-city woke lunatics. But it's bad marketing locking up academics. It makes you look like China. You can't then lecture them on human rights.

"Wait a minute. This John Grey … He's supposed to be on the NE2. Hmm. Anyway, how good is it that we have accommodation already available?"

On Turbott's orders, the detainees had been taken to hastily recommissioned onshore detention centres—run-down camps previously reserved for refugee boat-people before the Australian government set up more salubrious offshore internment facilities—facilities for persecuting victims of persecution so that other persecuted people would think twice before seeking asylum in Australia.

"We could be stuck here for years," said Kate. "They might send us to Christmas Island. It's a big camp, and there's no one there but that poor Sri Lankan family who've been alone for four years."

"You don't have to be a lawyer to know this is illegal," said Emma. "Australia isn't Russia. Not yet anyway."

"Potato Head would like it to be a police state," said Kate. "He's an ex-cop."

The right-wing media were ecstatically jubilant.

"So, Prime Minister, you finally listened to me," said Alan Williams of Radio 2GBH to his fellow septuagenarian listeners. "I trust you will remember to lose the key."

"We have Barney McDuff, Deputy Prime Minister, on the line. Barney, what do you think of this move?"

"I think it's bloody marvellous, and I told the Prime Minister it has my full support. What's more, I told him I'd like to see internment extended to all smashed avocado eating, soy latte drinking, climate warmist and other inner-city lunatic fringe wokes."

December 16

Burns briefed the team using a whiteboard and a PowerPoint showing aerial and 3D views. The task of his team was to wreck Western Australia's LNG plants. Big and highly flammable with pressurised gas, they were asking to be blown up. But doing the job and planting the explosives would be a little more challenging a task than the coal jetties. There were similar soft targets—the gas loading jetties—but wrecking the plants would do much more lasting damage. The coal industry lacked similar strategic targets, which could be crippled to the same extent. Perfect targets. Drones or rockets could destroy them in real time, but seeing to them with delayed action explosives meant breaking and entering.

"Okay, here's what they're all about, how we'll get in and where we'll leave our calling cards." Burns pointed out the most vulnerable targets rather than describing all the processes, conscious that when teaching karate, you didn't give a degree course in anatomy, you described how to knacker your opponent.

"There are three LNG plants in WA and one up here near Darwin. This is the biggest, on Callow Island, fifty kilometres off the coast, with three trains. Oatstone here has two, and Mercury has one with another being built. The Nipex plant near Darwin has one train. Most gas is liquefied and exported. Some is processed for domestic supply. As they're the biggest and not far away from each other, we will focus on Callow Island and Oatstone. Jannie and Jacques will see to Mercury.

"Nipex at Darwin will be last, the coup de grâce, before we bid farewell to Australia. First things first. Using the sub, we'll land a raiding team of four at Oatstone, and the following night, do the same at Callow. We'll plant the main charges here and here. We'll also plant a small charge in non-critical locations here and here and activate emergency evacuation plans before the whole lot goes up. They don't have many operators, but we want to minimise risk to people. Up to a point. We'll have to neutralise and dispose of anyone who interferes, for the operation's and our own protection. The timers will be set to allow us to finish our work and get out. When we're done, the Recce Boys will have their fun with Mercury. Any questions?"

December 17, Midnight

NE2 moored along the coast and the submarine was lowered into the water. With Mann and Martin driving, Burns, Moody, Simmo, Jonesy and Beattie boarded with their gear. Their faces were blackened so that they would be less visible in moonlight.

"Take it away, Mr Mann," said Burns.

"Aye, aye, sir," said Mann.

The sub reached the jetty, built for loading liquefied gas into giant pressured tanks on transporters. It parked under the jetty and the team found a ladder to climb up.

Burns went first. He signalled the all clear. There were no ships in. There was no one around. Lighting was limited, a regulatory requirement, so as not to attract nesting turtles. The silhouette of the giant LNG plant loomed ahead, also with limited lighting.

Good.

In his reconnaissance, Burns had looked out for security cameras and possible blind or shadowy spots. He had also acquired a clever little device that could temporarily 'freeze' security cameras. It was the sort of thing that Q would have cooked up for Bond.

Using their special scaling ladder, they went over the security gate and into the plant.

"Okay, boys. We'll meet back here in fifteen." They went their separate ways to plant the Semtex and timers in the designated locations.

They re-grouped. Beattie was about to cast up the scaling ladder when Burns saw a vehicle coming. He signalled to the others to conceal themselves.

The vehicle stopped and a man approached. Burns recognised the security guard he'd met at the gatehouse in July. He was looking suspiciously at the CCTV and looking around. He made a call.

He'd better not bring backup, thought Burns. *We don't want to blow the place up yet.* He had a silenced gun and knife ready if necessary. Only if necessary.

The guard drove off.

The following night, the NE2 moored off Callow Island. The blacked-out LNG plant was silhouetted against the spectacularly starry night sky—one of those you could only see in the Southern Hemisphere.

"Fucking amazing," said Mallon to Burns. "Meaning the stars, not that heap of tanks and pipes. That's a bit of an eyesore in a nice place like this, even at night."

The sub parked under the loading jetty and the same team scurried along and scaled the fence. Burns was the first on the ground on the other side. Moody was there already.

"How did you get here?" whispered Burns.

"Gate were open," said Moody.

The plantings were completed without incident and the sub returned to the NE2.

The NE2 continued north.

December 18, 22:00 WA time, December 19, 00:00 Queensland time

"Mr Mallon, would you care to do the honours? Press here, here and here."

An hour later, while Burns was just dozing off, listening to music on the radio, the news came on.

"Earlier at midnight, local time, there were simultaneous explosions at the coal ports of Straw's Point, Sadstone and Brisbane. The extent of damage has not been reported, but five ships are believed to have sunk. No casualties have been reported. The cause has not been established, but the attacks are believed to be the work of terrorists. More information will be reported in later bulletins …"

CHAPTER 38

The Recce Boys had kept a low profile, mostly driving during the night and early morning, resting out of sight by day and avoiding dusk when wildlife was out and on the roads. Recces were good at not being seen, good at reconnaissance, hence their name. That was why Burns had hired them. Their main job was checking that the port receptions were safe, but if the seaborne mission failed, they were equipped to take out any of the land-based LNG plants. Belt and braces.

They were enjoying the road trip after nearly eight weeks on the boat. The coast road from Perth was a bit boring—hours of flat, endless scrub—but they didn't care that there was no ocean view. They had seen enough of the Australian coast.

"Dis' is orraait, Jannie," said Grobbelaar, a look of contentment on his face. His heavy Afrikaans accent was combined with sparing use of the Queen's English.

"Yaah, we've had worse jobs, Jacques," said Boonzaaier, with his own look of relaxed reflection. His accent was lighter, and his English diction more correct. "If all goes well with the boat, all we must do is cruise to Darwin and get paid some lekke ching for it. It's a nice change to be on land."

"It's not bad, man," said Grobbelaar. "That Big Oz Bight thing was ruff, hey? Haven't peuked like that since I ate some overripe whortogg. That time, I could see it trying to get out and run back to the bush. On thee boat, it was like a bit of that servo curry pie trying to take off."

"Same, same," said Boonzaaier. "Talking of bite, we might stop for a 'tchaow soon, hey?"

Being of Boer bloodline and with survival skills developed in the South African Special Forces, the Recce Boys had a taste for exotic meats, or any meat. In Africa, their diet had centred on large steaks of beef—Kudu, Buffalo—around a kilo or so if they could. Pork or warthog was considered a 'heavy vegetable', and lamb, goat or Impala were 'light veggy'. Chicken or any poultry was a 'heavy salad', and anything fishy, a 'light salad'. The rest was just garnish.

They had noticed a lot of roadkill. "Thees dead roos look like they are all on the side of the road," said Grobbelaar.

"I read that it's a safety thing," said Boonzaaier. "It's unique to WA. Patrols go around dragging them off the road to protect drivers and the wedgies—the wedge-tailed eagle. They're big bastards and a bit slow off the ground when they come for a bite to eat. You don't want to hit one of them unless you're in a truck." He was a keen bird-watcher.

"Wouldn't mind trying some," said Grobbelaar, looking interested in the roos and birds. "Kood also make some interesting biltong, you know?"

As the sun was rising, they received a message from Burns. 'C2 G3 W84'. It meant 'take-out'. Not mines with long delays—blow up. 'G3' meant 'Mercury, Gas Plant 3'. 'W84' meant 'wait for the signal'.

"We're in business, Jannie."

They stood by near Onslow while Oatstone and Callow Island ops were completed. 'GI G2 AOK G3ISGO.'

"Looks like they've laid the eggs here and at Medusa," said Boonzaaier. "We're on next."

They drove on to Karratha, did the usual recce before the NE2 came in during the morning for a short visit, then found somewhere out of town to rest up. It was going to be a busy night. They stopped to refuel. They would need to do some hard driving after.

Then they heard the news from Queensland about the coal port bombings.

"That'll stir up a hornets' nest," said Boonzaaier. "They'll know now, if they didn't before, that pros are on the job. We'd best get the job done and be on our way."

The filling station in Karratha informed the police, and the police informant informed Hoxha, who then informed Nalder.

Grobbelaar and Boonzaaier drove to the Mercury LNG Plant at sunset. A lone Harley overtook them, sped ahead, then sped back, disappearing behind them. Suspicious.

"This will do nicely, Jannie."

They chose a spot that was concealed from the road but close enough for a quick getaway and a safe distance from the plant. You wouldn't want to be much closer than one kilometre when it went up.

"What do you think, Jacques?"

"I'm thinking the drones." Grobbelaar loved tech and fun toys, especially when they could blow things up.

"Excellent choice," said Boonzaaier. The other options with the gear they had were to break in and plant timed explosives or to fire a rocket into the place. Breaking in was possible but troublesome. You had to climb over or cut the wire, then reinstate it after. There was always a risk of detection. They might have to start killing people—messy—and blow up the place immediately, as they'd start looking for explosives and try defusing them. Firing a rocket was quick and dirty and would do the job, but it was not as accurate—a bit hit or miss—and it would give them little time to get away. Boonzaaier knew everything about using mortars or RPGs on fuel tanks in South Africa, from when the ANC military wing, uMkhonto we Sizwe, had tried to blow them up. He'd studied it extensively in his terrorist defence strategies training unit. It had never worked.

Drones were civilised and less trouble. You didn't have to fuss with breaking in. In the dark, you could drop a few around undetected and, with timers, blow them when you were out of sight and on your way. You could carry bigger bombs. You could plant them precisely. On top of the storage tanks was ideal. You could first blow a smaller one in a safe location to trigger an emergency evacuation and kill fewer people, if any. Humane. Not that there were many around anyway.

They also fancied trying the drones. They had practiced while on the boat.

"We have lift off!" Grobbelaar steered his drone to its location on top of a storage tank, GIS guided. "Now you."

Boonzaaier guided another to the top of the compressor plant. Grobbelaar sent another smaller unit, as a decoy. They were timed to go in ninety minutes.

"Okay, let's get out of here."

As they were about to join the highway, six Harleys drew up, forming a semicircle and blocking their way. All of the riders drew pistols.

"Get out with your hands up!" shouted Nalder.

"Better do as he says, Jannie," said Grobbelaar. "They look ugly. Like those Danville mommy's boys with the small dicks. You know … all they do is shoot lead bullets. No offspring, just death …" He was familiar with the rougher side of Pretoria.

"Well, not as ugly as us, my friend," said Boonzaaier. "Good evening, gentlemen! Can we be of assistance? We were just doing some birdwatching. Have you ever heard boobook owls? They sound like cuckoos. *Cook-who!*"

"Don't give me that shit," snarled Nalder. "Which of you is Mallon?"

"He's the mellon," the Recce Boys said together, each pointing decisively at the other with expressions of absolute honesty.

"I said keep your hands up! What's that in your hand? Drop it!"

"Is over there alright?" enquired Boonzaaier.

Boonzaaier lobbed the grenade into the middle of the gang while he and Grobbelaar ducked.

Five of the gang were killed instantly. Nalder was on the ground, wounded, but grabbed his gun and started shooting. Grobbelaar found his own gun in the glove compartment and put a stop to that.

Boonzaaier examined their insignia. "It seems they call themselves the Undertakers. They'll be needing one."

"Yah, and also a good scrap dealer for their Harleys," said Grobbelaar.

"This was a setup, Jacques," said Boonzaaier. "Someone knows something, hey. Too much of a coincidence. Wonder how they knew we were here. We better finish the job in case they do a search at the gas plant. Security would have heard that cracker go off and maybe called the coppers."

Without discussion with Boonzaaier, Grobbelaar set off the small bomb. They heard the emergency evacuation siren and saw vehicles racing to the muster stations outside the gate. They waited five minutes, and he fired the main bombs. There was a blinding flash, and the noise of the shock wave was deafening.

"Lékkerrrr …" marvelled Grobbelaar, with an 'up yours' expression at the pleasurable outcome.

"I like the way you make popcorn, Jacques," smiled Boonzaaier. "Now let's clean the kitchen … Master Chef."

Before leaving, the Recce Boys set up the scene so that it looked like there had been some sort of disagreement between Nalder and the others. They were experts at this sort of deception, knowing exactly what to do to make the forensic investigators believe the scenario they wanted. They worked quickly but meticulously, moving Nalder and one of the gang, planting the fired weapon and using branches to clean up shoe prints and vehicle tracks.

In the distance, Burns and others had seen the flash, like distant lightning.

"Here is the news. Last night near Karratha, Western Australia, there was an explosion at the Mercury liquefied natural gas plant. The cause is still being investigated, but the members of the Undertakers bikie gang are believed to be involved. No casualties were reported in the plant. The explosion follows multiple explosions in Queensland coal ports the previous day. It is not known if the west and east coast events are connected, but authorities are now concerned that there may be a coordinated group responsible."

Lone Pine Detention Centre, near Brisbane

Tim Gleeson found out where Emma was being detained after much obstruction from the Department of Homeland Security. He marched in, waving a piece of paper above his head. He'd seen an old newsreel of Neville Chamberlain in 1938 and had thought it was an impressive and dramatic move, even if a bit of a failure.

"I have a Federal Court Order for the immediate release of Emma Johnson, who has been unlawfully detained. Any obstruction and you face jail for contempt." A close inspection would have revealed that the document was not entirely kosher, but his good friend, Federal Court Judge Fred Horne, would sort out the legal niceties and secure the release of all the other detainees.

"Come on, Emma. Let's get you out of here before someone asks to read this."

"Tim, you're a legend. Will the others be alright?"

"Yes, they will. The government have broken half the constitutional law of Australia. They seem to think they're in North Korea. If they don't comply with a release order, the PM and Scroton will be threatened with jail."

The local police established a taped-off zone around what was left of the Undertakers.

Wedge-tailed eagles and crows were attracted to the roadside restaurant. After a great deal of shooing, the police found a tent to keep predators away.

It took fourteen hours to mobilise and transport a full police and forensics team to the site.

"What a bloody mess," observed DCI Papas. "What do we have?"

"This lot have been identified as members of the Undertakers gang. All with form. GBH, armed robbery, drugs, tattooing, you name it. One has been shot; the others blown up."

"Charming bunch," said Papas. "Could be a boy scout patrol. I nicked most of them in my time. I know the names but can't think of their faces."

"Looks like they had some sort of altercation. Maybe they were hired to blow up the plant and then disagreed on their payment?"

"Not sure," said Papas. "We'll need to get a weapons expert to take a look. This one must have been shot by one of the gang. Odd how he managed to blow them all up, perhaps shot just before the explosion? He copped a bit of his own grenade there … not a very smart bloke. Either way, all this confirms that the gas plant explosion was no accident. Personnel in the control room and the black box say there was no malfunction or gas leak. The security gate thought they heard a bang and shots out here just before the plant explosion, but no one is sure. Any news on Mallon and the campervan? A bit of a coincidence if he's in the area …"

"Not since the sighting of it filling up in Karratha the night before last. One man got out and paid by cash. It's not clear who the other one was."

"Get more cars out patrolling. Find that van. Tell them it's a priority. But tell them to keep their distance until we get reinforcements."

Damian Sproake was less than happy to hear the news of the destruction of Mercury LNG. He called his fixer.

"If this is their idea of protection … Well, with friends like that, who needs enemies? This Mallon is behind this. Get him and get him now! Or I'll find someone else."

The fixer called Hoxha.

For yet another day, PM Turbott's phone didn't stop ringing.

"Alexander … I know, it's a catastrophe … I'll see what I can do." Alexander Upham was ex-Foreign Minister and Chairman of the Stoneside Board, major donors to the Conservative Coalition. He had his hand out for a small donation from the taxpayer.

"Maurice," said the US President, "we have shitloads of beautiful, sweet, clean gas from all our fracking. We can do a deal …"

The Recce Boys continued north, the bullet-holed and grenade-blasted windscreen of the campervan held together with tape.

Using a secure satellite phone, Boonzaaier reported to Burns on the Mercury job and the bikie encounter. "The bikies were out scouting for the van. Must have known the rego. Asked if one of us was Mallon."

"You're doing a great job, boys. Better keep out of sight. We'll take our chances going into Broome. We'll see you in Darwin."

How did they know? thought Burns, tracing the van's movements. That house in Hamilton Hill was a bikie house. There was a connection to them—the Albanians and whoever had contracted them and Moore. Had to be someone in the coal industry. There must have been CCTV … a police leak? It couldn't be helped. Either way, the police would be looking for the van. It couldn't be seen during the day. He could pick up the Recce Boys at Broome, but it would be risky if the van was seen in town at the same time as NE2. They might be needed for a land attack on Nipex at Darwin.

CHAPTER 39

December 20, Broome

The NE2 slipped into Broome Port for the penultimate official reception. They kept a sharp lookout for any signs of naval vessels in the water, police cars and people who looked like spooks on the jetty. Rocket launchers and machine guns were at the ready.

"Shame we can't have one at the Roey. That's the Roebuck Hotel," said Mallon. "You'd like it. Good pub, good beer and cute backpackers on the bar." He wondered if Ulla had ever worked there. Nice girl. Bilebola seemed like a lifetime ago, before he was an outlaw.

After the reception, the NE2 departed for its two-day journey to Darwin.

The police lost the trail of the campervan. Then a service station at Kununarra spotted it heading north on the Great Northern Highway.

"Tell patrol cars to find and track the van. It's probably going to Darwin. Keep at a distance until reinforcements can be mustered. They're heavily armed."

Hoxha received a tip-off. "Darwin, you say?"

He had business associates up that way. The north-west coast of Australia was isolated and close to Asia, ideal for drug-running and people smuggling. But he couldn't trust anyone else to do the job. He had a contract to fulfill, vengeance for his boys to be exacted. He had to get to Mallon before the police did. He and his cousin Shefqet would also go to Darwin. If you wanted something done properly, you did it yourself.

Before leaving Perth, Hoxha had made calls to some of his contacts—half the lowlifes of Darwin. He needed that van traced.

December 23, Canberra

Commander Linda Crosby had received 'need to know' information on the various bombings. Although the case was under Homeland Security and the ACP, the discovery of a Chinese-made limpet mine directly triggered Australian Secret Service involvement, as did the combined scale of the coal port bombings, the oil rig and now a gas plant.

There was an apparent connection to Mallon in all of them, although the Pacific Islanders were implicated in Hunter River, the greenies in the oil rig and a bikie gang at Mercury. But there must be something more ... It was all too professional.

The van associated with Mallon in Fremantle had been seen in northern WA, albeit with another unidentified man. A gas plant had been blown up when the van was in the area and heading north. Coal, oil, gas ... clockwise around Australia. Was the fossil sequence complete or was there more to come?

Crosby was at a dental appointment. While in the waiting room, she flicked through a magazine and saw an article about the NE2. It showed a map of its clockwise course around Australia during December.

Before being called to the dentist's chair, she phoned Dennis Baines, her assistant. "See what you can find out about Mike Ryan, John Grey and the IMCF. And the whereabouts of the *New Endeavour*."

Her thoughts were racing as the dentist poked around in her wide-open mouth. If there was another attack, how big would it be? How long did they have? Why would anyone want to be a dentist? This was awful.

―――

Crosby called Lieutenant Steve McCall of Naval Intelligence, Darwin.

"Looks like they're arriving today and will be around for a couple of days," said McCall. "As the final visit on NE2's tour of Australia, there's been a lot of publicity and there'll be a reception tomorrow morning. We can't go barging in too soon and spoil the party. Anyway, it's up to the police to do any formal questioning. They get upset if we encroach on their territory. I'll look into it."

Crosby knew that his nickname was 'Mirrors' McCall, always looking into things and not known for fast action.

Just thinking about Darwin made her shake her head. Intelligence seemed to have become a stranger to Australian political, commercial and military affairs these days. The Darwin Naval Base was one of the most important military installations in Australia and, close to Asia, strategically important for the US. It was also next door to the Port of Darwin, which had—like half of Australia—been sold to the Chinese. "What the fuck?" the US Defence Secretary had enquired of the PM, after learning of the sale—made without consultation and even 'supported' by her own boss, for God's sake. Of course, the Port's CEO, Brad Bono, had once been the Australian Trade Minister, responsible for doing deals with China. The old revolving door was ever spinning.

She would await news from Darwin.

―――

Louise Brailly and Eddie were back in Brisbane. She was about to run a piece on the abductions and internments, 'The People's Republic of Australia'.

She held off when she heard that the internees had been released. Emma would have a great story.

She called, but there was no answer. She had Emma's address and was passing her apartment, so she decided to stop by. She banged on the screen door and the main door opened. She recognised Emma's friend Kate from when she'd been locked to the coal railway at Manstone.

"Oh, hi … Aren't you Kate? Remember me? I'm Louise Brailly. We met at …"

"Yes. Nice to see you. Come in."

"I was wondering if Emma was around?"

"She's gone to Darwin with John. He wanted to be at the final reception before the NE2 leaves, and she's gone with him. They're thinking of taking some time out in the Northern Territory—maybe going to Kakadu. She's worried about all the fracking projects being planned over there. They're all on Aboriginal land, and she wants to speak to the people about what they can do."

OMG, thought Brailly. The poor frackers didn't stand a chance.

"Did they intern you?"

"Yes."

"Do you mind if I ask you what it was like?"

―――

Brailly had been writing about climate protests and sabotage around the world, about the growing tension. Anti-fossil fuel protest had been repressed everywhere, not just in Australia. But when pressure built, you could only keep the lid on it for so long before it blew off.

In Australia, coal jetties, an oil rig and now a gas plant had been blown up, all around the coast during the NE2 tour, while at the same time, things were happening elsewhere. Ned Coaly had disappeared in Queensland, then reappeared in Fremantle when the NE2 was there. Was everything connected? Was Mallon on the boat? What was John Grey's involvement? Did Emma know?

"Pack your toothbrush, Eddie. We're going to Darwin."

December 23, afternoon

The NE2 entered the Port of Darwin and tied up.

Without the Recces there to do a recce, they all kept their eyes peeled for any suspicious naval activity and anything on the port. This was the final VIP reception, so it would be embarrassing for the government if anything happened before that. Burns had lost contact with the Recce Boys. He hoped they were okay. He couldn't hold the boat for them for too long …

December 23, early evening

Grey and Emma touched down at Darwin Airport, picked up a hire car and drove to the NE2. They came aboard.

"We wanted to show up for the finale and say goodbye before you leave," said Grey.

Ryan was especially pleased. "Good to see you, old buddy. And lovely to see you again, Emma. You've done a fantastic job. It's a relief that they released you."

They exchanged greetings and hugs.

Grey hadn't been allowed to tell Emma anything, but she'd guessed that the NE2 was somehow involved with the coal port, oil rig and gas plant bombings, which had followed in its wake.

Although it was now dark, Mallon still wasn't allowed to show himself up top. Burns knew that there would be surveillance everywhere in the port, not just by its Chinese owners.

Emma went below.

"It's good to see you, Sean." She hugged him. "I just wanted to say goodbye and good luck."

"All the very best to you too, Emma. Thanks for what you did for me. I'm sorry I didn't get to know you more, through David and all … I'm very happy for you and John. He's a great guy."

"Yes, he is. What will you do?" she asked.

"Mr Phelps will see me right."

Burns had mixed feelings about Grey and Emma being there. "Look, thanks for coming, John, and keeping up the front. But after the reception tomorrow, you and Emma must be away. The same with Mike here. You've done your job. Things could get hairy from tomorrow on, and you can't be involved."

"We understand," said Grey. "We'll make ourselves scarce. Maybe head off to Kakadu."

"I'll be leaving the boat too," said Ryan. "I have a flight booked to Brisbane and LA tomorrow night at eleven thirty."

Emma and Grey checked into their apartment hotel. "I don't know about you, but the old jetlag is really catching up with me," said Grey, stretching and yawning.

"We'd better have an early night, then," suggested Emma. Darwin was thirty minutes behind Brisbane.

Agron Hoxha and Shefqet Shehu arrived at Darwin airport after their flight from Perth, hired a car and checked in at the Rydges Hotel.

As Brailly and Eddie checked in at the Rydges hotel, Brailly watched two men leaving. They were smartly dressed in suits. She vaguely recognised one of them. He was a prominent Melbourne businessman, his picture in the paper at celebrity events. He was allegedly a mobster but had always strenuously denied it. Some time ago, she had drafted a piece about gangland killings and links to businessmen and police corruption after a child was killed in crossfire, but her editor had told her to drop it for her own good. What was Hoxha doing here?

***

It was late. One of McCall's assistants, Nigel Perry, watched the NE2 for any suspicious activity. It was just a hunch of the Chief, the circumstantial presence of the NE2 around the coast. The police needed reasonable grounds to get a warrant and it would be embarrassing for the PM if there was a raid before tomorrow's reception. The NE2 voyage around Australia was his special project.

Anyhow, the boat had already been cleared by Border Force. Okay, they'd also cleared that cruise ship before it had infected half of Sydney during COVID-19, claiming afterwards that it wasn't their job.

He lit up. Ed Dennis would take over at midnight. A spook's work was never done.

CHAPTER 40

December 24, morning

The Recce Boys had stopped at a roadhouse earlier to make some repairs. They were already running late. The camper wouldn't be caned, and it was hard to see out of a windscreen held together with tape, lucky to have survived blast from the grenade.

"That's the trouble with second-hand shit," said Grobbelaar. "No warranty."

They couldn't wait for the RAC. You could wait for hours on Australia's long highways. The satellite phone wasn't working.

"Hope they wait for us," said Boonzaaier. The Recce Boys knew that they were being tracked by the police.

"There's another one following us," said Grobbelaar. He slowed and sped up, and the police car did the same.

"They aren't going to stop us," said Boonzaaier. "Maybe they're waiting for reinforcements. We have a schedule to keep and can't detour or outrun them in a chase. There might be more options when we're near Darwin."

December 24, Darwin Waterfront, morning

"Over the past six weeks, the *New Endeavour* has done Australia proud." Bronwyn Porter, the Commonwealth Minister of Tourism, was summing up. "The brainchild of our wonderful Prime Minister, this ship's voyage around Australia has showcased our rich coastal heritage and the government's commitment to keeping our waters clean. It has reminded us of our nation's heritage—our proud connection with Captain Cook. Ladies and gentlemen, girls and boys, I'm proud to commemorate this historic voyage around Australia, this Odyssey, with this plaque." She drew back the curtain on the large plaque.

"They might want to forget this later," muttered Burns.

⌒

After they had taken some pictures, Brailly and Eddie joined the visitors on the boat. They were only allowed on the deck. If Mallon was aboard, he'd be concealed.

Burns was talking to Ryan as Brailly approached them.

"How do you do. George Phelps, and this is Mike Ryan."

"Hi," said Ryan.

"Hello. I'm Louise Brailly from *The Sentinel*, and this is Eddie Donnelly. We've followed your voyage with great interest. Do you mind if we take your picture?"

"Not at all," said Burns. They posed as Eddie got some shots.

What a pair of hunks, thought Brailly. *Especially Phelps.* He had a military air, didn't look like a boffin.

"What's that?"

"It's our submersible, for surveying the ocean floor."

"Oh, my." Although it was under wraps, she thought it looked more like a midget submarine. All the better to blow things up with.

"What's in there?"

"Crew's quarters. You don't want to go in there—it's full of smelly sailors."

Pity, I'm rather fond of seamen, thought Brailly. *He's hiding something, I know. But I'm not to ask and he won't tell. If the NE2 has done the big bombings, it and Mallon have done something amazing—drastically cutting Australia's greenhouse emissions at a canter.*

"Can I say, I think you've done a fine job, drawing attention to the plight of the oceans and reefs—an even more pressing concern with climate change and everything."

"Thank you," said Burns.

"Something drastic needs to be done," said Brailly. "It's our only chance. We won't get it from this government."

Burns recognised a knowing look when he saw one. Grey was trustworthy, but had he let anything slip? By now, any number of people might have their suspicions.

Grey and Emma joined them.

"Hi, Louise. Hi, Eddie," said Grey. "Nice to see you again." Grey always felt uncomfortable with Brailly, like he wanted to confess to things he hadn't even done. What were they doing here? She must know something by now. At least she seemed to be on their side. But you couldn't tell with journos. They'd sell their soul for a story.

"Hello, Emma," said Brailly.

"Hi, Louise."

"We're in NT to do an article on fracking on Aboriginal land and thought we'd drop by to see the NE2 leave. I saw Kate and she mentioned you'd be here. She told me about your and her ordeal. It must have been awful."

"It was," said Emma. "But thank goodness for Tim Gleeson and whoever's paying him. I pity the poor boat people in indefinite detention."

"Yes, poor devils. Tim's amazing. Would you mind if I did a piece about you, why the government is so afraid of you? People like you that they had locked up?"

"Of course not."

December 24, afternoon

Burns was getting concerned about the Recce Boys. They hadn't checked in or reported on any trouble or delay. Hopefully they'd show up after dark.

He waited for the signal from Command. The sandstorm was still delaying the start of global ops, but he'd press on with his plan to blow Callow and Oatstone at midnight and take out Nipex at the same time. They would need night running to get to international waters. If they were found out, the navy would give chase.

They would sail at ten pm and stand by offshore.

Late afternoon, near Darwin

"Time for some fun," said Boonzaaier. They had checked for alternative routes off the Great Northern. "In two hundred metres, turn left," said the robotic satnav voice.

He turned the camper and accelerated along the secondary road. The police car followed, blue lights flashing and sirens wailing.

The road was barely two lanes wide and Boonzaaier drove in the middle to prevent overtaking. The policeman in the passenger seat started shooting, like in the movies, trying to take out the camper's tyres.

Grobbelaar flung open the back door, brandishing a sub machine gun. He was about to grab the rocket launcher, but that would be overkill. He sprayed the police car.

"Fuck me dead!" said PC Hanson, swerving into the roadside ditch.

"That's one way to avoid a speeding ticket," said Grobbelaar. "We better check they're alright and stop 'em calling for backup."

The police officers were not seriously hurt, but mildly concussed. The Recce Boys tied and gagged them, drove on and waited in some undergrowth for the light to go. They didn't want another shootout, and so they took the backroads into Darwin. It would take longer, but they'd get there, hopefully in time.

"They can't have just disappeared!" yelled ACP Commissioner Robb. "Find them! Watch every road!"

Early evening

Brailly and Eddie were having a drink by the waterside. Earlier, they had seen a man sitting, reading, every so often looking at the NE2. He was still there two hours later. Now, he had just been replaced by someone doing the same.

"They're not very good at being spooks, Eddie."

Then they saw Hoxha and the other man walk by.

"I don't like it, Eddie." She thought of Siobhan's ordeal, how mobsters had tried to get Mallon through her.

Then she saw the two men who had driven off in the camper at Fremantle. They went up the gangplank.

December 24, 20:15 , Darwin Harbour

The Recce Boys turned up at the NE2 on foot.

"Where the hell have you been?" said Burns. "Why didn't you call? Where's the van?"

"Sorry, boss," said Boonzaaier. "Signal and mechanical probs, then chased by the coppers and had to exchange some pleasantries. The police have been following, but I think we gave them the slip. We parked the van down the road. Couldn't bring it here."

"Okay, well done, lads. I'm relieved you're here. We'll need to unload the gear from the van. It wouldn't do to leave it there with ordnance in it. Since those police officers saw you, there will be a description out for you. You'd better stay on the boat."

Grey and Emma had returned to the boat and were about to take Ryan to the airport. He was all packed and ready to go.

"John, do you mind if we borrow your car?" asked Burns. "The van is just along the road, but it will help in carrying stuff. Are you okay for time, Mike?"

"Sure. We have plenty of time. My flight is a domestic connector, and I'm checked in."

"I'd better come," said Boonzaaier. "I know where everything is."

As he watched them drive off, Mallon pondered on Burns's theory about how the police had picked up the trail of the van. It must have been picked up on CCTV at Freo. But how were the bikies involved at Mercury LNG? Freo must have been a bikie house connected to the Albanians.

Brailly saw Burns and one of the campervan men drive off. The watching man in the cafe was making a call. A man appeared on the boat ramp and was coming down. It was Mallon. Something was happening. She and Eddie needed to create a diversion. She had to think quickly.

"Eddie, take that man's picture and leg it."

Eddie walked up to the man and held up his small camera.

"Good evening. Take your holiday memory?"

"You can't take my picture," said Nigel Perry.

"Why? Will it take your spirit away?" Eddie took a snap and ran.

"Stop!" shouted Perry, leaping up and running after him. If his picture fell into the public domain, it was career over, at best a desk job for him. The cameraman could be a foreign spy, working for the Chinese. He ran and ran but couldn't catch the man. Damn! He'd better get back to watching the boat.

Brailly and Eddie met up away from the harbour.

"Well done, Eddie!" said Brailly. "I've always said you're pretty fit."
Eddie still had his two hundred metres trophy from school.

They heard an explosion and a gunshot.

20:36

Burns and Boonzaaier got out of the car behind the van. From the shadows, Hoxha and Shehu appeared, pointing guns at them. Hoxha's network had done their job.

"Take out your guns very slowly and drop them," said Hoxha.

They complied. There was no other choice. They both had concealed guns and knives and would pick their moment.

"Good, now kneel."

"Take me, but please leave what's in the van," pleaded Burns. "My girl's schooling and future depend on it."

"What's so special in there? Throw the keys to my friend!"

Normal people had car alarms. Ex-SAS left booby traps for unwanted guests, and these needed to be deactivated. Shehu turned the key and opened the door.

The van blew up. It was convenient for Burns and Boonzaaier that they were low down. Less so for Shehu, of whom little remained. Hoxha had been standing away but was still blown to the ground. Burns and Boonzaaier tried to grab their guns, but he had held onto his.

"Not so fast! Stay down!" Hoxha scrambled to his feet and looked at what was left of the van and Shehu.

"Shefqet! Shefqet! What have they done to you?" He was running out of relatives thanks to Mallon and his gang. Which of them was Mallon, anyway?

He crossed himself—he was strict Orthodox—for Shehu and for what he was about to do to these two.

"Time to say *lamtumire*."

Hoxha raised his Beretta. Then, something made him lose his head. Mallon had shot it away.

Barking dogs and police sirens responded to the explosion and shooting.

"Nice work, Sean. Where did you learn to shoot like that?"

"I didn't. It was the luck of the Irish. Anyhow, it was the least I could do. Two good turns deserve another."

"We'd better be going. Give me your wallet." Burns replaced Hoxha's with Mallon's. He removed chains, rings and other artefacts. "It's worth a try."

"Won't there be your name on the vehicle licence and rego?" asked Mallon.

"What? Michael M. House?"

Boonzaaier prepped the scene for forensics to find what he wanted them to find. He was good at that.

20:55

Burns hurried things along as the crew prepared the NE2 for departure.

"The place is going to be crawling with cops very soon and people asking questions. Seems like everyone is after us tonight. Look, John, you'd better take Mike to the airport now and lie low. There will be a lot of checking at airports after Callow and Oatstone go up and after our little surprise later. Mike and John, thanks a million for all you've done. You'll be paid with a bonus into offshore accounts, inheritance from a long-lost auntie." They hugged.

"Emma, thank you, too. Keep up your good work and try to stay out of trouble—I know, not like me."

She kissed him and Mallon. "Thanks. I'll always remember you. Good luck."

Burns took Grey aside and gave him a brown envelope. "We'll signal from Dili to say we've arrived safely. If you don't hear from us, give this to Louise Brailly. If you do hear, destroy it."

"I promise," said Grey.

"All right," said Burns. "All ashore who's going ashore."

The NE2 cast off.

21:05

The police arrived on the scene of the explosion and, after an initial inspection, reported to the ACP.

"It's the van, alright. The licence plate was in some bushes on the other side of the road. There are two bodies—at least one and bits of another. The face of the otherwise whole one is unrecognisable. But there's a driving licence. Looks like it's Mallon. Maybe his mate shot him, but he was then blown up when he tried to run off with the van. Don't know."

December 24, Stanmore, Sydney, 21:45 local time, 21:15 Darwin time

Even head spooks were allowed time with family on Christmas Eve. Linda Crosby's emergency pager vibrated and flashed. "Sorry, Mum, I need to make a call." She went into her bedroom, kept for her now infrequent visits to her parents. She sat on the bed next to the giant teddy she'd had since she was eight. She called Dennis Baines, who reported on developments.

"Mallon—or what's left of him—is in Darwin, less than three hundred metres from the ship."

"What? This is too much of a coincidence."

She called McCall. "What's going on? How has this happened right under your fucking noses?"

"I've had someone watching it. He heard an explosion and went to see what was going on."

"Get onto the ACP. They need to board the ship and do some real policing for a change, instead of raiding journalists' bloody knicker drawers and licking the sodding arses of pollies." She looked at Teddy, as if hoping he wasn't too upset by her grown-up language.

Perry returned to the wharf and called McCall.

"The boat's flown the coop. I think I can see it heading out."

"Shit!" said McCall. "Her Highness will have my balls on a gold platter."

"Should I get the water police to chase it?"

"I don't think so. This is for the navy. But it'll need to be cleared."

Crosby called Brian 'Horatio' Nelson, the Defence Secretary, who was not too pleased about being disturbed on Christmas Eve, especially when he had told his wife he had to be in the office to take a call from Washington.

"Who is it, darling? Tell them to go away," said his private secretary, Daphne, champagne glass in her hand and wearing her red lingerie—a Christmas present.

"I'll get someone to order a plane to search and a boat to intercept. They'll want to wait till it's light. Coastguard boats are fast, and it won't have gotten far. Coming! No, not you, Commander Crosby."

The NE2 slipped from the main harbour, lights dimmed, and moored two kilometres out and one kilometre from the Nipex LNG plant.

CHAPTER 41

December 24, 23:00

Burns briefed the team.

"This is it, lads. Once more unto the breach. But we're now on the home run. It's the last job." He paused. "I want to thank you for all of your grit and professionalism in getting the job done so far and I know we can nail this one. But you know me, I won't expose you to any risks without your knowing the score. I haven't been able to give details, but you are aware that our mission is part of a bigger plan, a bigger operation. The gas plants are all planned to blow at midnight, followed by facilities around the world. As you know, our plan is to drone attack the Nipex plant in one hour's time as our finale. But Saudi is pivotal, and a sandstorm has been blowing so that other ops are on standby, and we've been told to do the same. Here's the rub. We can abort, but not change, the timers on the gas plants. If we blow Callow, Oatstone and Nipex tonight, it could compromise global ops. More importantly for us, the authorities here will likely connect the coal ports and gas plants with us. They may already be on to us. The sandstorm could go on for days, weeks. We can delay or abandon the attack here, but if we're not heading for international waters in one hour's time, there's a chance we'll be intercepted. Questions? Comments?"

"We're with you, boss," said Simmo. "We trust you to decide. It'll be a shame to abort and waste all that good work and the bombs at the gas plants.

Speaking for myself, I was looking forward to playing with the drones and seeing a plant go up instead of hearing about it in the news."

"They might think it's that Ned Coaly again," said Mallon. "Or the plants got caught up in the bushfires. Half the fuckin' country's alight again, after all."

"Let the fuckers try coming after us," said Moody, grinning.

December 24, midnight

From the NE2, the Nipex LNG plant could be clearly seen a kilometre away, reflected in the calm, shimmering water of the bay.

"It's very seasonal," said Burns. "All lit up like a Christmas tree."

With Burns supervising, Simmo, Jonesy and Beattie prepared four armed, fixed-wing drones.

"Okay, send the decoy," said Burns.

Using GIS, Simmo directed the smaller device to a planned location at the edge of the plant. "It's there now."

"Fire it now." They heard the sound of a small explosion, followed by the sound of emergency evacuation alarms.

They waited two minutes.

"Send the others now."

They directed the other three drones across the water and into the main part of the plant, with its giant gas compressors.

"They should all be out by now," said Burns. "Anywhere around these coordinates should do. Okay, let's all light up."

The plant became a giant fireball. The explosion sent out a shock wave.

"I've always wanted to see the Sydney Harbour fireworks," said Moody. "That were almost as good."

"Now for Medusa and Oatstone," said Burns, firing the hidden decoy charges. He waited five minutes and fired the others.

"As I said, all you need is a box of matches."

At Callow Island and Oatstone, nocturnal animals and nesting turtles were confused as night turned to day.

At Durtis Island, Queensland, two limpet mines blew away the LNG loading jetty. A Semtex bomb under the gas flow line ignited the gas. The flame rushed along the line, like touch paper, to the waiting gas plant.

"We'd best be on our way. Give it all you've got, Mr Hoemberg."

"Very good, Mr Burns."

"Head for the state line," said Burns. "D'you know, I've always wanted to say that."

There was two hundred and fifty kilometres between the NE2 and international waters.

December 25, 03:25 local time, Kirribilli, Sydney

PM Turbott was in a deep sleep, dreaming about Christmas pudding, cricket and Baby Jesus, in that order. Christmas Day and the Boxing Day test match would be a welcome relief from all the troublesome events lately.

Australia was on fire again. Once again, when visiting affected people, he had been as welcome as a fart in a spacesuit. They didn't want to shake his hand. He had thought of extending police powers by obliging people to shake his hand. After all, during COVID-19, the police were fining people if they *did* shake hands.

Now his beloved coal industry exports were in ruins until they repaired the jetties and unblocked the Hunter River. He couldn't keep pretending to be out or in a meeting when his coal chums called. Oil in the Bight was out for now, and a gas plant had blown up in WA.

To cap it all, the Federal Court was threatening to jail him and Peter if they didn't obey the order to release all the greenies. Whatever was next?

He was woken by an urgent call. "Not now … What? … No! … How bad is that? … This is war! … An attack on gas is an attack on our feet … our nation … Surely not the *New Endeavour*? I just don't believe it … get me Brian!"

Defence Minister Nelson was back with his wife. "Who's that calling at this time? On Christmas morning too?"

Turbott put the nation on a red, maximum terrorist attack alert. He had considered a war alert but had been advised that to declare a full state of war you would need an actual, named enemy, usually another country.

"Who would stand to gain most?"

"Well, Qatar, I suppose," said Nelson. "They're our biggest competitor for LNG. But we need proof that they were responsible. We can't just declare war on them … can we?"

⌒

McCall briefed the liaison officer of the Royal Australian Navy.

"The coal jetties and Hunter River in the east, the oil rig, and now the gas plants in the west … There's still only circumstantial evidence of the NE2's responsibility. But it sailed close to all locations. And if they're innocent, they won't mind stopping and answering a few questions, allowing inspection."

He briefed the Marine Unit of Border Force.

"As it happens, we have a boat going out this morning on routine patrol. As you know, drug and people smugglers and illegal fishing boats don't take Christmas holidays."

He briefed the RAAF, who had been ordered by Canberra to send out a spotter plane.

"If they're responsible and are planning a getaway, they'll head out to sea. It doesn't in itself prove anything, but it's a bit suspicious going on Christmas Day, all the same. Start by sweeping out and if no luck, go along the coast."

06:20 Darwin time

An Orion radar and spotter plane took off from RAAF Darwin. There wasn't a lot of sea traffic, and satellite systems enabled a focus on vessels of a relevant size to be picked up on radar, followed by visual confirmation.

07:10

The crew of the NE2 were relaxing and enjoying Christmas morning, unwrapping their presents. "Oh, you shouldn't have! It's what I always wanted!" Burns had sent out to the bottle-o while they were in Darwin. They would save the Christmas dinner until they were safely away.

Fifteen minutes later, Burns saw what he had feared. A plane on the horizon. He looked through his binoculars. "They've found us. We'll have company before too long."

They were still some ways from international waters.

Lieutenant Commander Brian Adams was proud to be captain of the patrol vessel *Cape Leeuwin*, proud to be protecting Australia's borders. He was disappointed not to be on shore for Christmas, but it went with the job. They'd have a nice lunch later, with all the trimmings.

It was a routine patrol, pretty boring if he was honest. He'd always wanted to join the Royal Australian Navy from a young age. He'd imagined it would be more exciting, with more action and adventure, but it was good work stopping drug smugglers and illegal fishing. At least the boat people had stopped coming. That was pretty unpleasant.

He wasn't into politics; he thought it was boring. But he couldn't help thinking that in stopping the boats, the RAN had been used to serve the political interests of the Conservative Coalition. Turbott and other politicians had won elections and built political careers on stopping the boat people and generating anti-Muslim sentiment. Refugees, many women and children, had risked death in leaky boats to escape persecution in their home countries. Many were from the Middle East and Afghanistan, where the Yanks, dutifully supported by Britain and Australia, were responsible for the death and turmoil in the region. He'd read that many were fleeing from climate disaster, to which Australia was allegedly a contributor. Surely not. Anyhow, it was all pretty bad form. A lot of the refugees were drowning en route when their leaky boats sank, but the navy had to follow orders to turn the poor buggers back or escort them to offshore detention centres, where they were being held indefinitely. Apparently, they were like concentration camps, where conditions were so bad that leaking information about them, taking pictures even, carried a two-year jail sentence. He knew it was cruel, but at least it had stopped the people smugglers. It was a quiet day, but he could do without that sort of excitement. It seemed that there was more going on ashore than at sea, what with all these gas plants blowing up.

Then he received a message.

"Intercept, board and search the survey vessel, *New Endeavour II*. It is suspected of being involved in the bombings. Here are its bearings ..."

Time for some action, thought Adams. Unusual, they normally stopped people coming in, not boats leaving.

A chase would be exciting. Cape class naval patrol boats could do up to twenty-five knots.

⌒

10:24

Burns scanned the horizon. A large boat was approaching fast.

"Okay, boys, stand by for SOP4," announced Burns over the loudspeaker. The crew were trained for all eventualities and had drilled and memorised standard operating procedures during training throughout the voyage.

The *Cape Leeuwin* drew near. Its stern-mounted machine guns were turned towards the NE2, manned by two gunners, Leading Seaman Jason Drew and LS Diane Mullet. The Marine Unit of Border Force was an equal opportunity employer.

"This is Lieutenant Commander Brian Adams of the *ACV Cape Leeuwin*," blared through the loudspeaker. "Heave to. Request permission to board." The patrol boat was entitled to stop and search any vessel suspected of illegal activity, but Adams still considered it good manners to ask nicely.

"Sorry, can't stop," replied Burns. "We're late for an appointment." The NE2 continued ploughing through the waves.

"Failure to comply will result in you and your crew being arrested and detained."

The patrol boat overtook and veered into the NE2's path. If it had been a police car, its blue light would have flashed and a loud 'pull over' signal sounded.

"Gun crew, give them one round for'ard," ordered Adams. "And I'm not talking a round of turkey sandwiches." He remembered that it was Christmas.

Loud *rat-tat-tating* and water spattered ahead of the NE2.

"Strewth!" shouted LS Mullet. She and LS Drew saw the rocket coming and hit the deck just before it blew away the gun platform.

Jonesy was holding a rocket launcher on his shoulder as Moody reloaded. "I don't think we'll be getting a speeding ticket from them, somehow."

Burns scanned the patrol boat with his binoculars. "They won't bother us anymore with their only gun out. Let's hope there's nothing else in the area and we can make it to East Timor waters before they send something else. We won't have surprise on our side if there's another encounter."

His team resumed their poker game.

Adams decided to withdraw. He couldn't risk his boat. The 2X20 was the vessel's only major armament, and he knew that light automatics wouldn't cut it against rockets. He called for backup.

The frigate *HMAS Whyalla*, a much bigger vessel, was returning from patrol in the South China Sea.

Commander Stephen Smith received the message. By the time he intercepted, the NE2 would be in international waters. Different rules of engagement would apply. It would require international consultation.

December 24, 23:05 EST, Excelsior Golf Resort, Key Largo, Florida

"What the fuck, Maurice. I was already in bed. It's bad luck to see Santa on Christmas Eve. First your coal, now your gas industry. What you got left to trade? Sheep? Just kidding. Family is very important to me as well. What? Let me understand this. You wanna send your boys to go and sink a boat in international waters? Why would that be now? What, you're kidding me? You're telling me you invited this old tub to come sailing around Austria, and it may have fucked your coal, oil and gas industries and one of your ships, and you want permission to engage near to Asia, get us involved somehow and cover it up? Maybe if we can do a deal ... I already told you, we got tons of beautiful, sweet, clean coal and gas ..."

Timor Sea

The NE2 was within spitting distance of East Timor, but still outside Timorese waters. *Come on,* thought Burns. *Just a bit closer and we're there.*

He saw the ship getting closer but keeping its distance. It was a frigate. *Shit!*

The *Whyalla* pursued the NE2 and had a visual, but it was standing off. Commander Smith knew the survey vessel was armed with rockets and he was taking no chances coming up close. The lesson of the *Sydney* was not lost on RAN commanders. Shoot first and ask questions later.

"One salvo for'ard."

A large spout of water erupted ahead of the NE2.

Burns looked through his binoculars. All guns and missiles were trained in their direction.

A radio message came through.

"This is Commander Stephen Smith of HMAS *Whyalla*. Heave to and lay down your weapons, or you will be sunk."

"They mean business," said Burns.

He had already considered this worst-case scenario. There weren't many options. He knew that they were cornered. The frigate was firing in international waters. They would never do that without permission from the Yanks, including permission to sink. They'd want to cover up the government's negligence.

They'd like us to fight back. We might get a lucky shot, but it's unlikely. It will be an excuse to sink us, destroy the evidence. But if we surrender, they won't want all this coming out. We'll be detained indefinitely on Christmas Island or some other hellhole. We'll never be seen again. The Australian Navy don't seem to mind doing that to refugees.

Burns had arranged that if anything untoward happened to the NE2, the PM's involvement in sinking them would be disclosed to *The Sentinel*. But that wasn't going to help now. And if there were awards for lying, the PM would get an Oscar. Their only chance was to make a run for Timor.

"We carry on. Keep calm and run. Full ahead, Mr Hoemberg."

"Very good, Mr Burns."

Burns knew that in World War II, destroyers coming up against battleships would make smoke and hope to hide in that. But you needed heavy fuel oil for that trick. It was difficult with marine diesel.

Another salvo ahead. Another alongside. The next one will be us ...

Then the firing stopped. The *Whyalla* withdrew.

In all the noise, they had not heard the communications radio repeatedly receiving a signal.

Short-short-short-long, short-short-short-long ... the opening notes of Beethoven's Fifth Symphony.

C-Day was a go.

CHAPTER 42

Saudi Arabia, December 25, afternoon

The wind dropped as suddenly as it had started. The air was thick with dust, the sun invisible through orange half-light. All was still.

The silence was broken by a buzzing sound, coming closer, like a plague of giant bees, then multiple flashes and shock waves as fractionating columns and other refinery plants exploded, flames flaring all around.

The *short-short-short-long* signal flashed around the world. *Proceed as planned.*

On the NE2, they heard crackly snippets of news on the BBC World Service.

"Earlier today, there was an exchange of missiles between Saudi Arabia and Iran with extensive damage to the oilfields and refineries of both countries. Yemen has claimed responsibility for the attack on Saudi Arabia. Iran has declared war on Saudi Arabia and the United States, which Iranian officials claim are responsible for the attack on their soil. There have been explosions at gas plants in Qatar and unconfirmed reports of attacks in Russia and China, denied by both countries. These have followed earlier attacks in Australia, Singapore, Japan and India. It is believed that all events may be connected. Oil and share trading have been suspended as oil prices reached record highs with supplies collapsing, then record lows in anticipation of a collapse in demand. Global share markets have collapsed."

"Jaysus!" said Mallon. "I see what you meant when you said big things were happening."

The radio broadcast continued.

"The United States has sent a task force to the Persian Gulf with two aircraft carriers. Britain and Australia have each sent two frigates."

"The Brits and Aussies. Always America's bitches," said Burns. "Luckily for us, this time."

It was now safe for them to have their Christmas dinner. The galley crew had been hard at work.

Everyone sat down to dinner, pea-and-ham soup to start with, slices of roast turkey roll for main course. In Darwin, Burns had sent out for Christmas crackers, and they all had hats.

"Let the feast begin!" said Burns.

"This is a nice salad," said Boonzaaier to Grobbelaar, tucking into the turkey. "I wouldn't mind some meat."

December 26, East Timor

As the NE2 put into Dili, further radio reports came through of attacks around the world. The latest ones were in Nigeria, Texas, Louisiana and Alberta.

"I think we'll anchor here for a short while," said Burns. "At least until the dust settles."

Burns, Mallon and various crew members relaxed in the Castaway Bar, watching the sun set over the headland.

"This was a Portuguese penal colony once," said Mallon.

"What, the bar?" said Moody.

"No." Mallon laughed. "East Timor, Timor-Leste. Portugal used to send criminals—mostly political dissidents here. On a one-way ticket."

"We'd have fitted in well," said Burns.

"How do you know all this?"

"Ah, came diving with David once. The Nino Konis Santana National Park includes three hundred and fifty square kilometres of coral reef. There are over one thousand species of reef fish and hundreds of species of coral. The reef here is one of the finest in the world, but almost unknown. There are a few dive schools who'll take you around. Fancy going out?"'

"Love to," said Burns. "Another beer?"

Burns returned from the bar with beers for everyone.

"Cheers, boys. Well done." They all clinked glasses.

"What do think you'll do next, George? Can I call you Alex now that we're out of Australia?"

"Who's George? Never heard of him," said Burns. "I don't know. I could retire, but I'd get bored. I'll see what turns up next. In the meantime, I'll need to get the tub and sub back to their owners. You?"

"Well, I don't think I'll be at all welcome back in Australia. What I would really love to do is go back to Ireland. Make peace with my past. See family, friends—if they're still alive. Walk in the mountains."

"I might be able to arrange something."

The following day, they swam in the reef. Mallon, Burns and, in spirit, David

December 27

As the next of kin, Siobhan, still desolate, flew to Darwin to identify the body reported as her father.

She was taken to the mortuary, and the attendant pulled out the body.

The face was covered. "There's nothing to see there, I'm afraid. It's unrecognisable and we have no dental remains, but perhaps this tattoo …"

One of the Albanian kidnappers had had one exactly the same. Siobhan's heart leapt with joy, but she kept a sombre face.

"This is my father. I'd recognise that tattoo anywhere. He had it done at a bikie tattoo parlour."

CHAPTER 43

December 29, Zürich

Dreiser was physically and mentally exhausted. He'd hardly slept since C-Day, waiting for hourly reports from Command, and now he awaited the worry of hearing about casualties and captures among the operatives. There were thankfully none reported so far, touch wood. It seemed that all the payloads were delivered successfully and that the operators had made themselves scarce. They were well-trained to do that. The Australia mission had been a close call.

But no operatives were safe yet, nor were he and the other sponsors. There would be repercussions, reprisals. The world was in chaos. It could escalate to world war. The situation was very unstable and very unpredictable.

He had predicted some things. The Saudi Arabia-Iran war was critical and was going according to plan. He had closely following events; both were armed to the teeth with missiles pointing at each other, up for a scrap. The knife-edge situation was a miniature version of the Cold War, when the US and Soviet Union were poised to launch an all-out nuclear war on one other in an instant. Then, under the doctrine of Mutually Assured Destruction—MAD—accidental nuclear holocaust was only narrowly avoided, by luck rather than by judgement. This time, war was started deliberately, like seeding a cloud to make it rain.

As the drone bombs and rockets descended on refineries in Saudi Arabia, there were the planned simultaneous attacks in Iran. In both cases, the attacks were on key targets, but big enough in scale to cause serious damage. Both nations had assumed it had been an attack by the other and had launched an immediate, pre-programmed strike on each other's refineries. There was no diplomatic discussion or consideration about how this might be a stitch-up.

No matter that it was senseless. Men were driven by testosterone. When the balls filled, the brain emptied. The initial missile attacks were measured. Then, as each side's assets were hit, they had escalated to total, all-out war within two hours. Like punch-drunk, heavy-weight bruisers in a much-anticipated title fight, both sides had been slugging it out with missile attacks on each other's most vulnerable targets until there was little left to attack. They were running out of missiles anyway, so it looked like they were calling it a draw. They should have a soccer decider with a penalty shootout.

As Dreiser had predicted, the conflict at first escalated to Sunnis versus Shiites as oil states in the region took sides. Qatar had already taken a beating in the first bombings and was initially keen to join in. People joked that you could see Qatar from Nepal when its LNG plants went up.

Iraq had gotten off relatively lightly but had apparently fired a few pot shots at Kuwait for old times' sake. Seeing the commercial benefits of having the only supplies, others had backed off and were encouraging a peaceful settlement. It looked like it would all be over by New Years' Eve.

Dreiser was most worried about the potential for global military escalation. The world was an armed camp, full of boys with toys.

The United States had long taken a keen interest in the social and democratic welfare of the peoples of the Middle East—nothing to do with oil, of course. Like its friend Saudi Arabia, it had long been itching to have a go at Iran.

The US Navy conveniently had a task force on exercise in the Indian Ocean, ready to go in at the first hint of trouble. It would have already been on high alert from Intel reports that something was going on. The Task Force predictably sailed for the Gulf after the first missile exchange. It was joined by two British frigates that were in the area. Two more frigates were on their way from Australia—one from Sydney and one reported as 'on patrol' in the Timor Sea.

The main part of the conflagration was over by the time the Task Force arrived, and all it could do was watch the fireworks. Saudi was already doing a perfectly good job of stuffing Iran, and Iran was busy seeing to Saudi, not daring to provoke the US fleet.

Also in the military equation were the Russians and Chinese. This was more worrying; Arms Suppliers By Appointment and competing backers of Iran, both were potential allies in any conflict. There was potential for war, especially as much of China's production and refining capacity was in Iran. Or *had been* in Iran—its refineries were torched. Hopefully the US, Russia and China all had other issues of their own. They were too busy firefighting to start fighting, too busy dealing with their collapsing economies and the political fallout.

The economic chaos was the most predictable outcome of all. It might have been C-Day—Operation Phoenix, to him and his colleagues—but it was already being called Big Bang Two—BB2—around the world for its explosive consequences. He liked that.

The economic meltdown was immediate. The attacks on Christmas Day had predictably caught the world with its pants down. Leaders were with families, full of Christmas cheer. The role of politicians was marginal, anyway. It was what traders, markets and corporations did that counted. It was their job to run the world. After sluggishly mobilising, traders and markets did what anyone would do in the circumstances—they panicked. Shortage of supply meant the price of oil, a global commodity, immediately went through the roof, along with the prices of goods and services tied to it directly or indirectly through raw material, transport and other costs. As they offloaded stock, oil prices crashed and went negative. A similar rollercoaster of boom and bust occurred for most commodities until share and currency trading was suspended.

Petrol shortages were leading to gridlock in cities as queues at petrol stations overlapped. Unlike toilet rolls during the COVID-19 crisis, there had been little stockpiling. Most householders did not possess a home storage tank and bowser. Attempts to stockpile fuel in unsuitable containers in backyards and bathrooms had led to numerous housefires.

Countries, companies and many people had been bankrupted overnight. Speculators and other important people had been jumping off tall buildings in major financial centres. They would be sorely missed.

As Dreiser had predicted, the world was now in deep recession after just a few days.

Washington, DC

These are very bad, very nasty people who've done this, tweeted the US President as the US economy, already trillions in hock to China, collapsed around him. The main oil refineries in Texas and Louisiana were still burning, as were plants in Canada, Saudi Arabia, Nigeria and elsewhere.

Those responsible must be punished. Our fine oil industry must and will be restored, whatever the cost. If foreigners are involved, we will find you and bomb your country—see how you like it. I blame Iran. At least our Saudi friends have saved us the trouble of bombing them. Or is it our other enemies, like China, who are to blame? ...

... I hear they've all been bombed too. Okay, it must be home-grown communist traitors or jihadists here. I want a massive manhunt, a roundup of all suspects, and I don't mean the weedkiller.

There can't be that many in America who know about bombs and weapons and shit, and where to get them ... .

... so what, if we've trained a lot of military and our arms industry has made weapons freely available? Americans have a sacred right to bear arms. It's made us the greatest nation in the world.

Dreiser's first concern was his operatives. He would ensure compensation for the families of any of his crew that had suffered loss, legal aid for anyone captured and tried, including himself.

He was also concerned about the many others being rounded up and imprisoned in the US and elsewhere. China and Russia didn't need any excuse to do that without trial at the best of times, and this was the worst of times.

Agents reported on the situation. The operatives were highly trained specialists and skilled in making themselves scarce, but it would be necessary to move quickly where help was needed.

Russia's oil production and refineries were mainly where it liked to exile people it didn't like: in Siberia. It already had its known dissidents locked up, so it was hard to find unknown bombers who had just disappeared into the wilderness. All it could do was step up the general persecution and, not without some justification, blame the Ukrainians for attacks on its gas pipeline infrastructure in the west.

China needed no excuse to lock up or lock down millions of people at will. Everywhere, the perpetrators wrecking fossil fuel production were an unknown force—professionals, highly trained, anonymous, their tracks covered.

In the US, a massive manhunt and roundup began. Matt Coburg and others working for Phoenix were picked up but released with lack of evidence and smart lawyers, paid for anonymously.

Dreiser knew a major victory had been won, but not the war. The fossil fuel industry was broken, but there would be attempts to restore it. This must not happen. He had anticipated all this. The planned counter strategies would be implemented.

Victories must be followed through. This had been the mistake after the First World War—instead of disarming and occupying Germany, rubbing their nose in it, the Allies had allowed the German army to march home as if it had won or scored a draw. Within a few years, it was on the march again to another world war. You didn't let a defeated enemy rise up.

December 29, Weymouth, Massachusetts

Mike Ryan was visiting his mother, Martha, and stepfather, Jim.

The immigration officer at LAX had looked at him suspiciously and told him to wait. Did they know something, or was he just on a watch list anyway for being outspoken? There was a lot of security activity.

They let him go, and he got a domestic to Boston—just in time; flights were being cancelled for lack of fuel.

"It's wonderful to have you home, Mike," said his mother. "Especially at this special time. We really believe all this Armageddon in the Middle East is the foretold time when Jesus will come again. What was it you were doing in Australia?"

He loved his parents. They had brought him up with love and kindness in a homey home, but there were never Christmas decorations or presents—Seventh Day Adventists didn't do Christmas. As a boy, he'd sometimes felt he was missing out on the fun other kids were having, but he'd gotten over it. As a teenager it was especially at this time of year he'd think about his family and wonder about his real father. His mother had made him promise to never go looking. Yet, if he waited until after she died, he would never get to meet his father. He decided then and there that, after all this blew over, he would go searching for him.

Tonga

New Year celebrations started in the Pacific Islands and went round the world with the rotation of the planet. Many Islanders celebrated the wrecking of the Australian coal industry. In Tonga, the family and friends of Angah Tupou welcomed him home as a warrior hero. He had been acquitted of bombing the coal ships in the Hunter River but deported as an undesirable alien. Someone else would have to pick the fruit.

Australia

Many had suggested cancelling the Sydney Harbour fireworks as inappropriate, since the country had run out of luck and money. PM Turbott insisted that the fireworks should go ahead to boost morale, mateship and national pride. He liked to watch them from his Kirribilli residence across the water and go "*Ooh!*" and "*Ah!*" In any case, the fireworks were already paid for.

Some in Australia were not celebrating. Craig Tooley and other Friends of Coal Exporters were hoping for a better year ahead and looking forward to a time when exports could be resumed.

Coal magnates Greg Hutchings and Tina Nulhart were helping police with their enquiries, as was Damian Sproake. The bereaved families of the deceased mobsters and bikies wanted compensation.

Dili, East Timor

Burns had told Mallon to keep his head down and lie low for a while until he returned with documentation. He'd left plenty of cash.

Siobhan and Kieran paid a visit to Mallon, taking the one-hour flight from Darwin. They sat in the Castaway Bar, watching the New Year's Eve fireworks.

"What are you like, Dad? *Bliadhna mhath ur.*"

"And a very happy new year to you, darlin'. And to you." He blew a raspberry on Kieran's cheek. Kieran laughed.

"What will happen next? Will you be in exile here for ever, like in a penal colony? You know, like Devil's Island? Remember when we watched *Papillon*?"

"I do. Don't worry. George is making arrangements for us all to be together."

Bernese Oberland, Switzerland

Dreiser was enjoying a quiet new years' celebration with Anna, family and friends.

He reflected on the past year and especially the past week. A lot had happened, and the trouble was not over, but he had new hope for the future and for his grandchildren.

Deiter and Gunter were playing with their new train set and Sofia with her new doll's house.

London

The Brits were stoically optimistic.

"Mustn't grumble, it could be worse. Next year has got to be better. Things will soon be back to normal when they repair all those oil refineries. Cheers! All the best!"

The Trafalgar Square celebrations went ahead as usual.

Burns had arrived back that morning, and he and Galina had spent all day in bed. They were ready for a night out and were in the square with many others, waiting for the chimes of Big Ben.

"Come on," he said.

"What? No!" said Galina, laughing as they joined the revellers in the fountain.

"Who dares gets wet," said Burns, kissing her.

January 1, Musikverein, Vienna

Dreiser and Anna were standing, applauding the conductor Riccardo Muti and the Vienna Philharmonic. They smiled at each other. They were at the annual new years' day concert, with a programme of waltzes and polkas, happy dance music for the darkest time of the year.

Afterwards, they had champagne before sitting down to dinner.

"Wolfgang, it's been simply wonderful. I've wanted to come all my life. I can't thank you enough. However did you manage to get tickets?"

"Ah. That's a secret … a surprise."

"We don't really have many secrets now, do we?" asked Anna. "After all that has happened."

"No, we don't. You have been my bedrock, my support and inspiration through all difficulties. I don't think I could have done it without you. Your administration, communication and encryption skills are quite astonishing. But do you still want to associate with a criminal?"

She held his hand across the table. "You're not a criminal. You have been preventing a greater crime. How could I not love and admire a man who would save the world? Besides, I am a willing accessory and your assistant. They will have to get past me."

"Anna, there's no one I respect more, whose company I enjoy more. There's no one who makes me feel happier. I love you. Will you marry me?"

"I … I don't know what to say. Yes … I will."

They kissed.

"We should have no secrets …" Dreiser began.

"You don't have to say any more," said Anna. "I know you. I love and respect you for what you are."

"There's one thing you should know. I have a son, somewhere … in America … I was young, it was a long time ago."

"It's life. These things happen. You want to find him, don't you?"

"Yes."

"Then I will love him as my own."

CHAPTER 44

September, nine months later, Brisbane

Louse Brailly was still making sense of what had happened in the world over the past twelve months.

"I know it's a bit boring, watching me writing, Eddie, but you know it's what I do. This has been a momentous year, and you really inspire me to write. I always write best when I'm happy, and you make me happy ... Okay, that's enough of that for now. Go and make me a nice cup of tea, darling."

She started writing.

It started with Ned Coaly's first railway bombing. In its far-reaching consequences, it was like two historic shots heard around the world, which changed everything.

The first shot of the American Revolutionary War in 1775 led to the formation of the United States, the French and other revolutions, and to ending the Divine Right of Kings to rule the world. The shot at Sarajevo in 1914, which assassinated the Austrian Archduke Ferdinand, led to the First World War, which led to the rise of fascism and the Second World War, to the rise of communism and the Cold War and the rise of China and to God knows what. Delete. *'History, just one bloody thing after another,' as Alan Bennett wrote in* The History Boys.

Coaly's bomb echoed around the world. There were more coal railway bombings in Australia that bore Coaly's trademark, causing enormous damage to the coal industry without hurting anyone. It was alleged to have been the work of Sean Mallon, avenging his son David, killed by police in a climate protest. But the truth will never be known, since Mallon was never caught for questioning and was mysteriously killed in a shooting incident in Darwin. Like Ned Kelly, he came to a bad end. Like Ned Kelly, his story and name will live on.

Around the world, Ned Coaly was an inspiration—a revolutionary hero—to people who were devastated by climate change but felt powerless to do anything against the destructive force of the Fossilarchy—the Evil Empire of the fossil fuel industry and their political cronies—who would destroy the Earth for power and profit. The situation was desperate, but, apart from a few instances of minor damage to pumping stations, no one thought to break the law.

Then, thanks to Coaly, around the world people realised how vulnerable the Fossilarchy's assets were. Climate activists realised that power lines, pipeline ports and railways could easily be disrupted. There were copycat attacks all over, as people realised that everyone could do something more to reduce global emissions.

Dissidents and oppressed peoples realised that there is no political power without physical energy, electricity and fuel, and they soon learned that sabotaging was easy. At first, the attacks were small in scale, ad hoc, and governments clamped down hard. Then came massive attacks on fossil fuel facilities in Australia, as if it was the warm-up act for something bigger. Coaly was implicated in the first coal jetty bombing, but the scale of the bombings on other coal ports suggested someone else was involved—especially in the destruction of the Australian LNG industry and the mysterious sinking of the oil rig off Rottnest Island. There was initial ACP suspicion that the oceanographic survey ship, the *New Endeavour II*, may have been somehow involved, but the evidence was circumstantial. Was it a cover-up for Turbott, who supported and facilitated its voyage around Australia? No one will know until the information can be released, if ever. Either way, Turbott had bigger fish to fry with the collapse of the world and Australian economies.

The attacks in Australia were big but dwarfed by the seismic, Richter Nine attacks around the world on Christmas Day, forever known as BB2. They were clearly planned and coordinated by a person or persons with the resources to *finance the attacks, which seem to have been linked to the big attacks in Australia. Their identity remains a mystery. The attacks had the hallmark of professionals, but no one knows who. They struck and disappeared into the night.*

Then came the backlash as countries rounded up suspects, including many who had been involved in minor sabotage. In their rage, authoritarian governments stepped up their general oppression, but in the new circumstances, there were new limits, political and economic, to what they could do.

When people awoke from the stupor of their carbon drug dependency and the shock of BB2, they realised how much of a threat to the future the industry was and how vulnerable the whole fossil infrastructure was. The more they were oppressed, the more they fought back, using all prior established methods against the industry's railways, power lines and other infrastructure.

Then there were economic limits. Bankruptcy and skyrocketing oil prices limited the pursuit of power and capacity to oppress people. Tanks and warplanes needed fuel, and both cost money.

Then came the anonymous warnings that there would be still more attacks and damage if the manhunts and persecution continued. They went viral.

Before all this, governments liked to deny the power of these attacks. Now, they have been forced to back off because of threats to kill the hostage: fossil fuels. The Fossilarchy is over a barrel. An oil barrel.

The political and financial power of the fossil fuel industry has been broken, with many of its assets in ruins and with collapsed demand as the world economy has nose-dived. There has been little prospect of taxpayer bailouts from governments for their fossil friends. The industry begged and received during COVID-19, but governments are themselves bankrupt, and the cupboard is bare. Oil, gas and coal companies have filed for bankruptcy. Exploration projects have been canned along with bonuses and stock options for senior executives, political donations and the revolving door to directorships for politicians.

With the end of the Fossilarchy, the powerful have become powerless. The US economy collapsed around the US president, along with the likelihood that his party will see the presidency again soon. Their administrations have long been dependent on economic growth and funding from the oil magnates and the lobbyists who filled their governments.

Collapsed demand and high transportation costs mean that it is no longer viable to have everything made in China. At least for now, it seems that China has been forced to shelve plans to take over the world with the proceeds from making consumer goods for the West. As its economy has faltered, cracks have appeared in China's regional and ethnic divisions. Discontent and riots can only be repressed by the military for so long. Cracks have also appeared in the wall of China's biggest dam, which has been blocking water flow to downstream countries. Sabotage is suspected.

Closer to home, PM Turbott's re-election campaign was stymied by a collapse in fossil fuel donations to the Conservative Coalition and a collapse in advertising revenue to Moorcock News. Looking to the booming renewables and EV giants wouldn't have helped either, considering how his government had shunned them in the past.

The opposition made an election issue of Turbott's plans to restore the Fossilarchy with a massive bailout for his corporate chums, instead of investing in a green recovery and many more jobs. The opposition never lost an opportunity to congratulate him on achieving greenhouse emissions cuts at a canter, with the wrecking of the fossil industry under his watch.

Knowing he was on a losing wicket, Turbott resigned before the election, citing a will 'to spend more time with his family'. A more moderate leader, Michelle Smith, has taken over. As the first female leader of her Party, she purged the right-wing, climate-denier faction. George Magnussen, Craig Tooley and others were deselected. With friends like them, what was left of the coal industry didn't need enemies.

The geopolitics of the world have hopefully started to change. Overseas military adventures are being curtailed. In the good old days, if your neighbour had territory or resources you wanted, such as oil, you went and snatched it. But it isn't a good time for that sort of thing now that fuel to fill the tanks of ships, warplanes and other toys is in short supply. The US military, one of the biggest contributors to global greenhouse emissions, has been forced to cut back.

The world has changed dramatically in so many other ways—political, social and economic. It truly has been a revolution. New words have arisen, allowing *new understanding. No one knows who invented the term 'Fossilarchy', but it has become a symbol of all of the evils and excesses of the old world, a symbol of what we are all now fighting to recover from. BB2 broke not only the Fossilarchy, but corporate rule of the world. The COVID crisis was a warm-up for governments to show new leadership. Capitalism has shown itself to be entirely useless during an emergency, as has dog-eat-dog individualism. The crisis has also been a warm-up for at least some people behaving as responsible members of a global community, instead of consumers in the neo-liberal world. New economic models and ways of living have emerged out of BB2, which don't consume vast quantities of fossil fuels or other resources of the planet. Markets for sustainable, low-carbon products have mushroomed. Local producers have benefited, as long, fuel-dependent transportation supply chains have collapsed. People are starting to make important things again, instead of selling pointless items for profit. Thanks to cheap oil, air travel had been predicted to double in twenty years. People are now grounded and will have to make do with local holidays.*

"Oh, Eddie, every day with you is like being on holiday."

Before BB2, the world economy was a fragile, unsustainable bubble, ever-expanding chaos contained by a thin film of superficial order and stability. The bubble depended on cheap fossil energy to fuel everlasting growth, inflating itself by sucking the life out of the Earth. COVID-19 pricked and deflated the bubble for a time before it reflated as the world returned to its high carbon habit.

Now the bubble has burst. The world is doing what sooner or later it had to do—going through the pain and convulsion of cold turkey on the road to rehab, the fever and delirium of a viral infection before recuperation. Getting off the carbon habit was not going to happen without some pain and sacrifice.

In the days, weeks and months that followed BB2, the world descended into deep chaos. But that was where it was heading anyway, with little chance of recovery. Now, there is a chance for the future. Fire sometimes brings new shoots, new growth.

"Oh, Eddie, promise you'll never do a wombat to me."

"What?"

"Eats, roots, shoots and leaves."

"Never, I love you too much, Lou Lou."
"I love you too, Eddie."

December, Geneva, Switzerland

Dreiser drove the last stake into the heart of the Fossilarchy with the United Nations Carbon Charter. It came like a bombshell out of the blue, like the armed drones he had unleashed.

Initiated by him, the charter was drafted and brokered by the World Business Council for Sustainable Development. Its aim was a rapid and global transition to a global low-carbon economy. There were ten commandments, provisions to be enacted directly and through national laws:

1. An immediate global tax on carbon was to be initiated, applicable to all producers as well as products from life-cycle assessment. Revenues were to be invested in renewables, low-carbon alternatives and finances for climate mitigation and adaptation in poorer countries.
2. There were to be no more subsidies for fossil fuels.
3. New fossil fuel exploration and development was to be banned.
4. Existing projects in World Heritage and other sensitive areas were to be immediately run down and capped.
5. There was to be a total separation of fossil fuels from government, no ownership, lobbying or patronage political funding; the revolving door would be padlocked.
6. Governments, organisations, media and others intentionally disseminating false information on climate science would be subject to penalties and sanctions.

7. Laws would be enacted and enforced to protect young people and future generations from climate change.
8. Laws would be enacted and enforced to protect biodiversity and wildlife from climate change and to restore damage, a global fund would be established, and countries would contribute according to their means.
9. Laws would allow suing for damages.
10. No geoengineering unless proven safe.

The charter was tabled for all member nations to sign. It would be passed with a majority vote, unlike previous efforts, which allowed a veto from Fossilarchies. Dissenters would be subject to sanctions and other penalties.

It was not stated, but by now the industry knew that this meant more than trade sanctions or a slap on the wrist from governments.

Dreiser knew his history. He was not unlike the barons confronting King John, compelling him to behave better at Runnymede in 1215, when they signed the *Magna Carta*. The fossil industry was on notice.

There was much to do, fine words to say. Consultants would rub their hands with glee.

CHAPTER 45

January, twelve months post-BB2

The NE2 continued to be available for survey work. In the worldwide turmoil after BB2, it was quickly forgotten in Australia. With no defendants or witnesses, evidence of its involvement in the bombings around Australia was circumstantial. The story of the altercation in the Timor sea, resisting arrest, would never come out in its lifetime.

John Grey and Mike Ryan withdrew from academic research and formed a foundation to train scientists to communicate science and be politically active in conserving the oceans and planet. They were greatly assisted by an endowment from a rich relative of Ryan's.

They remained on security watchlists because of their wider activism and opinion pieces, but then, who wasn't on those lists?

Emma Johnson also remained on security watch, like all the protesters. She completed her master's and became involved in organising climate and biodiversity protection activism in Australia and internationally. With her beret, Grey called her 'Cher Guevara'.

Grey and Emma lived together in Brisbane. You could say they were still seeing quite a lot of each other.

―⁓―

Galway, Ireland

Mallon, Siobhan and Kieran lived in a house overlooking Galway Bay, just outside Galway. Mallon and Siobhan had chosen it. It would be a new life for the three of them, since he didn't exist in Australia anymore. He had always wanted to return to Ireland, but Newry was too close to a past he wanted to forget and to people he didn't want remembering him.

He had arrived from East Timor some months before. Siobhan had inherited and sold the house in Fremantle, and she and Kieran had joined him.

He'd traced and found his relatives. His brother Jim was still in Newry, and they'd had an emotional reunion.

"I was always waiting for you to come back," said Jim. "It's your round."

They'd gone to a pub for a pint of Guinness. Mallon was especially enjoying the real thing.

No one had recognised his photo in the news about Ned Coaly, and he didn't raise the subject. All the same, he told people to keep quiet about him. They all knew why he'd left.

He checked and found that George Moore's family were still around, others too from the old days. People were still wondering what had happened to George.

"He went on a holiday to Australia and never came back. Sure, it's a dangerous place with all those snakes, spiders, crocodiles and backpacker murderers and stuff. I wouldn't go there. Did you ever see *Wolf Creek?*"

He took Siobhan and Kieran to visit his parents' graves.

"Sorry, Mam and Dad. Just to let you know, I'm back. This is my family."

He was now Patrick Kelly and they were his Kelly gang.

January, Davos Klosters, Switzerland

Dreiser attended the World Economic Forum and viewed the scene with some satisfaction. In the economic meltdown following BB2, unbridled capitalism was on the ropes. Governments had to start serving the people, not their donors. Corporations no longer ruled the world. But the stinking rich and the self-important still liked to gather at the annual forum at Davos Klosters to do deals, make bold pronouncements and say fine words.

The previous January, immediately following BB2, the event had been cancelled. Many of the usual delegates had been bankrupt or too busy counting what they had still had left. One or two had even ended it all. Fine words were hard when everyone was speechless.

This year, the mood was more reflective amongst those who could still afford to come. The main resort accommodation and air travel were not cheap, but there were alternatives for those on a budget. The atmosphere was more relaxed than usual, delegates milling in cable-knit sweaters rather than suits and ties. The glühwein flowed freely, helping to keep out the January cold.

Economists, finance ministers and ex-finance ministers had all reinvented themselves. Everyone was now a Keynesian chameleon, talking about new deals, new economics, new technology, new this and new that. The last time he was here, Herman Hormann had been spruiking Australia's clean coal, helping to reduce global emissions and lift millions out of poverty, speaking on the wonders of the market, the evils of state intervention and deficit spending. Now he was stalking delegates, looking for a job— maybe with an international agency, like the OECD. "You know, during my time as Finance Minister, Australia reduced its greenhouse emissions quite remarkably …"

NGO people were there in force as delegates or at fringe meetings. Many were there to gloat, many to take their seats at the top table, believing that the time had come for them to deliver the promised land. Some had almost visible halos. Or was it afterglow from the glühwein?

Sustainability guru Jonathon Polkington was a guest speaker on the subject of 'Sustainability: Can Business Still Make a Difference?'

"In conclusion. Yes, business can and must make a difference. The key is leadership from top management. As I was saying to Wolfgang Dreiser only the other day …"

Dreiser met privately with a colleague over lunch.

"There has been progress in climate change, but we are far from out of the woods. There is still much to do on this and on other issues. The forces of destruction are still at work. We won a big victory, but not the war."

Belgravia, London

Alex Burns was dividing his time between his apartment in London and the south of France.

He also had a thing for Galina. He loved her company, and they were constant companions. She enjoyed the good life but was not a gold digger. She liked simple things, like being warm. "Can you turn up the heat, darling, I'm not a soldier," she would remind Burns, when he forgot to turn it on.

His phone rang.

"Don't answer it. Tell them you're busy, you naughty boy …"

Burns saw that it was Piers Hadley.

"Alex? Hadley. How are you? I have something that may interest you …"

The following day, Burns called Mallon. "Patrick! It's Alex. "How the devil are you all?"

Burns's team were all enjoying their new comfortable lifestyles, mainly in Spain. Each received a call from Burns.

A beach villa in San Vito Lo Capo, Sicily

The smoky aroma of a typical South African *braai* floated across neighbouring properties and towards the beach, complementing the herby, piney scent from the hillside. Boonzaaier was turning over a variety of meats on the open grill with his specially imported *braai tang* tongs. A Birra Messina in his left hand, he shook *braai* spices over everything as he cooked. Hot coals glimmered below, making cracking and popping sounds as the salt made contact, smoke whisping from the adjacent fire-pit.

"This is orraait, Jannie," said Grobbelaar, a look of deep contentment on his face.

"Yah, we've been in worse places, Jacques," reflected Boonzaaier.

"Is that your sat phone ringing?"

Arnold Zimmermann was still hiding in the woods.

END

ACKNOWLEDGEMENTS

I want to give special thanks to all of the publishing team at Aurora House for all of their professionalism, support and advice throughout the process: Linda Lycett, Lianna Heussler, Lucy Leishon, Ryan Waters, Amit Dey as well as Donika Misheniva of Art of Donika for the stunning cover design. I'm grateful to all the reviewers of earlier drafts of the manuscript for their helpful suggestions for improvement and for their encouragement: Jacques Boonzaaier, Peter Dawes, Andy Fallon, Patrick and Jayne Mallon and Eric Munden. Last but not least, extra special thanks to my wife, Pauline, for her patience when I disappeared into the Land of Lost Boys and Girls inhabited by aspiring writers.

ABOUT THE AUTHOR

Born in the UK, Tom has been a consultant in environment, sustainability and climate change since 1990 and been involved in environmental protection and campaigning since 1978. At last count, he has worked in twenty-eight countries for governments and many industries. He has a degree in civil engineering, an MBA, an MSc in environmental technology from Imperial College, London, and professional qualifications in environmental and greenhouse gas management.

He has many interests stemming from the many influences over his life. From a young age he has loved nature and wildlife. His father's front line experience throughout World War Two, as well as his own travels, led to an interest in modern history. The turbulent 60s and 70s, and being an exchange student in the US during Watergate, led to an interest in politics. Growing up in Swindon, once a great railway town, and seeing express trains screaming through, like fiery dragons, in the last days of steam, turned him into an incurable trainspotter.

He has had a long love affair with music. His much older brother, John, introduced him to early rock n' roll even before the amazing music explosion of the 1960s. John's LP of *Walt Disney's Fantasia* introduced him to classical music. Tom joined a local choir and has been a choral singer ever since, including over two hundred performances with the London Philharmonic, London Symphony and other orchestras under many of the world's greatest conductors. John's recordings of *The Goon Show* triggered Tom's lifetime love of comedy. His English and Irish heritage and worldwide travels led him to seeking out the pubs and beers of the world.

Since 1999, he has lived in Western Australia and helped raise a family—the best thing he has done—and has travelled and worked throughout Australia, appreciating its beauty and diversity. He has been involved in many campaigns there, including ending the logging of the ancient forests of the south-west and whaling in the Antarctic as well as working towards climate action. In this, he has observed Australian climate politics with a mix of amusement and horror. You couldn't make it up.

The Fossilarchy is his first solo novel. His first novel, *The Seventh Boat*, co-authored with David Ashbridge, is about whaling in the Southern Ocean and is an Amazon eBook.